By Xenia Melzer

GODS OF WAR
Casto
Love and the Stubborn

Published by DSP PUBLICATIONS
www.dsppublications.com

LOVE
AND THE
STUBBORN

XENIA MELZER

DSP PUBLICATIONS

Published by
DSP Publications

5032 Capital Circle SW, Suite 2, PMB# 279, Tallahassee, FL 32305-7886 USA
www.dsppublications.com

This is a work of fiction. Names, characters, places, and incidents either are the product of author imagination or are used fictitiously, and any resemblance to actual persons, living or dead, business establishments, events, or locales is entirely coincidental.

Love and the Stubborn
© 2016 Xenia Melzer

Cover Art
© 2016 Aaron Anderson.
aaronbydesign55@gmail.com
Cover content is for illustrative purposes only and any person depicted on the cover is a model.
Map © 2016 Xenia Melzer
Author Photo © 2016 Photographer: Andreas Eirainer, bildwerk; Make up: Kathrin Fuchsenthaler.

ISBN: 978-1-63477-189-4
Digital ISBN: 978-1-63477-190-0
Library of Congress Control Number: 2016911392
Published December 2016
v. 1.0

Printed in the United States of America
∞
This paper meets the requirements of
ANSI/NISO Z39.48-1992 (Permanence of Paper).

To my parents. For everything.

The Continent
The Valley
The Mines
The Hot
Heart
Arana
Eppirat
Ka'li'enn
Wa'na'Atoka
Srarrana
The Plains
Alemba
Medelina
Ummana
Ana~Raina

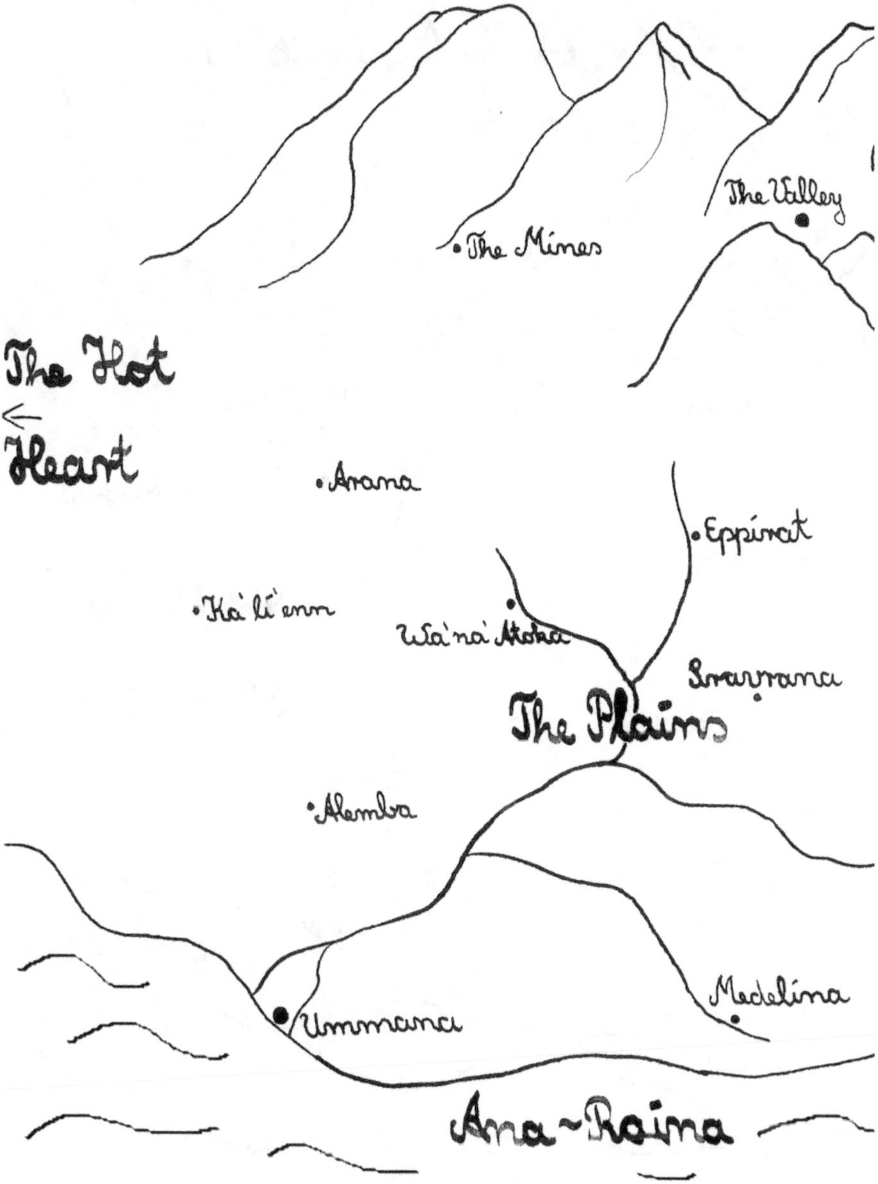

Wolf Mountains
The Swamp
The Dark Forest
The Eastern
Kingdoms
Kwool
Elam
Umman River
Hre
Ruins of Quell'Renar

MEASUREMENTS

Measurements of Length

1 hand = 4 inches = 10.2 centimeters (1 hand is the unit still used
to measure the height of horses.)
1 span = 9 inches = 22.9 centimeters
1 ell = 45 inches = 114 centimeters or 1.14 meters
1 pace = 5 feet or 60 inches = 1.5 meters
1 league = 3 miles = 4.8 kilometers

Measurements of Mass

1 ore = 0.85 ounce = 24 grams
1 clove = 6.4 pounds = 2.9 kilograms
1 quarter = 2 stone or 28 pounds = 12.7 kilograms
1 hundredweight = 8 stone or 112 pounds = 50.8 kilograms

As to readers who are familiar with the various measurement systems during medieval times, I would ask them to kindly turn a blind eye on any inconsistencies they may find.

LOVE
AND THE
STUBBORN

XENIA MELZER

KI'T

1. THUNDERSTORM

DAMON WAS alert when he entered the shady shed. Elwan and Sindal, the two former overseers, who'd hated Casto ever since their degradation, approached him slowly. The priest couldn't suppress a satisfied smile. Those men's hatred wrapped around his shoulders like a warm cloak.

"Damon, what do you want?" Elwan was terse. It was late, and they still had some work to do.

"I wanted to see how you're doing."

"Don't be ridiculous. You're not interested in anybody besides yourself. You're here because you need something, so spill."

"Elwan, I can't say I've missed your bluntness. But if you must know, I need your help. You do know Casto, don't you?"

Sindal spat out, "As if you don't know. What do you have to do with him?"

"Well, I guess you could say I'd like to teach him a lesson."

"Forget it. We've already tried, and look where it got us."

Elwan sounded gruff, so Damon treated him to a bright smile, which didn't fail to annoy the slave. "That, my friend, is because you two are as dumb as the day is long. I, on the other hand, have a perfect plan."

A dangerous glint sprang to life in the men's eyes. It hadn't been a wise move on Damon's part to disgrace them, but he hadn't been able to withstand temptation. Now he could feel their hatred bubbling up, swallowing their every sensible thought. It was exactly how Damon preferred his minions—easy to manipulate because they were oblivious to everything else around them.

"And what kind of plan do you have in mind?" Elwan sounded sly, on edge.

"It's easy," Damon said soothingly. "I want you to see to it that Casto gets delayed tomorrow noon."

"No chance. He's always punctual for training." Elwan had immediately understood what Damon was aiming for, a fact that didn't escape the priest. As much as the former overseer was consumed by hatred, he wasn't stupid.

"It has to be something pressing. Something he can't ignore. He's still riding that brown mare, Nirena, isn't he?"

"The loopy one? Yes. Although not even the Holy Mothers understand why."

Damon acknowledged the answer with an innocent smile. Finally his constant surveillance of the blond pest would pay off. "What would happen should she escape from her stall? Of course, it would be an unfortunate accident, but once she's outside…."

"Casto will try to get her personally." Elwan grinned broadly. "That we can arrange."

"So I can count on you?"

Sindal and Elwan shared a long glance. From their own painful experience, they knew what kind of risk they were about to take. Because one thing was for sure, should the Angel of Death ever find out about this, they would be denied a quick, merciful death. But the hatred burning in their chests enticed them to give in to Damon's plan.

They hesitated for one more moment, and then they nodded. "Yes."

Damon bowed to the two slaves in mockery. He hadn't thought they would deny him, but he was still surprised how easy it had been to win them over. "It's a pleasure to do business with you."

CASTO WAS about to go to his daily training with Renaldo when he became aware of the racket in the stables. He turned around just in time to see Lord Wolfstan's brown mare racing at breakneck speed toward the fields with her eyes rolled back so that only the whites could be seen. It had started to thaw during the last few days, so the ground was frozen over and extremely slippery. At the pace Nirena was setting, she could break her legs in no time. Experience had taught Casto that she was too crazy to slow down on her own. Once she started sliding, it would be too late, and Lord Wolfstan would lose his most valuable horse.

Casto gave a shrill whistle and Lys appeared at his side. They followed Nirena and finally, after more than half an hour had passed, managed to corner her by one of the paddocks. It took even more time until she calmed down enough so that Casto could take her back to the stables.

This time he closed the door himself before hurrying to the training hall. He knew he was awfully late. Renaldo didn't like waiting, and Casto half expected the demigod to be gone when he reached the training hall. Given how cranky Renaldo had been that morning, Casto secretly hoped he wouldn't be there.

Unfortunately, Renaldo *was* waiting for him, and he didn't look happy. With his right hand, he gripped the handle of the training sword so hard his knuckles turned white. "Where have you been?"

For once Casto realized that it would be wise to apologize. At this point, it didn't pay to ponder why Renaldo was so angry. Casto could either try to soothe the man or risk yet another argument. As much as he enjoyed fighting with Renaldo, he just didn't have the energy. So he bowed to the enraged Angel of Death. "Please forgive me, my lord. There was a problem at the stables, and I couldn't leave."

"A problem at the stables? How interesting. Straighten yourself!"

Casto obeyed immediately. The Barbarian's tone was icy, his countenance had become unreadable, but Casto felt instinctively that Renaldo was angrier than he'd ever seen him before. He felt his own anger rise in response and almost challenged Renaldo before he reminded himself that he didn't want that. At least not today.

Renaldo tossed him a sword with more emphasis than was strictly necessary, and while Casto was busy getting into position, he charged.

If Casto had ever had the illusion of being able to meet Renaldo on equal grounds in a fight, it was shattered. The Angel of Death was playing with him like a predator with its half-dead prey.

Renaldo drove Casto through the hall, time and again dealing him humiliating and painful blows while accentuating each one with an angry reprimand.

"You have to be punctual for training!"

"Nothing is more important than your training!"

"How dare you let me wait?"

On and on it went, the blows as well as the scolding coming in accelerating succession. After an especially nasty blow to his knee, Casto snapped. He managed to parry the next strike out of sheer anger. His voice cracked in fury. If the Barbarian wanted a fight that badly, he could have it. "I said I was sorry! I apologized! But I had no choice!"

"Of course you had a choice, but as always, you preferred to deny me."

"That's not true!" Casto wanted to say something more, but at that moment, Renaldo disarmed him with a flick of his blade. Renaldo pushed him against the wall, stabbed him painfully in the ribs with the tip of his sword, and looked at him coldly.

"Today was your last training session. I want you to get out of my sight, you ungrateful, arrogant little prick. Get lost, now!"

Casto couldn't believe the Barbarian was sending him away. He snapped back with all the ferocity of a rabid dog. "As you wish, Barbarian! I really hate you!"

Trembling with rage, Renaldo watched the retreating shape of his slave. Suddenly a crackling noise caught his attention. The heavy wooden sword in his hand was burning to ashes with a blazing flame. Cursing in the tongue of the Ancients, he tossed the blistering remains to the ground, his gaze fixed on the inferno he'd just caused with his fury. There was no doubt; since he'd met Casto, his powers were getting out of control. The last time he'd unconsciously flamed something when he got angry had been shortly after Ana-Isara had taken his and his brother's hearts. But his slave threw him so off-balance that he was no longer able to contain the powers inside him.

Once again he pondered if it weren't better to get rid of Casto—or at least to discipline him in a way that would teach him his place.

Renaldo sighed. A beating wouldn't tame the capricious blond, rather the opposite. And selling him was simply out of the question. The mere idea of somebody else's hands on his slave's flawless skin made him even more furious than Casto's behavior had. He would have to find another solution for this dilemma.

CASTO HAD barely left the training hall when he started to realize what a grave mistake he'd made this time. His anger faltered, paving the way for a despair so dark it threatened to consume him completely.

Crestfallen, he went to Lys, who greeted him reproachfully.

"I know, brother. Please, let's ride. I'm afraid it'll be the last for quite a long time." Even to his own ears, Casto sounded beaten.

During their ride through the Valley, Casto couldn't stop blaming himself.

How could he have been so stupid? The powerful Angel of Death, the most feared warrior on the continent, had agreed to train him. It was an honor only a select few had ever enjoyed and certainly wasn't normally bestowed on a mere slave. In his arrogance he had taken this generous gift for granted—and even worse, trampled it underfoot. There was no denying it; he owed the Barbarian a sincere apology.

Given how furious Renaldo had been, Casto wasn't sure whether it would be enough. He didn't want to think about what would happen to him should Renaldo decide to sell him. It was difficult enough for him to obey Renaldo; he wasn't able to imagine doing the same for another master.

Glumly he returned to the stables with Lys, said his good-bye to his friend, and lurked back to his master's chambers. Renaldo wasn't there, which gave him the chance to prepare for his apology. His deed had been so ignominious he wouldn't be able to get around a beating. Sighing deeply, Casto sat down on one of the lounges and waited for the return of the Barbarian.

When Renaldo entered his chambers, Casto got up from a lounge and knelt with his head bowed demurely. But Renaldo was still furious and not in the mood for games. "I told you to get out of my sight! What do you want?"

"Begging your forgiveness, Master. My behavior was inappropriate and lacked respect. I'm truly sorry."

"And you think that fixes it?" Renaldo's voice was pure acid. Deep inside he could feel his flame blazing again, and the urge to hurt Casto was almost impossible to suppress.

"No, of course not. You've been so generous as to make me your pupil, a grace I took for granted. That alone was wrong, as well as my delayed appearance and my reaction to the punishment you meted out. I'm fully aware that my insolence can only be expiated with blood."

Upon those words, Casto held up the leather whip with which Renaldo had punished him after his escape from the Valley.

Renaldo was rendered speechless. He'd never seen Casto so humble, a sure sign of how serious he was about his apology. Against his will, Renaldo felt himself forgiving the young man. Casto's behavior had been so unacceptable that he had to atone. With his mind now clear again, Renaldo took the whip from Casto's hand.

He threw it into a corner. "We both know that a whipping will only enhance your defiance. I'm really disappointed, Casto. I'd thought a highly civilized person like you would know better how to behave."

Casto lowered his head even more but didn't say anything.

Renaldo went on. "I want you to go to your room. At the moment I'm too angry to make a decision. I'll tell you tomorrow what I'm going to do with you."

In the oppressive silence following those words, Casto got up. His shoulders were slumped, and he was far from his usual, overbearing self. All the proud defiance Renaldo loved so much about him was gone. It took all of Renaldo's willpower not to hug and comfort his slave.

CASTO STOOD in front of the bed he hadn't slept in since he'd spent his first night with the Barbarian. He felt empty and exhausted.

Renaldo's disappointment had been like a knife in his chest that a cruel torturer slowly twisted. He was able to deal with Renaldo's anger in an offhand manner since he wasn't afraid of him like everybody else, but the mere idea that Renaldo could think ill of him made his stomach turn.

Casto hated himself for making Renaldo's opinion of him so important, but there was also no denying that he'd gone too far this time. No matter what else the Barbarian might be to him, as his mentor, Casto owed him respect and obedience.

Frustrated, he slumped on his bed. Even in Ummana, where every one of his teachers had been a monster, Casto had always shown perfect manners no matter what he thought about the people entrusted with his education. Renaldo, of all people, who'd been the first to teach him without trying to break him at the same time, had become the target for his ingratitude. Casto couldn't escape the insight that it was only just if Renaldo should decide to sell him. What use did Renaldo have for a slave like him anyways?

IN THE middle of the night, Renaldo startled in his sleep when Casto screamed.

He sighed, remembering those first months when Casto had woken covered in sweat every night. Since Casto started sharing Renaldo's bed, the nightmares had stopped, and even when he got restless sometimes, all it took to make him sleep peacefully was for Renaldo to caress him soothingly.

Renaldo had hoped the evil dreams were banished, but now it seemed that only his presence had kept them at bay. He wondered what horrors Casto had endured that they should follow him so far as the Valley.

The scream came again, high-pitched and wailing. Then Casto started talking in a tongue completely alien to Renaldo's ears. He knew it wasn't the language spoken in the area where they'd found Casto, but he was unable to connect the quick, melodic stream of syllables to anyplace on the continent. It sounded a little like Ummanian, but he wasn't sure. Renaldo had never bothered to learn the language of the merchants. Ummana was too far away from the Valley to justify the trouble, and those who came the long way into the mountains were usually fluent in four or five different tongues.

Without making a sound, Renaldo got up and went to Casto's chamber. The young man was kneeling on the furs, whimpering like a lost child. His azure eyes were wide open but apparently blind. He was fast asleep.

Renaldo approached him slowly so as not to startle him. When he reached Casto, he hugged him gently, pressed him back into the covers, and tried to lull him with soft words. "It's all right, my own. Shh. Everything's fine. It's just a bad dream. Relax, I'm here."

A last, desperate whimper, then Casto snuggled against his master with a sigh and slept on peacefully. Once Renaldo was sure the nightmare was banished, he returned reluctantly to his own room. Whatever it was that afflicted Casto so much had to be the reason for his stubborn behavior, his arrogance, and the way he always pushed his master away. But as long as Casto didn't confide in him, Renaldo wasn't able to help. The secrets surrounding Casto stirred Renaldo's interest more and more, but Casto had to tell him of his own free will. Should Renaldo try to force him, things would most definitely end in tears and misery.

THE NEXT morning, Casto waited nervously for his master to call him. He'd had a bad night. In his dreams he'd been back in Ummana, a helpless victim of his father's schemes. Just when his sire had started to humiliate him deeply again, the Barbarian had showed up and saved

Casto in the same way he'd done during Casto's escape from the Valley last year. Casto still was less than happy that Renaldo could follow him into his dreams, but last night he had been glad. He didn't know what he would have done without Renaldo's help.

As if he'd sensed that his slave had been thinking about him, Renaldo appeared and beckoned him to the main room. "Casto! Come here!"

The young man hurried to his master, his gaze demurely on the ground. For once, Casto knew it was better to yield. He knelt down, waiting for Renaldo's verdict and already mentally prepared for his master to sell him.

As if Renaldo wanted to torture Casto on purpose, he examined him for some time before he started talking. "I'm still furious, Casto. Your behavior yesterday was unacceptable. But I don't want to take rash measures based on my anger. For the time being, I'm going to keep you. However, one mistake, no matter how small, and I instantly sell you to the highest bidder, understood?"

Shocked, Casto stared at the ground. All he could muster was a hoarse whisper. "Yes, Master."

"Good. Then get to work now."

With that, Renaldo turned away from his slave so that he didn't realize how hard it was for Renaldo to treat him so dismissively when all he wanted to do was pull him into his arms and kiss him. He heard Casto getting up and leaving the room quietly. In that moment, the Angel of Death felt lonelier than ever before in his centuries-long existence. He missed their morning ritual, missed the arguments, the passion, and most of all, he missed Casto's pride.

But the young man had to learn that his actions had consequences, that he couldn't oppose his master any way he pleased.

If only it wasn't so hard to show the necessary strictness.

"YOUR PLAN has worked out perfectly!"

Elwan's taunting voice made Damon edgy. His week hadn't been too good so far. He'd hoped for a bombshell from his scheme against Casto, and all that had happened was a faint tinkle. Being mocked by the likes of Elwan didn't improve his mood.

Elwan continued to taunt him. "He hasn't even whipped him. The prick has gone unpunished, as usual."

Damon tried hard to hide his anger and highlight the few positive points. "I admit that things could've gone better, but you're wrong in thinking Casto wasn't punished. His well-being is hanging by a thread. Haven't you noticed how humble he's become? I bet you Renaldo's threatened to sell him—which means there's only one tiny incident keeping Casto from testing his arrogance against a master like Aegid or Noran."

Elwan's face lit up in malicious joy. "And you think you're going to create that incident?"

Damon ignored the mockery and the challenge attached to it. The man in front of him was nothing more than a gambling piece he could use for his own purposes. It didn't pay to get agitated because of a mere tool.

"That's not necessary. Regarding Casto's temper, I don't think he can keep up the humility for more than a few days."

"So we're just going to sit back and wait?"

Damon treated Elwan to a smile that made the slave shiver in fear. "That, my friend, is the fun part."

IN THEIR chambers, Wolfstan sprawled lazily on one of the lounges, sipping hot tea from a cup and watching his darling wife sharpening her favorite daggers with practiced ease. The sonorous sound of the grindstone had a meditative effect on Wolfstan and allowed him to let his thoughts go wandering.

He loved this time of year, when winter forced the normally hectic life in the Valley to a halt. It was time to lean back and reminisce about the past year and think about the decisions he had put on hold. When people first met him, many of them underestimated Wolfstan, thinking him slow and cumbersome until time taught them better. The armorer was a thorough man who didn't like to rush things. His never-ending patience also made him the perfect husband for Hulda, whose vivacious nature had drawn in—and then put off—quite a lot of men and women in the past.

Contrary to her husband, Hulda couldn't see the benefits of the quiet season. As an assassin, she needed a certain amount of activity for peace of mind. It was the time of year when she was irritable, and it wasn't a good idea to challenge her wrath. Now she stopped her work and put the dagger down with a little more force than necessary. Her expressive lavender eyes drilled into Wolfstan. "What is it?"

The armorer smiled. He had known his wife long enough to know that she wasn't really angry, simply bored. "Nothing, my sweet one. I'm just thinking."

"You do that all the time, armorer."

Despite the cool wording, there was tenderness in the voice of the Mother Superior of the Sisters of the Night, the most famous order of assassins in the history of Ana-Darasa. Even though the order was no more, Hulda still carried the honorific, thus keeping the memory alive. Hulda loved her husband deeply. She had a strong suspicion that he was the prize Ana-Isara had promised her before the kiss that had changed her life forever. She'd been married to Wolfstan for so long, she knew where his thoughts were taking him. "Don't worry about Casto and Renaldo. They'll make up soon enough."

A fond smile was the answer to this statement. "You always know what I'm thinking. But I'm still worried. Since that unfortunate incident, our leader is as irritable as a whore after an unsuccessful night. And Casto is sulking like a beaten dog. I've been expecting them to make up in less than a week. If this goes on, I'm afraid Renaldo might lose him."

Hulda cast her daggers aside, sauntered over to where Wolfstan was sitting, snuggled up to her husband, and sipped from his teacup. "I know what you mean. They're both so unhappy. Who would've thought it possible that the proud Angel of Death could fall so hard for a slave?"

"You've said it yourself. Casto is far more than a mere slave."

"That's a fact. Although I can't exactly pinpoint what it is about him that makes him so special. I don't like admitting it, but he's almost impossible to read."

"Harder to read than you, my sweet one?"

"Mmm. In comparison, I'm like an open book—for those who can read."

"Are you challenging me?"

Hulda kissed her husband passionately. Wolfstan was never able to resist her erotic assaults; she knew too well how to use her body. He returned the kiss with devotion. His hands spanned his wife's hips in a possessive gesture. Suddenly greedy, Hulda started to strip him, her beautiful face showing her lust openly. The so-far boring day was definitely looking up.

"YOUR SLAVE has shown admirable restraint over the past few days."

Canubis watched his brother intently. He was worried about Renaldo, who had gotten more and more introverted since that last argument with Casto.

"Yes. It's been almost two weeks." Renaldo sounded strained. He suspected what Canubis, the Wolf of War, was aiming at.

And Canubis confirmed it. "You're aware that he won't hold up for much longer? Sooner or later he'll decide that he has endured enough, and then he'll be back to his old self."

"I know."

"But you're not going to take any action?"

Renaldo sighed. He'd been pondering the very same question repeatedly without finding a solution. Casto's current humility was scary and awkward, and Renaldo preferred the young man rebellious and bold. How he should find a balance between Casto the way he wanted him and an obedient, uncomplicated slave escaped him. "I've explained to you already. There's no sense in whipping him. You were there when I punished him."

Canubis grumbled something Renaldo didn't hear. Then, "You have to come up with something, brother. He's making a fool of you. Your beautiful little slave needs to realize that he's your property."

"And how should I accomplish that?"

Canubis grinned. "Luckily, that's not my problem. But you're ingenious—you'll find a way."

"Idiot." Halfheartedly, Renaldo hit his brother; he was already busy trying to solve his aggravating problem.

THAT EVENING Casto returned to his master's chambers late. He was pale like the snow outside and some strands of hair had broken loose from his ponytail. The roughhewn shirt and the old leather trousers he'd worn since his punishment started were covered in dirt. He moved slower than normal, without the grace Renaldo had gotten used to.

Deeply worried, Renaldo approached him. "Holy Mothers! Casto, what's happened to you? You look like you've fallen off a horse."

"I haven't fallen off a horse, no."

"Have you been trampled?" Renaldo knew he sounded like a mother hen, but Casto looked as if he had been in some kind of fight.

With clumsy fingers, Casto tried to open the buttons of his shirt. "I haven't been trampled. I've been—under the horse." Casto made a face while taking off his shirt.

Renaldo's eyes narrowed suspiciously. "Let me guess. Crazy Nirena."

"It wasn't her fault."

"You always say that! How many times does she have to wound you until you realize that she's beyond hope? I'm seriously contemplating forbidding you to ride this stupid beast anymore!"

Under normal circumstances a statement like that would have been the opening act for Casto, and they would have gotten into a heated argument in no time. But now Casto lowered his gaze demurely and pleaded, "Please don't do that, Master. It was my fault. I overexerted her."

It made Renaldo shiver, seeing his slave subdued like that. It was high time to end the farce. Determinedly he helped Casto out of his remaining clothes and walked him to the bath. "Get into the water. The warmth will do you good."

Again Casto obeyed without a word and lowered himself into the pool that was more than one and a half paces long and almost as broad. To distract himself from the stunning sight as well as what he was about to do to Casto, Renaldo went into his bedroom, grabbed the jewelry he had been keeping in a small box on the bedside table, and returned to the bath. He watched Casto slowly relax in the hot water. "I've decided to forgive you, slave."

The blond startled in surprise.

"But I do ask for compensation."

Suspiciously Casto beheld his master. "What do you want?"

Renaldo crouched down next to Casto's head and showed him his open palm. Three studs made of pure gold, each as long as one of Casto's finger bones, were glittering there. Blue diamonds were attached on both ends, one of each suspended on a very fine chain.

"You will give your consent to being marked with these."

Casto's brows furrowed, but before he could say anything, Renaldo kept on talking. "This, and you're going to accompany me to the Spring Ceremony next week without any back talk. In return I'll forgive and forget the whole incident."

Abruptly, Casto sat up in the water. He was trembling with rage and the glances he shot his master were so spirited that Renaldo almost drew back. "What happens should I decline?"

Renaldo took a deep breath. He knew he was cornering his proud slave now. "If you decline, Noemi will come tomorrow morning to heal your wounds. Afterward I'll give you provisions, weapons, and gold, and then you'll leave the Valley together with Lys."

"That's blackmail, Barbarian. You know as well as I do that this is impossible for me!" Casto's voice was a hiss.

"I know. But you've said it yourself—I'm a barbarian. You shouldn't be surprised when I revert to low tricks. I'm weary of our games, Casto. Either you obey or you leave."

The internal battle Casto was fighting showed clearly on his face. After a breathless silence during which Renaldo started worrying whether his slave might decide to leave after all, Casto finally gave in. "Very well, Barbarian, I will allow you to mark me. But there's no way I'll accompany you to the Spring Ceremony. Never!"

Renaldo's eyes narrowed. He couldn't believe that Casto still wasn't giving up. At the same time, he was thrilled. Finally things were going back to normal. "You don't listen well, slave. You either obey or I'll send you away."

"And you don't seem to get it. I've absolutely no inclination whatsoever to spend an entire evening watching you fuck yourself silly with all the members of the Pack. I'd rather leave."

Instead of answering this heated declaration with words, Renaldo ripped off his tunic and glided into the water next to Casto in one swift movement. He grabbed Casto's shoulders violently, pulled him close, and kissed him hungrily. "Why in the world would I sleep with anybody else but you if I'm given the choice? I only want you."

Renaldo didn't know if Casto had heard his words, because his slave had nestled himself against him with a sigh, his wet skin rubbing Renaldo's own, his whole body an invitation. Renaldo gave in to the temptation. They hadn't shared the bed since the incident in the training hall, and the fire he had so arduously kept in check the past few days started blazing, burning them both to cinders.

Casto gave himself willingly: he didn't resist when Renaldo pressed him against the edge of the pool to take him first there and then later on the floor of the bathroom. His uncharacteristic obedience was a sure sign that he'd missed his master as much as Renaldo had craved him.

After both of them had sated their hunger, Renaldo spoke again. "I only want you, Casto. If you come with me, there's no reason for me to have intercourse with others."

Casto shot him an accusing look. "Those past three years you always attended the Spring Ceremony."

"Because it's my duty. I always left as soon as possible to be with you. You can ask anyone in the Valley, and they will all confirm that I have never done this before. And you know very well that I've otherwise been faithful to you."

Casto lowered his gaze, shamed by his jealousy. "I know. I'll do what you're asking."

Renaldo knew he had to take action before his own determination crumbled or Casto had too much time to think things through. He grabbed Casto's wrist, dragged him into the main room, and pushed him onto one of the lounges.

"You lie down. I'll be right back."

He returned to Casto carrying a sharp awl, a basin with glowing coals, and a pot of healing salve. Casto showed a stubborn expression as he rested in the pillows. Without heeding the reproachful looks, Renaldo bent forward and took Casto's right nipple in his mouth. When he started to suck, Casto drew his breath in sharply, and then his hips started to move invitingly.

Renaldo somehow managed to withstand the temptation Casto's naked body offered, and reached for the red-hot awl from the nearby brazier. Casto didn't make a sound while Renaldo pierced first his nipples and then the base of his manhood in order to push the studs through his flesh, but his hands clawed at the furs desperately and he was sweating all over. When it was done, Renaldo cast the awl aside and gently applied healing salve to the wounds before he started fondling Casto again.

Despite his anger, Casto allowed it and gave in to his master's wishes.

Renaldo enjoyed this docility, knowing full well it wouldn't last.

Later, when they were lying in the furs, drained from their exertions, Renaldo gently caressed Casto's smooth skin. "Once the wounds have healed, you'll find out that these studs aren't so bad. I know some interesting tricks you'll certainly approve of."

Anger crept into Casto's features. "Even if you knew a thousand tricks, the fact remains that you forced me to wear this trumpery. You've adorned me like a cheap tavern whore."

A condescending smile crossed Renaldo's face. "I wouldn't go so far, slave. Or do you know many tavern whores decorated with real blue diamonds in their flesh?"

Casto's eyes widened. He sat up and felt the three studs with trembling hands. Now that Renaldo had called his attention to them, he regarded the stones with more than just a casual glance. They were indeed blue diamonds, probably the most noble and rarest stones in the world. In his anger he hadn't noticed before. "Why are you doing this, Barbarian? These stones are worth a fortune, probably two."

Everything in Casto resented wearing such expensive jewelry. Aside from the humiliation the mere existence of the studs meant to him, he was reluctant to show off such wealth.

Obviously Renaldo had a different opinion. "That might be, but I think you're worth a lot more than this *trumpery*. I like adorning you with beautiful things. I enjoy giving you presents."

Those words, meant as a proposal of peace, rebounded from Casto's anger like water from a rock. "That the stones, as well as I, emphasize your power and status has nothing to do with it? You're simply demonstrating that nobody can keep up with you."

Renaldo sighed. He'd known Casto wasn't stupid enough to fall for flattery. He had seen immediately through his master's true intentions and was similarly angry. But Renaldo didn't know what else he could do. The studs were an obvious symbol for everybody in the Valley that Casto was Renaldo's and Renaldo's alone. That Casto had to bow to his will, however reluctantly.

Renaldo yawned. "You're probably right. I'd like to sleep now. My need for discussion with you is covered for today."

Casto didn't answer but turned in his master's arms in order to sleep.

2. ORGY

The morning of the Spring Ceremony dawned as bleak as Casto's mood. Immediately after breakfast, Renaldo brought him to the sweathouse, where he would be prepared for the evening. Frankus greeted them at the entrance, bowing respectfully to the Angel of Death.

"My lord, I'm honored!"

"Frankus! It's my pleasure. As discussed I'm bringing you Casto for the preparations. I'll leave him in your skilled hands."

With that, he pushed his slave toward Frankus, with one hand resting heavily on Casto's nape, reminding the young man of his promise.

"You know my preferences, Frankus. If everything is to my liking, you won't regret it."

Frankus smiled carefully. The tension between master and slave hadn't escaped him. "I've never doubted that, my lord. I'll look after your property with the utmost care."

Renaldo could feel Casto's back muscles tense when he heard those words, so he tightened his grip in warning. "Remember, you promised to behave."

The menacing glare Renaldo got for that made his blood sing in happy anticipation. Finally things were back to normal.

"I haven't forgotten it, Barbarian."

"That's all I wanted to hear. You can trust Frankus. He's the best. Everything he does to you is my will, don't forget that."

After those words of warning, Renaldo opened the collar around Casto's neck. "To mark the occasion, you'll get a different collar for this evening. Frankus."

He nodded toward the master of the sauna before turning away, glad to escape the accusatory glare of his slave.

Frankus gestured Casto to follow him into the building. Silent, with his brows still furrowed in anger, Casto followed the man at whose mercy he would be for the rest of the day.

Frankus wasn't unfriendly, he kept on talking as if he was afraid Casto would vanish into thin air should he stop speaking for even a second. "You'll be on your own during the preparations. This year there's only Lady Noemi and Daran as personal companions, so we have plenty of room."

"Lady Noemi is a companion?" Casto was surprised. He would never have thought the proud witch would humiliate herself like that.

"But of course. She loves her husband and enjoys being at his service."

It was obvious that Frankus was trying to give Casto a hint, but Casto had no inclination to start a discussion about his qualities as a slave with somebody like Frankus. Apparently Frankus failed to get the cue—or, as was more likely—chose to ignore it, because he kept on blabbering happily.

"It really is a great honor to be chosen as a personal companion by one of the lords. Every slave in the Valley would kill to be in your place."

"Committing murder isn't necessary. I'm more than willing to leave this privileged status of mine to anybody who wants to have it."

"Casto!" Frankus was so horrified he slapped a hand over his mouth. "What if your master hears you talking like that?"

"The Barbarian knows what I think of this. I've told him in detail."

Frankus felt his eyes bulging in terror. He already knew that the Angel of Death's slave wasn't one to respect social conventions, but that he was challenging the powerful warlord without a care was too much for a man whose life was entirely at the mercy of his masters.

Casto sighed. "But I've given my word to be good. So yes, it's an unimaginable honor, and I really don't know how I deserve it. Satisfied?"

Frankus had gotten a grip on himself; his voice was calm again. "One day your big mouth will cause you real trouble. I don't have to be a seer to know that."

Casto only shrugged in a dismissive gesture. He didn't seem to be too worried about his fate. "So, what's going to happen to me?"

ONLY A short time later, Casto was cursing the Barbarian with every swear word he knew, and that particular part of his vocabulary was vast. Frankus had brought him into a well-heated room where he helped Casto undress. After that, Casto had to lie down on a wooden bench where Frankus started to epilate all his body hair with a sticky mixture of honey and sugar. When he ripped off Casto's pubic hair, Casto had almost screamed at the pain. Even being whipped seemed tolerable compared to that.

Frankus had smiled maliciously. It hadn't escaped him how hard Casto had to fight not to show his agony. "I'm sorry, but the lord prefers smooth skin. Besides, the gold will stick better like this." The swear words with which Casto answered made Frankus laugh. "You know some nasty expressions. Is that what you learned as a merchant?"

There was no answer to that, and Casto was glad that Frankus didn't realize his sudden tension. When it came to the lies about his past, Casto always got nervous. He detested the sham he had to put on, but his and Lys's lives depended on how well he could act. Up until then, everything had gone smoothly; nevertheless, one day he would have to tell the truth to the Barbarian, and probably sooner than later. Since that would also be the day he spoke his own death sentence, he preferred not to think too intensively about it.

After the epilation he was sent to the sauna to sweat out the residue on his skin. He did several rounds before Frankus washed him with scented soaps in one of the pools. Casto was gloriously relaxed by then. His anger had not dissipated but had cooled considerably in the wet, hot air, and he felt a strange, undirected lust awakening inside him like he'd never experienced before. To his never-ending shame, even Frankus's gentle touch aroused him.

Frankus, on the other hand, was pleased. "This is a good thing, Casto. It's exactly what I was aiming for. You'll get a massage with nerula oil now. After that I'll finish your preparations. And Casto, the reason for this massage is to get you sexually aroused, so don't try to fight it. Lord Renaldo has expressed the wish that you should find your release at least twice before he picks you up, so please cooperate."

Casto furrowed his brows. He'd heard about the effects of nerula oil from stories. It was a mixture of different herbs blended with pure blacknut oil and then left to mature for at least half a year. The end product sold for horrendous prices and was mainly manufactured in the borderlands of the Eastern Kingdoms where most of the required herbs grew. The recipe was a well-guarded secret, and quite a number of people had died trying to steal it. Using it as a mere massage tool was akin to sacrilege for most people and showed once more how rich and carefree the barbarians truly were.

It irritated Casto to no end that he of all people should be treated with this precious oil after he'd already endured the surprised stares of others because of the jewels shining from his flesh. "Why would he want that all of a sudden? The Barbarian has expressed his displeasure on more than one occasion should I turn to somebody else. His jealousy borders on the ridiculous."

Frankus beheld the young man for a long moment. He wasn't as experienced as Hulda when it came to reading people, but it wasn't difficult to guess Casto's thoughts at the moment. "This is the Spring Ceremony, where different rules apply. You're going to have sex the whole night, and I can assure you, Lord Renaldo won't hold back. The feast in honor of the Mothers is an orgy of the wildest kind. You have to be prepared so that the Angel of Death cannot hurt you."

Casto gulped. Frankus's words made sense. From everything he'd heard, things got down to business during the Ceremony. In past years the Barbarian had always come to him after midnight and then taken him until the sun came up. Since Casto liked it rough and had always been angry at himself as well as at Renaldo, he hadn't minded the violence of those games. But when he imagined doing the whole night what they had done in much shorter time in the past, he couldn't suppress a shudder. He wasn't even sure if he had the stamina required to endure the whole feast.

Without further resistance he allowed Frankus to march him to a massage bench where two slaves started kneading his muscles. The nerula oil performed its duty; Casto came three times under the ministrations of the two seasoned women without feeling the slightest scrap of shame. After that, Frankus collected him again. In yet another room, Frankus opened a box filled with gold dust and took a brush in his hands to transform Casto into a living statue to honor the masters of the Valley. To crown his work, he highlighted Casto's eyes with kohl and dipped the ends of his hair first into a bowl of oil and then dusted them with gold. Then he stepped back and checked the outcome of his efforts with a satisfied air.

"I can understand why the lord is so lenient toward you. You truly are breathtaking. I could fall in love with you this very moment."

Casto pursed his lips. He'd heard that sentence once too often to believe it. "Beauty is only an illusion."

He sounded so derisive that Frankus looked up. His gaze bore into Casto's eyes. Finally realization dawned on him. "So that's why you can oppose him so easily. You're not affected by his beauty."

Casto preferred not to answer that, because the insight was too close to the secrets of his own past.

He was taken into the waiting room where the Barbarian would pick him up. Daran, the ex-thief, was already there. He wasn't covered in gold dust, but with silver, and wore the golden upper-arm bracelets he'd gotten from Renaldo and a collar made of pure gold with an emerald in the middle. The jewelry stood out even more because of his shining, silvery skin, which made Daran seem like a creature from a fairy tale. For the first time since Casto had met the young man, he understood why the two desert warriors, Kalad and Aegid, were so infatuated with Daran. Apart from his agreeable personality, Daran was stunning in his own special way.

He approached Casto with a friendly smile. "I'd have never expected to see you here! Isn't it fantastic?"

"What exactly should be fantastic?"

Casto's cold answer startled Daran a little bit. Imploringly he looked at his teacher. "I'm very happy that my masters have chosen me. What about you?"

"But of course. It's an honor."

The words were said without emphasis, but Daran was determined to not let it spoil his good mood. He was too excited that his masters had decided to let him participate in the feast. The past years they had gone without him, saying they wanted to protect him. Daran had been sad that he wasn't allowed to give them this special service, and it had also hurt him. Now he was truly happy, although his masters had warned him that the Ceremony would be tiring for him.

He didn't have to endure Casto's gloomy presence any longer because Kalad and Aegid came to pick him up. His masters were dressed in identical dark green tunics edged with the white fur of snow rabbits. Seeing their regal figures, Daran's knees went soft.

The warriors smiled at their slave endearingly.

"You look splendid, little thief."

Kalad's voice was so suggestive that Daran felt the blood rushing to his cheeks—and someplace else. "Thank you, Master. Frankus is very skilled."

"I imagine that he didn't have much work with you, Daran." Aegid, too, was full of hunger. He took out a length of golden chain, linked it to

Daran's collar, and then the three men left the room, but not before Kalad gave Casto a lusty examination.

"You, too, look stunning, Casto. Renaldo should be pleased."

Stubbornly Casto extended his chin, pretending he hadn't noticed the hunger in the warrior's eyes and that it didn't terrify him to be this naked and vulnerable in front of them.

Kalad laughed happily. He didn't often manage to get the better of the blond. He enjoyed this unexpected advantage and allowed his gaze to travel once more over the naked body in a blatant manner.

Casto's eyes sparked in anger.

"Kalad!" With a reproachful look, Aegid pulled his desert brother along.

The mocking laughter still resounded in Casto's ears long after the three men left.

In his chambers, Renaldo was listening to his brother's reprimands.

"I know I told you to find a solution, but I didn't tell you to force him to take part in the Ceremony. You know damn well that is forbidden!"

"And what else should I have done? You were the one who said he had to learn his place."

"But not during the Spring Ceremony! Damn it, Renaldo, there'll be an aftermath to this! He won't forget such a humiliation in a hurry."

"Then I should cancel his participation?"

Renaldo was furious. He knew how dangerous this game was, but getting it confirmed by somebody else was downright uncomfortable. By forcing Casto to take part in the Ceremony, he violated the very rules he'd sworn to defend. Should his slave view the evening as rape, Renaldo would be punished accordingly. Despite knowing all that, Renaldo had decided to take these measures, trusting his intuition about Casto and accepting the consequences should he be wrong.

Imploringly he looked at his brother. Canubis alone was allowed to witness Renaldo's weakness.

The amber gaze of the Wolf of War wandered around the room. Canubis was well aware of the predicament Renaldo was suffering and how difficult it was to assess the situation correctly and react accordingly.

"No, I'm not saying that. It'll do him good to bow to your power for one night. But you have to be aware that this won't be without consequences. Under no circumstances."

"I'm aware, brother."

The two men shared a long look that contained an entire discussion.

All of a sudden, a huge grin spread over Canubis's face. "I'm curious what your slave will look like. He'll certainly be stunning."

Renaldo, too, was grinning like a wolf. "Let's go and find out."

"It's really not as bad as you think."

Noemi's voice was soft; she placed a hand on Casto's wrist to placate him. "You'll see, as soon as Renaldo is here, you'll have different things to worry about than what might happen during the feast."

"Why's he doing this to me?"

The witch sighed. Noemi really liked Casto, but she could also understand her brother-in-law. "Because you're a stubborn, arrogant prick who challenges him in ways not even I would dare. Did you really think he'd let you proceed like that?"

The shining eyes sparked to furious life. "He could just whip me!"

Now Noemi laughed openly. "Because that would impress you so much! I'm sorry, Casto, but no matter how you think about this, you really deserve all of it. And the studs are truly beautiful."

The young man was about to give a vitriolic answer when he suddenly felt the presence of the Barbarian. He didn't understand why, but he always knew when Renaldo was close. A feeling of peace came over him, followed by a prickling along his spine. He turned his gaze toward the door.

The Angel of Death and the Wolf of War looked truly divine when they entered the waiting room and filled it with their overwhelming presence. Both wore identically trimmed clothes made of the finest silk. Canubis's outfit was black; Renaldo's such a dark blue it almost seemed black as well. Both men had broad golden belts slung twice around their hips. A ceremonial sword and a dagger completed the outfit. Their feet were clad in boots made of the soft leather of mountain chamois, that reached up to their calves. With exception of the swords, the warriors' clothing was plain; the value of the materials spoke for itself.

Seeing the formal attire made Casto realize his own nudity even more. He understood that he was part of the decoration to Renaldo's outfit, reduced to being there simply for his impact on bystanders. The thought made him angry but aroused him at the same time. Never before had anybody dared to treat him like that.

Canubis now went to his wife, pressed a kiss to her cheek, and then put a collar on her that was as high as a handbreadth and made from countless miniscule golden eyelets. Embedded in the middle was a black diamond as big as a walnut. On each side three more diamonds, the size of hazelnuts, bordered it. Casto worked out the value of the jewelry in his mind and decided that with the diamonds alone he would be able to buy half the harbor of Ummana.

Just like him, Noemi was reduced to being a mere decoration on this evening, but she didn't seem to mind. The Wolf of War linked a golden chain into an unobtrusive eyelet at the bottom of the collar before he turned to his brother with a questioning look. "You better hurry. We're running late."

Renaldo regarded Casto, full of hungry anticipation. "You look well, slave."

Casto made a face but refused to answer. Instead he stared daringly at his master. He felt a strange heat surge through his body, which reminded him of Frankus's and Noemi's words—that he would desire the Barbarian. He hated himself for it.

Renaldo came closer; his masculine scent seemed to caress Casto like a soft feather. In his hands Renaldo carried something glittering and heavy. Casto gasped in surprise. The collar was identical to the one Noemi was wearing, only the diamonds were blue, not black. It felt cool on his skin when the Barbarian put it on him, and when the fastener clicked into place, to Casto's ears it sounded like a dungeon door closing.

Renaldo's sensual lips widened in a satisfied smile. "Very well." He turned to his brother. "Let's go."

Canubis headed for the door, with his wife following him two steps behind, her gaze cast down demurely as if she really were only a slave.

Renaldo chained Casto with a similar shackle and dragged him into the night.

Although he was naked, Casto didn't mind the cold while they headed toward the main hall. He was too busy hating himself for the lust he felt toward Renaldo. Everything inside him longed to belong to the Angel of Death, and should Renaldo keep him at arm's length much longer, he would beg to be taken by him. The entire situation was so humiliating, so infuriating that Casto didn't register his master leading him through the rows of waiting mercenaries to the head of the table.

Although this was supposed to be an orgy, all the warriors were clad in their finest. On both sides of the hall stood tables that pointed toward the gallery at the front of the room. Situated there was another table where the Emeris, the counselors of Canubis and Renaldo, had taken their places. Except for Cornelia, the Emeris who had suffered so badly at the hands of a bunch of marauders, all of them were present, but only Kalad and Aegid had a personal companion with them.

In front of the gallery, Canubis turned left with Noemi in tow while his brother took the right-hand route. They reached the middle of the table at the same time, accompanied by the respectful bows of the Emeris. Noemi and Casto stopped behind the high chairs, their gazes trained on the backs of their masters. Casto was glad for having a spot he could concentrate on since he felt no inclination to confront the assembled warriors.

Canubis and Renaldo opened the festivities by pleading for the blessing of the Holy Mothers. They did so in a language Casto recognized as that of the Ancients. He only understood part of it and made a mental note to intensify his studies. It always paid off to be fluent in as many languages as possible, and this special dialect, outdated as it may seem, could help him to understand his captor better and might even provide some kind of leverage.

When the brothers were done with the surprisingly short ceremony—Casto had expected something more elaborate—they gave the signal for the orgy to start. Everybody sat down, and the naked, dolled-up slaves started serving the food. The mood was playful from the beginning; nobody seemed inclined to wait for the alcohol to do its magic and relax the mood. Eating and intercourse melted into a lustful, inseparable union.

Casto stepped forward to refill the Barbarian's cup, but Renaldo grabbed his wrist, pulled him onto his lap, and brought the full goblet to Casto's lips.

The moment Renaldo caressed the young man's upper thigh, Casto was lost. He felt a wave of lust washing over him, fired up by the sensual, sometimes rough sounds around him and the drug that had invaded his entire system. He gave up on fighting it. His eyes clouded with lust, his breath came in ragged gasps, his lips parted invitingly.

"Please, Master. Take me."

With a satisfied smile that under normal circumstances would have riled Casto up to no end, but that he didn't register at that moment, Renaldo leaned forward to kiss him.

When their lips met, the world exploded into a red-tinged rush, and for many hours Casto's feelings were solely concentrated on the Angel of Death. He didn't see how Canubis spread his wife's legs on the table, he didn't hear how Kalad and Aegid bent their thief over the backrest of a chair and took him numerous times, he wasn't conscious of all the people in the hall mating without shame or feelings of guilt. All he knew was that he belonged to Renaldo. All he wanted was for his master to take him.

The Angel of Death brought him to the highest peak over and over again. Casto only existed to please his master, was reduced to the lust Renaldo aroused in him. It was strangely liberating to commit himself so wholly, to think about nothing besides pleasing his master.

WHEN THE sun started to tinge the sky over the Valley a soft pink, Casto slowly woke from his intoxication. He felt sore and exhausted, his muscles ached, and his head felt light. He had problems thinking clearly and could but hope that his slowly returning memories were mocking him and that he hadn't really done all the lecherous things replaying in front of his inner eye.

Renaldo slung an arm around Casto's hips. "Let's go. It's enough for today."

Casto was too tired to argue. He followed his master obediently.

Or at least he tried to. His legs gave out, he was so spent he was unable to walk on his own.

Without hesitation, Renaldo picked him up and carried him back to his chambers. Casto wanted to wash, but the Angel of Death only shook his head. "We're both too tired for that."

Casto looked down at himself. The gold dust clung in slivers to his skin, his upper thighs were sticky with Renaldo's essence, and the nerula oil had entered into an inseparable union with his sweat. The mead Renaldo had spilt over him when he'd tried to feed him with it now pasted Casto's body.

Renaldo had licked off most of it, but Casto's skin stretched where the sugar had dried. "I'm going to ruin the furs."

The Barbarian only shrugged. "You're not the only one. That's what furs are made for." He grabbed Casto's wrist and dragged him to the bed.

Casto followed him without hesitation. He was too tired to give a damn about anything.

IT WAS early afternoon when Casto woke from a deep, dreamless sleep. He wasn't surprised that the Barbarian was already up again. Since he'd reluctantly accepted that Renaldo was more than human, all the little inconsistencies summed up to a harmonious whole. Renaldo's endurance, his unearthly skill with the sword, the speed with which his wounds healed, his ageless appearance that wasn't a side effect of youth but a fetching mixture of the experience gained in several lifetimes and the looks you expected from somebody still in their twenties.

Casto would never admit just how much he was drawn to Renaldo. It was a triumph that he didn't grant Renaldo, especially not after the previous night. Casto felt his temper boiling when he thought about what the Barbarian had done to him, what he'd made Casto comply with. Furiously he stomped into the bath, where he spent the next hour getting rid of the unpleasant mixture on his skin.

Afterward he returned to the bedroom, still naked because he couldn't stand being clothed again after his skin was so dirty. He fought the urge to puke when he gathered the ruined furs and crammed them all into a big sack he made from one of the sheets. Then he placed the bundle in front of the door, secretly wishing he could do the same with last night's memories. When he was done, he started pacing restlessly through the rooms, too upset to decide what to do.

The idea to visit Lys for a short ride only appealed to him for about a minute. He would have had to get dressed to do that, and he was too tired.

Casto's grumbling was interrupted. Renaldo entered the chambers with four slaves in tow who carried two heavy wooden trunks.

When Renaldo saw the angry tension in his slave's jawbone, he sent the men away. "Put down the trunks and leave."

Silently, like ghosts, the men retreated, leaving Renaldo and Casto alone.

Casto stared at his master in open fury. Renaldo had hoped the night of passion might have softened Casto's attitude, but that wish had obviously been in vain.

"What are those?" The blue eyes regarded the trunks with derision.

Renaldo sighed. "Those, my unruly slave, are your Spring Ceremony presents."

He offered the young man the keys that would open the trunks.

Still angry, but now also curious, Casto knelt in front of the bigger trunk and opened it. In silence he stared at the contents, his shoulders tense, his voice constrained. "If this is your idea of a practical joke, I'll refuse in future."

Renaldo placed a hand on Casto's nape; his voice was soft. "Do you really think I'd be so cruel?"

Casto spun around, his gaze an uneasy mixture of anger and guilt. "I think I'd have deserved it. At least before you marked and humiliated me publicly."

Renaldo ignored that comment.

"I've told you that I'd forgive and forget about the incident. You've made great progress in the past few months, that's why I'm giving you this. If you still want to go to battle with me, you're to be suitably equipped."

Both men stared into the trunk that held a complete armament, everything in the colors of the Angel of Death.

After a moment's hesitation, Casto bowed to Renaldo. "I thank you, Master."

Renaldo nodded. He knew that was all the concession he would get from the young man. "Come on. Look into the other one as well."

Dumbfounded, Casto looked at the treasure hidden in the smaller trunk.

Inside the chest was a goblet made from gold with inlaid work in lapis lazuli, several books bound in finest leather, new clothing made of soft linen and expensive silk, and to top it off, a warm coat from mountain deer leather dyed in blue and lined with sable fur.

Casto looked at the Barbarian suspiciously. He recognized a bribe when he saw it. "Although I acted so horribly toward you, you're surprisingly generous."

"I'm a generous man. Haven't you realized that?"

"Where's the catch, Barbarian?"

"Does everything have to have a catch? Can't you just accept the presents and be happy about it?"

"I'd love to. But I know there's a catch. So?"

Renaldo lifted his hands in defeat. "Perhaps a small one. I pressed you rather mercilessly, and I'm sorry for that. I hope to make up for it at least a little bit."

Casto stared at his master for such a long time that Renaldo started to feel uncomfortable. Abruptly Casto turned his back on him; his voice, when he spoke, was flat.

"I don't like to admit it, Barbarian, but it was your right. My behavior was dishonorable. I lacked respect, and it was right of you to punish me. Whatever there is between us, in the training hall, you are my teacher, and I disregarded your authority. You could have killed me on the spot for what I've done, so I'm grateful."

With an iron fist, Renaldo grabbed the young man who had brought him to a white heat more than once, and he kissed him hard. He only interrupted the kiss for a short moment in which they both glared at each other, panting. "Starting tomorrow you'll get the chance to show me your gratitude. Training is at the usual time."

Casto's eyes filled with sincere gratefulness. Then Casto tilted his head back, offered himself to his master like a sacrifice, and with that gesture, he made it known that he wouldn't fight back this time, that he would submit.

With a satisfied growl, Renaldo accepted the rare offer. He pulled Casto close, his tongue invaded the slave's mouth imperiously, and they both gave in to the lust that burned them to ashes.

IN THE bedroom of the desert brothers, Daran woke slowly from his exhausted sleep. He was vaguely aware that at some point his masters had taken him to the bath to get him cleaned up, but he'd been too tired to do more than leave himself in their hands.

As predicted by his masters, the past night had demanded everything from him, although he was aware they had held back. Daran blushed when he thought how much he must have disappointed his benefactors. Like a child he'd demanded to be taken along, and because they were so unbelievably kind, they'd given their permission. Deeply ashamed, he buried his face in the pillows and wished to turn back time and take back his selfish request.

Kalad's warm hand on his back startled him.

"Are you still tired, little thief? You can take another nap, if you want."

Daran hurried to get up. He didn't want to stress his owners' patience any more. "I'm fine, Master."

Kalad furrowed his brow in concern. "You don't look like it. It's been a long night, and we didn't hold back. You really should rest some more."

A flaming red invaded Daran's cheeks. Beaten, he lowered his head. "I'm sorry, Master. I served you badly. Please forgive me."

Gently, Kalad lifted Daran's chin with one finger; his voice was soft when he said, "You adorable idiot. You served us very well. We're pleased. You shouldn't forget that you're a mere human. Of course you'd be tired after a night like that. Aegid and I pushed you way past your limit to satisfy our lust."

Surprise crept onto Daran's features. "You're not angry? Or disappointed?"

"No! How could we be? We're just a little concerned because you're so pale. And now lie down and sleep some more before my bad conscience overwhelms me."

Gratefully, Daran kissed his master's hand. He was pretty sure Kalad was just trying to soothe him, but he was thankful for having such caring masters. Not for the first time did he thank the Holy Mothers for the unbelievable gift they had bestowed on him.

DAMON WATCHED, more surprised than angry, as Casto hurried toward the training hall. Only one day after the Spring Ceremony and the Angel of Death resumed the arrogant young man's training as if they had never had a fight, as if all of Damon's efforts had never happened. It was indeed interesting that the short-tempered and normally merciless warrior didn't seem able to resist the beautiful stranger. Damon wondered what kind of crime Casto would have to commit to be punished seriously.

Damon's suspicion regarding Casto was hardening the more he thought about him. It was time to start some research to confirm it. If his hunch proved true, then the Good Mother's victory over the two bastard brothers was only a matter of time. Even though the Good Mother had not created Ana-Darasa, as far as Damon was concerned, she had a stronger claim on the world than the two Mothers, its creators. Unlike Ana-Aruna and Ana-Isara, she was willing to allow her followers the use of magic. She even helped them, whereas they denied the humans the right to use their magical talents.

DEEPLY FOCUSED, Sic threaded the last two links into the damaged chain mail before he turned it around and riveted the still-open ends so that the armor looked as if it had never been impaired.

It was very placid inside the smithy. Traditionally nobody worked on the day after the Spring Ceremony, and Sic loved this day when the smithy was his alone. He treasured the tranquility and the peace, moving freely without harassment from the fellows and the apprentices. He enjoyed his work and knew he had to be grateful for being allowed to do other things than just menial jobs despite his lack of talent.

Days like this, rare as they might be, were perfect to work on his skills. Sic wanted to become so capable that Noran could be proud of him. He eyed his work critically but couldn't find a fault. With a satisfied nod, he turned aside to store the chain mail.

"Good job."

Startled, Sic spun around. Noran was standing next to the anvil, his dark eyes trained on him. The apprentice hurried to get on his knees. "Master."

"How long have you been here?"

"Since this morning, Master. Please forgive me, I didn't hear you."

"It's no problem. You were busy. Are you done?"

"Yes, Master."

"Then follow me."

Noran went in the direction of his private rooms with Sic rushing after him.

Noran's personal work space was located at the back of the smithy. Essentially it was just a big room divided by a forged folding screen. In the bigger part was a forge, and the other area was crammed with a worktable and two high shelves on which Noran stored his sketches, orders, and samples. For Sic the place was paradise, and he was always happy when he was allowed to watch his master during his work or when he had to clean up the workroom. It was as if somebody had given him permission to dwell in a treasure chest.

Now the master smith stopped next to the table, resting his hand on a trunk he had placed there. He scrutinized Sic. "How long have you been with me, Sic?"

The young man lowered his head shyly. "I'm not sure, Master. Seven or eight years, perhaps?"

"That's about the right time span." Noran hesitated for a moment since his next words were going to take him into uncharted territory. "I'm aware that I rarely praise you, Sic, but today I wish to tell you how very pleased I am with you. You've progressed remarkably well, and if you put your heart to it, you can go a long way."

Sic was so surprised he automatically looked up. Praise from Noran was indeed so rare he couldn't remember when he'd heard it last. "Master?"

With a smile, Noran pushed the trunk toward Sic. "This is for you. I wish you a happy Spring Ceremony, Sic."

The young man couldn't believe it. For the past seven years, he had wished time and again to receive a present from his strict master, but he'd never been worthy. He had already come to terms with the fact that he would never rise enough in Noran's esteem to get a gift.

"You're endowing me, Master? Thank you so much!" His voice brimmed with happiness. Sic fell to his knees again, his nape lowered in gratitude.

The master smith was strangely touched by the emotional outburst, a feeling he hadn't experienced in a long time. There was no doubt about his slave's genuine joy, even though he didn't know what he was about to get.

"Before you thank me so eloquently, you should check out what it is."

Hands trembling in anticipation, Sic opened the trunk's lid. When he saw what it contained, his eyes went wide. "Master!" Again he knelt down, but before he could lower his head, Noran saw the tears streaming down his cheeks.

"Please, don't start crying. It's just a set of tools, and you really earned them."

"I thank you, Master. They're truly beautiful."

"I hope they're useful as well. You didn't get them for admiring."

"May I try them right now?"

The young man's voice was so eager Noran could feel a smile creeping onto his lips. "But of course. Work with them as long as you like."

Sic carried the trunk to his working place with so much reverence it almost embarrassed his master. At the forge he put the tools in order and chose a workpiece he wanted to finish.

From his rooms, Noran watched Sic working skillfully on a dagger. The boy had truly progressed in a satisfying manner. A few more years, and he could become a master himself.

The master smith had pondered for a long time whether he should loosen the tight leash on which he'd held Sic ever since he bought him. But in the seven years since the boy had come to him, Sic hadn't shown any of the bad characteristics Noran was meticulously looking for ever since his humiliating experience with Arja. On the contrary, Sic was always eager to please his master, although Noran was a strict owner who didn't give his underlings reason to love him.

Sic was the most talented smith Noran had ever met, and he fostered this exceptional talent by keeping the young man under his thumb to give him the incentive to work even harder. The outcome spoke for itself. Sic was already better than any other man in the Valley. Very soon he would be able to compare to his Emeris master.

Noran was surprised about the impact his gift had on Sic. There was no doubt about Sic's genuine pleasure and gratitude.

Slowly, Noran started to realize that he could give more responsibility to the youth, that he could allow him to come closer. That cold, menacing voice that had been his companion ever since Arja's betrayal was indeed telling him that he could trust nobody, but Noran tried to ignore it.

Sic had earned his chance.

3. WOLFSTAN

WHILE THE last winter storms attacked the Valley, bringing with them the ice-cold air that was the season's harbinger, the mercenaries returned to their daily rhythm. In silent agreement, Renaldo had doubled Casto's training, knowing full well he wouldn't be able to keep the young man in the camp come next summer. His main target was to prepare him for every obstacle battle could throw at him.

Casto followed the same train of thought and threw himself into work. To drill him even more, Renaldo made him fight against other warriors, among them Kalad and Aegid. Renaldo almost burst with pride when Casto did well with all of them. He did not win every match but was able to seriously press his opponents.

With Kalad in particular, Casto reached an impasse they fought out anew every week. The spry desert warrior was honored to test his abilities with his god's favorite. In return, Casto took intensive care of Daran, whose progress was truly remarkable. It seemed as if the thief had had a warrior sleeping inside all this time.

Daran was so good that Casto advised Kalad and Aegid to give him a second horse, a wish they gladly granted.

While the cold still reigned over the Valley with an iron fist, Casto suddenly realized that he was truly happy. The feeling was so new, so unfamiliar, that it took him some time to understand what he was experiencing. Then he enjoyed it fully, for fear it wouldn't last.

After the last heavy snowfalls of the season, he even found time to return to the library. According to the chronicles, Wolfstan was the next Emeris who had joined the demigods. Casto didn't know Wolfstan, the silent, composed husband of Lady Hulda, very well but he felt oddly drawn to his level personality. Nothing ever shocked the man.

BENT DEEPLY, Wolfstan followed the stag's trail, clearly visible on the ground softened by snow slush. Apparently his prey was no longer ahead of him. It had been two days since he'd started to trail the magnificent twelve-pointer he'd first spotted close to the village where he spent the winter. He'd planned to give the animal to the villagers as a thank-you for their hospitality—should he ever catch up with the beast. Careful not to make any sound, he moved through the thicket.

It was uncomfortably wet and cold in the woods, winter fighting a ferocious battle with the first messengers of spring, resulting in earth that was frozen and softened at the same time. One moment you were treading solid ground, the next you were ankle-deep in mud. Wolfstan was grateful for his superb clothing, but even the cloak lined with rabbit's fur and the high, warm leather boots weren't able to completely banish the cold from his body. He only hoped he would find the damn stag sometime soon.

As if a kind deity had heard his wish, a small clearing opened in front of him, and the beast was browsing there.

Wolfstan froze. He checked the direction of the wind and moved in the opposite direction to prevent his prey from picking up his scent. With agonizing slowness he selected an arrow, put it on the bowstring, and then bent his bow with fingers clumsy from cold.

He evened his breath and drew air into his lungs one more time. When he was sure of his aim, he let the projectile speed toward the stag. Eyes still following the arrow's trail, Wolfstan saw another one zip through the air and find its target in the beast's throat. Hit by the two arrows, the proud stag went down. For a moment the long legs kept twitching in fruitless struggle, and then it was over.

Wolfstan placed his hand on the handle of his hunting knife and slowly entered the clearing, wondering who the second shooter might be. During unstable times like these, he assumed the worst and was prepared to fight for the prey as well as for his life if needed. In the thicket to his left, he heard a soft rustling before the wood spat out a slim figure clad in black leather.

He froze.

She was the most beautiful woman he had ever seen in his entire life. Her honey-blonde hair fell to her hips in a tight braid, and her lavender-colored eyes gazed imperiously at the world over a small, proud nose and generous, sensual lips. Her white skin was flawless. Black leather hugged her voluptuous curves tenderly and accentuated the long, slim muscles of her legs and arms.

The woman moved with the grace of a dancer, and when she spoke, her voice was soft and melodic. "Seems like we'll have to share the prey."

Feeling slightly guilty because he'd stared at her so openly, Wolfstan retreated a step. "You're right. Your arrow hit the throat, mine the heart. Both were lethal."

"Then we have an agreement. Or do you wish to fight me?"

Wolfstan hurried to shake his head. Although he'd met some truly amazing female warriors in his life, he usually tried to avoid fighting against a woman. It always made him feel as if he were doing something outrageous. "I'd never dare to! You're a lady!"

Her beautiful eyes widened in shock before she started to guffaw. The idea that she could be of noble lineage seemed to deeply amuse her.

"Lady or not, you wouldn't stand a chance anyway," she added.

Confidently she extended her hand. "My name's Hulda. I'm pleased to make your acquaintance."

Wolfstan took her small, cool hand, returning the smile with genuine joy. "I'm Wolfstan. And I'm pleased as well."

"Then let's cut up this fellow. But first—"

She whipped out a hunting knife, knelt next to the dead stag, and slit its throat. While the dark blood seeped slowly into the soil, she murmured something in a language Wolfstan didn't know.

Once she was done, he hunkered down as well to help her with the cutting. "A prayer for the beast's soul?"

"Something like that. I wished him a good journey to the Green Lands."

"You follow the Holy Mothers?"

The numbers of those following the goddesses had been steadily decreasing for some time now, which was why he was surprised to meet one out here.

"No. Or, to put it more accurately, only indirectly. I serve their sons."

Wolfstan paused in surprise. "You rank among the army of Lord Canubis and Lord Renaldo?"

"You've heard of them?"

"Who hasn't? But I've never been sure whether their divine ancestry is just a trick to lure naive folk."

"It's not a trick, of that I can assure you."

"May I ask what a beautiful woman like you does in an army of mercenaries?"

Hulda laughed softly. Again she seemed amused by his assumptions. "Thanks for the compliment. But you'd be surprised how well I fit in."

"I know about armies. I'm an armorer. And no, I can't imagine how you'd fit in."

"Armorer? We'll have to talk about that. And to soothe your curiosity, I'm a trained killer. Once I was the Mother Superior of the Sisters of the Night. I can assure you, I'm perfectly integrated."

Wolfstan gulped. His respect for the beautiful woman had just grown again. That also explained her relaxed handling of the hunting knife and the grace of her movements. She wasn't a dancer but a predator.

"You said you're an armorer. In which army?"

"At the moment, in none. My former master and I had some variance of opinion, and I preferred to spend the winter in a small village close by. I've been planning to go looking for a new master soon."

"Forget about that. Canubis is in want of an armorer. It would be best if you could come with me right now so that he can meet you."

"As much as I'd love to follow your invitation, I have to decline." Regretfully, Wolfstan eyed Hulda's shapely body. "I promised the villagers this stag in return for their hospitality, and I intend to keep my word."

"Is that all? Just wait here. I'm getting my horse, and then we can deliver this prime specimen to your village. Once we're done, you come with me."

"Just like that?" Wolfstan was amazed.

"Of course just like that. But it wouldn't hurt if you had a horse. It's a long journey back to the Valley."

"That's not a problem."

Still taken aback by the sudden turn of events, he watched Hulda disappearing between the trees. The villagers were more than pleased at his generous present and wished Wolfstan a good journey. Together with Hulda, he headed out to meet Canubis, the famous Wolf of War.

AFTER ABOUT ten days on the road, they reached the Valley. Canubis was thrilled to get a skilled armorer and engaged Wolfstan for the upcoming campaign in the Eastern Kingdoms. Throughout the summer,

Wolfstan fell more and more in love with Hulda, who'd bedded him every night on their way to her home.

It took some time until Wolfstan got used to the stunning assassin sharing her bed with others as well. For him, love, intercourse, and fidelity were inseparable, while Hulda viewed sex as something with the significance of a shared excursion.

After Wolfstan received the kiss from Ana-Isara that made him one of the Emeris, it took another hundred years until the blonde beauty chose him as her mate. But with the stoic perseverance that was built into his character, he waited for the woman who had stolen his heart the first time they met.

Hulda was the prize Ana-Isara had promised him for his service, and there was no way he would ever let her go.

WITH A smile, Casto set the book aside. The love story showed Hulda in an entirely new light, although Casto had to admit that she met his expectations. His valuation of the beautiful woman was reinforced by every word he'd read, and he renewed his resolution to never provoke her anger.

Yawning, he stretched his stiff muscles to shake off the fatigue before he went on his way back to the stables.

Lys greeted him with a content snort, looking forward to the ride they had planned for today. The stallion loved galloping through the deep, fresh snow, and the bright sunshine only enhanced their good mood. Casto didn't bother to saddle his brother or even give him a bridle. He reveled in the feeling of the strong muscles rolling beneath him while they were racing through the woods and along the slopes.

As soon as they left the vicinity of the stables and scattered houses, Lys increased his pace, not enough to make a random onlooker suspicious, but enough to at least partly satisfy their hunger for speed. Apart from the fact that nobody was to find out who Casto really was, it was the only drawback of living in the Valley—it was so unbearably confined.

Lys, as well as Casto, longed for the endless plains where he could run for days. They missed that flash of freedom they'd enjoyed on a regular basis during the year after their escape from Ummana, the one thing that had made their loneliness bearable.

They took a break at their favorite spot, the small lake at the foot of the ascending stone walls around the Valley. Everything was still icy at that time of year, and Casto's favorite place for sunbathing was buried under a pile of snow, but the sun set the snow crystals to sparkling almost as temptingly as the waves on the lake during summer.

Dreamily, Casto gazed at the spectacle of light in front of him. Almost automatically he was stroking his brother's hair in the weak winter sun. Lys was soaking it up with his eyes closed.

"Do you think we could stay here, perhaps?" Casto's voice was very soft. Lys could understand him without words, but Casto had to say it aloud to comprehend all the implications of the almost-inconceivable thought. Lys made a snorting sound. Apart from the missing range, he liked the Valley. Casto continued speaking softly.

"Renaldo isn't that bad. He's a Barbarian, no doubt about that, but I can deal with him. And nobody would ever find us here. It's a good place."

Lys was waiting. He already suspected what Casto was getting at but let his brother go on at his own pace.

"I'd have to tell him the truth. Who I am." Casto hesitated again before voicing his greatest fear.

"I'm afraid, Lys. He hates being lied to. What if he doesn't want me anymore? Or worse, hands us over? I can't stand lying to him any longer, but sometimes he makes me so angry I want to strangle him. I just don't know what to do."

Casto started pacing in front of Lys. With each word, he was getting more agitated.

"And then there's this stupid prophecy. Of course I don't believe in it, but even though it can't be true, a man like him will want an heir sooner or later. I don't think I could bear losing him like that."

With a determined whinny, Lys ended his brother's train of thought. His mind was as clear as the night sky.

Silently, Casto listened to the wisdom of the demon. With a whimper he buried his forehead in the soft hair. "You're right. We await the end of this summer. If he really lets me fight, when he sees that I'm his equal, perhaps I can tell him." Determined, he raised his head. "Let's ride back home. I'm getting cold."

CASTO'S RETURN was watched by more than one set of resentful eyes. Most of the slaves working in the stables didn't like him because of the way he treated them, but they kept their feelings hidden, mostly because it was imprudent to anger a personal slave—especially when that slave belonged to the Angel of Death.

Some, among whom were Sindal and Elwan, didn't hide their animosity. Nobody wanted to side with the losing party when it came to an open confrontation. Given how infatuated the Angel of Death was with Casto, there was no doubt who would lose out.

Damon assessed those emotions and stored them in some corner of his complicated mind as useful information. He was determined to bring Casto down after he had so eloquently turned down his offer of friendship. It wasn't that Damon hadn't expected that. After all, Casto was a man with firm principles and Damon himself did not fit into that category, but the open hostility with which Casto had responded to him had woken his anger. He didn't know how, but the slave of the Angel of Death had seen right through him, something Damon resented deeply. While Casto met the other slaves with complete indifference, he'd told Damon straight-out that he didn't want anything to do with him.

Fearing for his cover, Damon had been very reserved and made a hasty retreat. Nevertheless, he never forgot the ignominy. He would have loved to find out where the blond bastard and his beast went every day, but there was no chance he could follow them on foot. Apart from this small time span, Damon knew everything about Casto's daily routine. If he couldn't keep an eye on him, then Assani or one of the other six slaves in the Valley who also followed the Good Mother took over, and they told him every little detail about their target.

That was how Damon knew that Sic and Casto had established a very fragile friendship grimly tolerated by Lord Noran and constantly questioned by Casto. It was also how he'd found out—which Elwan had confirmed—that Casto was taking special care of the brown mare belonging to Lord Wolfstan, although the horse had a reputation of being completely bonkers. Neither Casto's visits to the library nor his lessons with Daran were hidden to Damon. He knew Casto better than anybody else in the Valley did, and he was sure he had him thoroughly figured out. Now he only had to wait for his chance to teach the arrogant bastard the lesson he deserved.

A plan started to form in his mind. A plan that would not only destroy Casto, but would also hit the damn Angel of Death and his cursed brother hard. Renaldo's infatuation with Casto was his greatest weakness, one Damon would use for the greater glory of the Good Mother.

FULL OF anticipation, Casto entered the small reading chamber in the library. He was eager to get back to his reading and find out more about the other Emeris.

Ever since he had witnessed Renaldo's miraculous return from the dead, Casto had slowly started to change his opinion about him. A part of him still refused to believe that Canubis and Renaldo could be demigods, but he was willing to set aside his skepticism for the time being.

Casto opened the chronicles at the marked page, made himself comfortable in the chair, and forgot everything around him for the next hour.

DEEPLY WORRIED, Bantu cleaned his sleeping sister's face with a wet cloth. Although she had assured him time and again that she was fine, he doubted it. And at the moment, their survival was inevitably linked to her endurance. The slave traders who had captured them two weeks ago weren't squeamish when it came to keeping their traveling pace. It had been only yesterday when they had left an exhausted slave with his throat slit open in the roadside ditch.

Cornelia had recovered from the wounds she had suffered during the raid on their village, but she wasn't completely healed yet. Bantu shuddered whenever he remembered how he had found his little sister on that fateful day.

Bantu was out in the fields with the other men, gathering the harvest, and hadn't even registered the raid. Only when they returned home in the evening had they found out what had happened.

The cabins had all been destroyed, everything of worth either stolen or broken. The elderly and the children, as well as the few women, had been raped and killed. Only Cornelia had survived, and for many days afterward, it had seemed as if she would follow the other victims. But his sister was tough. Day after day she fought her way back to life and conquered anew what the marauders had taken from her. She never talked about what had been done to her, but Bantu had seen the terrible wounds. Even now, almost a year after the raid, he still had to fight back the horror that tried to claim him at the memory of her injuries.

As soon as Cornelia felt better, she asked Bantu to take her away from the village. She simply wasn't able to cope with the horrors she had experienced. Even after the cabins had been rebuilt, all she could see was burned wood and the ground drenched in blood. During the night she woke from dreams that were so vivid she could smell the stench of the corpses. The only way to escape this never-ending nightmare was to leave the village.

And so the siblings had gathered their few belongings and started their journey south, in the hope of finding a place they could turn into a new home. But after less than a week, they had been captured by slave traders, and now Bantu's most pressing worry was again the bare survival of his sister.

Their group consisted of five slave traders and thirty slaves, all chained together at the ankles, following the Umman River in a northeastern direction. As far as Bantu understood, their destination was a mining city in the mountains. Should they make it there, they were as good as dead. The mines weren't a place you left alive. Once you passed into the dark maw, you were lost to the void. The blood of countless slaves was the price a vengeful god demanded for the desecration of the mountains that hid in their depths the raw material for blue steel—the hardest material the human race knew.

To sate the human hunger for steel and the divine hunger for blood, the stream of slaves had to be endless, a sad procession of the doomed. Bantu had never intended to stay with the caravan long enough to catch a glimpse of the mountains, but at the moment things looked grim. All his plans for escape were risky, if not impossible, especially now when all that was keeping Cornelia upright was her iron will. Bantu knew his sister's spirit was unbreakable, but even she couldn't endlessly force an exhausted body just recovered from terrible injuries.

He had to come up with an idea as soon as possible, or they both would meet their end.

At noon the next day, it looked as if their fate was sealed. Cornelia had tripped over a stone, fallen hard, and hadn't been able to get up again. When Bantu leaned over her to help, he was brutally yanked back by one of the slave traders.

"Out of my way, scum!"

In the man's fist, a dagger gleamed. He opened Cornelia's chain, ready to slit her throat. Desperately, Bantu attacked the man, determined to defend his sister to the last breath, to join her in death if necessary.

A second slave trader appeared and threw him off the first one. Bantu hardly felt the blows on his head and torso. He only had eyes for his sister, who fought her murderer's grip weakly without the slightest chance to get away. The dagger shimmered high in the air. Bantu reared up against his attacker, a desperate scream on his lips… and then there was suddenly a dark, gigantic shadow that caught the slave trader's wrist in a steely grip.

A shrill scream tore from the slaver's throat when his bones broke like dried twigs. He fell to his knees. With his left hand, he protected his broken right, his eyes glued to the newcomer in utter shock.

Or *newcomers*. Astonished, Bantu looked at the two men who had just saved his sister.

The one who had broken the slave trader's hand was a giant, about one ell and four spans tall, with white hair and milky blue eyes in stark contrast to his dark skin. His companion was almost two and a half heads smaller, with long black hair that hung in countless braids. The dark eyes sparked with humor, and he seemed to Bantu like a man who took everything in life as a game.

Now he shook his head, making his braids fly. "Tsk, tsk. Don't get your weapons. That's not a bright idea."

The slave traders gazed in fear at the heavy broadsword, which had appeared in the giant's hands as if by magic, and at the two smaller but no less intimidating weapons the braided one wielded.

He carried on as if oblivious to the superior numbers he was facing. "We don't want to detain you. We're here for business."

The taller warrior loosened a small leather bag from his belt. He threw it to the slave traders in a careless manner. "That should be enough gold to pay for the female and her brother, don't you think?"

Without opening the pouch, the traders nodded.

The warrior smiled encouragingly. "So we're in agreement, how nice. Please unchain them."

Bantu didn't move a muscle when the hated chain was removed from his ankle. Then he rushed to Cornelia, who was still lying on the ground. While he embraced her carefully, the slave traders and their cargo moved on.

The giant knelt beside the siblings, his eyes clouded by worry. "She's very weak, Kalad. There's no way we can transport her any length of time. She must rest."

The braided one shrugged. "It's okay. No drama. We'll set up our camp somewhere here. That's also what the wolves prefer."

The white-haired warrior wanted to lift Cornelia up, but Bantu stopped him.

"Who in the name of the Holy Mothers are you?"

"The men who just saved your lives. You're welcome, by the way."

The smaller warrior sounded amused, but Bantu felt his cheeks blush in shame.

"I'm sorry. Of course we thank you from the bottom of our hearts. But why did you help us?"

The tall warrior smiled at them amiably, a gesture that made him appear less intimidating.

"Because our masters sent us to get you. They knew you were in trouble."

"Your masters?"

"This we can discuss later. Now, let's get off the road. I don't want to attract unwanted attention."

With that, the giant picked up the half-conscious Cornelia and followed the other warrior into the thicket next to the road.

As the two warriors set up a camp, Bantu leaned against a tree with his sister in his arms and watched in amazement. They erected a small tent where Cornelia could sleep, then dug a fire pit, filled it with stones, and lit the fire. Bantu tried to help, but the two warriors were a perfect team and made him feel like a foreign body. In the end, he watered the four horses, just to have something to do.

As soon as the fire was burning well, the taller one put a small cauldron filled with water on an iron tripod and adjusted the height with a chain. From the thicket, two gigantic gray wolves emerged, carrying hares in their jaws. They dropped the prey in front of the warrior, who gave his thanks with a graceful nod as if it were the most natural thing on earth to have such huge, terrifying predators serving him. Then he started skinning and preparing the prey for the pot.

The braided one placed a gentle hand on Bantu's shoulder. "Don't be afraid. They belong to us."

Bantu managed a trembling smile. "I figured as much—but they're still unnerving. I've never seen wolves that big before."

"How could you? This special kind can only be found in the mountains."

He grinned broadly and suddenly extended his hand.

"I'm Kalad, by the way. And this is Aegid, my desert brother."

"My name is Bantu." He nodded toward the tent. "My sister, Cornelia."

"You've hit rock bottom, haven't you?"

Gloomily, Bantu watched his sleeping sister. "Oh yes. Our village was raided about a year ago. I wasn't there when it happened, but my sister… she was the only survivor."

Sympathetically the warrior placed a hand on Bantu's lower arm. Without saying anything further, he made clear how well he understood the hell the siblings had gone through.

"She couldn't bear it any longer. Staying at the village, I mean. As soon as she was better, we left. Then we were captured by those slave traders."

"Doesn't sound like you had a great time."

Bantu got the impression that Kalad was trying to keep their conversation on the light side, and he was grateful. To think seriously about the last few months was the last thing he wanted. "It wasn't. Thank you for saving us, although I don't know why you did it."

"As Aegid already said, our masters sent us. You're chosen ones and your death would be an inconvenience."

"And who are those ominous masters?"

"You've surely heard of them. Lord Canubis and Lord Renaldo, the mercenaries of the North."

Bantu felt the hair rise at the back of his neck.

"What would the Wolf of War want from two farmers?"

"I didn't ask him." Kalad's teeth blinked snow-white in his dark face. "Canubis doesn't appreciate it when his orders are questioned."

"No, brother. He doesn't appreciate it when you question his orders, because you always manage to be condescending."

Aegid hadn't even gone to the trouble of raising his head when stating that fact. It was obviously not the first time they'd had that conversation.

Kalad made a dismissive gesture. "Don't listen to him. It's always a good idea to be on good terms with the masters."

Bantu lowered his gaze. "I wasn't planning on anything else."

When the sun started to go down, they ate the stew, and then Bantu and Cornelia lay down to sleep.

They stayed one more day in the camp, and when Cornelia felt better, they started the journey to the mountains. It was a long way, but thanks to the horses, not as tiring as if they'd had to walk. Since Cornelia still wasn't well, they were pretty slow, which embarrassed the siblings but didn't seem to faze Kalad and Aegid. With their good-natured banter and an endless source of gripping stories, they managed to make the tedious hours in the saddle almost bearable.

Three weeks later, they finally reached the Valley.

"I STILL can't believe it."

Bantu offered his sister a mug of hot tea and glanced at the room they had gotten from Hulda.

For a month they had been the guests of Lord Canubis, and the powerful mercenary had seen to it that they didn't lack anything. Bantu still didn't understand what exactly Canubis meant when he said Bantu and Cornelia were chosen by the Mothers, but he was grateful for the kindness the two warriors bestowed on them.

Cornelia, too, was thankful, but she also worried how they would ever be able to pay back such a debt. With her eyes closed, she took a sip of the tea. "It seems like a fairy tale, doesn't it? But I still don't trust it. I want to know what those two could possibly want from us."

"You don't believe them?"

"I'm not sure. On the one hand, there has to be something. I mean, Aegid and Kalad found us. Then again, I'm asking myself what two simple peasants like us could do for such powerful warlords. You're a scholar, at least, but I'm nothing."

"Don't talk like that, my dear. You're my life."

Grateful, Cornelia leaned her head on her brother's shoulder. "It's nice of you to say that, but you can't spend the rest of your life protecting me. You have your own destiny to fulfill. I don't want you to give up on yourself because of me."

"Wouldn't you do the same for me?"

Bantu's voice was very soft when he asked that question. He already knew the answer. Cornelia and he had always been really close, even when their parents had still been alive. Bantu had neglected a promising career as a scholar just to be able to stay with her, and Cornelia hadn't taken the opportunity to earn big money with her golden voice because she couldn't bear being separated from her brother for any length of time.

"Of course I would," she said. "Nevertheless, I feel guilty sometimes."

"Don't worry about that, my dear. This is like a new adventure, and I'm looking forward to where our path is headed."

"As long as we're walking together, I don't care about the direction."

Gently, Bantu placed a kiss on Cornelia's forehead, and then they both watched the flames in silence, each cloaked in the comforting presence of the other.

Less than two weeks later, they met Ana-Isara, the Empress of the Dead, who gave them a new family and the home they had so desperately craved.

For a long time, Casto sat in silence, staring at the words in front of him.

The story of the siblings had touched him deeply, although Bantu had obviously tried to be as neutral as possible. But the tragedy behind the words and the deep connection between Bantu and Cornelia shone through the lines like the sun breaking through the clouds after a heavy storm. Because Casto had never felt such love—and had grown up with quite the opposite—he felt a twinge of envy. Although those two had gone through a lot, they had never been alone.

With a sigh that showed the greatness of the burden on his shoulders, Casto closed the book. It was time to return to his master.

THE MOMENT he entered the room, Renaldo realized the strange mood his slave was in.

Casto's gaze was clouded, but not in anger. He moved slower than usual, as if brooding over a problem that kept him fully occupied.

Renaldo approached him carefully, knowing from painful experience that this kind of mood could turn into rage at any minute. He didn't feel like fighting today, so he was willing to give Casto a break should he require it. But the young man surprised him, as he did so often. With a shy smile Renaldo hadn't seen on him before, Casto leaned his head on Renaldo's shoulder.

"Are you all right, Casto?"

"I think so, Barbarian."

They were silent for a moment, and then Casto seized Renaldo's hands. "Can you hold me? Just a bit."

Surprised, Renaldo slung his arms around this strange youth who had kept him busy ever since they'd first met. "If you want, I can hold you the entire evening." He could feel Casto tensing and hurried to soothe him. "I'm well aware that you do not wish to share your body tonight. But I'm still offering to hold you."

Casto looked up in surprise. "Really?"

"Of course. You please me so often that it's only just to do the same for you once in a while."

Casto's cheeks turned a lovely red; he sounded unusually timid. "Then I gladly accept your offer. Are you going to bathe with me?"

"Whatever you want. It's my pleasure."

It turned out to be one of the most peaceful evenings they'd ever had. Renaldo was surprised how much he enjoyed just having Casto close by, how rewarding it was to simply talk to him. He already knew that Casto was an agreeable talker, but their discussions usually ended in a fight or sex—very often with both. Just talking to each other without hidden agendas was new and stimulating.

When Casto was slowly drifting asleep in his arms, Renaldo whispered softly in his ear, "That was a very nice evening, Casto. I really enjoyed it."

Casto's voice was husky and came from a place deep within. "I enjoyed it as well. I thank you, my lord."

Then he fell asleep.

WHIMPERING, CASTO rolled onto his stomach.

Renaldo watched him with an innocent air, and only the telltale glittering in his eyes betrayed him. "Are you feeling unwell, slave?"

A venomous look was the answer. "You know all too well, Barbarian. I can't remember giving you permission to spank me that hard."

"You really don't remember? You begged for it quite eloquently. Every time I wanted to stop, you asked for more."

"Yes, because you couldn't keep your hands to yourself."

"Admit it, you liked it."

"Perhaps yesterday. But today I'm aching all over."

"Stop making such a fuss." Renaldo leaned over his beautiful lover and lifted him up. "Be a good boy and I'll take you to the bath. The warm water will be good for you."

With a satisfied sigh, Casto slung his arms around his lover's shoulders and nestled his head in the warm crook between neck and torso. "It's always nice when you can be manipulated so easily." His voice sounded dreamy. He could feel Renaldo chuckle.

"Why would you think you can manipulate me? I simply want to take a bath. With you."

The last two words were said with a certain conviction that startled Casto. "What are you planning? I'm telling you, I'm too tired and sore to play any games."

"Don't fret about it, my gorgeous. The water will relax your muscles, and I'll wake you up. In less than half an hour, I'll have you begging, slave."

Casto started to fight against him, but it was only halfhearted since the Barbarian's words had already aroused him. He knew well that there was no escaping from Renaldo's grip. He stopped his resistance when Renaldo eased him into the water.

A short time later, Casto was begging, as Renaldo had prophesized, which led to a prolonged, joyous morning that tempted Renaldo to keep his slave occupied in bed for the rest of the day.

Casto declined this wish, although it wasn't easy for him. But he had his hands full with training the horses and couldn't afford losing even one day. With that, Renaldo let him go, not without a certain regret, but he consoled himself with the thought that Casto would soon come back to him.

Thus the last weeks of winter passed quite peacefully, and except for two bigger fights, after which Casto refused to talk to his master for days, there were only single skirmishes that were hardly worth mentioning. It was indeed so tranquil that Casto couldn't help but remember—and long for—the excitement he and Renaldo had shared earlier in the winter on their first hunting trip together.

4. THE CHARMS OF WINTER

RENALDO WAS sitting on one of the lounges in his chambers trying his hardest to fight temptation while Casto stripped off the numerous layers of clothing he wore to fend off the cold. In the process, Casto kept grumbling about the chill, the early nightfall, the ugly color of his thick woolen socks in particular, and the injustice of the world in general. Renaldo had to bite his tongue more than once so he wouldn't disrupt the ranting with a teasing remark.

Aggravating Casto was always a risky thing to do. On a good day, it could lead to an agitated argument followed by hot, passionate make-up sex. On a bad day, it would inevitably lead to an open fight with the high probability of breakable items as collateral damage and no sex at all for a prolonged time. Since they had just left such a dry spell behind them, Renaldo was very reluctant about provoking the next one. He regarded the still-ranting but now almost-naked Casto closely in hopes of discerning his mood.

Casto sensed the intense gaze and his mesmerizing blue eyes darkened instantly. Renaldo hurried to look away and decided that this was not the time to test his luck. Trying a different approach was the wise man's choice. He filled a cup with hot tea and offered it to Casto, who seemed taken aback by the friendly gesture.

"Is everything all right with you, Barbarian?"

Renaldo furrowed his brows but ignored the aggressive tone. "What should be wrong?"

"You're being nice. And you've refrained from teasing me about the cold. Of course I'm a little worried."

Renaldo grinned with a hint of challenge in his gray eyes. "I've gotten pretty good at reading your mood, which is why I'm offering you not only a hot beverage to warm you up but also my strong arms to fall into and forget about the day's hardships. What do you say?"

For a moment Casto looked as if he couldn't believe his ears, and then he started to laugh so hard that tears streamed down his face. "I'd say you'd better cut it out, Barbarian. You're not suited to be a smooth talker, at least not where I'm concerned. I know you too well. What you could do, if you're serious about comforting me, is get in the hot water with me and help me warm up."

Delighted that Casto not only understood the joke but was also willing to take it further, Renaldo slung his arms around him and carried him to the bathroom.

TWO BUSY hours later, Renaldo pulled one of the furs over Casto's naked form. The young man was snuggled up against him, his wheat-blond hair a soft caress on Renaldo's broad chest.

"You're unaccustomedly compliant today."

Casto made a mewling sound deep in his throat. "Well, you're unaccustomedly caring today, so I guess it's fine."

"I'm really worried, Casto. The cold seems to be getting to you."

The sentence was only half a joke. Renaldo was truly worried. As a child of the Plains, Casto was used to all kinds of heat, and where he came from, a cold spell was when people had to wear long-sleeved tunics at night. The biting cold of a northern winter must be a shock for him. And the worst was still to come. The blizzards had stopped, as they always did around this time of the year, but temperatures had started to drop, every day a little more.

Since Casto already found the chill intolerable, he was in for a nasty surprise within the next few weeks. Although this was his third winter in the Valley, Casto still hadn't got used to the cold and the annual, sudden drop in temperature was still an issue for him. What this would do to his temper was something Renaldo didn't want to think about. He pressed a kiss on Casto's head. "Is there anything I can do to make this better for you?"

Casto sighed. "Since you can't change the weather, I guess you and I have to live with the consequences. I really hate it, though. Today the sun came out and I hoped it would become a little warmer, but the opposite happened! I really don't understand how you can bear this horrible weather!"

"It's not all bad. Of course it's chilly, but winter has its nice aspects as well."

"Tell me one. I dare you!"

Renaldo hesitated. He did have an idea how he could brighten Casto's mood, although it was not without taking another risk. He was almost sure that his short-tempered slave would not try to run away from him while they were nearing the peak of the cold season. Casto was no fool. Unfortunately he wasn't a coward either. If he sensed a chance to get away, he would definitely seize it. Casto could not run away from Renaldo, at least not for a prolonged time, but Renaldo didn't put it beneath Casto to escape just to prove that his first escape hadn't been a mere stroke of good luck. As much as Renaldo loved the chase, he still remembered too vividly the pain he endured when Casto was gone to even consider giving him a chance to do that again.

Renaldo pondered this dilemma as he distracted Casto with deep kisses until he came up with the perfect solution. "How about I show you how beautiful the landscape is outside the Valley? Everything's covered in snow, and when you let the horses run, they don't make a sound. Also, it's less confined, and I know how much you hate to be bound. We could try to hunt down a stag or two. It's the season for it."

Abruptly, Casto sat up. His blue gaze drilled into Renaldo. "Where's the catch, Barbarian?"

"Does there have to be a catch?"

Casto snorted. "As much as I hate to admit it, you're not stupid enough to present me with such a chance. So where's the catch? Are you going to shackle me the entire time we're outside the Valley?"

Renaldo chuckled. The image of Casto bound did have a certain allure. "Nothing so drastic. The two of us are going on a nice trip. I'll even give you a bow and a hunting knife. But Lys stays here. That should ensure your return without me having to chase you down in your dreams."

Casto's eyes narrowed, his expression a mixture of anger and involuntary admiration. "How sly."

"That's me." Renaldo was very pleased with himself. "You would never go anywhere without your stallion, so keeping him here is all I need to guarantee your obedience. Now, do you agree to my terms?"

Casto felt torn. He was eager to get out of the Valley, but leaving Lys behind was a serious drawback and not only because it meant he couldn't share this hunt with his brother. It also meant that he acknowledged the Barbarian as superior, something he tried to avoid at all costs.

In the end, Casto's urge to get a change of scenery won out over the calculating part of his brain. "Fine, I play by your rules, Barbarian. Don't let it go to your head. I'm not going to make a habit out of it."

Renaldo grinned and pulled Casto into his embrace again. "I never expected that. We ride tomorrow."

THE NEXT morning, Casto and Renaldo had an early breakfast and then hurried to get everything ready for their departure. Casto was in high spirits even though he had to leave Lys behind. The cold didn't seem to be as trying as before, and he enjoyed the reassuring weight of the hunting knife on his hip. Although Renaldo was training him, he was still not allowed to wield a weapon in the Valley, something that was among the greatest drawbacks his enslavement had brought with it.

Two stable boys led Ghost and Demon, the horses belonging to Renaldo and his brother, out of the stables. They were already saddled and eager to start.

Renaldo stepped next to Casto, who had his hands on Ghost's bridle. Even though Casto rode both horses during training, Renaldo felt more comfortable when his slave was on Ghost's back. It had something to do with his possessiveness. He had a radiant smile on his lips.

"I'm really looking forward to this. Let's ride."

Both of them mounted their horses. Once they'd left the Valley behind them, Casto breathed a deep sigh of relief.

Renaldo regarded him with raised brows. "What was that sigh for?"

"Somehow I was sure you'd find a reason to cancel this trip or that something would happen and we wouldn't be able to go. I'm just glad, that's all."

Flustered by Casto's honesty, Renaldo averted his gaze. "There's no way I would have canceled this trip. I was looking forward to it."

"Then we'd better enjoy it to the fullest. I would hate to make you regret your decision."

"As long as you don't regret it. I'm immortal, so I've had my share of disappointments and know how to deal with them."

"Spoken like the old man you are! Now let's go and find those stags."

Renaldo took the lead, and they rode briskly for about two hours until they reached the outskirts of a small forest on the way to Kwarl, the nearest city to the Valley. Renaldo dismounted Demon there and beckoned Casto to do the same. The two stallions nodded off under the cover of a huge oak tree while their riders ventured into the forest.

Under the trees the snow wasn't as deep as out in the open, so it was easy to navigate, and the tracks of the stags were clearly visible. It was almost too easy—locating the herd in a small clearing, selecting one of the majestic animals as a target, and then bringing it down with two well-placed arrows. Still, the rush of the chase managed to get Casto's blood boiling. He knelt with Renaldo next to the dead stag and watched as the Barbarian slit the animal's throat to let it bleed out. In silence they waited for the stream of life to subside, and then Renaldo spoke some ancient words, wishing the stag a good journey to the Green Lands.

When Renaldo finished, he looked at Casto, his gray eyes burning with lust. Shuddering, Casto realized that the Barbarian was as agitated as he was.

He didn't resist when Renaldo grabbed him with his bloodstained hands, leaving trails of red on Casto's clothes and over his face. The metallic scent in combination with their feral passion made him forget everything else. When Renaldo yanked his jerkin and shirt open, Casto perceived the cold as just another pleasant sensation on his heated skin.

Renaldo kissed him fiercely while his hands wandered boldly toward Casto's belt and opened it with frightening skill. Groaning, Casto dug his hands into Renaldo's back. He was drowning in the Barbarian's fiery passion, even more than usual. Just when Renaldo was getting serious, the ominous sound of a sword being drawn behind them made them both freeze. A deep, condescending voice doused their last embers of passion and put them on high alert.

"How very nice. I don't think anybody has ever made it so easy for us to rob them. Must be our lucky day."

Casto peeked over Renaldo's shoulder to see what they were up against. Four haggard-looking men dressed in rags, yet all armed with swords and daggers, eyed Casto and Renaldo hungrily. Casto pressed his finger four times into Renaldo's abdomen, thus indicating the number of their opponents, then slid his hand down toward his knife, which was concealed by Renaldo's massive torso.

The leader of the highwaymen started to speak again. "If you would be so kind as to turn around slowly with your arms raised? Given what you were about to do, I don't think your partner poses any threat at the moment, but we'd still appreciate it if he showed his hands as well."

Slowly, Renaldo raised his arms. He and Casto locked gazes. Casto smiled at him with grim determination. This was so much better than hunting stags. Renaldo felt a surge of heat swamping his body. Casto was simply too perfect to be real.

Both of them inhaled deeply, and then Renaldo jumped sideways so quickly the highwaymen had no chance to react. Casto's hunting knife flew through the air like a falcon and pierced the heart of the spokesman with a crunch. The leader of the robbers went down with a look of sheer disbelief in his eyes, his hands too feeble to hold the sword.

Before the other three highwaymen could get over their shock, Renaldo reached the first and killed him with a clean stab to his neck. He grabbed the dying man's sword and beheaded the third in one graceful motion. When confronted with the quick deaths of his companions, the fourth man tried to escape, but Casto killed him with a bowshot.

The whole incident had taken only a few minutes. Panting, Renaldo and Casto stared at each other, each assaulted by a range of conflicting emotions. There was joy about how smoothly they acted together, how easily they had eliminated this threat to their lives.

Casto also felt disgust about that very fact. He didn't want to admit how natural it was to fight at the Barbarian's side.

Renaldo, on the other hand, was torn. He was ecstatic that Casto had so willingly fought alongside him, and yet shaken to his core when he thought how easily he could have lost his beautiful, capricious slave. To make things even more complicated, both men were swamped by a passion fueled by the rush of a good fight. Only the fear of running into even more trouble and thus endangering Casto again made Renaldo hold back from taking him. He kept Casto at arm's length to resist temptation while he gave his orders.

"Let's get the stag out of here and return to the Valley as quickly as possible." When he saw Casto's questioning glance in the direction of the fallen highwaymen, Renaldo only shrugged. "Leave them here. They'll make a splendid meal for the scavengers."

In silence, Renaldo and Casto returned to the Valley, each lost in his own thoughts while trying to ignore the throbbing in his loins. Once they were back in Renaldo's chambers, they attacked each other like hungry wolves, burning away all their doubts and fears, their insecurities and anger, in a love that knew nothing but the will to possess the other completely.

5. RETALIATION

Canubis gazed calmly into the faces of the Emeris gathered in his chambers. Hulda sat next to her husband, Wolfstan, just caressing his arm. Aegid and Kalad talked to Renaldo; Bantu, Cornelia, and Noran were toasting with the wine Noemi had just poured them.

Canubis sat down. It didn't take more. Immediately there was silence; his brother and their closest counselors turned their attention to him.

"As you know, a messenger from Tanara arrived yesterday. The Eastern Kings are finally done with Count Markon's games. Conquering Elam was the final straw, just as we anticipated. We've been officially asked to conquer and destroy Kitona."

A hungry fire lit up the features of the Emeris. They all knew what this was really about. Kitona was one of the countries where the Good Mother had gained a foothold. It was going to be their pleasure to eradicate her followers down to the last man.

"Of course, the count already knows. He started assembling his troops in Ki't. The capital is heavily fortified, so it won't be a stroll like last year. But we're being paid exceedingly well, and we get the chance to rob the Good Mother of a great deal of followers."

"When do we ride?"

Hulda asked the question. As Mother Superior to an order, she was used to organizing people, and she was responsible for getting the troops on the road. Canubis smiled at her, his amber eyes glinting dangerously. He couldn't wait to go against this stronghold of his archenemy.

"In three weeks."

Hulda nodded. The other Emeris, too, gave their consent. There was no need for discussion when the target was as compelling as Kitona. Three weeks wasn't a lot of time to prepare, but they all were seasoned warriors and the mercenaries couldn't wait to get back on the road. They would make it.

"Have you sent scouts?" Aegid turned to Canubis.

"Of course. We don't want to run into trouble, do we? At the moment it seems as if the count really wants to face us in Ki't. Which is making things easier."

They all knew Count Markon, a ruler who'd given them lucrative jobs in the past, as a man of intelligence and deviousness. It was wise to deal with him carefully. Without a doubt he'd already made plans in case he should become the target of the Pack.

It was that worry Renaldo voiced next. "We've got to be careful. I don't trust that bastard."

Renaldo's perfect face was grim. He distrusted any situation that seemed too easy, especially when somebody like Markon was involved.

His brother nodded at him. "We always are." Canubis turned back to his Emeris. "You all know your duties. We ride in three weeks."

With that, their assembly was called off. The counselors left Canubis's chambers to fulfill their tasks. Only Renaldo stayed behind, mainly to enjoy another cup of wine with his brother.

Canubis toasted him and then focused on the topic he was most interested in. "It seems you've finally defeated your slave. He's surprisingly docile lately."

Renaldo's smile was sour. "That's just an act. He's still his old self, but now he stops to think before he opens his mouth."

Canubis laughed. "I know you don't want to hear this, but he suits you."

Renaldo furrowed his brow. Something stirred in his mind, a thought that slipped from him whenever he tried to grab it. Indignantly he shook his head, but the nagging feeling that he was missing something wouldn't cease.

"He has his strong points. And he's been putting up with me for some time now."

"It's going to be your fourth year."

"You're keeping count?"

"After the two of you cost me so much money? Of course. But nobody is inclined to bet on the end of your relationship anymore. Just recently Bantu said that Casto is too stubborn for that to happen."

Renaldo grinned. "I can confirm that."

"You're going to let him fight this year?"

Renaldo made a face that clearly showed how much he resented the idea. "Yes. He's too talented to stay in the camp, and I owe him."

Canubis knew immediately what his brother was talking about. "You know it isn't done with just that?"

"Yes, but it's a start. And since he knows he's allowed to fight, his motivation has gone up."

"He'll fit perfectly in the Pack."

Renaldo brought his cup down hard. "I won't allow him to get into undue danger. He will fight, but certainly not on the front lines. I was thinking more about the reserves."

"Does he know?"

Renaldo rolled his eyes. "We're still talking to each other and nothing has been smashed, so no, I haven't told him yet. It's perfectly fine if he finds out shortly before the battle begins."

"You've got to give Casto credit where credit is due. He's a never-ending source of entertainment. Never would I have thought that you'd allow a slave to run wild like that. I'm curious what he'll make you do next."

"Shut up, brother, or I'll have to beat you up."

Canubis laughed heartily. "In your dreams, little brother, in your dreams."

"WHAT'S THE matter, little thief?"

Kalad's amused voice pried Daran from his gloomy thoughts. With a guilty smile, he turned to his masters, who were giving him their full attention.

"It's just me being stupid. Please don't mind me."

Aegid's gaze darkened. "You were so lost in thought, Kalad had to address you three times. Whatever it is you're thinking about, we *do* mind."

Blushing, Daran knelt. Ignoring the masters was one of the worst things a slave could do. That the two didn't punish him immediately was akin to a wonder. "It's because of the campaign. I have a bad feeling about it. The thought that something could happen to you...." He swallowed hard.

Kalad stepped forward and pulled him up, touching Daran's cheeks lightly. "We've talked about this, little thief. We're Emeris, immortal. No harm can come to us."

"You can be hurt."

"What if I am? When I met Casto for the first time, his black demon smashed my shoulder to a pulp. It hurt, but it healed within two hours. You really don't have to worry." The warrior's lips split into a suggestive smile. "The only thing you have to worry about is that we'll be too busy to take care of you. Your precious self is going to face some empty nights."

Daran kissed his master's hands. "Nights I'll gladly endure as long as I know you're safe."

"You're so adorable! Relax, we've been doing this for eight hundred years. Everything will be fine, just like always."

Aegid started kissing Daran to prevent any further protest. Kalad, too, began touching him with skilled hands. Together they distracted him so effectively that he had no more time to think about the upcoming campaign.

"It seems like Count Markon is really staking everything on one horse by gathering all his troops here. I don't know whether I should admire his guts or mock his naiveté."

Musingly, Canubis viewed the obscenely high walls of Ki't, which rose toward the merciless sun like a man-made mountain range. They had arrived in front of the city only a few days ago, and now that the camp was erected, Canubis concentrated all his energy on finding the best strategy for defeating the count. He never liked it when his enemies found out about the approaching Pack too soon since it gave them the opportunity to prepare.

The count was neither a fool nor a weakling. It was obvious that he wouldn't be easy prey. The Eastern Kings had paid the Pack a large sum for the eradication of this comparatively small kingdom that had been an annoying thorn in their sides for about fifteen years, and all due to Markon's abilities.

Not that the count had a choice in the matter—to protect his people, he'd maneuvered through the jungle of foreign politics like a snake, always trying to secure a position that made it either unprofitable or too dangerous to attack his kingdom. Canubis wasn't overly interested in politics so long as he and his men got paid, but Markon had managed to gain his respect. The man was definitely a rat, but one with principles, and Canubis could relate to that. Up to a certain point, he could even understand why the count had made a deal with the followers of the Good Mother.

Kitona had always been a place where the schemers of Canubis's ancient enemy felt at home, but Markon had managed for a long time to keep them out of the government of his country. That had changed when the Eastern Kings' request became public. The count knew that his chances against the Pack were slim, and so he grabbed every straw he could reach. Even though the magic practiced by the followers always came with a hefty price, they were valuable allies in a war against two demigods.

Canubis wasn't so stupid as to underestimate them, although he was furious that the servants of the Good Mother dared to ignore the laws of the Holy Mothers so openly.

"He didn't have much of a choice. It was either gathering the troops here and hoping he could stick it out till fall, or trying to go for an open confrontation all over Kitona. I'd have chosen the capital as well."

Hulda's dispassionate voice woke Canubis from his musings. As always, she assessed the situation with the cool attitude of a trained killer. Canubis grinned at her with open fondness. He was truly grateful to have such a dangerous, and merciless, woman at his side.

"And what would you do to keep me off your walls?"

Her lavender-colored eyes betrayed nothing of the lethal intent lurking behind them. "I'd visit you in your camp during the night when nobody would disturb us—of course, you wouldn't be able to say a lot, but it would be a very intimate meeting."

Canubis snickered before he turned serious again. "Do you think they'll send a killer?"

"Only if they're really foolish. The Order doesn't exist anymore. The assassins you can get these days are second-class idiots of dubious origins. Nobody with solid training. Markon knows that. And he knows you're immortal, so he won't take the trouble."

"That's what I was thinking. But what's his plan? He's not an idiot. He won't rely on the strength of his walls alone, and he's too realistic to view the magic of the followers as more than a backup. He must have a plan."

Hulda's lips parted in a sensuous smile, her voice a seductive purr that had taken the Wolf of War to the peaks of pleasure more than once in the past. Only since he'd met Noemi was he able to resist Hulda's allure, but her tone evoked fond memories.

"I'm going to find out."

With an elegant gesture, she pulled the hood of her jerkin over her bright blonde hair. Then she checked the five daggers she was wearing and turned toward the besieged city. "Don't wait for me. This could take some time."

Before he could answer, she vanished.

"I hate it when she does that." Shaking his head vigorously, Canubis went back to the camp. Hulda's ability to step behind time had always been unnerving to him. He'd never had a problem with how, back when they'd first met, she'd dealt him a blow that would have been lethal but for his immortality. On the contrary, he admired her for her callousness. But the way she manipulated time itself however she pleased sent shivers down his back.

The Holy Mothers had introduced time to dam Chaos and to establish order. Hulda was a direct descendant of the most powerful witches of the First Aeon, and her power was a remnant of those times. She was the last witch to command such magic, and it was just like her to turn that gift into something useful. She'd become the most famous and feared Mother Superior the Order of the Sisters of the Night had ever known. And now she was using her talent to spy for him within the city walls and find out about Markon's plans.

Canubis wasn't worried; Hulda was the best. For a moment he'd even contemplated allowing her to assassinate the count, but he'd changed his mind. According to the contract, they had to conquer the city, and Canubis preferred fighting against an enemy he knew and could size up.

Just the idea of the Good Mother's followers taking the lead should Markon die had been so detestable that Canubis had spared the man's life— for the time being. Nobody could tell what would happen if the violations the followers committed to make their magic work got out of control.

Canubis had no intention of finding out while all his men were present.

SULLENLY, CASTO kicked off his dusty boots. He'd been on patrol since early morning to make sure that they wouldn't be surprised by

the count's scattered troops. The ride had been long, hard, and terribly boring, which had worsened his mood by the hour. Not even the prospect of a fight with Renaldo had managed to cheer him up.

Listless, he stripped to take a bath. Since they'd set up camp three weeks ago, Casto's life had been an endless succession of patrols, digging moats, and maintenance of weapons. It was so boring, yet exhausting, that Casto got the feeling his brain was slowly cooking in the unrelenting sun. To make things worse, he was missing the Barbarian, a fact that didn't brighten his mood.

Renaldo was so busy they only met sporadically to exchange a few words. Casto even found himself thinking things would have been a lot easier had they stayed in the Valley. Then they would be able to see each other regularly, have their usual fights, end up in bed, and he could get riled up over Renaldo's bad habits.

While he was pondering those gloomy thoughts, Casto washed himself with the ice-cold water from the tub. Since he'd started living in the Valley, he'd gotten used to the comforts of a warm bath, but in this heat, the chill was actually welcome. With ease of practice, he oiled himself. Naked, he returned to the front of the tent to enjoy the tingling sensation the oil caused while seeping into his skin. At that same moment, Renaldo entered the tent.

Casto didn't know that to Renaldo he looked like some fairy-tale creature. The four diamonds in his nipples reflected the light like little suns. The last rays of the declining, real sun caressed the perfect relief of his muscles, got caught in his still-wet, wheat-blond hair, and made his eerie blue eyes flame like ghost lights that lured the incautious wanderer to perdition. Renaldo extended his hand demandingly.

Casto's face contorted in defiance for the tiniest moment, but it was gone fast, as if it were nothing but a mere shadow. Casto tilted his head slightly, opened his lips invitingly, the glittering blue became darker, deeper, and then he stepped toward his master.

Renaldo pulled him close, the young man's naked skin rubbing against the steel-reinforced leather tunic he was wearing.

Renaldo's lips closed over Casto's own; his hands stroked the smooth skin. Whimpering, Casto obliged his master's will, allowed Renaldo to push him against the table and take him there. Then he turned around in his arms, helped him to undress in his usual, graceful manner, and followed him to their bed. They kept their silence while mating time and again, knowing full well that one word would be enough to break the spell that kept them prisoner so sweetly.

And so they expressed with their bodies what their tongues were unable to say.

"ARE YOU sure?" Canubis's amber eyes bore into Hulda's frozen expression.

"Yes, I am. Thinking about it, the plan is not half-bad. And Markon has definitely enough men to succeed."

Canubis crashed his fist on the table in frustration.

Renaldo placed a placating hand on his shoulder. "We're warned, brother. Thanks to Hulda we know what he's planning and when."

Aegid joined the conversation. "What fails me completely is where he'd stationed all those men. Two thousand soldiers need to be fed. How is he doing that?"

When she answered, Hulda's voice was hard. "A good question, Aegid. He's making use of magic. The followers of the Good Mother are helping him. There are more magical traps in this city than rats roaming the streets. That's why it took me so long to come back. I've also seen how some of the priests have fed the soldiers, which is one of the reasons why Markon is getting nervous. Even the old hag's followers have to obey certain rules, and they can't get supplies out of thin air endlessly."

"So the question is how do we defeat about two thousand soldiers backed up by magic with our meager eight hundred warriors?"

Kalad and the other Emeris looked at the brothers imploringly.

Canubis's expression was grim. "We're going to outflank them. They have to leave through the main gate. If Markon is wise, he'll open two more gates at the sides. Renaldo and I are going to hold the middle where our numbers are the weakest. Wolfstan, Hulda, and Noran will cover our flanks. Aegid, Kalad, as soon as all the men are on the battlefield, you will break rank in our back, attack their flanks, and keep them occupied. As always, Belnor is going to lead the mounted reserves and intervene where necessary. I want this army completely eliminated. We take no prisoners. Only Markon will be spared. I want to have a little chat with him."

The Emeris showed their consent with a slight bow, and then they all left the tent to prepare for the upcoming attack.

Canubis and Renaldo, too, went into the camp. The prospect of a long, merciless fight filled them with unrestrained delight that was only slightly marred by the worry for their men. Since they were gods of war, they did expect a lot from those who followed them, and the mercenaries knew about the risks they were taking when joining the Pack. They also knew about the rewards, which made obeying the demigods so much easier.

Renaldo and Canubis knew that those who died in their name were taken to the Green Lands by the Holy Mothers where they would live in eternal peace. For that reason they didn't pity the fallen too much.

They were the Lords of War. For them, humans were born to serve their gods. If it meant dying, then it was the price they paid for their servitude, for being allowed to follow Canubis and Renaldo. A price that went hand in hand with the reward. That might be arrogant, but from the viewpoint of the brothers, it was only logical. What kind of sense had a human existence if not for serving the gods?

But there was one mortal who Renaldo didn't want to lose—Casto. In his tent he explained to the young man where he would fight.

As expected, the conversation didn't go smoothly.

"I thought you wanted to let me fight, Barbarian? And now you're asking me to stay with the reserves?"

"Be assured, Casto, the reserves will fight. We are up against an army of two thousand men. But I want you first, to be mounted, because Lys would never allow anything to happen to you, and second, that you don't fight at the front. It's going to be tough, and it's possible I might lose sight of you."

Casto stared silently at Renaldo for so long that he started to feel uncomfortable, something only Canubis had accomplished before. Then Casto spoke in measured tones.

"I understand."

"Do you only understand, or are you going to obey?"

A menacing glint in Casto's eyes made plain how angry he was. "I obey."

Relieved, Renaldo pulled him close. This had gone better than he'd dared to anticipate.

Casto allowed the Barbarian to kiss him. He was furious that he'd been banished to the ranks of the reserves when he'd wanted to fight at Renaldo's side, but he knew Renaldo would never waver. Before Renaldo forbade him to fight at all, Casto preferred obeying him and using the opportunity to show him he was trustworthy.

INSIDE THE palace in Ki't, Count Markon sat on his throne, drumming a nervous rhythm on the armrest while listening halfheartedly to the statements of one of his provision officers.

Despite the magical assistance from the followers of the Good Mother, things were starting to look glum for his men. Their provisions would soon be gone.

Markon prayed that the Wolf of War would finally decide to take action. That was the only drawback in his otherwise flawless plan—he was dependent on his opponent making the first move. The count wasn't stupid enough to think that Canubis didn't at least suspect what he was planning, but he trusted that he would attack nevertheless to stop the uncontrolled use of magic taking place within the city.

Markon still wasn't convinced that the followers of the Good Mother were suitable allies, but he hadn't had that much choice in the matter, and he could at least trust them to hate the demigods enough to fight to their last breath.

Although he hadn't asked her for this, their leader, an ice-cold priestess called Rave, had read his future and predicted him a great victory. His plan was outrageous enough to end in triumph, but he preferred not to trust the ranting of a woman whose own destiny was so inextricably interwoven with his own.

Once the Wolf of War attacked, it would end. One way or another.

6. BATTLE

From Lys's back, Casto watched the battle begin.

As anticipated by Canubis, Markon had opened two gates next to the main one to allow his men to spread out quickly. Canubis hadn't tried to prevent that for fear the battle would turn into pure chaos that would obliterate all his plans. The two armies faced each other for what felt like an eternity before the count finally gave the command to start.

Everything had gone as planned; Aegid and Kalad had attacked the enemy flanks and started to broach the soldiers, allowing the hard-fought middle, where Canubis and Renaldo were, to gain some breathing space. As Lys and Casto watched the battle, Lys shook his head nervously. Although things went as predicted, something felt off. The demon could almost grab it but couldn't quite get a hold on it.

Casto shared his brother's hunch. He, too, was nervous. Disquieted, he searched the ranks of the warriors, allies and enemies alike, always on the lookout for what disturbed him, for the hook he suspected, and suddenly he knew what was wrong. *There aren't enough enemies.*

Hulda had said that Markon had about two thousand men gathered in Ki't, but only two-thirds of that number fought in front of the city gates. It wasn't immediately apparent since the Pack was so heavily outnumbered that the sheer mass of their opponents threatened to swamp them. At the same moment that Casto realized what that meant, an explosion shook the earth. On the northern side of the city, parts of the wall crumbled, but so accurately the damage had to be magical. The heavy stones sailed elegantly, controlled through the air, and they left a swath through which the attackers could reach their target quickly.

About five hundred enemies rushed through the breach and made a charge at Kalad's men. Now the desert warrior had to defend himself on two sides, and it became obvious that Markon had enforced that part of his flank from the beginning. He had managed to encircle Kalad, and none of the other Emeris were able to help him since they were still struggling with the superior numbers of Markon's army.

DOWN IN the heart of the battle, Renaldo swore under his breath. When he'd heard the explosion, he knew something was seriously wrong, and then word reached him that Kalad was outflanked. The count had used the same maneuver the Pack had, only his version was actually working. No way could any of them come to Kalad's rescue. The desert warrior was on his own.

Furiously, Renaldo ducked under the sword of an advancing soldier and killed him with a clean slash. He turned to Canubis, who was fighting next to him. "We need to do something!"

Canubis spun around in an elegant circle, fending off three attackers at once. "There's nothing we can do, as you well know. We can't even send Belnor down there since we're cut off. No messenger is going to make it through, and my connection to the wolves is disrupted. They're really going beyond themselves to take us down. You've got to give it to Markon, his plan isn't half-bad. All we can do now is wrap things up on our end as quickly as possible and hope the flank will hold until then." He parried another attack. "So go off and kill, dear brother mine."

Renaldo hefted his sword, a grim smile on his lips. As bleak as their situation might be, his heart sang out in joy. Brutal carnage was what he was born for.

KALAD, TOO, swore, but he did it aloud. Being cornered by the same trick the Pack had intended to use didn't sit well with him, let alone the fact that he was losing his men. Not even his well-trained mercenaries were able to hold against superior numbers like these. To top it off, Markon had positioned his elite right there, and those men were perfectly trained killers too. With a grim determination and merciless accuracy Kalad had to admire despite being its target, the enemy decimated his warriors. The Pack's rigid training still made it hard for the attackers—they did not give in easily—but with their numbers dwindling, the enemy gained ground and started to isolate Kalad from his men.

CASTO TURNED with gleaming eyes to Belnor, the seasoned mercenary who had led the mounted reserves for many years. "We have to help Kalad!"

Belnor shook his head. "We don't attack without orders from Canubis. I know this is your first battle, but believe me, it isn't in vain to wait for the orders of the Wolf of War."

Casto regarded the slaughter taking place in front of the city skeptically. Kalad was doing well, but the superior forces were crushing him, and his men fell one after another.

"I don't think Canubis is able to give orders at the moment. He's busy."

"He's a god. When he wants us to attack, he'll tell us. I didn't reach this age by ignoring the Wolf of War's orders. He told me to stay put, and stay put I will until I hear otherwise."

Angrily, Casto stared at the battlefield, his blood roaring in his ears. He couldn't let Kalad be overrun by the enemy. If Markon managed to break up their flank, then the end of the battle was becoming uncertain at best. Canubis's plan would go up in smoke, and the ensuing chaos would make victory questionable.

The thought that Renaldo was at the center of the slaughter made Casto heave. No matter how skilled and powerful the Angel of Death was, not even he was able to withstand such superior numbers forever.

Determined, Casto turned around to the other riders. There were a hundred of them, and twenty-five were sitting on horses he had trained. He'd taken great pains to imprint every horse on him. In the beginning that had been just another ace up his sleeve in case he wanted to escape. Later he simply thought it a good idea that these painstakingly trained warhorses that brought death to their enemies should be in the control of not only their riders but also Casto himself.

Right at that moment, he was glad he'd gone to the trouble. His voice unwavering, he addressed the riders of the special horses. "I'm going to charge. You fall back and keep open the breach. That should be enough to distract the enemy and give Kalad a chance to regroup."

Angrily, Belnor steered his horse next to Casto.

"Don't listen to him! He might be the Angel of Death's favorite, but he's still just a slave. We won't do anything unless we get an order, understood?"

Torn, the warriors glanced from Belnor to Casto, plainly wavering between the obedience they had been taught so mercilessly, that Belnor was now asking of them, and the burning desire to get down and help their brethren.

Casto smiled weakly. "Don't be angry with them, Belnor. They don't have a choice."

Before the mercenary realized what Casto meant, the young man had given a high, shrill whistle. Casto's horses pricked their ears and then, following his orders, deployed behind him—not entirely against their rider's wishes.

Casto led them to the enemy's rear, and after a moment's hesitation, the remaining riders followed, including Belnor.

Lys was like a force of nature coming down on the enemy lines. His hard, iron-shod hooves dealt pain and death while Casto ploughed a bloody breach through the soldiers. The black stallion was unstoppable, as if death itself had descended upon the enemy and made them scatter in blind panic. Those who weren't fast enough to dodge the whirling hooves were trampled mercilessly into the ground or fell prey to the warriors coming after Lys and Casto. Like hungry wolves they attacked the confused soldiers who had been completely taken by surprise by this new development.

Dealing lethal blows with his sword, Casto reached the spot where Markon's men had managed to isolate Kalad.

Markon's objective was definitely to get the Emeris down, but Kalad didn't make it easy for them. He struck as fast as a viper, his sword slashed out in quick succession, and the only thing that could bring him down was the sheer number of his enemies.

Lys broke into that circle like a hawk onto a flock of doves. With well-aimed kicks, he provided the desert warrior with some breathing space.

Kalad turned to Casto with a grin. "Does Renaldo know what you're doing here?"

"What do you think?"

"You'll be in trouble. In deep, deep trouble."

"Would you prefer I left?"

"No way!"

After the short exchange, they concentrated on fighting again. The surprise attack from Lys and Casto had confused Markon's men. Halfheartedly they defended themselves against the riders widening the breach in their ranks while Kalad regrouped his men and started a counterattack.

HIGH ON the walls of the city of Ki't, Markon witnessed gloomily as his army was slowly decimated.

The woman standing next to him looked aghast.

"It seems your talent as a seer was overestimated, priestess. We are losing."

"That's impossible. I've seen it! The desert warrior will fall."

"Did you see the demon coming to his rescue?"

"No. I don't understand this. It's as if he's able to elude my gaze, as if he's not really here. Who is he? If I didn't know better, I'd say he's protected by magic, but that's impossible!"

Markon's gaze grazed Casto's bright blond hair and turned into the distance. "I think I know, but it's no longer important. I'd advise you to make your peace with that goddess of yours. Because one thing's for sure, the Wolf of War is not going to show any of us the least bit of mercy."

CASTO DIDN'T know how long he'd been fighting. Judging from the sun's position in the sky, it was already past noon, but he didn't really care. The enemy's resistance had weakened during the last hour. Bit by bit the fight had turned from desperate self-defense into merciless slaughter.

After Kalad regained the upper hand, they'd stuck to the original plan and started to broach the enemy's flank. The riders made quick forays that scattered the soldiers like panicked sheep, making them easy prey for the mercenaries fighting on foot.

Aegid had done the same on his side, and the center of the adversarial army faltered under the attack of the demigods.

Casto's world had shrunk to killing his enemies. Ducking attacks, starting counterattacks, parrying swords, severing limbs and heads. He and Lys were covered in the blood of the fallen, the thick, metallic scent burning into Casto's nose. It was the first time in his life that he'd shed blood like this, and a small, still-innocent part of him was repulsed by his actions. But with every life he took, that part of him shrank and became weaker and weaker, until it died without Casto even noticing it. Before he knew it, Casto had transformed into a full-fledged warrior, baptized in blood and gore, heralded by the shrill sounds of metal upon metal and the eerie, mind-numbing choir of the dying.

The armor Renaldo had given him was superb, protecting him like a shell while his sword cut through soldiers' bodies without resistance, even late in the afternoon when he'd long stopped counting the bodies he left in his wake.

To his enemies, Casto was a fairy-tale monster, so completely in sync with Lys it was like they were one creature that bathed in the blood of those who dared to confront them. He killed with the cold precision of an experienced predator and appeared invincible. No matter who or how many went against him, Casto came out as unscathed as if protected by some powerful charm.

Not only the soldiers were dumbfounded. The warriors of the Pack couldn't help but admire the slave who had changed the course of the battle.

They all knew Casto. Every one of them had their personal opinion about the young man who was able to get along with the incalculable, aloof Angel of Death. Not everybody liked him, but they all respected his strength, his unbending will, and now also his abilities as a fighter. Watching Casto was like delighting in a beautiful, deadly dance acted out by a talented, rigidly trained dancer who was also extremely easy on the eyes.

It was as if amid all the blood and gore, Casto's true predatory nature shone like a beacon.

WHEN THE sun's last rays kissed Ki't good night, the area in front of the city gates was scattered with corpses. The mercenaries had won, but they'd paid an unusually high price. Quite a few of the fallen wore the armor of the Pack.

Exhausted, Casto slid from Lys's back and leaned against his flank.

The black stallion looked around with a satisfied air. The killing hadn't drained but revived him. Deep down, Lys would always be a demon of chaos, and what had happened that day was very close to his true nature. He was also proud of his rider's performance.

Casto took the water Kalad offered him.

"Nice fight." The desert warrior's voice was derisive as always; he regarded Casto with an unfathomable look. "You've saved my ass today, Casto. I won't forget that."

The young man grinned broadly. "It was my pleasure."

Kalad grinned back. He placed a hand on Casto's shoulder and punched him in the ribs with the other. As complicated as the young man could be, Kalad truly liked him.

Then Aegid approached them with long strides. The giant's voice boomed. "You stupid idiot!"

The two men embraced each other violently and shared a long, deep kiss.

Casto delighted in this rarely shown open affection, but the moment of peace didn't last long.

With anger oozing from every pore, Renaldo stormed toward him. Unlike Aegid, his voice was a barely audible hiss. "Which part of 'keep out of trouble' didn't you understand, Casto?"

He grabbed Casto with iron fists and started shaking him as if he were a rag doll. Casto's teeth rattled violently, which caused Kalad to intervene.

"Hold it, Renaldo. He's wounded."

Immediately Renaldo stopped shaking Casto, his eyes wide in worry.

"It's nothing big, Barbarian. Just a few scratches."

"You should've seen him, Renaldo. He fought like a lion. Not to mention Lys!"

Full of admiration, Kalad bowed to the stallion, who received this gesture of respect with a graceful snort.

Renaldo looked at his brother-in-arms coldly. "The two of us will have a talk later!" he said menacingly, implying that Kalad wouldn't like the content of that talk at all. Then he turned to Lys. "Get on your stallion, Casto. We'll go back to the camp."

Without a word of protest—now that he had stopped fighting, he was way too tired for that—Casto hopped onto Lys again. The stallion trotted contentedly next to Renaldo, careful not to step on the bodies lying around. Now that the battle was over, the steed behaved like a noblewoman who didn't want her precious sandals sullied.

KALAD AND Aegid watched the powerful warhorse and the two men with mixed feelings.

Aegid was just glad to have gotten his brother back in one piece. Although they were Emeris and immortal, it was still like a knife in his heart every time Kalad got hurt.

Kalad never wasted too many thoughts on the past. He'd been in a dangerous situation, but now everything was fine again, and with that the problem was done with. What bothered him more was a thought that had flitted through his head when Casto had crushed the enemy lines like death itself to rescue Kalad. At that moment Kalad knew who Casto was—but right then he couldn't remember what he'd thought during the battle, no matter how hard he tried. All he knew was that it was important. Very, very important. He shook his head vigorously. The more he concentrated, the blurrier it got.

"He's going to nag him badly."

Aegid's voice distracted Kalad from his musings. He shrugged. "Better him than me."

"He saved your ass."

"And I'm really grateful to the arrogant bastard. But I still prefer him getting the blame. You know what Renaldo can be like."

Aegid laughed happily. He was so relieved that his brother was fine he let his impoliteness slip for the time being. "You're insufferable!"

"Admit it, it's what you love about me!"

"Could be. Perhaps I've just gotten used to your presence over the years."

Kalad smiled, satisfied with how things had worked out. Suddenly he felt the urge to celebrate. "Let's go see Daran. I want him."

Aegid's pale eyes came to life. Merely mentioning their slave was enough to get him in the mood.

Arm in arm, the desert warriors went to get their reward.

WHILE RENALDO and his slave returned to the camp, they remained silent. One of them because he was so angry, the other because he was still exhausted from all the killing.

They left Lys in the care of an eager stable boy at the paddocks before they went to Renaldo's tent. Renaldo helped his slave to strip out of clothes slathered with blood and filth, still not uttering a sound. He took off his own clothes before leading Casto to the back part of the tent, where he started to wash him.

Carefully, Renaldo removed the traces of the slaughter from Casto's skin; he looked after the countless cuts and bruises that weren't as bad as they'd seemed and started to massage oil into Casto's velvet skin.

Only when Renaldo was done did he feel calm enough to talk to his stubborn slave about his behavior. "How could you do that, Casto? You endangered yourself without thinking, although I'd forbidden it. Why? Is it some kind of reflex with you that no matter what I say, you do the opposite?"

Casto narrowed his eyes in defiance. "How could I not have done it? How could I look into your eyes if something had happened to Kalad? You're my teacher. I couldn't endure disappointing you like that."

With a sigh, Renaldo took his beautiful slave's face in his hands. He kissed him tenderly and allowed himself to get lost in the emotions. He understood very well what had moved Casto, and he scolded himself for forgetting that the young man had the heart of a warrior. "I'm proud of you. You've been very brave today."

At those soft words, something changed, like a breeze stirring the air in the tent, like the drop of a small rivulet unexpectedly turning into a roaring flood. Casto had braced himself for a heated argument, but he felt a wave of affection flooding his soul, and for the first time since they'd known each other, the love he felt for the Barbarian was not accompanied by anger about that same fact.

Also, for the first time, he saw the Barbarian not as his oppressor, as the person who'd stolen his freedom, but purely as the man he was.

It was almost too much. Reluctantly, Casto pulled away from Renaldo's grip, not sure what he should do next. When he made up his mind, he took the sponge, suddenly not only willing, but indeed eager to please the warrior.

"Please, my lord. Allow me to wash you."

With a nod, Renaldo showed his consent and somehow managed to hide his excitement.

Casto dipped the sponge into the water, wrung it out, and started to wash the enemy blood off his master's skin. He did it with full respect, with all the devotion he had, completely overwhelmed by the love that he finally yielded to without resistance. He knelt to wash Renaldo's legs and feet, his mouth level with his master's pelvis. Only once had Renaldo tried to coax him into fellatio, but the thought of humiliating himself so completely had repelled him.

Now he wanted to do it, wanted to show his master how much he respected and loved him. His sensuous lips came closer to Renaldo's penis.

Renaldo held him back with one hand. "You don't have to do it, Casto." Renaldo's voice was soft, kind.

Casto smiled at him brightly. "I know. That's why I want it."

With that, he returned his attention to the Barbarian's wakening dick. Casto pressed small kisses over the whole length, marveling at the smoothness of the skin, and then he took the tip in his mouth.

A flood of emotion overwhelmed him.

Starting with the salty taste, followed by surprise about the texture, and ending with a strange feeling of power when he realized that Renaldo was giving in to him completely. For a moment Casto was shocked, but then he used all means possible to satisfy Renaldo.

Before Renaldo reached climax, he retreated from Casto's mouth, picked him up, and carried him to the bed. Their lips joined in a passionate kiss, and with his hands, Renaldo allowed Casto a first, relaxing orgasm using the semen to slick Casto's hole. Then he turned him around and entered him in one swift movement, only to pause and enjoy their intimate union.

Casto whimpered softly, longing for Renaldo to move inside him, but he didn't want to rush him, wanted to wait for him as Renaldo had done countless times for him, especially in the beginning.

Their lovemaking went on for hours, and the moon was already round and full in the sky when Renaldo poured his essence into his lover for the last time.

For a few wonderful moments, they stayed intimately joined before Renaldo retreated. He wanted to get up to clean himself, but his delectable partner held him back. With his eyes glowing softly with love, of his own free will and eagerly, Casto cleaned his master, a service that until then he'd regarded as the worst of punishments and that he'd resented with all his might.

For the first time in his life, Casto understood what it meant to respect somebody else from the bottom of his heart, to love him unconditionally. When he was done, Renaldo pulled him close, and together they rested on the furs, naked. Their bodies still radiated heat like dying bonfires.

Renaldo traced his lover's skin dreamily. "Thank you, my own."

Casto snuggled closer to his lover. "I thank you."

"What for?"

"That you didn't lose it, despite your fury."

"What good would it have done?"

Suddenly serious, Casto sat up; his eyes were shadowed. "You could've punished me. And though I probably wouldn't have liked it, it would've been your right. I disobeyed you."

"Who says I'm not going to do that? Punish you, I mean." The gray eyes sparkled in mockery. Casto sighed and Renaldo sobered up. He could feel something was amiss. "What is it, my own?"

"I killed so many people today."

Casto's voice was flat, as if he was trying not to show his emotions. Immediately, Renaldo started to worry. Because Casto was so arrogant and forward, Renaldo sometimes forgot how young he still was. "Do you regret it?"

A strange light shone in Casto's eyes. "No. Those men intended to harm you. They deserved death."

"Then what's the problem?"

Casto's shoulders slumped. "I'm not entirely sure. I was willing—I was so angry. But I wasn't out of control. I knew what I had to do, how to kill effectively. I did it to protect you, and if need had been, I'd have killed a hundred times more men."

Renaldo pulled Casto even closer, his voice soothing. "I'm glad you're thinking like that. You're an excellent warrior. I'm proud that you're my pupil, that you share my bed."

"Even though I'm stubborn and arrogant?"

"Especially then. You know me—I get bored easily."

They shared an amused grin that betrayed the depths of their bond.

With a sweeping gesture, Renaldo pulled the fur over them. "Let's get some sleep, my own. The coming days are going to be tiring."

"As my master wishes."

"Shh. Your sarcasm is out of place this late at night. Keep it for tomorrow."

With a light chuckle that matched his age, Casto closed his eyes. Although it would certainly take time until he came to terms with the events of the day, he was happy.

Renaldo pressed a kiss to his forehead, but Casto was already fast asleep.

"WHERE ARE you going so early in the morning?"

From their bed, Renaldo watched Casto getting dressed.

Casto shot him a gloomy look. "I owe Belnor an apology. I'd rather do it now than later."

"That's a good idea."

Casto wrapped a silk belt round his slim waist, caught his blond curls in a tail, and started to leave. Before he reached the front part of the tent, he hesitated. "Just out of curiosity, what would be the worst Belnor could do to me?"

Renaldo suppressed a smile. To anybody else, Casto's voice would sound cool and detached, and his demeanor would betray nothing of his true feelings, but Renaldo had known him long enough to spot the small signs of insecurity he was trying to hide. "The worst Belnor could do is leave you to me for punishment."

A relieved grin crossed Casto's features. "Then I'm at ease."

"Don't get too relaxed. I'm known for my brutality."

Casto narrowed his eyes and blushed slightly. "I can't say that is turning me off, Barbarian. To be frank, I'm counting on it."

Suddenly wide-awake and deeply interested, Renaldo sat up, a wolfish smile on his lips. His difficult lover's eyes lit up in triumph; he even bowed slightly to his master.

"I have to go now."

"Don't think I'm gonna let this slip, slave! Once you're back, brace yourself!"

Casto's answer was barely audible since he'd already left the tent, but Renaldo's godlike hearing picked it up. "Is that a promise?"

Amused, Renaldo leaned back in the furs. "You can bet on it, my beautiful little warrior."

Content with himself and the world, he allowed himself to doze again.

WITH HIS fingertips, Casto grazed the closed flap of Belnor's tent.

"Who is it?"

The warrior sounded tired. The battle had taken its toll on this seasoned fighter as well.

"It's me, Casto."

"Come in!"

Casto entered the tent.

Belnor was sitting on a small table, a meager breakfast of bread and cheese laid out before him. When Belnor made a gesture, the slave who was serving left with his gaze cast downward. "To be frank, I wasn't expecting you this early."

Casto lowered his gaze. "I like to resolve such things promptly. Dragging it out only worsens it."

"You're a brave man."

Casto swallowed, and then he knelt down. As Renaldo's favorite he didn't have to do that, but he respected Belnor as an experienced fighter, and it was one way to show his respect. "First and foremost, I'm a stupid hothead. I ignored your orders, and for that I apologize."

For a moment the tent was silent. Contemplatively, Belnor watched the strange young man who'd been like a demon in the flesh the day before, now kneeling in front of him so humbly.

"I assume you didn't do it because my orders were abhorrent?"

Casto raised his eyes, his gaze terribly intense. It reminded Belnor of a born leader, and all of a sudden, the prostration was no longer a sign of subservience but quite the contrary. Belnor shuddered when he imagined how strong a personality it took to accomplish such a thing.

Casto's voice, as clear and fearless as always, cut through his musings. "No. I did it because I thought it was the right thing to do. And because I didn't want to disappoint my lord."

"You may not believe this, but I understand. You're young and, let's face it, a better warrior than I'll ever be."

Casto opened his mouth to say something, but Belnor stopped him with his raised hand. "What you did yesterday wasn't exactly clever, but it was necessary. I've been serving the brothers for so long I've forgotten what disobedience is."

"What will be my punishment?"

Belnor smiled. He liked the young man's straightforwardness. "I'll leave it to Renaldo. But tell him I want one of the horses you've trained as compensation."

Casto stared at the veteran in disbelief. He hadn't expected to get off so lightly. "If that's your wish, I'll train one especially for you, Belnor."

"That would be nice. And now go back to your master before he misses you too much."

Gracefully, Casto got up. His gratefulness was sincere and his voice was full of respect. "I thank you, Master."

With that, he turned away. When he moved to leave the tent, Belnor stopped him once more. "Casto?"

"Yes?"

"We're all very glad how happy you're making Renaldo. Thank you."

Casto smiled, and his answer surprised himself probably more than the warrior in front of him. "I'm just giving the Barbarian back what he's bestowed on me."

Belnor's eyes widened in surprise, but before he could say anything, Casto had already left.

"I CAN see that Belnor has been truly cruel to you."

Renaldo's voice dripped with good-humored banter, which Casto acknowledged with a smile. Although he'd seen and done things during the battle that would haunt him for some time, he felt free and easy.

Which was mostly Renaldo's doing. "He leaves my punishment to you, Barbarian. But he's asking for a horse trained by me in exchange."

"The old crook! He's known me for too long. Anyway, Canubis wishes to ride to Ki't in an hour. That means there's not much time left to start your punishment."

With the grace of a cat, Casto approached Renaldo. He dropped the silken belt from his hips and the tunic followed with a soft rustling. Casto's eyes burned with lust, he caressed his naked body temptingly. He hesitated for a moment at the studs in his nipples, still unsure whether he welcomed them or not, then trailed his hands farther down toward the third jewel Renaldo had driven through his flesh.

Hungrily, Renaldo followed every little movement his lover was making. No matter how much they fought, when it came to the bed, they were so perfectly tuned to each other it sometimes spooked him. Casto seemed to always know what Renaldo wanted, and Renaldo was almost better acquainted with Casto's body and limits than with his own. Right then, words were unnecessary, but Renaldo gave orders in a deep, husky voice nevertheless, to heat up the mood even more.

"Lean over the table."

Obediently, Casto did as asked. He tilted his head, an inviting smile on his lips. Renaldo stepped behind him, touched the muscular back and lingered on Casto's butt. He placed the little bottle with oil next to Casto's head. A whimper of anticipation escaped Casto's throat, which made Renaldo smile with a hint of cruelty. Casto wouldn't appreciate what was to come next.

Renaldo spanked the willingly offered flesh with a light slap and entered Casto with two well-oiled fingers at the same time. "You've been very cheeky this morning."

The back in front of him arched, and Casto's voice was as raw as it could get. "I know."

"You'll pay for that, just as I promised."

With his fingers, Renaldo grazed Casto's prostate, and Casto slid his hands helplessly over the wood.

"Please, Barbarian, please!"

"I know. It's terrible, isn't it? Being so hot and not able to find relief. Tell me what you want me to do."

"You know what I want."

"Yes. But you have to say it."

"Damn you!"

Renaldo moved his fingers vigorously. He could feel Casto's inner muscles tense in anticipation. He really enjoyed torturing Casto like that, even though it meant stretching his own self-control to its limit. "What was that? Did I mishear?"

Casto's back muscles trembled, and he grabbed the table so tightly his knuckles turned white. "Please, Master. Punish me and then take me. I want to feel you."

Renaldo took a deep breath to keep his cool. Hearing Casto beg like that was more than he could bear, but somehow he managed to hold back. If he lost his control, the whole game would be in vain. By imagining what they would be doing that evening if he could keep his urges in check, he managed to resist Casto's alluring scent, his pleas, and his appealing body.

"Mmm. An interesting request. Let me think about it—somehow I don't feel like devouring you at the moment. Later, perhaps."

A frustrated groan was his reward, and then Casto started to pump his hips. Laughing, Renaldo pressed his hand flat on Casto's back to keep him from moving while he kept teasing him with his fingers. After a moment's thought, he allowed Casto a shallow orgasm before taking his fingers out.

Wheezing, Casto got up, his eyes burning with anger. "You cursed bastard!"

"Silence! While you keep talking to me like that, you certainly won't get anything today."

Casto was ready to give a sharp retort, but Renaldo was faster. Imperiously he sealed his lips on Casto's and invaded Casto's mouth. Slowly, Casto started to relax.

Renaldo drew back. "View it as a game. You've been really cheeky, and I promise the punishment for that will be severe. But right now I want you to think only about me, about the things I'm going to do to you."

"You're cruel, Barbarian."

"You only realize this now?"

"There's no way I can change your mind?"

Renaldo grinned broadly. "Even if you could, it would be too late now. We need to get dressed if we want to make it in time for our trip into Ki't."

Casto's eyes lit up. "You're really taking me with you?"

"Of course. Needless to say you have to stay close to me all the time."

A tantalizing smile was the answer. Never one to let a challenge go, Casto was ready for battle. "Don't worry, Barbarian. I'm not going to leave your side, you've seen to that yourself."

"Why do I get the feeling I should've taken you just now?"

Casto's smile grew even brighter. "Perhaps you should've done that. Perhaps not. I'm a great fan of games too, so let's have one. We'll see who's going to be the winner."

Violently, Renaldo pulled him closer, barely able to keep his flaming urges in check. "Have I told you how much I love it when you challenge me like that?"

"No, never. But I'm taking it as a compliment."

7. NEW BEGINNINGS

ALL THAT was left of Ki't was smoking ruins. Wherever Casto let his gaze wander, there was nothing but destruction. Not a single house was unmarred. In the narrow streets, debris and muck were scattered around, and rats almost as big as cats scampered through the chaos without any signs of fear. The hoarse calls of carrion crows fighting over the corpses were a fitting music to the overall devastation. The crows and rats fed greedily from the countless corpses littering the streets.

Knowing well how merciless the demigods were toward the followers of the Good Mother, many had preferred to kill themselves before the brothers could render their verdict. The whole city was drenched in a terrible stench of decay, fire, and death that made Casto's stomach turn. Compared to that, the battle from the day before was like a stroll in the sunshine.

Involuntarily he steered Lys closer to one of the persons responsible for the carnage. For the first time since he'd met Renaldo, Casto realized how powerful and merciless he truly was. After the city had fallen to them, without batting an eyelash, Renaldo and Canubis had ordered their men to kill every follower of the Good Mother and to take all the remaining citizens as slaves.

The only consolation was that death came swiftly to those who had dared to oppose the divine brothers, although Casto was not entirely sure whether this was due to Canubis and Renaldo feeling merciful or because they wanted to be done with Ki't and its citizens as soon as possible. Still, the gurgling sound when the throats were slit made Casto shudder. This was different from the battlefield, where an enemy had at least the chance to defend himself. This was slaughter, plain and simple, and it showed yet another facet of Renaldo—one Casto found difficult to deal with. He understood why Canubis and Renaldo were so cruel: they had to protect their own and make sure anybody who wanted to go against them thought twice about it. Casto was no stranger to ruthlessness, he had been both on the receiving and giving end of it, but the blatant brutality Renaldo and Canubis showed then was new to him, and he wondered if he would be able to get used to it.

During their trip through the ravaged city, Casto also realized how unbelievably lenient his almost almighty master was toward him. When he imagined what Renaldo could have done to him in answer to his stubborn behavior, he felt his stomach turn. Casto still wasn't afraid of him. He didn't know where that courage came from, but his instincts told him he was absolutely safe with Renaldo.

THE PERSON still waiting to pay the price for Ki't's hubris was Count Markon. The mercenaries had made him a prisoner in the palace, and now he knelt in his own throne room on the bloodied and dirty floor, in front of Canubis and Renaldo.

At their first meeting, Casto had deemed the man a weasel, albeit a very intelligent one who had managed to survive as a ruler for a surprisingly long time in the borderlands of the Eastern Kingdoms. Casto recognized a cunning politician when he saw one, and the man was shrewd. Involuntary admiration mixed with pity when he thought about the hopeless situation the once-lively schemer had gotten into. When he knelt in front of the warriors, the formerly vigorous man just seemed tired. Markon had dusky locks and a plain face in which his dark eyes were too close to be pleasing. He had lost in one day what he had built in over twenty years.

Standing amid the ruins of one's life's work seemed more than cruel to Casto. For some time, everybody present remained silent, and the mood in the throne room was hushed. Neither the triumph of the victors nor the desperation of the defeated gained the upper hand. Then Canubis raised his voice, but not in anger, as Casto had anticipated.

The Wolf of War sounded detached, as if the conversation wasn't about the destiny of an entire kingdom. "Count Markon, you allied yourself with the Good Mother. I think you know what that means."

The count shrugged, a gesture that conveyed his hopelessness. "Of course I know. I'm not stupid."

"Why did you do it? You must have known what would happen."

A bitter smile appeared on the count's lips. "Believe me when I tell you, Lord Canubis, that if I'd had a choice, it wouldn't have fallen on the old hag. But my options were limited. After I found out that you would oppose me, my allies fled like rats from a sinking ship. The priestess Rave was the only one who offered help."

Renaldo furrowed his brows and looked at Markon. "Why did you face us? You could have just kept a low profile."

"And leave everything I've fought for all these years to the Eastern Kings? No, I couldn't do that. And my plan could have worked. It was risky to stake everything on the turn of one card, but if things had played out differently—"

"Then you'd be a powerful man now." Canubis ended the sentence.

Markon nodded glumly. His gaze fell on Casto. It was difficult to tell whether he was angry when he addressed the young man, but he was definitely agitated. "If it hadn't been for you, you and that black demon! I knew you were different when I met you the first time in the Valley, but I'm still surprised that you're responsible for my end."

Casto opened his mouth, but Renaldo beat him to it.

"It has nothing to do with Casto. You've fallen prey to your own arrogance. We're the sons of goddesses. We can't be defeated."

"That has still to be proven, as you well know."

Canubis raised his hand. "Enough! These things are in the distant future. You, on the other hand, are surprisingly relaxed for somebody who has to face the Eastern Kings very soon."

The count laughed. For the first time since the confrontation started, he sounded like his old, arrogant self again. "That's not going to happen. Although I hoped to get the better of you, I still prepared for the worst. The kings will never get their hands on me."

Canubis's amber eyes lit up knowingly. He didn't seem surprised at all. "What did you take?"

"Balnar. It takes effect a little slowly, but it's indolent, and the corpse isn't too terrible to look at. Another upside is the anaesthetizing effect, something I fancy quite a lot. I wanted to talk to you one last time, but I really can do without the torture."

Casto gasped. The count was talking so dispassionately, as if it were not his own destiny he was discussing but that of a stranger. He was an enemy who had threatened Renaldo, and that alone was reason enough for Casto to kill him on the spot, but he couldn't help admiring the dignity with which Markon had shaped the last moments of his life.

Casto was obviously not the only one impressed by the man's verve. Canubis got up from the throne, stepped toward Markon, and helped him up. "I promise you an honorable funeral. You've been a worthy opponent. I respect that."

A cynical smile played around the dying man's lips. "And here I thought you knew no mercy. It seems you're more than meets the eye. I thank you."

His body went limp in the arms of the Wolf of War, and his eyes stared unfocused at the ceiling.

Reverently, Canubis laid the count down. Even more reverently did he close his eyes. After a few moments during which he stared at the corpse with an unreadable expression, he turned to two of his men. "You heard what I said. Give him a proper funeral."

The two mercenaries nodded and carried the body from the throne room.

Lost in thought, the most powerful warlord in the world stood amid all the chaos and devastation he'd brought upon this city, a lord of perdition such as Casto had never seen before.

Renaldo stepped next to his brother, death and doom united on the once-polished marble floor. "A worthy end."

The Wolf of War laughed drily. "Whether it was worthy or not, the outcome is always the same. Mother had a good harvest, so I think she should be satisfied."

"Then we should be too."

Silently the brothers held each other's shoulders, a gesture that showed Casto plainly how close the demigods were. No matter how intimate he got with the Barbarian, the Wolf of War would always be closer to him. The thought irritated Casto, but he got no chance to ponder it further. Renaldo stepped away from his brother and took Casto's hand.

"Let's go. I want to take a look at the booty before we return to the camp." A teasing smile appeared on his lips. "As I recall, I still owe you punishment."

Casto stepped closer to his master, glad for the distraction. His breath fluttered across Renaldo's perfect face, his voice a soft and challenging whisper. "Punishment? I don't know anything about that. We'll have to talk about it."

Heat flared between them, shot right through Casto and sent him into raptures. It suppressed his jealousy as well as the horrors he'd witnessed during the last two days.

Renaldo's answer was a purr. "I'm going to refresh your memory, so don't worry, my own."

With that he placed a hand on Casto's back, waved to his brother standing smirking in the middle of the hall, called a short good-bye, and took his slave back to the camp.

AFTER THEY returned to their tent, Casto took off the full-length, dark blue coat Renaldo had given him as a present. He got rid of his boots and leather trousers next. Only his tunic remained on his body.

With a bright smile, he helped his master out of his clothes and led him to the table. "Sit, my lord. I'm going to attend to you."

A little irritated by such sudden zeal, Renaldo followed Casto's every movement. First Casto served him a cup of wine; then he filled a plate with fruit and small pieces of honey cake. Every time he passed Renaldo, he touched him randomly. During the meal Casto stood closer than was strictly necessary and didn't seem able to get away from him.

Finally, Renaldo had enough. He grabbed Casto's wrist and pulled him closer. "I've had my fill. It's time for dessert."

Softly, but determinedly, Casto withdrew. "Oh, but that won't be possible. I don't want to do it today."

Renaldo froze. That was far from what he'd anticipated. "You must be kidding me."

Casto turned to him with an innocent gaze that told Renaldo how deeply in trouble he was.

"Of course not, my lord. I'd never dare." Casto leaned forward to refill Renaldo's cup. His lips grazed Renaldo's right ear, his voice a soft, teasing purr. "It must be terrible being so aroused, so hungry, yet unable to get sated."

With a growl, Renaldo grabbed the young man and pulled him onto his lap. He was running out of patience fast. "You little tease, that's my line."

His lips made contact with Casto's, demandingly, as usual, he entered Casto's mouth.

Casto whimpered but pried himself loose. His breath was ragged, yet his voice remained firm. "I've already told you, I don't want it today."

"Really?"

Renaldo stroked Casto's penis through the cloth. It rose to the touch obediently, just as it always did. "Because to me it looks like you want it desperately."

With a shudder, Casto lifted his hips and dug his hands into Renaldo's shoulders. "No, I really don't.... Perhaps a little bit."

"Just a little bit?"

Renaldo moved his hand, increasing the pressure, and Casto gave in. The game had been fun, but he was still frustrated from what had happened that morning, so he was inclined to let the Barbarian win. Besides, he'd managed to make his point, which was the most important thing. "All right. I want you. Satisfied?"

Renaldo kissed him again. "Very much. And as a heads-up, tonight I'm going to make you pay for everything you did. You've been a really bad slave, disobeying your master, entering the heart of a battle and then keeping said master yearning. I'm truly angry. It's going to take some time until I forgive you."

Whimpering, Casto snuggled closer. He loved the sound of that. "I'll do everything you want me to, Master."

Renaldo smiled contentedly. There were quite a few things he wanted from Casto.

"THAT WAS pretty exhausting."

"You're still able to walk on your own, so don't complain." Renaldo sounded amused and slightly tired. It had indeed been a long night. He and Casto lay huddled up to one another on the bed. With his fingertips, Renaldo traced the soft, naked skin of his slave. He loved the moments of quiet peace right after the act when they were both too complacent and exhausted to start arguing again. Lately those moments of tranquility lasted longer and longer, and because of their growing intimacy, Renaldo got more forward regarding his discussions with Casto.

Right then, too, he was wavering between the urge to keep the peace and talking to the young man. He finally decided on the second. "That was really nice today, Casto. I enjoyed our game a lot."

With a sigh, Casto nestled closer to him. "Me too. You're a worthy opponent, Barbarian."

"You know how much it irritates me when you call me that?"

"Yes."

"Earlier, while we were doing it, you called me master. I liked that, though."

"That's no surprise."

"If I ordered you, would you stop calling me Barbarian?"

Casto thought about it for a moment, and then he shook his head. "No, I don't think so. I've gotten used to it by now, and frankly, I think you'd miss it."

"Smartass."

Again they remained silent for some time.

Renaldo started anew. "You once told me there are happy days for you. Are you happy today?"

Casto got up, his eyes as bright as the sun. He didn't know where the conversation was headed, but he could sense the tension in Renaldo's body language. "Very much."

Renaldo hesitated. What he was about to say now could lead to catastrophe in the blink of an eye, but he'd been pondering this for some time, and he wanted to finally voice it. "If you could, would you still leave me?"

With his brows furrowed, Casto moved away from his master. His face showed his confusion but then cleared quickly. "I can't, so there's no sense in discussing it."

"Let's assume you could. Would you do it?"

Silence. When Casto finally answered, his voice was strained, his face stubborn. "No. I wouldn't leave you. Not any longer."

"Does that mean you're happy with me?"

Renaldo's tone was so ripe with hope that Casto held back the snippy retort he wanted to give. Instead he reached for Renaldo's hand and kissed it reverently. "There are still days when I curse my fate and wish the pestilence on you, but their numbers are dwindling."

The answer seemed to please Renaldo because he suddenly smiled brightly. "It pleases me to hear that."

He extended his hands, and Casto first thought he would embrace him again, but instead, Renaldo took off the leather collar around Casto's neck. Speechless, with trembling fingers, Casto reached for the spot that was bare again for the first time in four years. He widened his eyes. "Why?"

"Because you make me happy. And you've earned it. Besides, you're the worst slave I've ever had. Now I don't have to be vexed with you anymore."

Then Casto leaned forward to kiss Renaldo fiercely. "I haven't said this often, but I thank you—Master."

Renaldo grinned happily. "See, you can do it. But don't let it go to your head. You aren't a full member of the Pack yet. That ceremony is always held in winter, and I still have to talk to my brother about it. But you're free, Casto. Just as you've wished."

A shadow crossed Casto's features but was gone so fast it could have been an illusion. He rested his hands on Renaldo's muscular chest, and his voice came from a place deep inside. "If you allow me, I'll show you my gratitude, Master."

Renaldo leaned back, suddenly immensely aroused. "Go on, my own. Indulge yourself."

"HEY, LITTLE thief, are you glad that we'll be leaving soon?"

Daran smiled at Aegid so happily it was answer enough. Even though Renaldo and Canubis were eager to get back to the Valley, there were still some things that had to be taken care of before the Pack could leave Ki't. "Yes, I am. But I'm even gladder that you both are still in one piece."

Aegid, the giant warrior, pulled Daran closer with a sigh. "Stop brooding about it. We're both here. Everything's fine."

Daran made a hiccupping sound. He still hadn't gotten over the terrors of the battle. "But it was close. The mere idea…." He trailed off as he buried his face in Aegid's tunic and inhaled deeply the soothing, familiar scent. "I couldn't stand losing you. The thought that you had to endure hardship…. I simply can't think about it."

Thoughtfully, Aegid caressed his slave's back. When they'd returned from the battlefield, Daran had been devastated. He'd heard the news about the battle and knew exactly what had happened. It had taken the whole night to comfort him until he fell asleep. Ever since then, Daran had been haunted by nightmares in which he saw his masters lying cold and dead on the battlefield.

The warriors hoped that their return to the Valley would banish the bad dreams. As flattered as they were that Daran was worked up over them, little did they want him tortured.

To take Daran's mind off the sore topic, Aegid asked after Casto. "How is your teacher doing? Was today's lesson good?"

Daran made a face when reminded of his beautiful but bad-tempered teacher. "Depends on how you look at it. Rajan and I weren't bad, but Casto was in a terrible mood today. I think he and Lord Renaldo had a fight—again."

"That's nothing new."

"No. But I don't like it when I'm at the center of the storm. Casto usually makes no bones about it."

Aegid laughed. "No, you definitely can't accuse him of that. He's going to calm down soon. Although I thought he'd gotten a little more lenient after my brother gave him his freedom."

"On the contrary. Now that he's free, the Angel of Death has more chances to piss him off."

As soon as the words left Daran's mouth, he lowered his gaze with a guilty expression. He rarely spoke so brazenly and then never about the Pack's leader.

Aegid pulled him closer with a smile. "That was pretty cheeky, little thief."

"I know." Daran didn't dare raise his voice above a whisper. "Please forgive me. I don't know what came over me."

"Oh, I know pretty well. The truth has come over you. Still, it would be better if you didn't repeat such words in front of witnesses. That could lead to a painful lesson for you."

Contritely, Daran lowered his head. He knew all too well that his words, should they reach the wrong ears, justified a whipping. He was glad that Aegid was lenient in this regard. "I certainly won't, Master."

The warrior took Daran's face in both hands. "I guess it's better that I seal these lips before you can talk yourself into more trouble."

He kissed Daran so deeply that the young man's knees gave in.

"You're having an orgy without me?" Kalad feigned offense as he stood in the entrance to the tent.

Aegid looked up for a moment, a saucy smile on his lips. "You're always welcome to join in."

It didn't take more. Kalad stepped behind Daran, Aegid started kissing Daran again, and Kalad caressed Daran's half-naked body.

Daran closed his eyes and groaned. He enjoyed feeling both his masters close, their bodies warm and alive. The thought of losing either of them made him freeze inside. He knew he wouldn't be able to survive such loss. Without knowing how it happened, he'd fallen irrevocably in love with both men, unable to escape or to even prefer one over the other. Aegid and Kalad were a unit, and Daran saw them as one soul residing in two bodies. He didn't understand how that could be, but for him one of them couldn't exist without the other.

It was that inexorable devotion to both warriors that chained Aegid and Kalad to Daran without them knowing it. The tie Daran had offered them so willingly grew in strength with every day they spent together, a connection none of them would be able to refute.

Sic, too, was busy preparing for the journey back home. After a battle the smiths always had a lot to do, and Noran hated having to transport back unfinished work. For that reason his men were working almost nonstop. Sic had last slept two days ago, and it still wasn't enough. They wouldn't be able to finish before the departure. Sic resented disappointing his master like that, but the Pack had paid an unusually high price for this victory.

A price the smiths now had to pay as well.

Critically, Sic controlled the sword he'd been working on. It belonged to Casto. Renaldo had made it clear that his lover's armor had priority over everything else. The weapon was beautifully crafted, one of Noran's masterpieces, and it hurt Sic deeply to see all the dents and nicks it had acquired during battle. But now it was back to its former glory, an adornment for anybody allowed to wear it.

"You've done a pretty good job with that." Noran's voice sounded almost kind.

Sic hurried to turn around and get on his knees. "You're very generous, Master." He handed the sword to Noran so that he could inspect it.

Noran tested the edge with his thumb. "Very good. But you still have to sharpen it."

"Yes, Master."

"How are you progressing?"

Sic squirmed. "Not as well as we should, Master. We won't be able to finish. I'm sorry."

Without looking at him, Sic knew his master was getting angry. He could almost feel the fury of the master smith rolling over him. He tensed, anticipating a scolding, but to his utter surprise, it never happened.

Instead, Noran lifted his apprentice up. He looked into the tired, hollow-eyed face of the young man for what felt like an eternity, and then he caressed his cheek. "You should take a break. You look tired."

Sic was so surprised he didn't know how to answer.

The ghost of a smile appeared on Noran's face. "Come with me. I have some food in my tent."

Still speechless, Sic followed his master from the smithy, knowing well that all eyes were on him. The other smiths didn't like that the young man they'd all known as a mere runaround had gotten so much attention since the last Spring Ceremony. They were jealous of Sic's obvious talent that, to their surprise, hadn't been fostered by Noran. They all knew how much their bad-tempered master adored the pleasant young man who served him with so much devotion and awe it made everybody who knew Noran think twice.

"What is it? Stop gawking and get back to work, you lazy lowlifes."

Noran's angry rebuke woke the slaves from their daze. They hurried to do their master's will. Noran wasn't squeamish when it came to punishing misbehavior.

"WHAT ON earth could you still be fighting about? By now you should be through with every possible topic!" Saying that, Canubis offered his brother a cup of wine, an amused smile on his lips.

Renaldo took the beverage with a grimace. "If you think Casto is done with a topic after just one argument, you're even more naive than I thought. He's the king of repetition."

"What was it about this time?"

"I said something he didn't like, one word led to another, and I missed the point where I could have ended it with sex."

"Listening to you when you're talking about your relationship beats every comedy."

Renaldo's gray eyes flashed at his brother. "You wouldn't be so gleeful if you had to endure it."

"Probably not. Luckily for me, I don't have to endure it. I just have to comment on it." A rude gesture was the answer to that banter. Then Canubis turned serious. "I thought he'd be a little more grateful after you'd given him back his freedom."

"Oh, he was grateful, I can assure you. But according to him, I've just given him back what he'd lent to me."

Canubis shook his head. "Casto truly is special."

Each man took a sip from his cup.

Canubis regarded his brother from half-closed eyes. Although he'd just fought with Casto, Renaldo, the beautiful, lethal warrior, looked happier than ever before. Canubis knew how hard it was for Renaldo to bear their world. He, too, had problems with the loneliness his natural dominance brought in its wake, but he didn't have to put up with a perfect face that blinded everybody and an inner fire that could burn everything to ashes.

In addition, Canubis had his heart. Noemi was his anchor, the safe harbor from which he could go about his seemingly endless mission without losing his sanity.

His irascible brother had nobody. Casto was like a gift from the Holy Mothers, a stabilizing factor despite, or perhaps even because of, his stubbornness.

Canubis placed a hand on Renaldo's arm. "I'm very pleased, brother. Casto is a perfect match for our army, and it's my honor to welcome him to the Pack. I'm glad he's making you happy."

Renaldo grinned. Giving Casto his freedom had been a spur-of-the-moment thing, but it had been the right thing to do. The longer he thought about it, the happier he was that he'd finally taken that step.

Casto wasn't suited for slavery; it was better to bind him with other, less obvious chains. "That he is doing. I better start thinking about the gifts I'm going to get him for the ceremony."

"Knowing Casto, I don't think you need a lot. He's surprisingly immune to finery."

That too was something Canubis thought strange about the capricious blond slave. In the beginning he assumed that Casto refused presents out of sheer stubbornness, but he'd had to revise that opinion. Casto really seemed oblivious to the riches Renaldo had showered on him. He only showed true gratefulness for the books he was allowed to choose on a regular basis. Everything else was seemingly of no interest to him.

Whether Renaldo knew how pointless it was to give Casto presents or not remained a mystery to Canubis, who usually knew his brother inside out. Renaldo's next words didn't shed any light on the puzzle.

"He's very modest. That's why it's vitally important to get him something special."

"I'm sure you'll find the right thing." Canubis toasted his brother in mocking salute.

Both content with how things had turned out, they emptied their cups in one go.

TREASON

1. NORAN

"I CAN'T believe it! He's really given him his freedom!"

Assani was trembling in righteous rage. When the Pack had returned to the Valley, the news about Casto no longer wearing a collar had spread like wildfire. As well as the rumor that he had been honored because he'd fought as a hero in Ki't.

Damon was deeply amused by the slave's indignant reaction. "It doesn't surprise me in the least. I actually expected it from the moment I first saw those two together. The more worthwhile question is, why is Casto still here? Considering that he's a free man who could already be somewhere in the plains by now. But he has returned with the bastards, which is unexpected."

Assani regarded him with small eyes. She hated it when Damon patronized her like that, but she could tell he was keeping something important from her, so she refrained from going against him. "You know something."

"No, I've got a hunch. A suspicion, if you want. And it's becoming more and more substantiated. I still have to check a few things, but if I'm right, the Good Mother's victory is close."

"But you won't tell me."

"That would be premature. And it could be that I'm wrong. Plus, I like keeping my secrets. This way, I minimize both our risk."

Assani spit on the ground. She wasn't a patient person to begin with, and Damon managed to draw her out on a regular basis. "You are, and always will be, an abominable power seeker. Don't think you can fool me."

"And you're a whore who'd stop at nothing for your own benefit. We're a match made in heaven, don't you think so?"

"YOU LOOK displeased, free man." With raised eyebrows, Renaldo watched Casto's unsettled tread.

Casto fell onto one of the lounges with a sigh, and a few strands that had gotten loose from his leather hair tie at the back of his head flew up. "I'd have never thought the only difference between a slave and a free man could be a collar around the neck."

Renaldo smiled mildly. "I take it from your words that today was taxing?"

"You take it right. I don't seem to be able to remember my own name anymore. I even had to cancel the ride with Lys."

Renaldo hugged Casto in alarm. He knew how important the daily ride on the black demon was for his lover's mental well-being. If Casto had to relinquish it, it dampened his mood, to put it mildly. "What can I do to make it up to you?"

Like a young cat, Casto snuggled into Renaldo's arms. It made him happy that Renaldo showed concern for him so openly even though he would never admit it. "You could tell me that Cornelia has baked some honey cake. That would be a good start."

"I'm afraid I have to disappoint you, my own. No honey cake today." Casto vented his displeasure with a sigh, which caused Renaldo to pull him even closer. "No sweets. But if you promise to show me a smile, I'll see what I can do to lift your spirits."

"I promise."

"That's all I wanted to hear."

Renaldo took his lover's face in both hands and kissed him deeply. It didn't take long until Casto had forgotten all about the day's hardships under Renaldo's knowledgeable ministrations.

Their relationship had deepened considerably after Renaldo gave Casto his freedom. There were prolonged phases of peace during which they treated each other with loving care. Those intervals were disrupted by fights that had, oddly, gotten fiercer than before.

Although Casto was officially a free man, their affiliation hadn't changed. To his own amazement, Casto still saw himself as Renaldo's slave, a fact that made him sometimes claim the proof of his independence in a reckless manner. Renaldo reacted with his usual dominance and thus fueled an explosive mixture they were only able to handle in bed, like at the beginning of their relationship. There were days when their physical interaction was so violent that Casto would carry the proof on his skin for days.

The precarious master-slave balance they had fought so hard to obtain had been shattered with Casto's release. They had to rediscover their position in regard to each other, a feat additionally complicated by their deepening feelings for each other. To outsiders they seemed like two dancers who were trying to find the right step sequence with their eyes blindfolded and an unknown melody to guide them. The outcome was an emotional mix of harmony, heated discussions, and open violence that the other members of the Pack tried to avoid as best as they could.

TROUBLED BY Casto's complaint, Renaldo saw to it that Casto's workload was reduced drastically in the following days. In no case did Renaldo want to risk losing his lover because he felt overworked.

And thus Casto found time to devote himself to the history of the Valley and its inhabitants again.

According to the chronicle, the next one to join the divine brothers had been Noran, and although Casto had no sympathy for the dark, brooding master smith, he was still curious about how a man like him had come to fit into the Pack.

STUNNED, NORAN stood in front of the ravine that led to the famous Valley of the Gods. Full of awe he stared at the mighty cliffs that presented an insuperable obstacle to anybody who wished to enter the place unseen. Their sheer size reminded him how insignificant and evanescent human life truly was, and their rough beauty, born from untamed ferocity, touched his heart. Noran had always had an eye for aesthetics, and here, in this unwelcoming but hauntingly beautiful landscape, he was rendered speechless at almost every turn. The sight of the light alone, when it broke on the rocks and glowed like fire, was worth a painting. The rocks contained mica that permeated the stone like veins and glowed in the sunlight, and Noran was so fascinated, he simply stood there and took in the unique beauty. He was in paradise.

A threatening growl interrupted the silence and woke him from his admiration. In front of him, a gigantic gray wolf had appeared seemingly out of nowhere—the biggest wolf he'd ever seen, as stunning as the landscape around them. Its fur was like silk, and its golden eyes gleamed almost as brightly as the sun. Less stunning were the impressive fangs the wolf presented with its lips drawn back in a snarl. Should it decide to do so, the animal was certainly able to crack a man's skull like a nut with the strength of its jaw.

Noran had been traveling on his own long enough to know he was in trouble. Wolves rarely hunted alone, and he didn't fancy meeting the rest of the pack if they were like that one. Slowly his hand wandered down to his belt where a long dagger sat sheathed in an intricately decorated scabbard.

The growling grew in intensity.

"If I were you, I'd stop right now. He can't take a joke."

Noran's head whipped around.

From the entrance to the Valley, a tall, good-looking man approached. In Noran's vocabulary the term *good-looking* was usually reserved exclusively for women, but the stranger was more than just easy on the eyes or handsome—both words suitable, for Noran, to describe a male. No, the man was outstanding. Perfect. His dark brown hair fell to his shoulders in a shimmering cascade, gray eyes stood dominant in his harmonious, flawless face, the lips were an invitation for kissing, and the athletic, elegantly muscled body moved with the grace of a predator.

Noran lowered his hand, bewitched by this wonderful sight. The stranger was like the landscape around them, rough and strong, fascinating and perfect, a dream incarnate, and deep in his bones, Noran knew he would never grow tired of admiring it. "I didn't really think I'd stand a chance. But I also didn't want to end with my throat torn out. That would have been embarrassing."

A bright smile parted the soft lips, showed blinding white teeth, and made the stranger's eyes light up like stars in the night sky. "You're lucky I happened to drop by. My name's Renaldo. What do you want here?"

Noran took the hand offered to him, and at the same time he tried to bow, rather awkwardly. A free man, he wasn't used to lowering his head, but he instinctively realized that the stranger deserved the sign of respect. "My name is Noran. I'm a smith, and I've heard there's work for the likes of me here. My lord."

The man had given his name, and Noran scolded himself for not recognizing him. The rumors about Renaldo's beauty didn't do him justice.

The Angel of Death was regarding him sharply. "Your information is correct. Our last smith left us, and my brother would like to replace him before winter comes. You're aware we're looking for somebody who's in it for the long run?"

"That's how I understood it. I don't have any ties or duties that could pry me away, so I'm the ideal candidate."

Happy laughter sounded, as untroubled as that of a child, as if this man weren't the most dangerous warrior on the continent but a mere boy delighting in a joke.

The fascination about the contradictory character traits would never cease to entertain Noran for the rest of his life.

"How ideal you are will be Wolfstan's decision. He's our armorer. Let's go. It's quite a trek to the main hall."

HALF A year later, Noran stood behind his anvil, working on his Spring Ceremony present for Renaldo.

About four months after Canubis had taken him in, Noran had started a steamy affair with the Angel of Death. They shared the bed in irregular sequences, mostly when Renaldo was fed up with his constantly changing partners. Noran had known from the beginning that it wouldn't last; he simply wasn't able to give Renaldo what he was seeking so frantically. By then he seriously doubted if anybody could accomplish that feat.

Whatever it was Renaldo needed so desperately, it was directly linked to the fire burning deep inside him, the fire that made it impossible to deal with him sometimes. Despite those problems, they'd managed to develop a deep friendship that could be mistaken for love. Intercourse was an outlet to them, for Renaldo to escape his loneliness, and for Noran to generate a kinship he craved almost as fiercely as Renaldo did his unknown target.

Noran's parents had died early, and he'd grown up with a distant relative who taught him blacksmithing and the meaning of coldness.

Noran couldn't complain: his mother's great-uncle had never left him lacking. Noran was always well fed and clothed. But a boy of eight years needed more than just food and clothing, something his uncle never understood. To avoid the coldness in his new home, Noran buried himself in work and set out to become the best at his craft. He had an eye for beauty, and it helped him achieve his goal at an early age.

By then Noran could claim that no one could match his skill with a hammer. Sometimes he asked himself whether it had been worth the price, but it was useless to muse about that. Things were the way they were, and he had never been the type of person to dwell on what-if questions. Before Noran came to the Valley, he'd been traveling for five years, always trying to learn something new and to better himself. He'd never stayed at one place for long—an inner restlessness always forced him to keep going.

With the Pack he found tranquility, a home, and a family for the first time since he lost his parents, although the strict hierarchical structures had deterred him in the beginning. But he found out quickly that while those structures were important for coherence among the Pack members, they played a surprisingly small role in daily affairs. That was why it was possible for a simple master smith like him to have an affair with the powerful demigod, the Angel of Death, without anybody batting an eyelash.

Noran was grateful. Being with Renaldo gave him a feeling of being appreciated, of being loved for who he was, something he hadn't known until then. The sex was a bonus or perhaps an excuse for the closeness he craved so badly, he couldn't really tell.

Noran was genuinely happy with the way things were at the moment, and nobody could ask more of their lives.

With pliers he lifted the work piece to his eyes, inspecting it. Renaldo loved simple but elegant things, probably a reaction to his own outstanding beauty. For that reason the dagger would be bare except for some sparse patterns on the blade. A weapon that convinced with its functionality and was not overloaded with ornaments such as those often seen among people who mistook conspicuousness for status.

When he lowered the pliers again, a woman Noran had never seen before stood in front of him. Her skin was as pale as marble, and her black eyes and red lips stood out starkly from the noble, strangely lifeless features. Her snow-white hair hugged her body like a veil.

With fingers as cold as ice, she caressed the back of Noran's hand. "I am pleased to meet you, Noran Mastersmith."

Noran put the dagger down. More than one alarm was going off in his head, but somehow, at the same time, he knew that the woman posed no danger to him. His insecurity stemmed from a different source, more primal, something he wasn't able to name.

Quickly he ended the embarrassing moment. "That's very kind of you, my lady, but you have the advantage of me. Unfortunately I don't know who you are."

A smile parted the wounded-looking red lips, and again Noran wondered if he should be afraid, but he couldn't find out of what. The woman was beautiful, so beautiful that small discrepancies didn't matter, provided you didn't look too closely.

"My name is Ana-Isara. I am the Empress of the Dead."

The words cleared Noran's feelings at one stroke. Naturally he felt uneasy in the presence of a goddess. Till now he had regarded the stories that Canubis and Renaldo were of divine origin with skepticism, but he didn't doubt the beautiful lady's words for a second. Reverently, Noran bowed to the goddess he had already heard so much about in the Valley. "I'm honored, my lady."

"It is my honor as well, Noran. I am very glad you have found your way to the Valley. My sons have been impatiently awaiting your arrival." She extended her hand invitingly. "Come here so that I can welcome you to the family."

Meekly, Noran obeyed the goddess's order. Her hands lay cold on his face, and he lost himself in the depths of her black eyes, which he then noticed had no iris.

"You know my son is not the one you are looking for?" Hypnotically, Noran nodded. "You'll find your love, that I promise, Noran. But be careful. Inside you is a great darkness, and it has the power to vanquish your light. You cannot let that happen. Do you understand?"

"Yes, my lady."

"Do not be afraid. My sister and I are guarding you. From now on, you will never be alone."

Then she placed a kiss on his cheek, and it burned with ice-cold fire.

TREMBLING WITH rage, Casto tossed the book aside. He couldn't believe that the Barbarian had had an affair with the grumpy, cranky smith. Even less could he believe that the Noran from the story should be identical with the one living in the Pack, the man who had once tried to beat him up.

Casto had always known Renaldo hadn't lived a life of celibacy, and up until then, it had left him mostly unperturbed about who had warmed Renaldo's bed. But Noran was a different story. Casto didn't like the grumpy man, maybe even hated him. It had always been Casto's policy not to squander his feelings, be it of hate, or love, or friendship, but the smith made his skin crawl. Whenever he met Noran, he had to restrain himself from challenging him, because he loathed the way the man viewed the world. It nettled him no end that Noran had shared with Renaldo what Casto had viewed as his exclusive right until then.

Angry with himself for getting so worked up over the information, he left the library. If possible, he would have gone for a ride with Lys, but night was already descending on the Valley. If he was late, Renaldo would certainly make a fuss again.

Casto stopped abruptly.

What did it concern him when the Barbarian got angry? He clenched his fists so tightly the knuckles shone white while he answered himself—it concerned him a lot. He didn't want to cause the Barbarian trouble. He wanted to serve him appropriately.

With a furious scream, Casto started walking toward the main house again. How on earth had it come to this? Why had he bound himself to a Barbarian? He'd been born free, and nobody could enslave him!

Agitated, Casto entered Renaldo's chambers.

Renaldo was waiting for him. "Casto. You're late today, my own. I've been waiting for you so we can take our bath together."

"Don't touch me! I want to be left alone!" Casto spat the words as if they burned his tongue.

Stunned, Renaldo retreated. He had accepted a long time ago that Casto's mood swings were as unpredictable as the weather in springtime, but it had been some time since Casto was so fierce. Only a year ago, Renaldo would have backed down to give him the breathing space he needed to calm down. But the growing intimacy of their relationship made Renaldo reckless. "What's the matter? You look as if you've stepped into a wasp's nest."

That question was met with pure anger. "It's none of your business. Just leave me alone."

"Okay, okay. Calm down. I'm going to leave for the bath. Although it's a pity. I had planned something special."

Those words, meant to redirect the mood, turned out to be oil to Casto's flame. Casto could feel his rage getting the better of him, and he started to talk without thinking. "Ha! It's certainly nothing you haven't done with others before!"

Renaldo's eyes lit up dangerously. He'd kept his cool for an atypically long period of time, but Casto's irrational behavior ignited his own fury. "What was that?"

"You heard me clearly, Barbarian. Is anything of what you've done with me truly original, or did you simply repeat what worked with others before? It's not as if you lack *training*."

"Watch your mouth, slave. I don't like the tone of your voice."

"I'm not your slave anymore, so stop calling me that! And is it just my tone or what I have to say? Am I hitting a sore spot when I remind you of my predecessors? Tell me, am I as good as Noran between the sheets, or do I need to be taught?"

The silence following those words was so intense it was almost noise.

When Renaldo finally spoke, his voice was as icy as his face, his whole body stiff. "How do you know about Noran and me?"

Casto froze. He could never admit he was reading the chronicles; that would be another defeat at the hands of a man who had already beaten him so often. "I heard it today. And it doesn't really matter, since the only remaining question is what you could want from me when you can have an Emeris in your bed anytime you wanted."

Renaldo approached Casto and urged him against the wall with his sheer presence. He dropped his hands heavily on Casto's shoulders. He didn't know how Casto had found out about that special relationship, but Casto's anger was obvious. Seeing Casto jealous like that was a balm on Renaldo's own possessive nature. On the other hand, he feared the consequences, so he decided to draw the battle lines once and for all.

"What I want from you?" A hard, demanding kiss. "I think you already know that by heart. The only remaining question, as you put it, is whether you acknowledge it to yourself or not."

Again a kiss that made Casto's knees weak. In order not to fall down, he had to cling to Renaldo. He could feel a tension in the warrior's body, identical to his own, through his fingertips. Heat flared between them, ignited by their mutual anger, and turned into a darting flame that burned them both in blind lust.

Again their mysterious attraction, the origin of which both men were oblivious to, overwhelmed them.

Casto didn't have to answer his master with words: his body took on that duty for him when he snuggled submissively against Renaldo, obedient only to his lust.

With his strong arms, Renaldo scooped up Casto and carried him to the bath, ripped off his clothes as if they were only made of cobwebs, and threw him into the warm water. In the tub he pushed Casto against the edge and snaked his arms around him, forcing him into submission. Whimpering, Casto gave in, offered himself willingly while all-consuming lust wiped away the last vestiges of his anger and left nothing but a terrible, never-ending hunger that only grew worse every time they sated it.

Several hours later they separated, both exhausted, both still angry. They'd already left the bath and exchanged it for the bed.

Renaldo loomed over Casto, pinning him down mercilessly. His gaze pierced the flaming blue of his difficult, mysterious lover. "Why are you so upset about my affair with Noran? Until now you couldn't care less who I bedded before you."

The eerie blue in Casto's eyes darkened. In vain, Casto tried to escape the Barbarian's grip. "It's different with him. He didn't just amuse you for one night. With him it lasted."

"It lasted?" Renaldo made a short, barking sound. He didn't sound amused. "Casto, our affair *lasted* for about three months, and during that time I definitely wasn't monogamous. It only persisted for so long because the sex was noncommittal."

"He's your friend and brother-in-arms."

"The connection's not as deep as it used to be." Renaldo loosened his grip and pulled Casto up, engulfing his face in his hands. His voice was soft now. "There's only you for me, my own. You're all I need." He watched the blue lighten again, only to be shadowed by sorrow.

"Am I? I warm your bed, but I'm neither your friend nor your brother-in-arms. I'm just a body you use, nothing more."

"What do you mean, Casto?"

Now Casto was crying. Tears streamed down his face like a river, but no sob escaped his lips. "That means I want to be more than just a nice fuck. Because that's what it always comes down to. We have a fight… and then we end up in bed because we're unable to solve our conflicts otherwise. You're keeping me because I'm amusing… and you've made me the way you want. I'm a creature molded by your will… I'm unable to leave you. How utterly pathetic."

Shocked, Renaldo lowered his hands. He avoided Casto's gaze— the young man he thought he'd known. "That's not true, Casto. You're far too strong to be formed by me. I like your strength."

"Yes, because it submits to you."

Casto's voice was barely audible. The words sounded as if they'd been forced out of him with a poker, the summary of his misery. Casto had been successful in deceiving himself for a long time, had lulled himself into believing that he had at least a scrap of control over what was happening to him, but faced with the things he'd found out about himself today, it was no longer possible to ignore the facts. As much as he resented it, to Renaldo, Casto was nothing but a toy, an amusement along the way.

And Casto had been stupid enough to fall in love with him, to grant him an influence nobody had possessed over him before.

In that moment, Casto hated himself with all his might.

"It's not true." Renaldo sounded stubborn. He reached for Casto's face but stopped in midair. Lost for words, they knelt on the bed, staring at each other without finding what they were looking for.

Casto waited desperately for Renaldo to finally tell him that he loved him.

Since he read the prophecy, he'd been longing to hear those words from Renaldo, the confirmation that he wouldn't have to worry about being replaced someday. But it seemed as if Renaldo wouldn't do him that favor. Casto cursed himself, cursed the whole situation, cursed his fate that had bound him to a man he couldn't escape from and who was holding his heart in his hands, carelessly hurting it time and again. His inability to leave both wounded and enraged him, but he was too tired to deal with the insoluble problem any further.

He left the bed, keeping his gaze down so Renaldo couldn't see how much he was troubled. "I'm going to wash myself. It may take some time."

Renaldo let Casto leave without protest, glad for the opportunity to be alone. Casto's outburst had surprised him, and it pained him how accurately he had described their relationship. Ever since Renaldo met him, he'd fought against the undertow that pulled him closer to his former slave, his lover.

It couldn't be that he had fallen for a mere mortal. The powerful Angel of Death could not have given in to the charms of a young man on the brink of maturity.

The feelings he harbored for Casto were so overwhelming and disturbing, Renaldo tried to ignore them as much as possible so he wouldn't become vulnerable. He knew all too well how time itself would crush this love. Not for the first time did he contemplate it might be better if the young man left the Valley. But the thought of having to live without Casto was like a dagger to his heart. He'd already gotten too used to having Casto around to send him away now, even though he knew how egoistic that was.

It was partly because he was a god and every human's destiny was to serve him. Casto was no exception to that rule. And even if it made Casto unhappy, it was his master and god's will that he stay by his side. Nevertheless, Renaldo would try to repay Casto for his sacrifice.

Determined, Renaldo got up to make peace with Casto.

Casto was floating in the water with his eyes closed. He looked almost at ease. Renaldo joined him, pulled him close, and kissed him on the cheek. His lips were close to Casto's ear when he started to speak.

"I'm sorry, Casto. Right from the beginning, I've never been fair towards you. When I saw you for the first time, I knew I wanted to possess you. I've lived for so long, I've gotten used to getting whatever I desire. I know you're not here of your own free will, and I'm aware of how much you resent having to serve me. That, too, is my fault. But it can't be changed. Even if I wanted to, I just can't let you leave. You're mine."

Renaldo could feel Casto tensing at those words. He hurried on. "Please believe me when I say I'm going to make it up to you. Please allow me to. I want you to be happy, and I swear to you, I'll do everything in my power to ensure it."

Casto started to tremble in his arms. He buried his face on Renaldo's shoulder. His voice was flat because he didn't want Renaldo to hear the unshed tears in it. There was no escape for him anymore, and the severity of the defeat made him despair.

"It's me who should be sorry, Master. I was stupid. Please forgive my unreasonable behavior."

"You're never unreasonable, my own. And now allow me to reconcile with you."

For a moment Casto hesitated, but then he let Renaldo sweep him away in a gale of lust, although he still felt a semblance of self-loathing.

2. NOEMI

"I HAVE good news!"

Pleased with himself and the world, Damon leaned against the dusty wall of the shed in which he usually met with Assani.

She regarded him hungrily. She knew him well enough to know that his news was going to delight her. "Your investigations have been successful?"

"Not only my investigations, which, as I want to humbly point out, have verified my suspicions. I already have a plan. This time it'll be the bastards' downfall—and I do mean that literally."

"Share."

At Assani's greedy voice, Damon couldn't suppress a condescending smile. The woman was so ice-cold it impressed even him. "You're terribly nosy, but since I'm going to need your help… you're going to play a vital part in my plan. When the time is ripe, you'll go to Renaldo and tell him you're having an affair with Casto."

Assani's eyes widened in terror. Even her ruthlessness seemed to have limits. "He'd never believe that. It would be my death!"

"Not when you have proof to back up your story. And when a certain dupability has taken hold of Renaldo."

"Magic?"

"We'll change the shrouding spell slightly. It's going to cost us a little more blood than usual, but it's worth the price."

"I still don't get you. The law states that Casto can have sex with whomever he pleases. The Angel of Death can accuse him of bad style, but he has no right to kill him for it."

"We know that, but the bastard won't see it that way. He'll believe that Casto has no right to get involved with others."

After a moment's silence, Assani's mouth formed a perfect O of surprise. Her face was highlighted by a malicious gleam that made her almost attractive in Damon's eyes. "Casto is his heart, isn't he?"

Damon made a mental note to never forget that the woman in front of him was no fool—her intuition and sharp mind could be dangerous in the future. "I'm sure of it. Or at least as sure as I can be under the circumstances. The hearts are protected by powerful magic, but their true nature can only be seen after they've been acknowledged by Ana-Isara. As far as I know, even the goddess has to wait for certain conditions that allow her to reveal the heart. The spell we've cast strengthens that protection—that's why it took me so long to recognize the truth. All signs are indicative of Casto being the one we've been searching for."

"And when Renaldo kills him in a fit of temper…."

"Then they die together." Damon couldn't suppress his malicious grin. He didn't understand why Ana-Isara and her sister had tied this special condition to the finding of the hearts, but since it was perfect for his plans, he certainly wasn't sad about it.

After their hearts had been taken from the brothers, the Holy Mothers had entrusted them to chance. It was entirely possible that Noemi, as well as Casto, had already wandered Ana-Darasa several times just to die a natural death. That didn't pose a problem since their divine natures had placed them outside the cycle of life and death. They would be reborn as many times as it took until they found their masters. Only when one of the brothers killed his heart with his own hands would that cycle finally be ended.

After all, only a god was able to destroy a god.

It was simply too good. Should the hot-tempered Angel of Death kill Casto in his rage, they both would die and the Good Mother would triumph. Without his brother it would be impossible for Canubis to win the war. Even if Renaldo didn't kill his heart with his own hands, Casto's death would still grant the followers of the Good Mother a reprieve that would allow them to gather greater strength. A triumph for the Good Mother, no matter how you looked at it—

"What do I have to do?"

Assani's voice pried Damon from his dreams of glory. He eyed her greedily. "First, I need blood. Yours and mine will flow tonight so the spell can reach its peak come the next new moon. That's when we'll strike."

Wordlessly, Assani offered her unmarred arm to the priest of the Good Mother. Compared to Damon she was nothing but a child when it came to using magic, trained well enough to know what he was doing, but never herself able to achieve anything remotely similar.

The other followers they had brought into the Valley had no magical powers at all. They were there to obey Damon and, to some extent, Assani. Should the priest's plan be successful, all would be rewarded greatly.

"Take as much as you need," Assani murmured.

"Your willingness for self-sacrifice is admirable."

While their mingled blood dripped into the ceremonial cup and burned up with an angry hiss, Damon explained their further course of action.

"We need something from Casto that you can use as proof of his infidelity."

"How shall we get that? None of us is allowed into the Angel of Death's chambers, and even if we were, the wolves would sense a theft immediately."

Assani shuddered. The powerful predators were the biggest problem in the Valley. They moved around like shadows, appearing suddenly in unexpected places only to vanish the next instant. They were not only bigger than normal wolves but also a lot more intelligent, and they were absolutely loyal to Canubis. Whatever the wolf pack knew, the Wolf of War knew too.

Damon answered her. "That's why we're going to send somebody who won't attract attention. I admit it's a little risky, but it's worth it."

"Who do you want to use?"

"Sic. He's dumb enough to be fooled by me. He has a strict master, which means he'll never betray us for fear of what will happen to him, and he has free access to the chambers of all the Emeris. He's the perfect candidate."

Assani agreed with him—Sic was made for the task. And since she hated the little bootlicker, she would enjoy watching him suffer. "You're truly vicious. I like it."

Damon bowed to her in mockery. "Years of experience. But we have to be careful. The spell protects us, but still one wrong word can destroy it all. It's almost two weeks till the next new moon. We have to make good use of that time."

"I will lie low and leave everything to you. Only contact me when it's necessary."

"Good girl. Prepare for your part. Even though Renaldo's senses are confused, he's no fool. You have to be convincing."

"Can't you put a spell on him directly?"

"Unfortunately not. He's a demigod. He would sense immediately when magic targeted him. I'm sure you can imagine what would happen to us should he find out."

Assani blanched. The methods of torture used by the brothers were infamous. Although it would be hard to hide her glee, she had to do it. After the bastard demigods' downfall, when the Good Mother finally appeared in her full glory, Assani could celebrate the end of her enemies.

The final days were drawing near.

"SIC, HOW nice to see you here."

Slightly startled, Sic looked up. He hadn't expected to meet anybody in this shed at the edge of the wood. Noran had sent him to do an inventory of the tools stored here, and Sic had assumed he was alone.

Damon stepped out of the shadows, a slave Sic knew but always feared a little. Sic's nature was too indulgent to actively talk bad about somebody else, but Damon made him shiver. Involuntarily Sic retreated a few steps from the malicious aura, which the man registered with a faint smile.

"We need to have a little talk, you and me." Damon placed an arm around Sic's shoulders, a gesture that could have been friendly were it not for his fingers digging painfully into Sic's flesh.

Although Sic was definitely stronger than Damon, he did not fight back. Noran hated every kind of disturbance, and if Sic hurt another slave, his master would definitely punish him severely for it. "I don't know what we should be talking about. And I don't have time to be idle. My master is waiting for my return."

"You will take the time," Damon hissed. He, too, was aware that Sic could still gain the upper hand simply because he was physically stronger, something Damon had to prevent at all costs. So he used all his authority as a priest to render his victim helpless. When he saw fear in Sic's eyes, he forced himself to smile. He needn't overdo it. "Calm down. It's nothing major. I'm just asking you to do me a favor."

Sic's whole body was wreathed in suspicion, but he remained silent. That was a positive sign, and Damon kept on talking. "You have free access to the chambers of all Emeris. I want you to bring me something from Casto's belongings."

Sic's eyes widened in fear and a hint of anger. He understood better than anybody else in the Valley about the consequences of such actions since he served the strictest master of them all. "You want me to steal from the Angel of Death's favorite? That's not a favor, that's madness! If you let go of me right now, I might forget that you made such a suggestion."

Damon's grip hardened. "Be careful who you threaten, you pitiful dog. You either do what I say, or your precious master dies."

With a violent motion, Sic freed himself from Damon's grip; his eyes were now alight with anger but also the first hints of worry. "You're talking nonsense. Lord Noran is Emeris. He can't die."

Damon laughed. It was a sound so terrifying that Sic could feel the hair on his nape rise.

"How unbelievably stupid of you. The Emeris are protected from death by a human's hand, so much is true, but I would use magic to end Noran's life. There will be no way to save him."

"Magic is forbidden in the Valley."

"Do you think I care? You're going to do what I say or Noran dies."

Trembling, Sic clenched his jaw. "I don't believe you. You're lying. I'm going to leave now and tell my master about this."

He turned away, but Damon grabbed his sleeve.

"I'm going to prove it. You don't want to risk that I could be right, do you?"

Sic stopped, hesitating. He knew he should go straight to Noran and tell him everything, but the fear of losing him, of being responsible for his death, kept Sic back.

Damon saw his chance. As merciless as a hawk stooping on its prey, he seized Sic. "Come with me. I'm going to demonstrate my powers to you."

Damon dragged Sic from the shed toward the huts. At a well, several slaves had gathered to draw water. Damon halted between two huts so that the women couldn't see them.

"Do you see the brunette over there? The one who looks so young and vibrant?" Sic nodded, bemused. "Keep an eye on her."

Frozen in terror, Sic heard Damon murmuring in a language he didn't understand. The air surrounding the priest's outstretched hand flickered for a moment, and then everything was like before.

The young woman at the well was laughing at some joke when her features suddenly froze. She grabbed her chest with a whimper; the bucket fell to the ground. The woman sank to her knees, her body seized by violent convulsions. She hit her head on the well. A strange shiver ran through her muscles and left her lying motionless.

Panic broke out among the other women. One started running toward the main hall, no doubt to get Lady Noemi.

Damon dragged Sic back into the shed. "Have you seen enough? You either do what I say or your precious master shares her fate."

Sic stumbled against the wooden walls of the shed. Tears streamed down his cheeks and he kept his gaze down. All reason had died inside him; his mind was swamped with the fear of losing his master. He knew how wrong it was to let Damon blackmail him, but what choice did he have?

Losing Noran was the one thing he would never be able to endure. "What do you want me to do?"

Damon made a triumphant sound. Once he had won, he didn't trouble himself with hiding his contempt. Manipulating Sic had been easier than he'd anticipated, and he had never been gracious in victory. "I already told you. You'll bring me something that belongs to Casto. It has to be valuable, but he mustn't miss it the next few days."

"I'll do what you want."

Disdainfully Damon patted Sic's cheek. "I had no doubt. Hurry, I want the thing by tomorrow noon. You come back here and deliver it to me then. After that, your master is safe."

"Do I have your word?"

Damon's face hardened. "Don't challenge me, little doggie. Go and do what you're told."

With slumped shoulders, Sic hurried to escape from the horrible man. He knew very well that Damon hated Casto from the core of his heart and that he would use whatever Sic brought him to harm Casto. But Sic had no choice. The mere thought of Noran being hurt caused him physical pain. He would do whatever was necessary. Even if it meant betraying someone he really liked.

THE SAME day, Sic went to Lord Renaldo's chambers. Unfortunate coincidence had it that Lord Noran had just finished a repair for Lord Renaldo. With his heart beating loudly, Sic entered the room. He hoped Lord Renaldo was there so he would have an excuse to leave immediately, but Sic was alone. He placed the package on the table, then went into the room where Casto kept his things. Opening the trunk posed no problem since the keys were lying right next to it.

Sic's eyes widened when he saw the riches in front of him. The Angel of Death was indeed a generous master. He only wondered why Casto never wore any of the treasures piled up so carelessly within. Sic doubted it was pure modesty that kept Casto from wearing the finery. The reason was probably Casto's sheer stubbornness, which forbade him to accept even the smallest favor from Lord Renaldo.

Carefully, Sic dug into the trunk until he found a splendid golden cloak pin set with sapphires. Given how deeply this jewel was buried under the rest, Casto wouldn't miss it anytime soon—should he even remember that he owned it.

With trembling hands, Sic hid the pin under his work coat, painfully aware that he was not only sinning against a friend but also against his master and his gods. He didn't see another escape from his predicament other than doing exactly what the obnoxious Damon asked of him.

On his way back to the smithy, Sic ran into Casto. "Hello, Sic! Noran keeping you busy?"

Sic's bad conscience howled, and he couldn't meet Casto's eyes. "I'm sorry, Casto. I'm in a hurry."

"Don't fret it, Sic. I don't want to cause you any trouble. We can talk some other time."

Sic cringed. He hurried into the smithy, hoping he could find some peace there.

Casto watched Sic worriedly. He had come to like the apprentice smith. He hated how Sic had to suffer under his master, but he didn't know how to help him either. Strictly speaking, Casto wasn't even able to help himself, so it was futile pondering what he could do for others. Since that fateful night when he'd almost given himself away, he'd become more careful around Renaldo again, horrified at how close he'd been to telling the Barbarian everything and confessing his love to him.

How low had he stooped to long for those words from somebody like Renaldo?

Renaldo, too, had changed since that night. He'd stuck by his word and did everything to make Casto feel at home: showered him with expensive gifts, reined in his possessive streak as much as was possible for himself, and held back massively when it came to intercourse.

All of which led straight to the next problem: Casto loved getting physical. He sighed. At this rate, they'd never have a normal relationship.

To divert himself, Casto visited the library. After the disaster that had unfolded when he'd read Noran's story, he'd hesitated to read the chronicles through to the end. But he was too curious to find out how Lady Noemi had found her way to the Pack to stop reading now.

In anticipation he opened the book at the page where he'd left off.

WITH CLOSED eyes, Noemi Amerasu listened to the steady rattle of the coach's wheels carrying her through the night toward her destiny. Opposite her sat Mother Vana, a priestess of the Good Mother and her inquisitor, propped up with soft cushions.

She, too, had her eyes closed, thinking about the enormous amount of money the girl's parents had paid to have her accused of practicing witchcraft without belonging to the Order of the Good Mother. They had been desperate to get rid of her, desperate enough to accept the girl's death.

Vana smiled when she remembered the fear within the father of the girl and his second, beautiful young wife. It was hard to tell if they were more terrified of the wrath of the Good Mother or the things the girl could do. Noemi was a snake witch, and a powerful one at that, and Vana would be the one to sacrifice her to the Good Mother.

Noemi Amerasu was probably the last of her kind, a relic from the times before the Good Mother came to Ana-Darasa. Back then, the healers had forged a pact with the snakes, a pact blessed by Ana-Isara and Ana-Aruna. In exchange for sharing their power of healing, the snakes were allowed to take up residence in the hearts of the healers. Such a double gift— witch and snake—would be rewarded greatly by the powerful goddess.

A muffled impact followed by a piercing scream tore both women from their musings. The horses whinnied in agitation and quickened their pace. Another impact sent the coach careening onto two wheels.

Noemi tried holding on to the cushion of her seat as well as she could manage, but the chains that tied her to the floor didn't allow much movement. Mother Vana clung to the door handle, berating the coach driver in her unpleasant, high-pitched voice.

They stopped. The coach swayed for a moment like a drunk trying to find his balance. When it finally stood still, absolute silence ensued. The door was yanked open brutally.

A man with countless braids on his head peeped inside. When he laid eyes on the two women, he grinned. "You were right, Aegid. This is a coach of the Good Mother's followers."

Saying that, he grabbed Mother Vana and dragged her into the darkness. The high, enraged screaming was music to Noemi's ears, although normally she didn't make a habit of being vindictive. However, the woman had taken immense pleasure from telling her in sordid detail the things that would happen to her before she found her death as a sacrifice for the Good Mother. Noemi's pity was very limited in this case.

The braided warrior reappeared and moved to grab Noemi when he noted the chains. Frowning, he turned away again. "They're transporting a prisoner here."

"Let me see."

That voice was full of calm authority. The braided one obeyed immediately, a sure sign that the man entering the coach held great power. Noemi only glanced briefly at a harmonious face bordered by pitch-black hair and dominated by imperious, amber-colored eyes before she lowered her head in humility. Under no circumstances did she want to anger the man. He emitted a strong aura of power and dominance, and she felt the irrational urge to kneel in front of him.

When he started talking to her, his voice was surprisingly gentle. "Don't be afraid. I'm going to open the chains now so that you can leave the coach."

"You're very kind, lord, but I'm afraid I don't know where Mother Vana keeps the keys."

Soft laughter spilled through the coach. "I don't need keys."

A jangle and the chain fell to the ground, broken into pieces. Noemi was so bewildered that she stared directly into the man's face. "How did you do that?"

His sensuous mouth smiled subtly. "One of my many talents."

He sounded so salacious that Noemi felt her cheeks redden. "Please forgive me, lord."

"Never mind. Give me your hand. It's dark and slippery out here."

She followed the warrior out of the coach and froze. Illuminated by the flickering torchlight, Mother Vana lay in the mud, her throat slit so violently that her spine was visible. The trunk with the blood money Noemi's father had paid to get rid of her stood next to the dead priestess.

The braided warrior approached Noemi and her escort. His teeth were white, in stark contrast to his dark skin. He sounded more amused than threatening. "Just what did you do to piss the Good Mother off?"

Noemi didn't look up. Her hand was still entwined with the black-haired warrior, and she felt kind of safe. "I was accused of practicing witchcraft. Mother Vana took me with her to have me tested."

"Seems like somebody wanted you dead. Those hyenas know no mercy."

"Enough, Kalad. You and the others can share the booty. I'll take this one with me."

The warrior bowed to his leader in mockery. "As you wish, my lord Canubis."

"Sometimes you really get on my nerves, do you know that?"

Although his words sounded harsh, Noemi could hear the amusement in the man's voice. When she'd heard his name, her heart stopped for a moment. Even secluded in the tower where she'd spent her past six years, she had heard about the famous Lord Canubis, leader of the most powerful army of mercenaries on Ana-Darasa.

She knew her fate then and steeled herself against the pain she would experience soon. A man like Lord Canubis certainly wouldn't take a woman with him just to wine and dine her.

INSIDE THE tent of the famous Wolf of War, Noemi stood lost while her new owner rummaged through his trunks to find something for her to wear. He finally gave up.

"You're too small. I can't find anything that could fit you."

For a moment he seemed to stare into thin air, and then he returned his attention to her, a satisfied expression on his face.

"The problem will be solved. Sit down, and tell me your name and how you ended up in the clutches of the Good Mother."

Shyly, Noemi looked up at the powerful man. She wondered how much she should tell him. It certainly wasn't a good idea to be caught lying, but the divine brothers' opinions about magic were well known. Should he find out that she was indeed a witch, her fate was sealed. It was a thin line she had to tread.

"I am Noemi Amerasu. My father is the leader of Amman. It's just a small city you've probably never heard of. My mother died shortly after giving birth to me, and about eight years ago, he got himself a new wife. We never got along well. She wasn't able to drive me out of the city entirely—my ancestry offered some protection, after all—but she managed to isolate me from the court. A few weeks ago, Mother Vana came into the city, and my stepmother must have sensed her chance. I was accused of being a witch, and for the payment of a certain amount of gold, Mother Vana agreed to take me to a shrine of the Good Mother and test me."

"That's a death sentence."

"I know. To be honest, I'm quite relieved you ambushed the coach, my lord."

"That's the first time somebody gave me thanks for a raid." Canubis grinned broadly. "I like you, Noemi."

His friendly words encouraged Noemi to express her greatest fear. "I'm still a virgin, my lord. Are you going to hurt me?"

Canubis's amber eyes lit up in hunger, and Noemi feared she'd just dug her own grave, when the powerful warrior gently touched her cheek.

"You mustn't be afraid. Nobody in this camp will touch you unless you give your express permission." When he saw her confused expression, he continued. "This is the Pack. We follow strict rules, sweet one. We serve the Holy Mothers, and they abhor nothing so much as forced sex. Regarding the bed, you're absolutely free. You can choose whoever you want, and nobody is allowed to force you. Not even me."

"Is that true?"

"I do not lie!"

Ashamed, she lowered her head. "Please forgive me, Master. I didn't mean to be insolent."

"Don't worry. It was a long day for you. Now go to rest. Everything else, we'll talk about tomorrow. Or sometime soon, since we're in the middle of conquering a city."

A wolfish grin accompanied those words as if a campaign was some sort of holiday. For the Wolf of War, it probably was.

With a sense of unease, Noemi lay down in the place she'd been shown. Although she was at the heart of the most feared army in the world, in the tent of the leader of that army, she slept deeply and soundly.

For reasons she wasn't able to comprehend yet, Noemi felt safe in the presence of the mighty Wolf of War.

THE NEXT day, Canubis left the tent right after sunrise, decked in full battle armor. For some time, Noemi sat there, bored. Then she got up and decided to look around the camp. So long as she didn't try to flee, she was free to move about as she pleased, a concession she was determined to enjoy. In the distance she could hear the sounds of battle, and the thought of all these pointlessly wasted lives made her sad.

In one of the biggest tents, she found the infirmary where the healers were busy. Noemi was just about to move on since it was none of her business, but her natural kindness shortened her stride. People were suffering there; it was her duty to help them, although it might endanger her. Not without a certain feeling of doom did she enter the tent. The mixed smells of blood, herbs, and, above all, pain were like old acquaintances from the time when she had undergone training as a healer, before she was locked up in the tower. The woman who raised Noemi in place of her mother had realized her talent and her connection with the snake, and she saw to it that Noemi started training at twelve. Even while she was locked away, the kind woman had brought her books about the healing arts so that she could complete her studies.

Two mercenaries were just carrying in one of their comrades, whose right leg was twisted at an unnatural angle. Automatically switching into healer mode, Noemi beckoned them over. The man was still conscious, which was surprising given the severity of his wound. With ease of practice, she cut away the clothing to reveal the entire laceration. After she had assessed the severity of the damage, she turned to one of the shelves to her left, selected a vial and gave the man a potion to make him sleep. It took her some time to cleanse out all the bone splinters and the dirt, then she used her power to heal the bone and close the wound enough to prevent it from reopening. The snake, her soul's companion from the day she was born, eagerly helped. Shaa-Azar, the snake, was also glad that they could finally follow their calling again.

After Noemi had taken care of that warrior, the next one was already sitting on her table, and before she knew it, the line of wounded fighters before her became as long as those of the other healers.

Without her noticing it, the day passed and night descended on the camp. The noise from the battle had ceased. Noemi was exhausted and longing for a break and something to eat. Before she had the chance to sit down for a moment, Lord Canubis entered the tent with a beautiful warrior at his side. Both men were covered in blood and dirt, but it only made Canubis more awe-inspiring. His companion was so perfect that the dirt only enhanced his beauty.

The Wolf of War's gaze fell on Noemi, and with a gesture, he called her closer. Noemi obeyed with her eyes cast down.

"What are you doing here?"

He sounded tired, which wasn't surprising after a day like that.

"I've been looking around the camp and found this place by chance. It seemed as if I could be of help, so I stayed. I hope I didn't do anything wrong, Master."

"No, of course not. I'm just surprised. You didn't mention that you're a healer."

"I'd say she's a lot more than that."

The calm voice made Noemi flinch. Behind her stood a small, tired-looking man with hair the color of sand and big, friendly eyes. She had seen him several times during the day. He was obviously the master of the infirmary since the other healers obeyed his commands.

Canubis watched him with narrowed eyes. "What are you implying, Bantu?"

"That your prisoner is a snake witch, if I'm not mistaken."

Frightened, Noemi staggered away from the gazes of the Wolf of War and his companions. Her heart beat so fast she was afraid it would burst at any time. As unhappy as her life had been so far, she didn't want to die yet; she was too young to give up. "Please, don't kill me. I'm not evil. I just wanted to help."

Canubis's bloodied hands grabbed her upper arms. "Calm down. You won't be harmed. Are you really a snake witch?"

"Yes. The last one."

"That's a surprise. We thought the last snakes had left this world years ago." The voice of the good-looking warrior was as charming as his looks.

Canubis seemed satisfied. "And what a happy coincidence that she found her way into the Pack."

"You're not mad?" Noemi couldn't believe it, but if anything, the warlord seemed happy.

"A little, because you lied to me. But I can understand your fears. You were afraid I would burn you as a witch, weren't you?"

"Yes, since you follow the Holy Mothers. I thought you disapproved of any kind of magic."

The perfect one was amused.

"Not compulsively. We're against the forcible use of magic against the rules of this world as the followers of the Good Mother practice it. We don't threaten those who are blessed by right of birth."

"Then I'd like to apologize for my lie."

Canubis placed his arm around her small shoulders. "You've already made up for your mistake. But you do look like you're in dire need of a break. Come with me, and I'll take care of you."

Relieved and still surprised, Noemi followed the Wolf of War to his tent, where he first bathed himself, and then he treated her to a delicious meal. When their eyes met over the table laden with food, the last snake witch had already fallen irreversibly for the powerful warlord.

On THE night after her wedding to the Wolf of War, Noemi was visited by Ana-Isara.

The goddess met her in the Green Lands, Ana-Isara's original home. Next to Noemi, Shaa-Azar, her inseparable companion, made soothing sounds.

The goddess bowed to the reptile. "It has been some time since I last met one of your kind. I'm truly honored and highly pleased."

Shaa-Azar's neck frill opened to show its full glory. She, too, was happy about this meeting.

Ana-Isara took Noemi's hands in her own. "I welcome you, heart of my son. He had to wait for you for so long, but now you are united again."

Shyly, Noemi returned the gaze from the black eyes. "I thank you, my lady."

A shining smile brightened the features of the Empress of the Dead. "Come to me, so that I can welcome you to my family. You are my son's heart, and from this day on, you are under the protection my sister and I offer to you."

Noemi curtsied deeply to show the goddess her thanks, and then she let herself be kissed. She was only able to bear the pain because Shaa-Azar was with her.

3. LOVE'S DEATH

"WHAT HAVE you gotten for me?"

Greedily, Damon grabbed the small package Sic held out to him. When he opened it, he couldn't suppress an evil snicker.

"This is perfect. You did a good job, doggie."

Sic kept his gaze averted in desperation. Now he was truly damned, and nobody could ever take the weight of that guilt from him. "I did what you wanted me to do. Please leave my master alone."

"But of course. You can leave."

Damon's thoughtful gaze followed the quickly retreating figure of Sic. Next to him, Assani emerged from the shadows.

Damon said, "I guess it's better if we see to it that he doesn't get any ideas in the next few days. We don't want to risk him spilling anything to Casto, do we?"

"What should I do?" Assani was anxious to make Sic miserable. It was one of her best features, her will to trouble others just for the fun of it.

"It will be enough if Noran thinks that his apprentice has been tardy. He abhors laziness and punishes it brutally."

"That shouldn't pose too great a problem. I'm on it."

"Assani?"

"Yes?"

"Don't lose concentration now. It's still three days until the new moon. Three days till we triumph."

"I know, Damon. You can count on me."

FOR THE last time, Renaldo went over the preparations he had made for this evening. Since their last argument, his relationship with Casto had become as tense as at the beginning. It had hit him hard that his lover thought he was just a distraction for his master. Of course the sex was an important part of their relationship, but Renaldo was willing to let go of it to keep Casto at his side. To prove it to him, he had planned something special for that night.

First they would eat all of Casto's favorite foods, followed by an entire plate of honey cake. Then Renaldo had found a special book for his lover, which they would read together. He only hoped that was enough to pacify the complicated young man.

A timid knocking disrupted his preparations. Slightly annoyed at the disturbance, he asked the guest to come in. The woman was a slave he didn't know. She was quite easy on the eyes, with a beautiful but cold face, long dark hair, and a voluptuous body. She kneeled in front of him, her gaze on the ground.

"What do you want?"

Renaldo wanted to put an end to this as quickly as possible. It wouldn't be long until Casto returned. The woman was whimpering.

"I'm here to beg your forgiveness, Master."

"Forgiveness? What for? What have you done?"

A hysterical sob escaped her lips. "I swear I didn't know! And he was so charming!"

Renaldo had had enough. He didn't have time for this kind of game. "Listen to me, slave. Either you tell me what the matter is right now or I'll leave you to the overseers to beat it out of you, understood?"

Trembling, the woman cowered on the ground. "Please have mercy, Master. If I'd known that you didn't have a clue, I'd have never done it with Casto. Never."

Renaldo froze. "What are you talking about?"

The slave was now talking so fast it was like a torrent flowing from her lips. She could obviously feel how angry he'd become. "Two years ago he started flirting with me. I was flattered because he's really good-looking. When he asked for more, I wasn't averse, and he was your favorite as well. Before you went to Ki't, I found out that you never knew about our little trysts. I wanted to end it, but Casto asked me to give him some time. He gave me this cloak pin as a token of his affection."

With trembling hands, the slave held up a golden pin Renaldo recognized immediately—one of the many treasures he had given Casto during the last four years that Casto had neglected. Obviously on purpose.

"When you returned, he told me that he was free now and could do whatever he liked. But I can't take it any longer. You're my god. I cannot lie to you. I'm so sorry."

Dazed, Renaldo stared at the whining woman at his feet. All of a sudden, so many details about Casto made perfect sense. The little bastard had lulled him into a sense of security, had lied to him and betrayed him, and Renaldo had fallen for it, taken in by a pair of glinting blue eyes and a beautiful body.

But that was the past. He clenched his fists in anger. Casto would find out this very evening what it meant to invoke the wrath of the Angel of Death.

On the ground, Assani had to concentrate not to start laughing. The heat in the room told her even more clearly than the tension in the bastard's body that the plan had worked. When he spoke now, his voice was strained and hardly audible.

"Get lost! I don't want to see you again."

Assani hurried to obey. She had no inclination to face the rage of the Angel of Death.

She would leave that to Casto.

THE FIRST thing Casto noticed when he entered his master's chambers was the unnatural heat. Usually Renaldo didn't bother with heating because the cold didn't faze him as much as it did Casto. One more thing they would never agree on.

He closed the door and was grabbed by strong hands at the same moment. Before Casto could get over his surprise, a blow hit him. Casto knew immediately that the Barbarian was serious: his fist had smacked Casto's chin, and for a moment he felt dizzy. He shook his head to regain his bearings and was just in time to block the next blow Renaldo aimed at him.

"What is wrong with you?" Casto dodged another blow and landed a punch on Renaldo's jaw.

The pain seemed to distract the Barbarian because he actually hesitated with his fists hanging in midair.

Renaldo's voice came out as a hiss. "You dare ask me that? This time, you've gone too far. You will pay!"

The next blow landed on Casto's ribcage and drove the air out of his lungs. He staggered sideways, lost his balance, and was just in time to catch his fall with his right hand, narrowly escaping the vicious kick

Renaldo aimed at him. When Renaldo moved forward to kick him again, Casto rolled out of the way and used his legs to swipe him off his feet. He rose into a half crouch to lunge at the Barbarian, but Renaldo was faster and caught Casto around the waist. Again they went down in a tangle of limbs. By then, Casto had abandoned his confusion about Renaldo's strange behavior and had gone straight to furious. Knowing that Renaldo was stronger, he tried to land as many blows as possible.

Renaldo was seething. How dare Casto defy him and fight back when he was the one who had wronged Renaldo? Something inside of him snapped. The tight restraints he kept on his inner beast crumbled as it reared its ugly head. On a level so primal it was virtually devoid of humanity, Renaldo understood that Casto was his and his alone. The young man had no right to look at anybody else, let alone touch them.

The beast wanted to punish Casto, eager to show the world that it could do to him whatever it pleased, simply because it was so strong. Nobody had a right to oppose it, least of all the slave who was glaring at him with open hatred.

"And this is why I hate being with you so much." Casto spit the words out as if they left a bad aftertaste in his mouth. "Just because you feel like it, I have to put up with your violence. I hate you, Barbarian. I really do."

The spiteful words were enough to send the beast into a greater rage.

Renaldo felt his fire blaze. He only had moments before he lost even the last shreds of control he still clung to. When that happened, Casto was dead. The thought made Renaldo shiver in fear despite his anger.

He lunged forward and knocked Casto unconscious.

The beast was not happy about that. It wanted to see the pain in Casto's eyes when it punished him, wanted to feel Casto's body tremble in fear when Casto finally understood what kind of power he'd challenged. Seeing Casto's prone form on the floor was not enough. Renaldo grabbed Casto's head to see if there was a chance to wake him, but the young man hung limp in his arms.

Knowing it would take some time until Casto woke up, Renaldo let go of Casto's head and directed his fury toward the room.

He burned the logs in the fireplace to cinders, and when that was not nearly enough, he directed the blaze to the lounges, the carpet, and the chairs. When every wooden item was nothing but ashes, he concentrated on the weapons on the wall. Under his power they turned cherry-red and then started to melt. The liquid metal left a smoldering trail on the stone walls before pooling on the wooden floor, destroying the planks. While he witnessed the power of his flame, Renaldo felt the beast inside him calm down, still agitated, but no longer out of control. When he was sure he had regained a semblance of restraint, he turned to Casto.

Casto was still unconscious. A lump the size of a hen's egg had formed on his temple. Blood trickled from his slack mouth, and more dripped onto the floor from a wound Renaldo couldn't see.

Renaldo felt like somebody had dropped a bowl of burning coal inside his chest. The pain made him realize how much he cared for Casto. If he didn't love him, then Casto's betrayal wouldn't hurt so badly.

In a fresh rush of anger, Renaldo ripped Casto's clothes open. He stared at the studs he had given the traitor, and their sparkle seemed to mock him. It was all he could do not to rip the jewelry out, and he wasn't too careful when he removed them.

Suddenly, Renaldo was overwhelmed by disgust. He didn't want the traitor to remain there, in his chambers, which Casto had sullied more than enough. Renaldo didn't even want him to remain in the Valley. Casto had to be taken far away, where his presence couldn't faze Renaldo anymore and where his death—for that was what he deserved for his treachery—would no longer be in Renaldo's hands.

He called for two overseers to carry the almost-lifeless body to the dungeons. He sent another slave to Noemi to explain everything and to ask her to heal Casto enough that he would survive transportation to the mines.

Empty and burned out, Renaldo sagged to the ground, sat in the pool of blood, and leaned his head against the metal-spattered wall. He inhaled the scent of his lover that lingered in the air like a last, cynical farewell, and stoically bore the all-consuming pain that rushed through his mind in crashing waves.

WITH A shrill whinny, Lysistratos tore at the door of his stall. The wood reinforced with steel groaned under the strain but withstood him. The stallion turned around, his flinty hooves crashed against the walls, and he bit into the iron bars that capped the top of the wood. The stable boys kept a safe distance from the rampaging demon, unsure what they should do. They couldn't understand why the usually relaxed stallion had suddenly gone crazy.

They didn't know what Lys knew, didn't feel the pain he was enduring as his brother was hurt both physically and mentally.

The link to Casto's mind inside Lys was getting weaker, buried under an avalanche of agony. When Lys thought about what Renaldo had done to his brother so far, his rage doubled. Again he crashed against the walls, but in vain. Not even Lys's exceptional strength could free him from that prison. His shrill screams resounded through the stables and were heard all over the Valley, but they brought no consequences.

Then Lys fell silent.

Casto was gone. Lys couldn't feel his brother anymore, and given the blow to his head, Lys, Emperor of the Storms, assumed that Casto was no longer part of this world.

Lys stood stock-still, a terrible void growing inside him, a void he had never known before. Even when he had still roamed the world alone, a newly born creature of chaos in orderly space, he hadn't felt so lonely.

His brother was gone, his anchor in this world. Deep down, at the bottom of the numbing despair Lys felt, the wish for revenge stirred. At that moment it was still too weak to take form, tamed by shock and grief, but soon it would rise, cold and clear. Then the sons of the Holy Mothers would pay the price for their hubris.

The black stallion, the Emperor of the Storms, the child of chaos, didn't move. Like a statue, Lys stood in his stall, ready to rain death and destruction on the Valley.

SLOWLY, CASTO emerged from the darkness he had fallen into. He felt rough stone under his body and knew without opening his eyes that he was in the dungeons. The memory of how he'd gotten there and why he was enduring such terrible pain in his head and in his side returned in fragments. Renaldo, beside himself with rage as Casto had never seen him before. Their fight, the insults, and then… darkness. He shuddered. Never would he have thought the Barbarian would hurt him so brutally.

It was Casto's own fault for trusting him. He really should have known better.

Cool hands touched his forehead, a familiar tingling ran through his body, and the pain subsided. Casto opened his eyes. Noemi's face was serious and distant.

"I thank you, my lady."

Her expressive green eyes darkened. "I'm not doing this for you. For all I care, you could rot down here."

Surprised by the unusually violent outburst, Casto retreated. "What are you talking about, my lady?"

"You know that full well, you miserable piece of shit! He trusted you! I trusted you! How could you?"

"I haven't got the slightest clue what you're talking about."

"Ha! I don't believe you, Casto. I don't believe anything you're telling me. The only good thing is that we now know your true colors, and this time you won't be able to soften Renaldo's heart again. Tomorrow you'll go into the mines, and then we'll see how long you'll survive there."

The hatred in Noemi's voice startled Casto even more than the news of what would happen to him. Desperately, he held out his hands.

"Please, my lady. I really don't know what you're talking about. Please tell me."

"Forget it. That silver tongue of yours isn't going to save you this time. I only healed you enough so you can endure the transport. Your fate is death in the mines."

With that, Noemi got up and left the cell.

Casto stared at the closed door for a long time, unsure about what to feel. He was angry, desperate, and surprised.

Into that chaos stumbled Lys, relieved that his brother was still alive. After he had made sure Casto was more or less all right, he let his anger out. Casto submitted to the emotion without hesitation. His situation didn't allow for insecurities. If he wanted to survive, he had to focus on the basics, and unbridled anger had always been his best ally.

"I'll be taken to the mines tomorrow. It would be good if we could escape before that happens."

Lys showed his brother a picture of the stall that was his prison. Casto cursed loudly. Without the stallion, he had no chance to escape. He pondered several possibilities, but none of them was remotely viable. Finally he gave up.

"We have to take a different route. Can you call a storm that stops the transport? Or at least delays it? I'm going to try to escape on my way to the mines. If you aren't free till then, I'll get you, and then we turn our backs on this cursed place forever."

Lysistratos wasn't happy about that plan, but he couldn't come up with an alternative, and so he started calling a murderous thunderstorm.

That very night the first gusts invaded the Valley like hungry predators. They ruffled the trees until their crowns bowed to them, and everything that wasn't meticulously secured was swept away. And yet those winds were mere harbingers of the powers Lys had unleashed on the Valley to save his brother's life. On that day, the sun did not brighten the Valley for even a minute, and dark clouds mounted along the steep mountain walls to crash down on the Valley and its inhabitants like waves on a stormy sea. In his cell, Casto didn't notice much of the chaos. Only now and then did a muffled thumping reach his ears when something heavy was hurled against an obstacle. Eventually an overseer arrived and brought him some bread and water along with the bloodied and torn clothes he'd been wearing when the Barbarian had betrayed him so brutally.

The man shot Casto glares full of hatred but didn't say a word. He obviously had orders not to talk to his prisoner.

Casto couldn't care less. Along his connection with Lys, he could feel the storm's raging deep in his bones. The raw force was like a balm for his wounded soul, and it fed his anger about the unjust treatment he'd endured. Casto hadn't survived for so long to be defeated by a mere Barbarian. He would escape. He and Lys would be reunited, and then the Angel of Death would be nothing but an unpleasant memory, a reminder to never give in to temptation again. He could only rely on himself and Lys. Nobody else was worthy of his trust.

For four days and nights, the storm raged through the Valley before it started to lose its power. Even Lys couldn't ignore the laws of the Holy Mothers forever. But those four days had been enough to give Casto new hope. He was still weak, although his wounds had healed so far that they seemed to be weeks old, not days. He felt strong enough to face his future.

It was early morning when the overseer took him upstairs. A coarse man grabbed him and chained him to four other men on a heavy oxcart. Renaldo was nowhere to be seen; the whole Valley seemed to have died out.

The overseer shot Casto a poisonous glance before he turned to the coarse man. "Don't forget, this piece of trash goes into the mines. You won't sell him, no matter what you're offered. The Angel of Death has been crystal clear in this regard. Should he find out that you went behind his back, you'll wish your grandparents had never been born. You'll curse the day on which your mother conceived you, and you will—for an unpleasantly long time—beg for the privilege to die. Do you understand?"

During that speech, all color drained from the coarse man's face. "Of course. Please tell Lord Renaldo that everything will happen according to his wishes."

"He assumes that. Now go—scram! In this weather it'll take you extra time to get to the mines."

The cart started to move slowly. With an empty gaze, Casto stared through the slush at the place that had become his home for the last few years. But even that sanctuary, which had almost made him forget what it was like to grow up in hell, had now been taken from him. He would never be able to think about the hills, the dark forests, or the steep mountains without being reminded of the betrayal he'd had to endure. This haven, too, had been taken from him.

And it had been by the hand of the Barbarian.

Casto wondered what the chances were to be so cruelly betrayed twice by those he loved the most. Fate was indeed a vicious mistress who delighted in his misery.

Only his brother's presence managed to lift his spirits a bit, but he didn't know how long their connection would last when he was taken farther away. They'd already spoken about every eventuality should that happen, but Casto was horrified by the thought of being alone.

FROM THE window in his chambers, Renaldo watched with shadowed eyes as the first person he had ever truly loved was transported to the mines. When he laid eyes on the familiar figure being loaded into the cart, everything inside him tensed. He felt as if his whole body had turned to stone, a hard, cold mass unable to show the slightest emotion.

Casto had betrayed and used him. Those beautiful blue eyes, the generous, sensual mouth, the willing, well-shaped body had deceived him. He felt bile rising in his mouth when he realized that a slave, a child, had played with him.

But Casto would pay dearly. He would die a miserable, dishonorable death in the mines, executed by the will of the man he had so shamelessly deceived. Then all the world would know not to challenge the Angel of Death, the lord of the eternal fire. He was a god, destined to rule over this world. Casto was nothing more than a disobedient servant, a nobody who had attracted his master's wrath and would now pay the price for it.

Trembling, Renaldo slung one arm around his waist. With his eyes closed, he braced himself against the pain that for days had washed over him in waves. He only hoped the agony would cleanse him, taking with it the despair of Casto's betrayal and leaving him purified.

4. THE MINES

ON THE third day on the road, Casto lost his connection to Lys. It came as a shock even though he'd known it was inevitable. One moment his brother was still in his thoughts, albeit weakly, the next he was gone, leaving an emptiness that forced a pained whimper from Casto's throat.

"Shut your damn mouth!"

Elk, the man escorting the prisoners to the mines, was in a bad mood. The overseer's threat hadn't left him unfazed, especially since that guy seemed to have read Elk's mind. When Elk had seen Casto's well-shaped body, he'd started to estimate how much he could get for him on the slave market. But not even he was greedy enough to challenge the Angel of Death's wrath. Instead he made his prisoners pay for his bad temper.

Casto was too caught up in his own pain to spare Elk more than a glance. He concentrated on the task before him: his escape and reunion with Lys. It would be best if he managed to flee before they arrived at the mines, but the prospects looked rather glum. Not only was the chain around his wrist secured by a complex lock, they were also moving through mostly open terrain that made it hard to find cover. Even if he hadn't been weakened by his wounds, Casto would have thought twice about taking such a risk.

As much as he resented it, he had to let himself be transported into the mines.

IT WAS a cold, foggy morning when they finally reached their destination. The mines were situated above a pitiful little town where small huts huddled like a flock of frightened sheep under the shadow of the mighty mountains that nurtured the precious blue steel in their depths.

A gigantic wooden gate secured the entrance to the mines and opened into a compound of about four hundred paces in diameter, where the barracks for the guards, a small smithy, and a bigger, almost-grand house were situated. Between the barracks and the house, a black hole, like the ghastly jaw of some monster, ripped into the flank of the mountain—the entrance to the mines.

Whoever entered that dark world never returned.

Casto only had to look at the void to know that he had to stay on the surface at any cost. With half-closed eyes he scanned his surroundings and assessed the guards who were now approaching to receive the new slaves. Casto always felt contempt for those who used their looks as a weapon; that seemed an unfair practice, but now he had no choice. He was too weak to fight, too exhausted to run. He inhaled deeply before he looked up, ready to play a role as he had been forced to do so often in the past.

The leader of the guards was his target. With the infallible instincts he'd had to hone during his childhood, Casto knew this man was his chance. He regarded the soldier with a soulful look, which he spiced up with a hint of fear.

The guard's green eyes widened and his tongue darted nervously across his lips, a sure sign that Casto had already hooked him. Casto was ready to proceed when a tall pale man dashed out of the grand house, his clothes fluttering behind him like a flock of hysterical hens.

"Stop! Lord Golob wishes to talk to one of the prisoners personally."

Casto saw his victim's eyes harden.

"Which one?"

The tall man pointed at Casto. "That one!" A derisive smile played around his lips. "You should've known! He prefers them young and blond."

The guard turned away, but not without shooting Casto a last, regretful look. "You heard the scribbler. Untie Blondie and take him to Golob."

Slightly unsure about this turn of events, Casto followed the tall man into the house and into a splendid room that contained a huge desk, two lounges covered in silk, heavy brocade curtains, sumptuous carpets, and all kinds of useless trumpery. The whole room was so flamboyant it was easy to overlook the unimpressive man behind the desk. But Casto ignored the distastefully displayed riches and concentrated on the fat man.

He knew this kind of human all too well. Even if the man's taste concerning his surroundings hadn't already told Casto everything about his personality, it would be enough to take one look into his face, ruled by small beady eyes and thick meaty lips, to realize that the man was a tyrant who reveled in others' weakness.

Casto hurried to lower his gaze—nobody would notice his smile. Manipulating that kind of man was easy, and he'd done it before. Even though he hated debasing himself, he was willing to do it for his freedom.

The guard hit him hard between the shoulder blades. "Come on! Kneel to the Master of the Mines!"

Casto obeyed immediately. He bowed so deeply he almost touched the ground with his forehead, his hands held flat at his side.

The fat one's voice was hoarse, as if he had just recovered from some illness. "That's all. Leave us alone."

The two men made haste to leave the room, which meant that this joke of a man commanded more power than Casto initially thought. He could hear Golob leaving his chair and approaching him.

"Get up so I can have a look at you!"

Casto's jaw tensed. It took all his self-control not to punch the presumptuous cretin. Instead he got up obediently, his gaze still lowered.

Golob circled him like a horse trader would a new steed. His fat fingers wandered over Casto's muscular biceps in admiration. "Look at me!"

The young man raised his gaze, and Golob was blinded by two soulful eyes swimming in tears.

"Please, noble lord. Don't hurt me. I'll do everything you want, I promise. I'm a good slave."

With glee, Golob patted the cheek of the dainty morsel who had been swept into his arms by some friendly deity. He enjoyed it when others cowered in fear before him, when they acknowledged his power.

The youth in front of him was trembling, a fact that increased the cruelty in the Master of the Mines. "How do you know whether you're good or bad? You're a mere slave. And I'm sure there's a reason for you being here." While saying that, he took the bloodied shirt from Casto's shoulders. "You've been beaten up quite badly. You have bruises all over your body. Few do this for the sheer fun of it. Do you want to tell me what happened?"

The young man started to sob. "It was my fault. My master is— *was* a powerful barbarian leader. He was very strict, but I always tried my best to please him. He wanted—" A snivel interrupted the sentence before the blond managed to carry on. "He wanted me to serve him in bed. But I had never done that before. I was afraid, and I begged him not to hurt me. He was so angry because I wasn't doing it right…."

Now the youth sank to his knees crying, his hands extended to Golob in a pleading gesture as if he hoped to find forgiveness for his sins from him. "I wanted to be obedient, really. It was so fast. It hurt so much."

The complete defenselessness of his prisoner, combined with his beauty, touched the darkest side of Golob's character. With the instincts of a predator, he recognized the unique chance to get himself a perfect toy. Once he was done with the boy, he would belong to him completely. Such a prize made the game he intended to play all the more alluring. Gently, Golob caressed the blond locks.

"It's fine. I believe you. I do know how coarse those barbarians can be. But you're lucky. You're with me now. I promise, everything will be fine."

With eyes wet from tears, the young man looked up. "You're so generous, noble lord. I promise I won't disappoint you!"

"I don't doubt that…. What was your name again?"

"Whatever you deem fit, Master."

Golob froze, and for a moment Casto was afraid he'd overdone it, but then a strange light shone in the creep's eyes.

"If that's the case, then I'll find a suitable name for you, my beauty. You've had a long journey. I'll send for a healer to look after you. Then you'll have a good meal and get some rest."

"Master! I cannot accept that. I want to serve you!"

"You can serve me more than enough once you're rested. You have to regain your strength, because the things I'm going to ask of you require stamina."

The young man's cheeks reddened, his breath sped up.

"I don't wish to disappoint you, lord. You only have to tell me what to do, and I'll happily bow to your will."

"Oh, you will, my beautiful one, you will. I'm going to form you the way I prefer, train you to be mine. As long as you're obedient, you'll have a good life here." A cruel smile played around Golob's small lips. "And when you anger me, your life ends down in the belly of the mountains. Pretty as you are, they'll give you a warm welcome down there."

"I'll be good, lord. Definitely. I'm a good slave."

Fat, distastefully ringed hands patted Casto's cheeks patronizingly. "I know, my beautiful one, I know."

Golob called for a servant, who led Casto first to the bathroom and then to a small chamber adjacent to that of his new master. He was served a rich meal, and a healer from the nearby town came to look after his wounds, which had already healed very well but were still taking their toll.

After the healer left, Golob came by again. He was satisfied. "According to that charlatan, you'll be right as rain in no time at all. Rest tomorrow, and then we start with your training."

"You're truly generous, Master. I thank you."

"Don't mention it. I'm sure you can't wait to repay my kindness."

"I'm looking forward to it, Master."

"Me too." Golob's eyes wandered suggestively over Casto's body. "It's going to be a feast. Sleep well, my beautiful one."

Casto bowed low and stayed in that position until Golob had left the room. Only then did he allow himself to clench his fists in anger. He would have loved to kill, or at least beat up, that slimy pig right on the spot, but he had to wait. He had bought himself an entire day, and he intended to put it to good use.

He had to gather his strength, because one thing was for sure, he would never belong to such an obnoxious man as Golob. *Never.* He was solely the property of Renaldo; nobody else had the right to touch him—

Casto froze. The Barbarian too, no longer had the right to touch him. He'd given up that privilege when he had betrayed Casto.

Reluctantly, Casto shook his head. It was high time he and Lys went their own way again. While he was thinking about where he and his brother could go once this whole situation was done with, a persistent voice kept telling him that he only wanted to escape from the mines to return to Renaldo. He still didn't know what he'd done wrong, but he would do everything to atone for his sins so long as his master would take him back again.

Appalled by his thoughts, Casto hit the pillow with all his might. It couldn't be that he even wanted to look at the Barbarian after everything that had happened. The man had betrayed him, beaten him without reason at a time when Casto had started to trust him. That Casto had managed to land some good punches himself didn't matter. Renaldo simply had no right to start a fight without proper warning and a very good reason.

Casto would never return to Renaldo's side.

CASTO USED the entire next day to regenerate. He ate as much as he could, slept late, and got acquainted with his surroundings in an unobtrusive way. He was already allowed to move freely inside the house, and from his room he could see the front courtyard and the entrance to the mines. The huge gate was closed early in the evening but stayed open throughout the day. The guards concentrated on the entrance to the mines, which would make it easy to slip through the gate. Casto only had to wait for the guard to change, and then he could sneak out without attracting attention. The only risk was the small road back into the town. It was wide open, and should he be spotted there, it would take a great deal of luck to survive. As soon as he reached the town, though, he would be safe. It shouldn't pose any problem at all to steal a horse that could carry him back to the Valley.

Regarding the wolves that guarded the Valley, he still had to come up with a solution, but that was something he would bother himself with once he was out of here. He swore not to waste another thought on the Barbarian. As soon as he was reunited with Lys, they would turn their backs on the whole mess.

After a sumptuous dinner, Casto went straight to bed. He was facing some strenuous days ahead that would take all his strength. As he suspected, Golob was hot on training him. A servant escorted Casto to the Master of the Mines right after he got up the next morning. There, under the hungry gaze of Golob, he had to put on tight pants in a terrible shade of red that reminded Casto of rotting entrails. It took all of Casto's self-restraint to give his demure thanks for the gaudy crime.

With a careless gesture, the fat creep ordered Casto to serve him. Casto did so with his natural grace, knowing well that his perfect manners weren't met with unalloyed joy. When he realized how irritated Golob was, Casto did him a favor and knocked over a cup of tea. The amber-colored liquid quickly soaked into the fine linen while Casto kneeled down, whimpering. "Please forgive me, Master. I didn't do it on purpose. Please."

Golob's voice was cruel. "It seems to me you're not as good as you claimed, slave."

"I'm so sorry, Master! Please tell me, how can I conciliate you?"

That was the cue the sadist had been waiting for. His hand was heavy on Casto's head, and excitement tainted his voice. "Strip!"

Seemingly frightened, Casto obeyed. He looked right ahead at the man's paunch imploringly. "Please, Master. I'll do everything you want me to. I only want you to be satisfied."

"Then shut up and spare me your whining. This is your first lesson." The meaty hands groped Casto's upper arms greedily.

Casto allowed Golob to pull him close, then snaked his hands upward and closed them around the man's neck like claws of steel.

Golob's eyes widened, he tried to scream, but Casto had been trained by the Angel of Death. Without mercy, he squeezed the creep's larynx so that all that could escape Golob's lips was a weak whimper. Feebly the fat hands clawed into Casto's muscular arms, the voluminous body was seized by spasms. Stunned, Golob stared into the blue eyes that now returned the gaze without pretense. Golob shuddered when he realized how dangerous an opponent he had gotten involved with. The last thing he heard before darkness consumed him was the cold, steady voice of the warrior he had underestimated so badly.

"My name is Casto, and before I'm bedded by the caricature of a man like you, I'd rather die."

With difficulty, Casto dragged the unconscious body to his bed and draped him among the pillows. For a moment he'd entertained the thought of killing the creep, but in the end, he couldn't murder a helpless man. All he did was hit him over the head with a little more force than necessary to keep him unconscious. He arranged the furs around Golob as if he was asleep, which should fool any servant passing by.

Naked, Casto sneaked back into his own room, dressed in the warm, simple clothes he had received the other day, and set off.

He met nobody on his way to the small chamber where the weapons were stored. It wasn't what he'd call a satisfying assortment, but for the time being, it had to be enough. Casto put a dagger in each boot and attached two more to his belt. His shirt was just long enough to hide them.

Finally he selected a sword, which he carried as if he didn't know the tip from the hilt. Anybody who saw him had to believe he was running an errand. Since the smithy was closest to the gate, his path was covered till there. He was electrified by anticipation while he waited for the first guard change. Even though he had hit Golob pretty hard, he couldn't be sure how long the disgusting bastard would stay unconscious. Casto did not want to be around when the man finally woke up. When the time came, he started walking nonchalantly toward the exit, hoping that his calm self-confidence would scatter any doubts a curious onlooker might harbor. Having his goal right in front of his nose, Casto had to force himself to keep a slow pace.

Everything was fine. In a few minutes, he would be free again.

"Stop him! He's trying to escape!"

Never in his life had Casto hated and cursed a voice more than that of Golob, Master of the Mines. Like a raven's croak it rang out and drew everyone's attention to Casto.

Golob had obviously recovered faster than Casto had calculated. For a moment Casto chided himself for not having killed the man when he had the chance, but it was fruitless to muse about past mistakes.

Alarmed by the shout, the guards came rushing. Casto knew that escape was now impossible, but he would be damned if he would give in without fighting back. If he couldn't live, he would at least die like a warrior. With his sword raised, he waited for his opponents. The first two attackers experienced a short, deadly surprise when, with a certain carelessness, they went against the seemingly inept slave.

Considering the bloody corpses, the other guards regrouped and were a lot more careful. Casto fought concentratedly and defensively. He would have liked to be more forward, but he could feel his strength waning with every move he made. He was still weak, and the events of the morning were starting to take their toll.

His opponents, too, realized his growing weakness and tried to tire him. Casto managed to kill one more guard, but when he tried to duck away from the next blow, he lost his balance on the slippery ground and fell. The men saw their chance and seized him. With one of his daggers, he eliminated one more, and then he felt night descending upon him. The darkness lurking at the edge of his vision now assaulted him like a hungry lion. He still tried to fight back, but his strength was no longer sufficient.

Just before he lost consciousness, he thought of Renaldo. The beautiful gray eyes looked at him calmly and full of love, and Casto felt a strange peace coming over him.

The moment he was ready to give in to that peace, Lys was suddenly back.

AWARENESS

1. THE VEIL OF TEARS

Covered in sweat, Sic woke with a start. His gaze wandered through the smithy and paused at the forge where the coal was still glowing softly from the previous day. Panting heavily, he concentrated on the hazy light and tried to forget what he'd seen in his dream. But Casto's bright, azure eyes haunted him, drilled into his mind in silent accusation, and tortured him even now he was awake. It had been six days since his friend had been sent to the mines, six days during which Sic was torturing himself with self-reproach. He had saved his master, but at what price?

Sic had betrayed Casto and watched his friend chained to an oxcart taking its sad cargo to the mines—and ultimately death. The sight of Casto, still in his torn, bloody clothes, his formerly proud gaze lowered in desperation, was something Sic couldn't forget. Lord Renaldo hadn't left his chambers since then, and Damon paraded around with such a gleeful look on his face that Sic wanted to throw up whenever he saw the man.

Damon was an enemy who only caused mayhem in the Valley, but until today Sic had been too afraid to confide in anybody. Damon, who took pleasure from the misery of others, just seemed too powerful. But Sic couldn't stand any longer to be haunted by Casto's accusing gaze, and he couldn't even look Noran straight in the eye without feeling guilty.

Sic had known from the moment he took the cloak pin that his life was forfeit. That one simple act had damned him forever. Sic had betrayed his master, his friend, and above all his god. No matter the reasons, he deserved worse than death for that. All that was left for him to do was set things straight.

Determined, he got up. Morning was close; he could already see the first shades of red in the sky. Before the sun had risen over the mountains, he said his farewell to the smithy. He loved this place that had been his home, his safe haven. For the last time, he caressed the anvil his master had given him, arranged his tools, put them in their leather bag, and then went to meet Lord Renaldo in his chambers.

Sic's reluctant knock was answered by an ungracious "Come in" that made him doubt his decision. But it was too late to go back now; it was time to take responsibility for his actions. Trembling with fear, he took a deep breath and entered his god's chambers.

Lord Renaldo was sitting in a broad chair, his brown hair hung unkempt around his tired face, and his tunic looked as if he hadn't changed it for days. He held a cup of wine. What disturbed Sic the most was that despite his devastated state, Lord Renaldo was still breathtaking. His sorrow was like an exquisite cloak turning him into a tragic beauty, a creature who breathed grace and dignity even in a situation like this. Lord Renaldo was like a character from a famous ballad of desperate lovers that enthralled every listener even though it could never end happily.

With tears in his eyes, Sic knelt in front of his god, knowing that Lord Renaldo's pitiful state was his fault.

The gray eyes regarded him without any interest. "What do you want, slave?"

Sic pressed his forehead to the ground. "I'm here to tell you the truth, Master."

He heard Lord Renaldo shifting in his chair and hurried to keep on talking before he lost the last strand of courage he still possessed. "Casto hasn't betrayed you, Master. He would never do such a thing. The pin used as proof against him—I stole it from his trunk."

The chair fell down with a crash. Sic heard Lord Renaldo approaching him, and he hurried on. "A man called Damon forced me to do it. He's a slave here in the Valley, but he prays to the Good Mother. At least I think he does, because he threatened to kill my master should I not do what he wanted me to do. To convince me, he killed a slave with magic. He practices the forbidden arts."

The dark spell that had shrouded Renaldo broke at those words with a sound like a giant's sigh. Considering the damage the spell had caused over the years, an explosion would have been fitting, but like the fog it imitated so perfectly, it dissipated in the first rays of the morning sun.

The spell's all-pervasive veil simply could not hold together when hit by the blinding light of truth.

Renaldo stood frozen. The parts of the complicated puzzle that was his relationship with Casto finally fell into their right places. The veil lifted from his eyes, and the realization of what he'd ignored for the past four years made him shudder.

He loved Casto, and it was entirely possible that the young man was his heart, his chosen mate. He cringed at the thought of what he had done to his heart, what pain he had caused him. His own behavior was unforgivable. He had sent Casto to his death.

Frantically, Renaldo counted the days.

Casto had been gone for six days, and usually it took three to four days to get to the mines. In this case probably four, because of the storm that had come down on the mountains like the wrath of the Holy Mothers. So Casto had reached the mines either yesterday or the day before, depending on how fast the oxcarts had traveled.

There was still a chance to get him back alive, but Renaldo had to hurry. He looked down on the trembling slave in front of him and felt anger rising inside. "I'm going to take care of you later. Now get out!"

Renaldo hastened to get dressed. He put on his riding boots, threw on a warm cloak, and left his chambers. In the hallway he met his brother, whose amber eyes were bright with rage.

Canubis, too, was no longer deceived. "You go and get Casto. I'll take care of the traitors."

As if to confirm his words, a deep, threatening howl rang out from the Valley. The wolves were gathering, ready to catch those who had dared to challenge the masters of their world. Thinking about how the pack would bring down every person responsible for Casto's suffering, a dark smile appeared on Renaldo's face. How he would punish himself, Renaldo had yet to decide, but if anything happened to Casto, then the pain he'd feel would suffice as just retribution. He knew he would never be able to recover from that blow. And if he got him back—Renaldo was sure Casto would make him pay.

On his way to the stables, Kalad joined him.

Kalad, too, was wearing warm clothes, and his face was grim. When Renaldo looked at him inquisitively, he said, "You're gonna need help."

It didn't take more. They'd known each other for too long—Kalad had been his brother-in-arms for more than eight hundred years. Renaldo thanked the Mothers he had Kalad at his side. No matter how tiring the lively, earthy humor of the warrior was, how nerve-racking his sarcasm could be, he was a friend every man could only hope for, always willing to do anything for those he loved.

Renaldo smiled with gratitude. "Thanks. Please get Ghost and Demon. I'll go to Lys."

"He's gonna kill you."

"I hope not. And I'm sure we're going to need him."

NOW THAT Renaldo's thoughts were no longer obscured, he remembered a talk he'd had with Casto not long ago. They had been lying in front of the fire, Casto naked and warm in his arms, relaxed by their sex play. They had been silent for some time, simply enjoying being able to spend time together. Out of the blue, Renaldo had remembered a question he'd had on his mind for some time.

"What I've always wanted to ask you is how far did you get? During your escape, I mean."

Casto had frozen in his arms, and Renaldo had thought it was because the memory of that time didn't make him happy. Carefully, Casto had answered as if he might discover an aching tooth that he expected to cause him terrible pain. "What would you say if I told you Lys and I had reached the border to the Eastern Kingdoms?"

Renaldo had laughed because he'd thought Casto was joking. No horse was able to cover that much distance in only two weeks. Then he stopped pursuing the matter since it was obviously uncomfortable for Casto. Which was only logical in hindsight, because Casto hadn't wanted to lie to his master but hadn't been able to tell him the truth either. Seen like that, Casto had solved the problem deftly.

Other memories layered their talk: the race in the desert when Lys had beaten Demon and Ghost, something that hadn't happened in centuries, the battle of Ki't where the black stallion had carried his rider safely through enemy lines without suffering a single scratch, the fact that Lys's stamina seemed to be inexhaustible, his intelligence obvious.

Renaldo had always admired Casto for his close bond to the steed, amused by the discussions the young man had with Lys. Now he realized that the stallion had understood every single word. Renaldo cursed the spell that had made him blind to the obvious.

At the stables he was led to Lys's stall by a stable boy. The black stallion glared angrily, and his hooves thundered against the walls.

The boy drew back. "He does that every time somebody gets too close. He's out of his mind. He lets us feed him, but as soon as he has his fodder, he starts kicking and biting."

With a gesture, Renaldo sent the frightened boy on his way. Then he slowly approached the stall, his hands outstretched in a calming gesture. "Please, Lys. I'm sorry. I know you don't trust me, and why should you? But I need your help. I've made a mistake, a very stupid, unforgivable mistake, and if I don't hurry, Casto pays for it with his life. Please help me!"

Lysistratos's big, far too intelligent eyes bore into Renaldo's face, and his flint-hard hooves trampled the ground threateningly. Then Lys's head shot forward with the speed of a snake, and his teeth closed a handspan in front of Renaldo's face.

The message couldn't have been clearer, and Renaldo was ready to admit defeat when the stallion gave a snort.

Lys turned his side to Renaldo, a silent invitation the warrior accepted hastily.

"I thank you, Lys. And I swear by my honor, when we make it, if Casto is still alive, I'll never disappoint him again."

That time the stallion's snort was definitely derisive, and Renaldo realized that he was trying to justify his actions to an animal. A very intelligent animal, but Renaldo was a demigod, after all—a demigod in dire need of this animal's help, his dry inner voice reminded him.

He hurried to get the stallion saddled and led him outside. Kalad was already waiting for him, leading two powerful horses: Demon, Canubis's steed; and Ghost, Renaldo's own horse.

Renaldo nodded his approval. "Try keeping up with me, but don't overdo it. You know the route I'm going to take."

Kalad rolled his eyes. "I know Lys is fast, but the same goes for Ghost and Demon. We'll never be far behind."

Renaldo nodded, although he suspected that wouldn't be the case. Swiftly he got into the saddle. "It's a long way, Lys, and we don't have time. A rider usually takes two to three days to make it to the mines. I know you're fast, faster than Casto had me believe, but I only hope you're up to it."

The black stallion shook his head indignantly. Then he started to run.

Kalad managed to keep up till they reached the entrance to the Valley, but when the horses arrived at the open plains, Lys tossed his head back before stretching his neck and starting to gallop in earnest. He left the other two stallions far behind in no time at all, his hooves drumming a beat on the snow-covered ground. For a long time, it seemed as if Lys would never cease accelerating, before he finally settled at a pace no ordinary horse could ever reach. Despite Renaldo's astonishment, he tried not to disturb Lys while the landscape flew past them.

Renaldo had assumed Lys would keep his dizzying pace for one, perhaps two hours before he had to slow down to recover. But Lys galloped through the afternoon as if it was nothing but a relaxed ride. Inwardly, Renaldo bowed to the exceptional beast and admired and cursed Casto equally for hiding Lys's talents from him for so long. He was no longer surprised that Casto had managed to escape so easily from the Valley.

Not even the wolves were able to keep up with this breakneck speed.

"One thing's for sure, you're not a normal horse. Where do you really come from?" Renaldo only murmured the words, but the black stallion must have heard them. Lys bucked warningly; an angry snort rumbled in his chest. Renaldo hurried to soothe him. "I understand. It's none of my concern. Please forgive me."

Again a huffing sound.

They resumed their journey in silence.

WHEN TWILIGHT descended, Renaldo started looking for a place where they could spend the night, but Lys wouldn't have it. He stubbornly kept on galloping. Renaldo was glad that the moons were high in a clear sky so they wouldn't break a leg—or their necks. Although that seemed unlikely, given how confidently Lys moved through the night. It almost seemed as if the stallion was a part of the shadows.

In the morning, Renaldo could see in the distance the smoke from the village at the foot of the mountains.

"We're almost there, Lys," he whispered into the pinned-back ears of the exceptional steed.

As if that sentence had unearthed additional strength, Lys shuddered and picked up his pace. Less than an hour later, they left the village behind and galloped through the gate into the hell that was the mines.

RENALDO IMMEDIATELY saw that a fight was in progress at the slush-covered entrance area. Three guards lay motionless on the ground, apparently dead, and three more thrashed around whimpering in the snow. Only a few feet away, a group of four or five men was engaged in heated battle. Above the tumult, a high-pitched, enraged voice rang out.

"I want him alive, do you understand? He has to pay for what he did."

Lysistratos shot forward, teeth bared. With a well-aimed kick, he shattered the skull of the nearest guard. The momentum made the corpse fly through the air like a rag doll. Cursing, Renaldo suddenly glimpsed a mane of wheat-blond hair on the ground in the midst of the fighting men. He dismounted the demon Casto called his best friend, drew his sword, and killed the bastards who dared to attack his lover.

Only minutes later everything was over, the ground slippery with blood, the corpses grotesquely twisted in the trampled, red snow. Casto had half gotten up from his prone position; surprised but also annoyed, and his blue eyes bored into Renaldo's gaze.

Renaldo felt relief and love flooding his senses, accompanied by an irrational claim of ownership. Casto was hurt, his face was smeared with blood, and the simple tunic he wore was stiff with dirt and torn in various places, but as long as Casto was able to shoot him looks so full of scorn, he had to be mostly well.

Renaldo stepped forward, his hand outstretched to help Casto up, but Casto only turned his head in contempt.

"Just leave me alone, Barbarian!"

A huff resounded at Renaldo's back, and he was tossed aside by Lysistratos as the stallion stepped forward to help up his true rider.

With ease of practice, Casto grabbed his brother's mane and got to his feet. For a moment he closed his eyes. His breath was ragged, his face pale, and he was obviously hurt more badly than it had seemed.

Before Renaldo could take a closer look at him, a fat, stocky man stumbled into his line of sight, his porky double chin trembling in rage.

His high-pitched, nagging voice reminded Renaldo of a vulture that had failed to reach the carcass in time.

"How dare you? You've killed my men, so I demand compensation! And this little rat stays here. I'm planning on punishing him *severely*."

A dangerous light crept into Renaldo's eyes. "And you are?" he asked with raised eyebrows.

The creep straightened up to his not-very-impressive height of one ell and two spans. Next to the tall, perfectly muscled Angel of Death, he looked like a caricature.

"I am Golob, the Master of the Mines. And this one"—he stabbed his finger in Casto's direction—"has dared to oppose me. He has raised his hand against me, killed four of my men, and wounded three more. For that, he has to be punished."

Renaldo turned to the young man. "Is that true, Casto? Did you really hit the master of this place?"

Casto rolled his eyes in annoyance. It didn't escape Renaldo that he was still very pale and hadn't yet let go of Lys. But his voice was firm and as condescending as ever.

"This despicable swine wanted to bed me. I declined, and then he tried to use force. I only defended myself."

"You wanted to bed him?" Renaldo's voice was deadly calm and so intimidating that even Golob realized something was amiss. He held up his hands in defense.

"Everybody who comes here is sentenced to death. I only take my share of those to whom I want to grant a reprieve. And look at him! Even now, wounded and dirty, he's still a stunning sight."

"I am aware of that."

Renaldo kept his gaze trained on Golob until the man trembled in fear. Golob, Master of the Mines, finally started to realize who was standing in front of him.

Renaldo reached for his belt, took the purse of gold from there, and threw it carelessly to the ground in front of Golob. "This should cover your losses. It's more than enough to get new men and pay for a whore to grant you the joy Casto has denied you." Without sparing Golob another glance, Renaldo turned back to Casto. "Can you get onto Lys on your own or do I have to help you?"

Anger and defiance flitted across Casto's expression for a moment, and then Casto turned to Lys and mounted—without his usual grace. He had no desire to go with Renaldo; for that, he was still too angry. Unfortunately, he knew he had no choice. Without provisions or gold, and as weak as he was, he had little chance of survival. As much as it galled him, he had to stick with the Barbarian for the time being.

Renaldo had to suppress the instinct to reach for the reins to lead the horse. For one thing, it wasn't necessary—Lys would never allow any harm to come to Casto—and for another, Renaldo knew his amnesty was over. Lys had grudgingly tolerated him while they were on the mission to save Casto, but he had no more reason to be nice to Renaldo. He was pretty sure the stallion would bite off his arm should he get the chance.

And so the three of them left the mines. Renaldo took the lead on foot, and Lys followed with the pale Casto on his back.

They passed through the town, stopping and getting new clothes for Casto, who changed behind one of the shops but refused any help. Renaldo acquiesced with clenched teeth, and only a short time later they resumed their journey in icy silence.

That evening they reached the small inn where Kalad had stopped with Ghost and Demon.

Kalad welcomed his leader and Casto in his usual laid-back manner. "I'd have never thought you'd be so fast! Lys must have run like the wind. I didn't want to believe you, Renaldo, but that horse sure is one of a kind." He smiled at Casto. "Nice to get you back in one piece. Is everything all right?"

Casto returned the smile halfheartedly. "Depends," he murmured with a sidelong glance at Renaldo, who now turned to Kalad with a sorrowful look.

"Casto is wounded, but he refuses my help. Perhaps you can talk some sense into him."

"I see you two haven't had the chance to talk things through yet. Come on, Casto. I've already taken a room, so let me have a look at your wounds."

For a moment it seemed as if Casto wanted to refuse, but then he sighed and followed Kalad to the first floor of the inn, where the guest rooms were situated.

An hour later, Kalad entered the public room alone. Renaldo, sitting at a table with a cup of wine in front of him, looked up in alarm.

Kalad nodded reassuringly. "He's still bathing. For the third time. I got the impression that he wants to scrub off the last few days. If he continues like that, there'll be nothing left of him come tomorrow morning."

"How badly is he hurt?"

"Outwardly? Nothing serious: some deep cuts, many scratches, lots of bruises and contusions, but nothing that won't heal quickly if treated thoroughly. Since he was in a fight when you found him, his condition is not surprising. The wounds you inflicted have healed quite well as far as I can tell, but that's no surprise either since Noemi took care of them. He's tired out, weakened, and I wager he hasn't had enough food."

"And how is he doing?"

"He's in shock. He's angry and frightened, never a good combination, especially for somebody as proud as he is. You know him far better than I do, Renaldo. You should know how he's doing."

Renaldo stared intently into his wine. "I didn't even realize he was innocent. I no longer dare to pass judgment on him."

"My lord." Kalad put his hand on his leader's forearm. His voice was soft while he addressed him so formally. "You've been cunningly misled. We all have been. None of us doubted Casto's innocence for even a second."

Renaldo's gray eyes were full of pain. "I should have *known*. Should have at least allowed doubt. He's been with me for almost five years, and yet I blindly fell for the lies of a slave I didn't even know. Tell me, how can I ever forgive myself? I almost killed my heart and endangered everything we've been fighting for all these years."

For a moment, Kalad was taken aback. Renaldo rarely opened up to anybody. It had been obvious how close Renaldo and Casto were, but never would he have expected the blond to be Renaldo's heart. Kalad recovered quickly from his shock and tried to soothe Renaldo. "But it ended well. The Holy Mothers have protected us as they always do. Casto's alive and fine. He'll come back home with us, and then you can marry him. You can become one with your heart."

"I doubt he'll ever let me get close to him again. Why should he?"

"Yes, why should I?"

Casto's voice was cold and bitter at Kalad's back. Without the two warriors noticing, he had stepped up to the table.

Renaldo got up hastily. "Casto, how are you?"

Casto made a derisive sound, but before he could make a snippy retort, Kalad got up as well.

"I suggest the two of you go upstairs and talk this out. Casto, if you want, you can come and sleep in my room then, but first you're going to talk. I've no intention of being the buffer on our way back to the Valley."

"Assuming I decide to go back with you."

The words didn't bode well for Renaldo.

"Whatever. Talk about it without killing each other. That's all I'm asking." With that, Kalad retreated to his room.

Casto and Renaldo stared at each other silently for a long time. After a while, Renaldo reached for his lover's hand with a sigh.

Casto flinched as if he'd burned himself. "Don't touch me! I'll follow you."

They climbed the stairs to the small chamber Renaldo had rented for the night, entered the room, and then stared at each other again.

Renaldo broke the spell. "Are you going to murder me with your gaze for the rest of the night, or do you have something to say?"

Casto didn't try to hide his anger. "I don't know what I could tell you or what you might want to hear from me, Barbarian. I sure as hell won't thank you for rescuing me, since it was your fault I ended up in that pigsty."

"I know, Casto. You have to believe me, I'm really sorry. I should have known you'd never betray me with someone else."

"You thought I was cheating?" Casto sounded surprised. "*That's* why you tried to beat me up, knocked me unconscious, and sent me to this forsaken place?"

"Yes—I'm sorry."

"You're repeating yourself, Barbarian. And what exactly are you sorry for? That you obviously fell for a liar? That you almost killed me? That you did things to me you had no right doing? That you've been keeping me as your property against my will for almost five years? That you forced me to participate in your feast dressed up like a cheap whore? What *exactly* are you sorry for?"

Casto had talked himself into a rage; his eyes shot fire, his chest heaved, his hands trembled.

Renaldo reached out for him but then lowered his hand again. He could understand Casto's anger only too well, and if he were in Casto's place, he would never forgive himself. What Renaldo had done to Casto, his distrust and the jealousy he acted on, were so horrible it screamed for punishment, and he knew the consequences of his actions would haunt him forever. The best thing he could do was to try and make up to his lover and then let him go. But the mere thought of losing his heart made his insides constrict.

And so, for the first time, Renaldo tried to explain to Casto what he felt deep inside.

"I'm sorry that I didn't trust you. I know this is unforgivable, but if only you could understand. When I was presented with the proof of your guilt, it seemed as if night had descended on me. An invisible torturer had ripped my heart out and piled glowing embers into my empty chest. All joy was gone, as if I had been banished to a place without sun, warmth, or life. The only thing left was this terrible pain, a pain I'd never known before.

"I've been walking this world for a long time now, Casto, but I've never suffered such agony. You're the first and only one to wield such power over me. This insight made me furious. All I wanted was to make you feel the same pain, to show you how much you had wounded me. I was so overcome by agony and anger I was unable to have even one clear thought. I only knew I had to get rid of you so that I wouldn't be killed in the maelstrom.

"I sent you to the mines because I couldn't bring myself to kill you directly. And then you were gone, and I was in even worse pain than before. I was dying. And that was when I had to face the truth.

"I love you, Casto. I love you more than anything else in this world. You are my life. And no matter what you do, nothing will ever change that."

With his eyes open wide, Casto listened to the Barbarian. He had never expected to hear those words from Renaldo. He didn't think it possible that the feared Angel of Death would ever show weakness so openly, make himself so vulnerable. This frankness swept away his own justified anger and revealed the love he felt for Renaldo. Admitting to himself that he indeed loved Renaldo was the hardest thing Casto had ever done. It was so much easier to cling to his anger about the unjust treatment and to hate the Barbarian for taking him prisoner. Casto also knew that in their twisted relationship, he had always given as good as he'd gotten. Even during their last fight, he managed to land some serious blows against Renaldo before the man took him out. The betrayal still hurt and would do so for a long time to come. After all, Casto was not a person to easily forgive even small insults, let alone such a big one, but knowing that they both loved each other, he decided not to deny himself the chance. If things didn't work out, he could still use this incident as leverage to get away from the Barbarian.

For this to work, he had to reveal the truth about himself.

Casto swallowed hard. It was his last chance to trust Renaldo, his last chance for a life free of his father's shadow.

Even though Renaldo would never truly be his, Casto could still make the best out of the time he had until Renaldo's heart was found. All he had to do was jump into the void and hope the impact wouldn't shatter him.

He searched Renaldo's eyes and steeled himself for what he was about to say. "I, too, love you." Renaldo's gaze lit up with happiness, which made it almost impossible to keep on talking, but he persisted.

"It's like you said. Without you, the sun doesn't rise. Everything is eternal night. I can't imagine a life without you. And that makes it even harder to tell you the truth. All these years I've spent with you, I've lied to you. I am not who you think I am."

He hesitated for a moment, knowing his next words could mean his end. But if he didn't take the risk now, he would be lost to the darkness forever.

"My real name is Castolus. Prince Castolus of Ummana, son of Queen Isiris and rightful heir to the Twin Cities."

The light faded from Renaldo's eyes, and Casto could almost feel his spirit sinking.

"I'm sorry," he whispered, barely audible. He wanted to say more, wanted to explain why he had never talked about this, but Renaldo spoke first.

"Why didn't you tell me? You hated being my possession, and yet you kept your silence. If I'd known who you really were, I would have freed you for ransom money—at least in the beginning."

Casto laughed bitterly. "Did you forget where you found me? Do you really think a royal prince earns his living as a mercenary? I was on the run and had no intention of ever going back home."

"Why?"

Such a simple question, and yet it reawakened so much pain and suffering. Now Casto closed his eyes; he didn't want to see how Renaldo reacted to his deepest disgrace. "Because my father tried to break me, to enthrall me.

"The rule over the Twin Cities goes through my mother's line. It automatically falls on the firstborn. My mother died when I was only six years old. My sister Anesha was two at the time. As the firstborn, I was the heir, but far too young to rule. My father was—is—a power seeker who only sees his own advantage. My youth was the perfect opportunity for him to gain control in the Twin Cities. To lull my father and keep him occupied, the Council let him do as he pleased. He was appointed my guardian, and I was left in his care, although they all knew what kind of person he was, what he was planning.

"The Council removed my sister from the court and started to train her as the new queen in secret. I was the sacrifice they made to back their own interests.

"In the beginning I thought my father was so strict in order to turn me into a good, strong king. But I realized his true intentions very soon and swore that I would defy him. I bowed to him, did what he wanted, bore his sadistic punishments, and begged whenever he wanted me to.

"I behaved like the well-trained puppy he wanted, and at the same time, I tried to learn everything that could be useful to me one day.

"When I turned fifteen, I made the mistake of openly defying him. I really thought I was strong enough by then, but I was wrong, horribly wrong. My own father had my arm broken as a punishment. I had to kneel in front of his desk for an entire day and beg him for forgiveness before he called for a healer.

"A year later I escaped, and after another year, you took me prisoner. I was only seventeen then, and yet it felt as if I'd already suffered through a lifetime."

Casto fell silent, exhausted by his confession and strangely void of emotion after the past tiring days, during which he'd gone through so many different emotions, that he thought the strain would turn him insane. He waited for a reaction from Renaldo, and when none came, Casto finally looked up.

Renaldo was watching him was an impenetrable gaze. "Why did you never tell me?" His voice was oddly gentle. "I understand you couldn't trust me in the beginning, but at least after your escape, I'd have expected you to confide in me."

There was disappointment in Renaldo's voice, a disappointment that tore at Casto's heart and annoyed him at the same time. He didn't try to keep the sharp undertone out of his voice. "Are you serious? I had just found out that I couldn't leave you. I was panicking that you would cast me out. You had shown me clearly what you think about lies and even though I knew I was bound to you, I had no reason to trust you with such important information. I simply couldn't risk it."

Renaldo exhaled slowly. And then he surprised Casto. "Oh, Casto. I'm so very sorry. I should have taken better care of you. But I couldn't admit to myself how much I love you, and because of my neglect, I wasn't there for you. It's all my fault. Can you forgive me?"

With those words, Renaldo approached Casto, his hands stretched out, almost pleadingly.

Casto still hesitated. So much had happened between them, not only during the past days, that he wasn't sure what he really wanted. A part of him longed to be back in Renaldo's arms, to ignore the pain the Barbarian had caused him and return home to the Valley. Another part wanted to make Renaldo pay, determined to never forgive him. And a tiny little voice at the back of his head told him he could have both and even gain some kind of leverage if he played this right.

Eager to end this situation, Casto took Renaldo's hands. "If you can forgive me?" Insecure, he looked into Renaldo's gray eyes that were now so close.

Renaldo smiled brightly. "Of course I forgive you. I'm just glad we finally talked. I've been waiting for this. Or is there something else you didn't tell me—apart from the fact that Lys isn't a creature of this world?"

Renaldo was teasing him, but Casto reacted in a unaccustomedly shy manner. This was a thorny question for many reasons. He didn't avert his gaze but couldn't stop a flaming red from invading his cheeks. "No, I don't have any more secrets. Now you know everything about me. Concerning Lys—he's my brother, and I was trying to protect him. I couldn't imagine you would stick to your word if you knew his true power."

Gently, Renaldo stroked his prince's cheek. "I admire how you managed to protect him for so long, and I respect that you're so loyal to your brother. But in the future, I expect you to trust my word, like I will trust yours."

"Whatever my lord wishes," Casto murmured with half-closed eyes.

Renaldo perked up. "Really everything? Then I'd like to kiss you now."

Casto didn't bother with an answer but raised his face so that his lover could kiss him more easily. When Renaldo's lips touched his, when his tongue entered Casto's mouth carefully, then more dominantly, claiming him again, Casto felt the hardships of the past days fall off him like dry mud. Groaning, he snuggled closer to the man who had stolen his heart.

He searched for and found the belt around Renaldo's hips.

Renaldo retreated. "No, Casto. We can't."

Confused, Casto looked up. His voice trembled. "You don't want me?"

"Don't want you? Damn, Casto, you have eyes, don't you? Of course I want you. But you've been through a lot. You're wounded. I'm pretty sure the injuries I inflicted aren't healed well enough to take you without causing you pain. Your ribs must be killing you. No, we're going to wait till we get back to the Valley. There Noemi can heal you fully, and I can deal with you without a guilty conscience." Casto opened his mouth, but Renaldo put a finger over his lips. "Shh. If I remember correctly, you were the one who accused me of treating you as a sex object. I'm determined not to repeat the blunder."

Casto raised an eyebrow. "So, you do admit I was right?"

"Not entirely, but in part. We do tend to solve our problems with sex, but I don't think that's because we don't have other options. It's just that we've gotten used to it." A teasing smile crossed his lips. "And to be frank, it's much better than talking."

Casto's eyes became hungry again. "Then what are you waiting for?"

The teasing tone didn't fail to challenge Renaldo, but he kept his urges in check. His fingers trailed gently over Casto's cheeks; he spoke softly. "Because I want to show you how serious I am about you, how much I love you. You're not just a sex object for me, you're my lover, and I won't subject you to my unrestrained urges when you're not up to it." He grinned broadly. "But I do wish to hold you as tight as possible. I've been without your warmth and scent for too long."

Casto sighed. "Then hold me. I've been missing you as well."

Renaldo snaked his arms around him, lifted him up, and carried him to the bed.

With a content purr, Casto closed his eyes and let himself be engulfed by the warmth of the Angel of Death.

Finally, he was home again.

THE NEXT morning, Casto woke with the wonderful feeling of being utterly safe. The Barbarian had his arms still slung around him and pulled him close to his broad chest. Casto closed his eyes and inhaled deeply the familiar scent of Renaldo. When Casto moved, the grip of the strong arms tightened, keeping him in the embrace and making escape impossible.

Casto winced when his wounds, both old and fresh, reminded him of what he'd had to endure the past few days, but given how things had turned out, it didn't matter. All that mattered was the knowledge that he still had a home, that he was still loved, even though the love might be fleeting.

Now that he had finally admitted to himself how dependent on Renaldo he was, everything seemed easier. He would enjoy his life at Renaldo's side as long as possible, and when he grew too old to please his lover, or when Renaldo found his heart, then he would die, because without him Casto was nothing but an empty shell without reason or aim. This didn't mean he wouldn't seek any advantage he could get over the Barbarian. Being submissive was not a part of Casto's character, and he knew for a fact this was one of the reasons Renaldo was so drawn to him. They both craved the fight as much as the passion. Often, it was indistinguishable.

Of course it would take some time until he finally got used to nominally being Renaldo's possession. It went against everything he was, but he was determined to accept this fact as soon as possible.

Renaldo was moving behind him, snuggling even closer. He opened his eyes and blew warm breath onto Casto's nape.

"Good morning, my own. Why are you already awake? You must be tired."

Casto smiled lazily when he heard those loving words. Being pampered by Renaldo made him feel treasured.

"A good morning to you as well, Barbarian. I'm awake because a lot has happened to me and I'm still busy processing it. Don't worry, I'm well rested."

"And what have you processed so far?"

Casto snickered. "A lot. But nothing you should be worried about. I still haven't come to any conclusions."

"Tell me when you're done thinking. I'd like to know the outcome." He buried his nose in Casto's neck and inhaled deeply. "Until then, I'm fine with how things are right at the moment."

2. HOMECOMING

"Finally, you're here. I was afraid you'd kill each other." Kalad was in as good a mood as always when he greeted them the next morning. "I ordered breakfast for you. But you better hurry because I want to go home quickly."

Without reacting to the teasing, Renaldo grinned contentedly and pulled Casto next to him on the bench. "As you wish, Kalad." He bowed mockingly to the desert warrior. "And no, we didn't try to kill each other. We made up."

Casto felt crimson creep into his face when Kalad watched him closely, and he berated himself for being so stupid. As if Renaldo had really taken him yesterday! But yesterday had been the first time he and Renaldo had interacted without the secrets Casto had hidden for so long between them. In that regard, it was different from their previous, sexually loaded encounters.

Kalad winked at him. "I understand that kind of making up. And here I thought you were too badly hurt."

"Leave him alone, Kalad. Everything's fine. We didn't do anything intimate!"

"Ha! As if I'd believe such an obvious lie. Just looking at you two is enough to get my own blood boiling."

Renaldo rolled his eyes heavenward. "No, we really just made up. Get your mind out of the gutter. My guess is you're missing your thief, and that's why you're projecting lewd ideas on us."

"And why do I miss my thief? You can babble all you want. I've known you for far too long to be fooled by you, O mighty Angel of Death."

Renaldo considered answering again but settled for just shrugging instead. Once Kalad had made up his mind about something, it was difficult to convince him otherwise, and Renaldo had no problem when the man's misconception was flattering to his sexual prowess. Casto was still too exhausted from his ordeals to pay much attention to Kalad anyway.

While Kalad kept raining amused banter on them, they enjoyed a simple but sating meal consisting of thick oatmeal enriched with dried fruit. It was food for the poor, but after everything he'd gone through, Casto thought it the most delicious he'd ever tasted.

The journey back to the Valley cost them two more days, because although Casto tried to hide his weakness from the two warriors, Renaldo—who'd acted like a mother hen ever since they made up—saw through him immediately.

After the first unhurried gallop, Renaldo challenged Casto. "You look as if you're about to fall off Lys, Casto. Why didn't you tell me this is too strenuous for you?"

"I can do this. I don't want to delay you."

"You stubborn idiot. How much do you think we'll be delayed when you fall off Lys because you've lost consciousness and we have to carry you all the way back? We'll slow down. It doesn't matter if we arrive back home tomorrow or the day after."

And so they slowed their pace despite the good-humored nagging from Kalad, thankful that the time of the heavy winter storms was coming to an end and they could ride in normal weather.

"CASTO, I'M so glad you're back home." Noemi sounded shy, not sure how Casto would react to her after their last encounter. Casto did stiffen when he looked at her, and she knew it would take time before their relationship would be back to normal. "I'm really sorry, Casto. The things I said—my only excuse is that I couldn't bear Renaldo's hurt. Please forgive me. I promise I won't disappoint you again."

Casto stared at the witch for a long time. It still hurt him how easily she had taken the Barbarian's side without giving him so much as a chance to explain himself. He also knew she was genuinely sorry and that if he played his cards right, he could use that to his advantage one day, just like with Renaldo. So he plastered a smile on his face and opened his arms. "It's fine, Noemi. I do forgive you."

With an expression of pure relief, Noemi slung her arms around Casto's neck, pressed a sisterly kiss onto his lips, and took his face in both hands.

Casto had to bow down in order for the small witch to do so, but he didn't complain because a by-now-familiar tingling down his spine told him that she was busy erasing the traces of the last few days from his body.

She furrowed her brows for a moment when she realized that Casto had new wounds added to the ones she'd already treated, but before she could voice her distress, Casto shook his head gently.

"It's fine, Noemi, believe me. It was hard, but it's fine now. I'm back home, and that's all I needed."

Tears streamed down her face as she listened. "You poor thing! I'm so sorry. I, too, believed you were guilty. I thought it strange, but I didn't doubt the evidence. I'm so sorry about the way I treated you. You do deserve better friends."

Casto took her petite hands in his own and smiled reassuringly. He was so relieved everything had turned out well that he found it easy to be generous. He would never forget. It was his nature to stay wary of others, and after everything that had happened, he would be even more careful in the future. But at that moment, Casto wanted peace to recover and gather new strength.

"In all honesty, my behavior did leave some openings for doubt."

Before she could answer, Canubis appeared next to her. His amber eyes were as hard to read as always, but Casto thought he could see a hint of relief in them.

"I, too, am glad my brother found you in time. I apologize formally that this hardship happened to you in my Valley. I'm in your debt, Casto."

Only with the iron discipline born from years of living in court could Casto stop his jaw from falling. The powerful Wolf of War was apologizing to him! He had trouble believing it, but he knew how to react adequately to this concession of fallibility and, at the same time, how to deepen the debt Canubis felt toward him.

He bowed low and then looked at the demigod openly while talking in measured tones and picking his words very carefully. "Your apology honors you, Lord Canubis, but I'm merely a servant of my master, and every obligation you have toward me is really toward him."

At that, Canubis's jaw was slack. Could this demurely speaking young man, who had just offered him a politically elegant get-out from an unpleasant situation, be the same man who had, not two weeks ago, driven his brother to madness with his obstinacy? He watched Casto closely but wasn't able to find any deceitfulness in his face.

While Canubis was still musing about Casto's sudden change in attitude, Renaldo stepped toward his lover, smiled at him happily, and slung an arm around his hips. "Well said, my own. I guess it'll take my brother some time to recover from his shock. As long as he's busy, we'll get you to bed. No back talk! I know you're exhausted."

And wonder of wonders, the stubborn, arrogant young man acquiesced to his will without a fight. As Canubis watched the two of them retreat, he heard Kalad whispering to Aegid.

"They've been doing this the whole time. It's truly mortifying. I wonder how long it's going to take till Casto reverts back to his old form. In any case, that would be more interesting." Then he noticed Canubis's reprimanding gaze and shrugged. "What? Don't tell me you don't think it's weird."

Against his will, Canubis had to smile. "I do. Nobody is as surprised as I am, believe me. But I wouldn't begrudge my brother some domestic peace."

"We all wouldn't. Still, it's more fun when Casto is his true self."

AN HOUR later, Canubis entered Renaldo's chambers. He found Renaldo in the doorway to the sleeping chamber, lost in contemplation of his sleeping lover. Canubis stepped next to him and watched Casto as well.

Sleep had relaxed Casto's features, and he looked even younger than he was.

Young and vulnerable and beautiful. If Canubis hadn't loved his wife with all his heart, he would have surely fought his brother for the exceptional young man. Even with that difficult character, Casto was still the most desirable male human Canubis had met during his long life. His wheat-blond hair was like a crown around his head, and his lightly tanned skin glowed in the light of the single candle as if the sun shone from within him. His elegant long muscles were relaxed but still hinted at strength and grace.

Canubis had grown up with the most beautiful man in the world, so he was used to perfection, but he'd never expected to meet a human equivalent of Renaldo's eternal beauty. It wasn't just Casto's youth or his noble face, but an inner strength that drew the attention to his obvious blessings. In that regard Casto wasn't unlike Renaldo, although the inner power of his brother was destructive, a flame that seared so hot it burned everybody who got too close.

Everybody except Casto. He, too, had been almost consumed by the flame, but it had hardened him, steeled him for living with a man who always seemed close to exploding from within.

Now the young man sighed in his sleep, turned aside, and pulled the blanket over his head in an unconscious gesture, as if he wanted to banish the two men who were staring at him so blatantly, from within his dreams.

Renaldo closed the door carefully and led his brother to the main room.

In silence Canubis watched him fill two cups with wine, offer him one, and sit down on one of the lounges, closing his eyes.

"When I think that I almost lost him, I feel panic to ever leave him out of my sight again."

"I understand you better than you might think. The idea alone that something could happen to Noemi makes my heart stop."

"No harm can come to her. She's your heart, your wife. Our mothers themselves are protecting her."

"I know. Still, the thought is disturbing. Do you think Casto is really your heart?"

Renaldo swished the wine around in his cup. It was a question he had been pondering ever since the shrouding spell had dissipated. "If not, I don't want to know how I'll love when I find my heart. For me, there's only him. The thought of replacing him is—well, unthinkable."

"Why do you think the Holy Mothers haven't confirmed him yet?"

Renaldo shrugged. It was bothering him deeply, and reassurance was slim.

"You know there could be dozens of reasons. Perhaps it's the spell's fault because it prevented me from realizing who he really is. Noemi, too, was only confirmed after she became your wife. And Casto had been keeping a secret from me. Perhaps they wanted it to be out first."

"A secret?"

Canubis's voice had an undertone of alarm. At that moment he was solely the worried leader who feared a possible threat to his people.

Renaldo nodded at him reassuringly. "Nothing serious. At least not in my opinion. Casto is a prince, heir to the throne of the Twin Cities. He withheld it because he had escaped from there."

"A prince, you say? So many things make sense all of a sudden."

Renaldo had to smile. He thought exactly the same thing. Casto's arrogance that was like an invisible cloak around him, his training, the superiority he radiated in everything he did, his talent to make even the Emeris feel like they were inferior to him, his polished manners that had won over Noemi and Hulda so easily—all of it was completely logical when one knew he was of royal ancestry.

"Why has he never said anything? For a suitable ransom, he could have been free."

"He didn't want to go back there. So far, I've only heard the short version of his story, but it's already so ugly that I'd love to leave for Ummana this very minute to make those who made him suffer pay. And pay dearly."

Canubis furrowed his brow. "You're very worried for Casto. But don't forget, if he hadn't been forced to run away, you'd have never met him."

"I know. Still, the thought that the crimes against him shall go unpunished is hard to bear."

Suddenly Canubis grinned maliciously.

"If it's sins you want to punish, I know a way for you. I haven't taken the chance to confront the traitors directly yet. Why don't we pay a little visit to the dungeons?"

Renaldo narrowed his eyes. "I don't like the idea of leaving Casto alone. Although I have to admit your offer is tempting."

"I thought so. That's why I asked Hulda to come here. She's going to look after your precious prince."

As if on cue, there was a knock on the door. Hulda entered with a wicked smile on her lips. "Don't worry, Renaldo. I'm going to take good care of him."

"Careful, Hulda! He's mine alone!"

Hulda started to laugh. "I know, I know. I'm just teasing you."

Canubis grabbed his arm and dragged him outside.

"The news about the happy outcome of your mission hasn't reached the dungeons yet, I've seen to that. Do you think it possible to banish that goofy smile from your face for the time being and act as if you'd lost Casto for real? I believe that would be the easiest way to get our information."

Renaldo pulled a disappointed face. "What's become of the noble tradition of brutal torture?"

"I know. The good old times. We could indulge ourselves, but I thought you wanted to get back to your lover as fast as possible?"

Renaldo raised his hands in defeat. "As always your arguments are convincing in their wisdom."

A truly wolfish grin was the answer. "I know, brother. If it makes you feel any better, I do plan to torture the dirty scum thoroughly, but that's always better when you already have your answers. Then it doesn't present a problem when, for instance, a tongue is lost."

"Wise words from a dangerous man. Sometimes I'm really glad you're my big brother, Canubis."

Canubis placed his hand for a brief moment on Renaldo's shoulder. "And I count myself lucky to call you brother. This world is ours, Renaldo. It's time to remind everybody of that."

The door to the dungeons swung open, leading into a world that was a bleak counter to life in the Valley. All the laws that protected even the lowest members of the Pack were nonexistent down here. In the twilight of the dungeons, the law of the jungle reigned. Life was divided into those who could use their powers as they pleased and those who had to bow to it, whether they were willing or not. A reality from the beginning of time, buried in the soul of every human being but only truly alive in the memory of the divine brothers. It was a state of affairs they had emerged from and to which, should fate favor them, they would return. A world bowing to their will alone.

The leader of the traitors, Damon, had his own cell where he was chained against the wall with his arms spread wide. He was naked; his body was covered in angry welts from a brutal whipping. Despite those marks, he showed no traces of further torture. On the orders of the Wolf of War, the wardens had grudgingly held back.

When the two brothers stepped in front of Damon, he looked up at them with a smoldering look. Greedily he took in the sorrow in Renaldo's expression before starting to laugh mockingly. "Let me guess, barbarian. You were too late."

The pain showing on the obnoxiously perfect features was enough for Damon. "So the triumph is mine although I'm here in chains. Your heart is dead, barbarian, and though I hoped to kill you at the same time, I can be content with my work. My mistress is going to reward me richly."

"How can that be?" Canubis's voice was as soft as silk. "Ana-Isara is the Empress of the Dead, not that bloodless image of a woman you worship."

Again Damon laughed in mockery. "Now that your brother has lost his heart, it's only a question of time until my mistress seizes power in this world. You know that as well as I do, barbarian."

Canubis looked indecisive for a moment. When he resumed talking, his voice was threatening. "Since you're so sure of having defeated us, tell us how you did it. How did you know that Casto was my brother's heart? What kind of dark magic did you use to get that information?"

Damon regarded them for a long moment, unsure what to do, but then he decided it would benefit him to answer their questions. It would give him the opportunity to feast on the pain surrounding the Angel of Death like an impenetrable wall. Nobody had to tell him that his own life was forfeit. But before he met his surely unpleasant end, from which his mistress would redeem him, he might as well delight in the demigods' pain.

"I didn't know. No magic is strong enough to break through the protection surrounding a heart. We weren't able to do it with the witch either. But we knew when the heart was born, and our seers were able to tell when it would find the way into the Valley. I infiltrated you a few years before, so as to not raise suspicion and to cast the shrouding spell. When the time came, I was on the lookout.

"First we thought it would be a woman as it was written in the prophecies, and we assessed all possible candidates. While doing that, I ignored Casto completely. I couldn't imagine that he could be of any significance. Only when he escaped and returned on his own, and was neither killed nor crippled, nor even seriously punished by you, did I start to pay him more attention. I soon realized that he was at least important enough to you to be used against you."

Renaldo's gaze was so shocked, it made Damon snicker maliciously. "Except for you, everyone in the Valley knew that you were in love with the little scumbag. So I had some leverage against you. I started to isolate him, a task that wasn't too hard since you played into my hands so nicely. Even before his escape, the little bastard had no friends among the slaves, but afterward it was easy to stir their hatred.

"He was all alone, so lonely and forsaken—so grateful for every scrap of friendliness. And you never noticed, did you, barbarian?"

Now Renaldo's eyes flashed in anger. "You damn bastard. I'm going to—"

"You're going to do what? Torture me to death brutally? Find something new. That threat is already old.

"In any case, I started being friendly to him now and then. Nothing pushy, just enough so he wouldn't feel threatened. Then I saw to it that he missed one of your training sessions. Both your temperaments escalated the situation, as I had hoped. But I would have never guessed that the arrogant thickhead would apologize to you—or that you would forgive him.

"At that moment I realized he was more than just leverage. I started to see he could be your heart."

"But you weren't certain." Canubis voice was as velvety as flowing honey.

The priest shook his head. "No, I wasn't certain. But I had a strong suspicion. I trusted my instincts and started to inquire. Did you know Casto was the first slave in the history of the Valley to successfully flee? And that he was the only one to survive an attempted escape? You two never let a slave get away with it. The others all died miserably.

"The other thing puzzling me was the fact that he came back on his own. The arrogant little pup gave up his precious freedom and risked his death only to be able to return to the Valley. That was so totally out of character, it enhanced my suspicion. At that point, my doubts were already so great I was willing to question even the prophecies."

"Impossible. You can say whatever you want about the seers of the Ancients, but they never lied or made a wrong prediction. Never."

Renaldo felt his heart sink when he heard his brother's words. Perhaps Casto wasn't his heart after all, although he couldn't imagine ever loving somebody else like he did Casto.

Damon coughed drily before he kept on talking with a hoarse voice. "My thoughts exactly, barbarian. Which was why I took a closer look at the original. Since the first writing, the prophecies of the seers have been translated at least a dozen times. Language is a petulant lover, she can undergo dramatic changes in the course of time, and she influences our thinking to the point where we no longer realize how we think. In the times of the Ancients, for example, there was no distinction between the sexes. There was only one article, *ana*, to describe a person or thing. We always thought the hearts had to be female because that's how the translators wanted it to be. They never spared a thought about the fact that *ana blod brester stratatos* means 'kindred of the wind' and therefore can also stand for 'brother of the wind.'"

"The brother of the wind." Canubis's voice was full of awe. "Of course. The Ancients really were careless in that regard. And we didn't realize because we don't make the distinction either, but everybody else in the Valley does. How stupid of us!"

"I can only attest to that. It really was exceptionally stupid that you never thought about it. On the other hand, it doesn't surprise me at all." He shot a look full of hatred toward Renaldo. "You were so used to getting everything you wanted just because you're beautiful, it had to be a shock meeting the bastard. If he hadn't been as arrogant and righteous as you, I might have even liked him. Simply for the fact that he had thrown you off-balance."

Canubis's voice was soft as he spoke to Damon as if to prevent a frightened animal from running away. "But Casto kept his distance, didn't he? Although you were friendly, as you claim, he kept away from you."

Damon spat out, "He thought he was something better, too good to socialize with the likes of me. But I made him pay for his arrogance. He's dead now, killed by the will of the man he so reluctantly loved. And you say the Good Mother knows no justice!"

"Yes, you really showed him. With a very cunning scheme. How did you manage to get it going so smoothly?"

Canubis sounded almost sly. He wanted to know at any price how the priest had managed to produce such beguiling proof and stay in the background at the same time. Silence descended on the cell for some time, and the brothers started to fear that Damon had stopped talking altogether, but then he raised his voice anew, no longer with contempt and glee but with naked hatred dripping from every syllable.

"I wanted the idiot to pay for his pride. I wanted him to experience what it means to go against me. I wanted to take away from him everything he was so proud of with the very nice side effect that you would be eliminated as well, barbarian. Since you were away all summer long, I had enough time to come up with different scenarios to get rid of him.

"I wanted him to die by your hand. For that, I had to make you jealous. Jealous enough so you wouldn't be able to think clearly anymore. Luckily, Assani is a loyal servant to the Good Mother. It wasn't difficult to win her over. But to be successful I needed watertight proof—which forced me to rely on Sic, the stupid oaf. He was the only one who kept being friendly toward the arrogant bastard, and he even defended him in front of the other slaves. It wasn't easy to keep him at a distance to the blond idiot, but fortunately your master smith is an unforgiving master. All it took were some muttered comments, and dear little Sic had things to worry about other than the well-being of Casto."

As he remembered the trouble he had gotten the young smith into, Damon started to smile. "The little doggie didn't even try to defend himself, although he knew the accusations were pure invention. He simply accepted the punishment his precious master encumbered him with."

"Why did he help you in the end?" Renaldo's voice was tense. He wasn't happy about what he was hearing.

Damon regarded him with a pitying look. "Because I used his greatest fear against him. I threatened to kill Noran if he failed to do what I wanted."

Canubis's eyes were narrow, thoughtful. "Why would he believe you? He knows Noran is Emeris."

"In the beginning he didn't believe me. But after I killed a slave with magic, he surrendered. From that moment on, I had him under my thumb."

"It was a great risk to use magic in the Valley."

"I'd have preferred not to. But I needed Sic's help, and he would have never come to my side willingly.

"But after my little demonstration, I could force him to steal the jewelry I needed to break Blondie's neck. The rest was easy: you reacted exactly like I planned, barbarian, and the shrouding spell took care of everything else. Although I have to admit that I was a little disappointed when you didn't kill him with your own hands. But death in the mines was surely worse than anything you could have done to him. I bet he died with a curse on his lips."

"Damon, Damon, Damon." Canubis shook his head as if he were talking to a misbehaving child. "So clever, so shrewd, and yet in the end you were discovered. Could it be your goddess is not backing you up in the way you've been hoping?"

"The Good Mother only rewards the strong—she doesn't tolerate weakness. And here in the Valley, her power is limited. Who'd have thought that the idiot Sic would gather the courage and go to Renaldo himself? I'd have bet my life that he didn't have the guts to turn himself in."

Now Renaldo was smiling brightly. "He had the guts. And I'm sure you'll be delighted to hear that Casto is doing just fine. At the moment he's sleeping warm and safe in my bed, recovering from the strain of the past days."

It took a moment until the priest understood him. Then his eyes bulged so much, it seemed as if they would fall out. "He's alive? How can that be? You tricked me!" With every short sentence, his voice got more hysterical until it turned into a squeal.

Canubis patted Damon's arm. "The followers of the Good Mother aren't the only ones versed in the fabrication of schemes. My brother and I have been walking this world long enough to be able to participate in the game."

"No, it's impossible. He's dead. He must be dead!"

Renaldo grinned maliciously. "I'm sorry, dear enemy. Casto is alive, and your goddess is not going to be happy with you. But I promise, in the days to come, you won't have time to waste even one thought on the false goddess. You'll be occupied with dying. And believe me, I won't make it easy for you, not in the least."

With that parting shot, Renaldo and Canubis left their defeated enemy. Two absolute leaders who'd left the twilight of their reign to step back into the light.

"What are you going to do now?" Canubis shot his brother a sidelong glance. Renaldo turned his gaze toward him, his face an impenetrable mask as always. But Canubis didn't have to rely on outward appearances to understand his little brother. He could feel the turmoil inside Renaldo as if it were his own.

"I'm going to talk to Casto. He's always been quite skeptical about our ancestry, but it's time for him to face the truth."

"Does he even know about the prophecy?"

"If so, then not from me. I told him who we are, but he was so dismissive that I avoided the topic from then on."

Canubis smiled crookedly. "Well, it does sound strange. By the way, we're two demigods who were waiting here in the Valley to be reunited with our hearts. After this has happened, we'll be subjugating the world. I'd declare anybody who tried telling me such a tale a lunatic."

"You're not the only one. We'll see how he reacts."

Canubis looked pensive. "The only thing about this entire affair that I still don't understand is the name used for your heart. *Ana blod brester stratatos.* Kindred of the wind. What does Casto have to do with the wind? Do you know if he has any siblings?"

When Renaldo heard his brother reciting the passage from the prophecy, he suddenly felt as if a light had been lit inside him. "Of course! That's it! *Ana blod brester stratatos. Stratos*! Lysistratos. Casto once told me the name of the stallion means 'Emperor of the Storms.' And you can believe me, he surely is. You should have been there when he carried me to the mines. Despite that, he and Casto are like brothers. That must be it."

His brother still seemed skeptical but agreed with Renaldo. "Could it really be so simple? But Noemi, too, was *ana dragda slan,* the daughter of the snake. And we'd been racking our brains what it could mean for so long because we thought the snakes had left Ana-Darasa."

"In any case, it all fits neatly. In some sense he's the brother of the wind and you know about my feelings for him. I've never felt like this before, never. I only know this kind of intensity from you and Noemi. It would be truly strange if I harbored such feelings for anybody else but my heart." Canubis smiled at his brother with fondness. Renaldo furrowed his brow. "What?"

"Oh, nothing. You're just reminding me of myself when I admitted for the first time that Noemi was more than just a passing infatuation. A wonderful feeling, isn't it?"

"Wonderful indeed. But also frightening. What am I going to do if he doesn't believe me? Or even rejects me because he thinks I'm completely insane?"

"He won't reject you, no way. Remember, he called himself your slave today, which can only mean that he has accepted his fate."

"That, or he was so weakened from the journey he didn't know what he was doing."

Renaldo was pessimistic. He knew Casto well enough to consider that a valid option.

LATER THAT evening, Renaldo lay down next to his sleeping lover, hugged him tightly, and basked in the knowledge that Casto was doing fine, safe and secure under his care.

Even in his deepest sleep, Casto reacted to him. With a sigh, he snuggled closer to Renaldo's chest. Casto's soft blond hair was like a caress on Renaldo's naked skin. For a moment, Renaldo contemplated waking Casto to take him, but he restrained himself.

Casto had gone through a lot. He deserved a full night's undisturbed sleep.

3. TRUTH

THE NEXT morning, Casto felt refreshed and full of energy as he hadn't in a long time. One night of peaceful sleep in Renaldo's arms had done wonders, although he knew that their relationship was still leagues from reaching calm waters. But right then he couldn't care less.

He was sitting on the bed with Renaldo, enjoying a sumptuous breakfast of sweetened oatmeal, honey cake, bread, and fruit, when he realized Renaldo was staring intently at him. "What's the matter, Barbarian? You look troubled."

Renaldo sighed. Having Casto already using that name again didn't make things easier. If anything, it was a bad omen for their upcoming discussion. "I have to talk to you, Casto. It's a difficult topic."

Casto stopped eating. Hearing Renaldo's tone, he suspected nothing good and prepared for the worst. Not to show any weakness, he reacted with his usual arrogance. "Practically every topic is when you're a barbarian. But don't fret. I'm well educated—I'm going to understand."

Instead of reacting to this half-serious challenge and lightening the mood, Renaldo decided to grab the bull by the horns. He didn't think Casto's reaction would be any better should he hesitate longer. "What do you know about the prophecies of the Ancients?" He watched Casto closely, anticipating an angry, stubborn answer, and prepared for an outburst of rage and a heated battle. What he didn't expect was Casto suddenly turning as pale as a sheet of linen and trembling so badly that he knocked over the tea mug he'd been about to pick up. The hot beverage trickled over the small bench on which the mug had been placed, but before it could stain the furs, Renaldo put it away quickly.

Anxiously he turned to Casto, whose unforeseeable reaction reminded him once again of how little he knew about the person who'd been at his side for the past five years. "My own! What's the matter? Are you hurt?"

Casto shook his head silently. He looked as if he had just been dealt a serious blow. "No, Barbarian. Or yes—but this is pain not even Noemi can heal. You've found her, haven't you? *Ana blod brester stratatos?* Your heart."

Renaldo stared at Casto in stunned silence. He'd expected a lot but never those words from him. "You know the prophecy?"

"Bantu gave it to me. After my escape from the Valley—after I realized that I'm unable to run from you—I went to Lord Bantu. He told me everything and gave me the prophecies. That's when I found out that—that there wasn't any hope for me."

"And yet you stayed with me."

Casto's chin went up in defiance. "I didn't have a choice. You called me, I'm bound to you. It took me a while, but I finally accepted that you would never feel for me like I do for you and that I would lose you one day. It's just, I didn't expect it to happen so soon. I somehow hoped you would find your heart when I'm already old and gray—or dead, for that matter."

With his finger, Renaldo stopped the tears flowing down Casto's cheeks. He could imagine how that insight must have hurt the proud young man. It was astounding that Casto had still decided to stay at his side. The bond between god and heart had to be even stronger than Renaldo had imagined. "My own! You've carried this burden all that time? I'm so sorry. Come here."

And he pulled Casto closer, caressed his back soothingly, and whispered breathlessly into his ear:

"I love you, Casto. More than anything else in the world. I love you like I can only love one person, and that is my heart."

Casto sat up abruptly. Anger and hope fought for dominion in him. "Please, don't play with me. I couldn't bear it."

Casto's voice was as desperate as Renaldo had ever heard it. His stomach twisted when he thought about the weight his heart had had to bear alone. "I would never play with you!" After a moment's thought, he added in a slightly mischievous tone, "At least not like that. But it's the truth. Yesterday my brother and I questioned the man who was responsible for the accusations against you. He had some interesting things to tell.

"The reason why he attacked you was because he thought you were my heart. If I had killed you in my rage, we both would be wandering the Green Lands now."

"How could he ever think I'm your heart? The prophecy speaks of a woman."

When he remembered how blind he'd been, Renaldo closed his eyes in shame. The shrouding spell did have a part in his oversight, but it still was unforgivable how ignorant he and Canubis had been. "It doesn't. At least not in the original sense. It's a mistake in translation. 'Ana' is a neutral article and *ana blod brester stratatos* is not necessarily 'the sister of the wind.' In the language of the Ancients, it means something like a 'kindred of the wind,' where *kindred* can mean a woman as well as a man. The translation can equally be 'brother of the wind.'

"Considering that you call the fastest horse in the world your brother—a horse named Lysistratos, of all things, the Emperor of the Storms—it's logical that only you can be meant. It's just too perfect. And as I said, I've never felt like this before I met you. It only took me so long to discern it because Damon's spell had clouded my sight in the truest sense of the word.

"You're my heart, Casto. And that means that you're bound to me for the rest of eternity."

Casto looked at him. Hope fought against insecurity in his expression.

Hope finally prevailed. "Is it really true?"

Renaldo kissed him gently. "Yes, my own. It's true. You're mine. Mine alone."

A groan escaped from Casto's throat, full of hunger and lust. He still resented being viewed as a possession, but after everything that had happened during the past few days, after the immense emotional and physical pressure he'd had to bear, he longed for reassurance that things were getting back to normal.

The longing was so strong that for the time being, he was willing to subordinate everything else to it. Renaldo seemed to follow a similar train of thought. He pulled Casto closer, gliding his hands over Casto's naked back, his tongue delving demandingly between Casto's lips.

Casto nestled closely to him. He clung to Renaldo's torso and rubbed his hips against the sturdy muscles of Renaldo's legs.

Renaldo laid him down on the furs, stripped off his linen trousers, and looked at him lovingly. "You're so gorgeous, my own."

He traced Casto's abs, which started to tremble under his touch. Goose bumps appeared where he'd inflamed Casto's nerve endings. Whimpering, Casto raised his hips, begging silently for more.

Renaldo skimmed strong hands over Casto's pelvis, touching it briefly, bringing his cock to life, and then he retreated, following the curve of Casto's legs down to his knees.

Helpless in his lust, Casto reached for Renaldo's shoulders, trying to pull him close, but Renaldo resisted, with a deep, lustful laugh.

"Oh no, my beautiful one, my precious love. I've just started, and I'll be damned if I don't enjoy myself to the fullest."

Casto whimpered in frustration but ceased when Renaldo's lips closed over his right nipple and he started to suck.

"Please, my lord. You're torturing me."

Instead of answering, Renaldo started to fondle Casto's cock in the same rhythm as the sucking on the nipple. It didn't take long until Casto yelled with lust. His hips bucked helplessly under Renaldo's skillful attack, his whole body wreathed in flames. Every fiber of his being longed to be possessed by him. When Renaldo let go of his cock and started penetrating him with fingers slick with oil, Casto started to beg, breathless this time and incoherent, completely overwhelmed by his longing for this man whose very existence he had cursed from the bottom of his heart only a few days ago.

"My lord, please. Whatever you want. Everything. But please don't stop. I'll do anything. Everything!"

Renaldo moved up and kissed him, silencing his pleas effectively. His fingers were still buried deep inside Casto, moving around and sending bursts of pleasure through his body every time they grazed his gland.

Casto undulated beneath Renaldo, unable to bear the sweet torture any longer. He wanted—no, he had to feel his lord. He managed to turn under him, to offer himself like a gift that fate itself had given the demigod.

A muffled sound escaped from Renaldo, like a sigh suppressed at the very last moment. He, too, was at the limit of what he could bear. The knowledge of who Casto really was, why Renaldo felt so drawn to him, only heightened his eagerness for his body.

"*Casto*." Casto's name was like a prayer on his lips, and he drank in the sight of him like a dehydrated man would a cup of water. He caressed Casto's back—his precious heart. Renaldo wanted to savor the moment as long as possible, but then Casto started begging again, his voice dark with lust, his ass a tempting invitation, and Renaldo couldn't resist any longer. He grabbed Casto's hips and penetrated him deeply.

As he thrust into Casto, Renaldo lost control. A red fog, similar to the first time he'd had sex with Casto, clouded his thoughts.

Before he knew it, the world exploded in ecstasy.

Casto felt his Barbarian finally penetrating him, ending the torture. He shouted his consent and arched up invitingly, his whole body turned into a recipient vessel. Seeing how Renaldo was taking him, how hard and recklessly he thrust into him, Casto figured he had lost control. But he didn't mind, since it meant that he, too, could give in completely. After everything they had been through, it was a heady feeling. Casto was surprised at how easily he trusted the Barbarian again—at least in bed.

They came at the same time, the climax of one catalyzing that of the other, a sweet torment that seemed to last forever until Casto was too exhausted to move.

For some time they lay there, still intimately joined, until Renaldo got up slowly and pulled out of Casto. He grabbed his shoulder, turned him around, and kissed him, full of love. "Did I hurt you?" He sounded worried.

Renaldo hadn't forgiven himself for what he'd done to his most precious possession, and the thought that he could have taken the sex too far, even though Casto had wanted it, made him queasy. It was so hard to maintain his self-control around Casto, but if he wanted the young man to ever forgive him, he had to tread carefully.

"No, you didn't hurt me, Barbarian. You exhausted me. It was wonderful."

Again they kissed. Renaldo's lips traced Casto's neck up to his earlobe, and lovingly he blew his breath over the soft skin.

"That's a relief. I've got to admit, I lost control. It was simply too much, having you again. You've no idea how much I missed you these past two weeks."

Sighing, Casto cuddled against Renaldo's massive form. "And I missed you, my lord. It's wonderful being back home."

Renaldo laughed contentedly. Since the mood was so relaxed, he dared to tease Casto. "It has a nice ring when you call me lord. You should do it more often."

Casto's eyes glittered. He was feeling playful as well and enjoyed challenging his normally aloof lover. "So that you can get used to it? No, it's better when 'my lord' remains special, for example, as a reward for satisfying me in bed."

The mighty warlord tenderly spanked his lover's backside. "Do you want to tease me, my own?"

"Teasing the powerful Angel of Death? Why would I do something so outrageous?"

Renaldo barely managed to suppress his laughter. He struggled to keep up a dignified front and laid his hand heavily on Casto's chest. "You're incorrigible. You leave me no choice but to punish you for your impertinence. Perhaps you'll finally learn your lesson when I give you a good spanking." Shaking his head, Renaldo pulled Casto across his lap in one swift motion. "This hurts me more than it does you."

Casto stiffened. The playfulness was gone, replaced by nervous agitation.

Renaldo realized, too late, that a spanking was probably not the best idea after the fight he had with Casto. Hastily he pulled back while Casto struggled to get up again. The young man was panting, and a fine sheen of sweat that had nothing to do with lust covered his body.

Renaldo felt like a monster as he watched Casto fighting the panic. "I'm sorry, Casto. I'm really sorry. That was stupid of me. I forgot—"

Renaldo stopped when Casto glared at him. There was something in his eyes Renaldo couldn't quite grasp. Fear and anger were obvious, and Renaldo could understand both emotions, but what he didn't get was the longing he glimpsed underneath. The realization of all the things he had lost in one act of stupidity made his heart stutter. There was no telling how long it would take until Casto would trust him again—if ever. With trembling fingers, Renaldo reached out for Casto and touched him, ever so lightly, on the cheek.

Casto closed his eyes. When he spoke, his voice shook. "I want our old relationship back. I want to have our sex life back. I don't want us to tiptoe around each other. We have enough baggage as it is. We don't need this shit!" He opened his eyes and they were full of anger. "Why did you have to hurt me? Why couldn't you believe in me, trust me? Why did you have to fall for the lies of a stupid slave? You ruined everything, Barbarian, and I honestly don't know if we can go back to what we had. Damn, I'm not even sure I want that. I'm so angry with you, I'd like to punch you in the face!"

Renaldo listened to Casto's outburst, unable to say anything in his defense. What was there to say? Casto was right. No words in the world could repair the damage his actions had caused. "If it helps, you can punch me. I deserve it. I'd do anything to get our old relationship back."

Casto stared at Renaldo as if he'd lost his mind. "And what good would me punching you do? I could only do it if you allowed it, which brings us back to the main problem: you're always the one in control, the one with all the power. When you first spanked me, you told me I could stop you anytime I wanted. I didn't want you to hit me, but you didn't stop. You violated the foundation of everything we have together, and it is me who has to take all the risk when I want us to reconquer what we had." Casto inhaled deeply. "I'm sorry, but I'm not ready for this yet. I need time. I don't know if I will ever allow you to spank me again. I'm too afraid to trust you."

Renaldo nodded. He didn't know what to say, didn't know how to react. "Of course, Casto. I promise I won't push you. You set the pace."

As if his words had been some kind of spell, the smile returned to Casto's face. "That's all I'm asking, Barbarian. Now come and show me how much you worship me."

When he saw the stunned look on Renaldo's face, Casto grinned. "I said I'm not ready for a spanking yet. I didn't say I wasn't ready for sex at all. Especially when a certain someone has a lot of groveling to do."

"You're enjoying this, aren't you?"

Casto's grin spread even wider. "I am. And you're in no position to complain."

"That I am not." With a mixture of relief and unease, Renaldo bent forward to indulge his complicated lover. He had an inkling that the precarious balance of power they had established after the battle of Ki't was once again shattered.

AN HOUR and another orgasm later, Renaldo and his heart were sitting in a heap of pillows in front of the open fire, drinking wine and enjoying the glorious exhaustion that only good, intense sex with the partner you love can evoke.

Casto sprawled comfortably in the pillows, his head rested on his lover's lap. Renaldo drew lazy circles on Casto's bare skin.

Casto watched Renaldo above him and decided it was time to find out more about what had happened to get him sent to the mines. He wouldn't be pleased about the details, but it was in his nature to face even uncomfortable facts without showing fear. "Why did you think I was cheating on you?"

Renaldo stared at him intensely. For a moment, Casto thought he wouldn't answer. When Renaldo finally started to speak, he sounded tense, as if he was afraid to give away too much.

Renaldo was painfully aware of how ugly the circumstances that had led to Casto's visit in the mines were, but he was too proud to use the shrouding spell as an excuse. Because when you got to the bottom of it, he had been unable to recognize his own heart. There was no way that could be forgiven. Nevertheless, he didn't want to lie to Casto. As painful as the truth might be, lying to him meant betraying him again.

Renaldo took a deep breath. "I was presented with proof, undeniable proof that I had no reason to doubt. A slave named Assani approached me and claimed that you had made a move on her, that you had an ongoing affair with her. To confirm her story, she showed me the golden pin with the sapphires, which I gave you last winter."

He looked directly at Casto. "The same pin you rejected like everything else I've given to you."

Casto turned pale. The unspoken reproach in Renaldo's words hit him hard because it was true. With a mixture of defiance and anger, he met Renaldo's gaze. "I swear to you, Barbarian, even though I never wore the pin, I'd have never given it or any of your other presents to somebody else. I treasure them too much to do such a thing."

Renaldo felt warmth spread through his body. He'd always suspected that Casto's stubbornness was the reason why he rejected all the gifts so vehemently, and he'd never given up gifting them in the hope of finding something that would melt Casto's pride. It seemed his efforts had not been in vain.

"I know, my own. I know. The pin was stolen from your trunk so that the cursed whore could use it to deceive me. And if I had given it a moment's rational thought, I'd have known you would never give away a gift given as a token of your favor."

Casto ignored the last part of the sentence since another detail had aroused his suspicion, a detail that made him shiver in cold premonition. "How? I thought the wolves…."

"The wolves scent every theft in the Valley, but there are humans who have free access to all chambers because they pick up laundry, deliver food—or return repaired jewelry." Renaldo hesitated, knowing well that his next words would hurt Casto deeply. "It was Sic who stole the pin. When he took it from your room, the wolves didn't even notice since he's moving around doing such things all the time. He's responsible for you being sent to the mines."

Casto had gone pale. He retched. His shock was apparent. "Not Sic."

He sounded so desperate it reminded Renaldo of his talk with Damon. *"So lonely and forsaken…. Sic… only one who kept being friendly…."*

Renaldo slung his arm around Casto's shoulders. He understood his desperation all too well. Being betrayed was never fun, but when it was somebody you trusted, it was like a knife thrust into your guts. "I'm sorry, my own. But it was Sic."

"No, I don't believe it. He'd never do such a thing."

"Damon blackmailed him, Casto. He threatened to kill Noran if Sic didn't do what he wanted. I hate to admit it, but the scheme was thoroughly planned and executed."

"That bastard! I knew he couldn't be trusted!" Casto punched a pillow in rage, his voice full of anger. He had known Damon was trouble from the moment the man tried to befriend him. "How did you find out I was innocent?"

Renaldo sighed. The discussion was getting more unpleasant, and the worst was still to come. "Sic told me. He sought me out six days after you'd been sent to the mines, and he confessed everything to me. He couldn't bear the thought of being responsible for your fate."

As Renaldo dreaded, Casto's features lit up. "He saved me, then?"

"No. He brought you into that situation in the first place. Strictly speaking, you've been saved by me and Lys, although I'm willing to credit the demon with the main part of your rescue."

"But if he hadn't confessed to you, you'd have never come to my rescue, isn't that right, Barbarian? Where is he now? What's going to happen to him?"

Renaldo's face became an irreconcilable mask. "He's in the dungeons, together with the other traitors. And like them, he's going to die."

Desperately, Casto shook his head. "No, this can't be! He told the truth and made up for his mistake. You have to let him live for that."

"Because of him I almost killed my heart. Thanks to his doings, the Good Mother was only a hairsbreadth away from being victorious. I don't care in the least that he told the truth in the end. For what he's done, he deserves the most painful death I can imagine. And believe me, on my way to the mines, I had plenty of time to think about the most dreadful punishment."

Anger flared in Casto's eyes as he reacted to the rage in Renaldo's voice. "He was *forced*. He didn't have a choice. If I had been in his shoes, I'd have done the same. I can understand him."

"Damn it, Casto. Because of him, you almost died. Don't tell me you've forgiven him?"

"No, I haven't. Actually, I'm so furious with him that I'll probably never forgive him. But in the end, he did the right thing of his own free will. He made up for his mistake, and he deserves a second chance. I surely won't allow Damon the triumph of taking Sic down with him."

Panting heavily, Casto paused. He resumed talking, with a hint of accusation in his tone. "Despite everything, *you* were the one who sent me to the mines, not Sic."

Renaldo's eyes narrowed. Casto's reasoning was well founded, which only made him that much angrier. "That was a low blow. I'm still your master and your god, so you had better watch your mouth."

Casto reared up to his feet. The old fire, doused by his ordeal, flared again, as hot and wild as ever. "My master and *god*?" His voice was full derision. "You didn't even realize I was innocent! What kind of god is it who trusts the accusations of a stranger more than his own lover?"

Renaldo had gotten up too. As always, Casto managed to find his weak spot without apparent effort, but after everything that had happened, he couldn't shake off the feeling that Casto should be more compliant. Renaldo was his god, the man who held his fate in his hands. Unfortunately it wasn't like Casto to let something like that stop him when he was in a full rage.

Over the pillows they stared at each other; the flames from the hearth drew flickering shadows on Casto's angry features and Renaldo's motionless mask.

Only Renaldo's gray eyes betrayed his feelings. "You said you'd forgive me."

"So that's how it is. I'm supposed to forgive you, but you can't do the same for Sic? He's young and inexperienced. How should he have known Damon didn't have the power to kill Noran?"

"You forgave me because I did you the same favor, *Prince Castolus*. The crime Sic committed is huge in comparison and cannot be excused with ignorance. He will die with the others. That is my final word."

Casto was about to speak, and Renaldo held up his hand in warning. "My final word, Casto. Don't challenge me."

Casto's blue eyes flared in rage, but no snippy retort followed. Instead, he turned and started walking away.

Renaldo clenched his fists in order not to hit him. Even though he knew now that Casto was his heart and after the things Renaldo had done to him, Casto was still able to make his blood boil with rage. Renaldo only hoped this was some twisted proof of their mutual love, because if not, they would likely kill each other. "What do you think you're doing?"

Casto stopped. He answered without sparing his master a glance. "I'm getting dressed to go see my rescuer. By the way, my brother is the only one who never doubted my innocence, Barbarian."

Casto started moving again and left Renaldo sitting alone at the fire.

CASTO'S THOUGHTS were racing. He was so furious, he was trembling all over. In his haste to leave Renaldo's chambers, he had put on the first clothes he could get his hands on, which turned out to be a dumb move. So clad only in a thin woolen tunic and light trousers, he was freezing.

The air in the Valley was icy, and a chilly wind heralded one of the last heavy snowstorms of the season. Casto was glad when he finally reached the stables that welcomed him with their warmth and, above all, their familiar, comforting scents and noises.

Lysistratos stood in his stall; two stable boys were busy brushing him. Casto smiled at them. "You can leave. I'll take over."

The two boys retreated silently, and Casto picked up one of the brushes. "My brother. I've missed you."

Lys snorted happily. He took a step toward Casto, who rested his forehead on the stallion's blaze. They stood like that for some time, enjoying the connection between them, all the stronger because it didn't need words.

"Thank you for getting me, Lys. Without you, I would be dead by now."

A snort, backed up by stamping.

"I know. I would have done the same for you. Still, I'm grateful that you revealed your secret to the Barbarian."

The stallion raised his head, and his big brown eyes drilled into Casto's.

Casto sighed. "Yes, he knows my secret as well. And we had a fight. I feel terrible. Angry and sad at the same time. It's disgusting."

Lys turned sideways when he heard those words, a silent invitation Casto gladly accepted.

"I hoped you would suggest this."

With his usual grace, Casto hopped onto his friend's bare back. He was barely seated when Lys started to run, out of the stables and along the narrow, snow-covered path that led to the mountain range that protected the Valley in the north.

Since Renaldo knew both their secrets now, the stallion had no reason to hold back. Across the icy fields, he galloped at a speed no ordinary horse would ever be able to reach.

Casto sat firmly on Lys's bare back, so used to his movements that he didn't even need to keep his hands on his brother's mane. Some surprised shouts followed them, but they soon left them behind, as well as the huts and the claustrophobia the protected world meant to them. Lysistratos tolerated the stables and the limits of a life with humans only because Casto was his soul mate. The stallion remembered all too well the times when he had roamed the world alone, his only pleasure the races he had with the wind.

But then he'd met Casto. Some invisible force had driven Lys to Ummana and to the side of the young man who he'd understood from the moment of their first meeting as if they had really grown up as brothers. Lys would never desert his prince; he needed him far too much for that.

At the mountain lake, Lys finally stopped. His warm breath condensed in the cold air. Against the midday sun, it seemed like a messenger from the other world Lys had once called his home.

Casto slipped from his back, his cheeks red, his hair ruffled by the wind. He leaned against his four-legged brother and started to talk, as he always did when he was upset.

"Till this morning, it was surprisingly peaceful except for one minor outburst on my side. Which was completely justified, by the way. I'm still slightly shocked by what's happened and I think he really regrets that he suspected and treated me so obnoxiously. We probably both tried to compensate for everything in bed. And it's not that absurd. I mean, I've forgiven him, but that doesn't mean that the memories just vanish. And you know how hard it is for me to make allowances. There's still a nagging little voice inside my head that keeps reminding me how deeply the Barbarian has betrayed me. So far, I haven't been able to silence it."

Lost in thought, Casto played with his brother's mane while he told Lys about Sic selling him out and then trying to make up for it by telling the truth. Lys rubbed his head sympathetically on Casto's shoulder while the young man kept on talking.

"Despite that, he wants to kill him, just like the other traitors. But I don't think that's right, and I told him as much. One word led to another, and before I knew it, I said some very hurtful and ugly things to him.

"Damn, Lys, I was so angry. This whole situation is such a complete mess that just thinking about it makes me furious. I was unfair to Renaldo, something I regretted the moment I slammed the door behind me. And now I don't know how to make up for it—or if I even want to.

"I still think Sic deserves a chance, and I have to make it clear to the Barbarian as well. The problem is, I can understand why he's so relentless. What shall I do?"

The powerful stallion rumbled deeply, a sound that soothed his human friend immediately. Lys knew what to do. It had always been like this. Perhaps because, as a creature of chaos, he looked at things from a different perspective than his human brother.

Silently, Casto listened to the demon's mental counsel. "You're right. The problem is the way we interact. Neither one of us is good with words. But how am I supposed to change that? I mean, it's part of who I am!" He slumped his shoulders miserably. "No matter what kind of conversation we have, it ends in disaster. We almost always get each other wrong. In the beginning I thought it was because of our different cultural backgrounds, but it's not just that. We're both used to not giving in—he even more than me. When I bend, I always get the feeling of being defeated. I can hardly stand it, especially after our last fight."

Now Lys rested his head comfortably on Casto's shoulder. His warm breath huffed across the prince's face, engulfing him in the scent of fresh herbs, his body heat keeping Casto from freezing. For almost half an hour they stood there, each lost in thoughts of a very different nature, and then Casto caressed his brother's nostrils.

"I know now what I have to do. But we have to get back right now."

Lys snorted adventurously, and Casto hopped onto his back with a broad grin.

"How fast do you think you can go back to the stables?"

The mighty muscles beneath Casto shuddered and the stallion ran.

Only a short time later, Casto entered Renaldo's chambers and looked cautiously around.

Renaldo was nowhere to be seen. He, too, seemed to have carried his anger into the Valley.

In Renaldo's private casket, Casto found what he was looking for.

Hoping that for once he was doing the right thing, he went to find Frankus.

WHILE CASTO had been cooling his head with a ride, Renaldo had gone to the training hall for the same reason.

He had been practicing for about an hour on his own, not going easy on himself, when Aegid and Kalad entered the room with a dozen trainees. The two warriors were responsible for training the recruits, a task they fulfilled so efficiently that the Pack had been able to defend its reputation as the best army in the world for a couple hundred years.

The young men were armed with training swords made of wood. The thin layer of sweat on their faces suggested they already had a healthy run in the snow. Full of awe they watched Renaldo, who just ended a complicated sequence with the grace of a wildcat.

Kalad spoke admiringly. "And here you can see a master at work. Strictly speaking, he's the best among us. Lord Renaldo, the Angel of Death."

Renaldo shot Kalad an angry glare for his pompous, and not entirely serious, introduction. "I'm sure the men know who I am. After all, they've sworn fealty to me. You can cut the cute talk." Renaldo's voice dripped with venom.

Kalad grimaced. "Aren't we Mr. Sunshine today?" Then he narrowed his eyes and really looked at Renaldo. "Tell me, when did you fight with Casto?"

"What makes you think we had a fight?"

"Because you're as irritated as two cubs with only one honeycomb. You're only in that kind of mood when you have trouble with your beautiful, arrogant lover, who thinks he's better than the rest of us. So tell me, when did Casto go back to his old self?"

Renaldo was looking daggers at Kalad. He didn't like it in the least how Kalad was talking about his heart, and he would pay for his impertinence. "This morning. It was loud and ugly and unnecessary. Satisfied?"

Kalad held up his fist in a gesture of triumph. He turned to Aegid, who'd been watching Renaldo warily. The giant was a very sensitive man, who could clearly feel the anger emanating from Renaldo.

Kalad, on the other hand, seemed oblivious to it. "I told you Casto would never be able to keep up the obedient front! Ha! So the pot's mine!"

"Wait a moment. Are you telling me you had a bet on when Casto and I were going to fight again?" Renaldo didn't know if he should be enraged or amused.

Kalad shot him a disarming smile. "As of late, you haven't given us much opportunity for bets. Your relationship was too stable. But that you would fight again was as sure as the next sunrise, so we dared it once more.

The bet isn't only between Aegid and me. The other Emeris wagered as well. But of course I was right. Can you imagine that Noemi seriously thought you'd persevere till the end of this week without getting at each other's throats? Sometimes she's truly naive. I'm still surprised that Casto was so obedient on our way home, but he was tired and wounded then."

"And you're stepping on thin ice, Kalad."

Renaldo's voice had a menacing quality. He didn't hold it against the others that they'd joined the bet—he would have done the same—but he was still angry about his fight with Casto and needed an outlet for his feelings.

Kalad still seemed oblivious, and even his leader's last sentence didn't faze him. "I never step on thin ice. If anything, I dance on quicksand."

"Which just ceased to support you. I need some exercise. You, Aegid, and your trainees against me. Strictly for training purposes, of course."

Kalad smiled broadly. He still hadn't realized how seriously pissed Renaldo was. "Don't you think that's a bit unfair?"

Renaldo watched the faces of the young men, some of whom looked as if they would throw up at any moment. Their antennae for impending danger were working well. "Very well. Nobody can call me unjust."

He handed Aegid the heavy wooden sword he'd been using, stepped aside, and blindfolded himself with a silken cloth somebody had left in the hall. He went back to Aegid, took back his sword, and stopped in front of the warriors. "Let's begin."

Kalad turned to the ten young men. "Today's your lucky day. You have the chance to fight against Lord Renaldo himself. For the time of the fight, you forget that he's your leader and a demigod. He's nothing more than an enemy you have to defeat. Whoever manages to bring him down can be sure to receive a generous reward. Fight like we've trained you and listen to our commands, understood?"

A many-voiced and slightly trembling *yes* resounded from the ranks of the recruits.

Kalad turned to Renaldo, his own training sword ready. "We're good to go."

Renaldo nodded, and the fight began.

Of course, it still wasn't fair. The blindfold wasn't really a handicap for Renaldo. If anything, it excluded all distractions and helped him to focus solely on the fight. His opponents were no greenhorns—the Pack only accepted the best, and each young man had undergone excellent training before coming to the Valley. In addition they had been under the care of the desert brothers since last fall. The merciless discipline that was a big part of the success of the Pack was already engraved into their very being.

Like a well-oiled machine, they followed their instructors' orders, and once or twice they even managed to trouble Renaldo. But one after another was defeated by him, and Renaldo noticed that none of these men could come close to Casto's fervor or ability. Not to mention the shrewd unpredictability that made the prince a serious opponent even for Renaldo.

After Renaldo had disarmed Aegid and Kalad too and shown them all their place, he pulled off the blindfold.

The recruits' eyes were full of respect and awe, while Kalad made a rude gesture when Renaldo looked at him.

Renaldo had disarmed Kalad quite forcefully and sent him stumbling to the floor, which hadn't pleased the desert warrior in the least. Involuntarily, Renaldo had to grin. If Kalad hoped it was over now, he was in for an unpleasant surprise. "Not too bad for a start. You're quite disciplined and very well trained. Now, let's work on the details."

For two more hours he pushed the recruits and the two Emeris, until the young men sank to the ground exhausted, unable to lift a finger. Aegid and Kalad were covered in sweat and panting.

"Don't tell me you're tired already? For Casto, this is simply a warm-up."

Renaldo's voice was full of mockery. Of course it was exaggerated, his gorgeous lover would be tired too after such intensive training, but he definitely had more stamina than those recruits. What Renaldo had really intended was to make clear to everybody present, and especially to Kalad, that Casto's position in the Pack was even more privileged than before, and he had been successful in that.

Kalad bowed to him, as always willing to admit a mistake. He even sounded apologetic. "I'm sorry, my lord. I didn't mean to be irreverent."

With a smile, Renaldo stepped forward. He couldn't really hold a grudge against Kalad, the Emeris who had been his friend for so long. He gave him a friendly pat on the shoulder and hugged him briefly. "Don't fret it, my dear brother-in-arms. This felt good. It was exactly what I needed. I'm feeling a lot better already. I owe you thanks."

He turned, tossed his training sword to Aegid, and left the hall. Outside, it was already getting dark. The wind had grown stronger, a messenger of the storm to come. Renaldo hurried back to his chambers.

CASTO WAS already there, sitting with his back to the door in front of the chimney. He was holding a cup of wine. When he heard the door open, he turned around and got up.

Renaldo watched him closely. Casto had already taken a bath: his hair lay damp against his skull. He wore a dark blue woolen tunic with gold pins at the shoulders.

With a hint of insecurity, Casto put down the wine and approached him. His lips were trembling slightly, and Renaldo had to suppress the urge to kiss him. Right in front of him, Casto stopped.

When he started talking, his voice was firm, determined. He extended his chin as he always did when he'd made a decision that didn't make him happy.

"I'm sorry, Barbarian. I didn't want to fight. And I surely didn't intend to confront you with all those ugly things I said. We have forgiven each other, and I had no right to dig it up again. I apologize for my foolish behavior."

That Casto meant what he was saying was reflected by the vulnerability in his gaze. He had just shown weakness and was waiting to see how his lord would handle it. Renaldo couldn't discipline himself any longer. He took the beautiful, serious face in both hands and kissed the lips that had just submitted to him. He hated to admit it, but seeing Casto demure like that gave him a feeling as if he had just drunk sparkling wine. It satisfied a side of him he hadn't been aware of. "I, too, am sorry. You're my heart, my lover. It wasn't fair of me to use my standing against you. I apologize for my behavior as well."

Casto reciprocated the kiss hungrily and rubbed his hips against Renaldo. Now that Renaldo was giving in as well, he felt more comfortable apologizing. "I really didn't want to fight," he said, his voice breathless. "My temper got the better of me. Can you forgive me?"

"If you can forgive me? I, too, have to learn to control my temper. It seems we both have a long way to go." He caressed Casto's back casually.

"My lord."

Again they kissed, and then Renaldo looked right into the heated face of the man who was his heart. "You already took your bath, but what do you think about accompanying me into the water?"

Casto nodded with that faint smile Renaldo knew was reserved only for him. "With pleasure, my lord."

In the bathroom, Casto helped Renaldo to get undressed. He was unusually clumsy, which was why Renaldo grabbed his wrists and pulled him close. "Why are you so nervous? Have you done something? You're never that awkward!"

Casto blushed deeply as if Renaldo had indeed caught him red-handed—or just made him angry again, it was always hard to tell with Casto. He tried to evade Renaldo's gaze, something he normally wouldn't do. But before Renaldo could get any more suspicious, Casto started talking again.

The slight tremor in his voice betrayed his nervousness. "I'm insecure. So much has happened, I'm no longer sure about my feelings or actions. Today I did something that I thought was a good idea, but now I'm already doubting whether I've done the right thing."

"What are you talking about?"

Instead of an answer, Casto stepped back. Now he stared at Renaldo in defiance as he opened the pins on his shoulders. The woolen tunic fell to the ground without making a sound, and Renaldo could only stare speechlessly at the unexpected present his lover had given him.

Overcome by his emotions, he didn't know what to say. The prince's name was like an incantation on his lips. "Casto."

The young man looked at him slightly hesitantly. In the light of the candles, his blue eyes seemed eerie. "I didn't do this solely for you. It's for me as well. About a year ago you forced me to wear the studs because you wanted to teach me that I'm yours alone. Now I've pierced myself to show you that I'm indeed willing to accept you as my lover and master. It's partly to take back some of the control you took away."

He paused for a moment and then went on. His tone made clear how much the topic hurt him. "In Ummana I lived by one rule alone—don't let them break you. That was my mantra, my maxim that accompanied me through eleven years of loneliness and pain. It was also a rule I made by myself, for myself.

"As your servant and lover, I have to obey the rules you lay down. This doesn't come easy to me, since I've spent most of my life dismissing everything that was forced on me from the outside. Sometimes I react to your dominance with defiance out of reflex, not because I necessarily have a different opinion, but just because it's you.

"I hope that, in the future, these studs will remind me that you don't have anything in common with my father or my upbringing, and that, on the contrary, you deserve my obedience. Where I come from, I'm a prince, descended from a long line of kings and queens who were used to having their every command obeyed. When I oppose you, it's not because I lack respect, but because I'm a king.

"I love you, I hope you know this."

Renaldo could only stare at his beautiful lover with his mouth hanging open. He had trouble regaining his composure and took the young man in his arms. "My own! My beautiful, precious heart. I love you so much! First and foremost I love you just the way you are because you are like this. Anything else would bore me to death. Also, I do have to admit I was only a hairsbreadth from strangling you this morning. I'm more than thrilled that you've decided to wear my marks again, but I hope you're aware that I would have never asked it of you again. It was wrong of me to force you in the first place, but I wanted to prove to myself and the world that I'm able to control you.

"Except for my brother, you're the only one who dares to challenge my anger. The only one who isn't burnt by my flame. I'll never give you up again." A mischievous grin spread on his lips. "We'll have to learn how to discuss things like mature adults, even though it means we won't be the object of malicious bets among the Emeris anymore."

Casto, too, was grinning now. "Don't you think they'll be shocked when we start acting responsible all of a sudden?"

"Surely, but they'll get used to it."

Casto wanted to say something more but furrowed his brows and looked at Renaldo with a hint of concern. "What about make-up sex?

When we stop fighting, we can't have that anymore, which would make me very sad. I have some very pleasing memories about sex in anger."

Renaldo's eyes lit up hungrily. "Rest assured, my shameless prince. I've been living for a long time, and I promise you, the best sex of your life is still to come."

"Really?" Casto's voice was raw with a hungry fire that not only unveiled his true, predatory nature, but also blazed in his eyes.

"Definitely. I'm going to prove it to you right now."

THE STORM had already reached its peak when Casto and Renaldo finally left the bath.

Renaldo had kept his word and given Casto a night he wouldn't forget in a hurry.

Ravenous, they fell on the cold dinner that had been served while they had been busy.

Across plates loaded with cheese, cold chicken, thick slices of bread, and slabs of butter, Renaldo regarded his lover with affection. "When you're done, we can try to take our first steps as responsible adults," he suggested.

Casto shot him a surprised look. "Barbarian?"

Renaldo smiled weakly. "I assume you're not yet done with the topic of Sic, and I'd rather discuss it now, when we both are still determined not to let it get out of hand again."

Casto glared at him suspiciously. "I seem to remember that you were already done with the issue. Why would you discuss a topic with me that you regard as closed?"

"Because I had time to think. Just as you oppose me out of reflex, I do things simply to make you angry. Don't get me wrong, I still think Sic should die for what he has done, but I'm willing to listen to your reasoning and think about it again. Although I might not like the outcome."

Renaldo didn't know what he'd expected from Casto, but surely not that he would get up from his chair, approach him, and press his forehead against Renaldo's palms in a gesture of respect.

"Should I ever doubt why I bow to your will, I hope I remember this day," he murmured to his master.

Then Casto returned to his place and started listing his arguments in favor of Sic. "Believe me, Barbarian, I'm certainly as furious with Sic as you are since I was the one who had to bear the consequences of his actions. But I can also understand why he did it. I know how much he adores Lord Noran. He would never allow anything bad to happen to his master. Besides, in the end he decided to do what's right, and he didn't have a demigod talking some sense into him in his dreams. The decision to save my life was his alone.

"Sic is a good person. He didn't stand a chance against Damon. You know that as well as I do."

When remembering Casto's escape and return to the Valley, Renaldo couldn't suppress a smile. In hindsight, that had been the moment when they had been irrevocably chained to each other. With some effort he managed to pry his thoughts from that particularly fond memory.

Casto was still speaking, his voice urgent. "Sic is not like Damon. He just wanted to protect someone he loves. That's why I think he deserves a second chance."

"Is that everything?" Renaldo looked calmly at him.

Casto nodded. "Yes, that's all. As I said, I don't ask you to not punish him. I only ask you to spare his life." He had listed everything that was there to be said.

"Your arguments are good, Casto. They carry weight. And if this wasn't about you, about the fact that I almost lost you, I'd pardon him. But it *is* about you, and that's why I can't feel any pity for Sic."

He held up his hand when he saw Casto open his mouth to interrupt. Casto closed it again.

"But I can understand how you feel, which is why I'll make a suggestion. If Noran agrees to take Sic back, then I will spare his life. In all honesty, the chances are small. Noran was betrayed by a young slave named Arja some hundred years ago. It almost ended in a catastrophe back then, which is why he reacts to treason even more sensitively than I do.

"If you manage to convince him, Sic is pardoned. But Noran has to take him back as his possession. I will surely not reward the little traitor with his freedom for his actions, and as a masterless slave, he wouldn't survive for long in the Valley.

"It won't be easy for him, Casto. Because of his actions, he lost the protection of the laws in the Valley. He's fair game. Strictly speaking, everybody, even the other slaves, can do to him whatever they please. Of course this won't happen when he belongs to Noran. Then he's only at the mercy of him, for better or worse."

Casto listened to the Angel of Death in silence. Then he showed his consent with a nod. Aware of the consequences of his decision, he was convinced that the life-loving Sic would prefer punishment, no matter how cruel, over death. "I accept your conditions. And I thank you for listening to me." Casto closed his eyes for a moment. When he opened them again, there was a wicked glint lighting them. "I have to admit, it feels good to have a level-headed discussion. Unfamiliar, but good. And definitely better than sex."

Before Casto could enjoy his little joke, Renaldo had reached him, yanked him up, and kissed him hard while he shredded Casto's clothes. He drew back to speak. "I'm more than willing to have a serious discussion with you, but I will surely not allow you to be impudent like that and leave you unscathed. Since spanking is still off the table, I have to find other means of showing you the error of your ways."

Casto ignored the underlying question. "What are you waiting for, Barbarian? Show me how ingenious you can be."

The words were an explicit invitation that Renaldo took without hesitation and a peace offering he was glad to receive.

4. DIVINE WRATH

EARLY THE next morning, Casto went to the smithy on his own to talk to Lord Noran and convince him to reclaim his slave. That it wouldn't be easy was clear to him even without Renaldo's explanation. Noran was a man who could hold a grudge over a past humiliation forever. Given the constantly dark mood and the verbal brutality Noran usually displayed, it was obvious that the sun would rather rise in the west before the master smith changed his opinion.

Casto had done some discreet inquiries and found out that Noran had beaten his unfortunate slave personally and then taken him to the dungeons. Ever since then, he was even more unapproachable than normal and blew his fuse over the smallest incident.

Renaldo had asked Casto why he even contemplated getting into such a confrontation, but Casto had a feeling that he somehow owed it to Sic. Even though he was still furious about the betrayal, he simply couldn't picture the life fading from those smiling, kind eyes. With a sigh, he straightened up, turned his face into his most arrogant, unwavering mask, and went to battle it out with a man he despised from the bottom of his heart.

WHEN CASTO entered the smithy, the master smith was busy working on a piece of red-hot metal. The hammer struck the anvil in a steady, unrelenting rhythm; the powerful muscles on his forearms bulged threateningly. With his more than one and three-quarter ells in height, Noran was the biggest man in the Valley after Aegid, and his sheer body mass made him a forbidding presence. His height alone was enough to induce fear in others, especially slaves.

Upon spotting Casto, Noran handed the still-glowing steel to an apprentice and motioned Casto to his private chambers behind the smithy.

Scattered rather carelessly on two desks were drafts for weapons and jewelry, steel samples, blanks for swords, hammers, and a bunch of other items that Casto wouldn't have expected to find in a smithy. Three chairs, each of which looked old enough to have seen the birth of Ana-

Darasa, were situated around the bigger table. Noran led his guest there, offered him the chair that appeared the least shabby, and then looked at him expectantly. He could guess what Casto wanted from him, and he didn't like it in the least. His aversion to Casto was as great as the dislike Casto felt for him.

Still, Noran tried to keep up appearances. "Casto! What brings you here? Are you feeling well? We're all very glad that you've returned to Renaldo safely."

Casto flashed a calculated, shy smile. He, too, wanted to keep things calm. "I'm fine. Thank you for your concern, Lord Noran. I'm here for a special reason, which, I'm afraid, is not going to please you."

The master's face darkened. "What would that be?"

Casto took a deep, mental breath before he went into battle. There was no sense in beating around the bush, so he cut to the core right away. "I've talked to my lord. He has informed me, in detail, about the circumstances of my punishment as well as my rescue. I was able to convince him to spare your slave Sic, but he'll only do it when you agree to take him on as your own again."

"That will only happen the day this world faces its end!" Noran got up abruptly, his face twisted in anger. He smashed his fist on the table, which started to shake as if it were about to break. "How dare you even think about asking me such a thing? I gave the obnoxious little rat my trust, and he returned the favor by helping the Good Mother! No matter what kind of fate Renaldo has planned for him, it's surely still too good compared to what he's done."

Casto had involuntarily backed off when Noran exploded. The man's physical presence was like a battering ram that obliterated any opposition, but now Casto leaned forward again, angry with himself that he'd been affected by it. His voice was calm and clear, a stark contrast to Noran's outburst. "Sic did it because he thought he could protect you. That has to count for something, even in your opinion, Lord Noran."

"Even if he'd done it to protect Ana-Isara herself, treason is treason, and he'll pay for it fair and square."

Casto realized he wouldn't get anywhere with rational reasoning, so he straightened up to his full height, tilted his head back, looked Noran directly in the eye, and spoke with all the authority his ancestors had accumulated through centuries. As if what he was about to say wasn't his last, desperate resort. "You don't seem to understand, Lord Noran. This wasn't a request. You owe me, and I'm claiming the debt now."

Noran froze. He was so used to slaves ducking in terror before his angry outbursts that it came as a physical shock when he met resistance. But he gathered himself well. A piercing look hit Casto. "What kind of debt would I owe you? I can't remember you ever doing anything for me. But I can assure you, had I won you back then in Arana, you'd now know how to behave toward a lord."

Casto regarded him calmly, trying hard to hide his contempt. Treating him as if he were nothing but a nuisance came naturally. "Thank you, but I do know how to behave. I just sometimes decide that it's not to my advantage to do so. And in case you think you can impress me with your shouting, I want to remind you that I fight with the Barbarian on a regular basis. I can assure you, once you're unperturbed by the wrath of the Angel of Death, the fury of a master smith is not impressive at all.

"To get back to the debt you owe me, it was your fault I had to go to the mines. So I definitely have a right to ask for satisfaction."

Noran hesitated. The calm Casto radiated had unsettled him, and he saw a cold, ruthless determination in Casto's eyes that commanded his reluctant respect. With the exception of Canubis, Casto was indeed the only one who dared to oppose Renaldo, so he was brave enough not to be intimidated by a few loud words. And if it was true and Casto was really Renaldo's heart, then it was wise to tread more carefully around him.

Noran decided to switch tactics. "Why would you think it was my fault? I wasn't the one who stole the pin."

Casto reacted to the change in Noran's behavior like a bloodhound to the scent of its prey. If he played it smart now, Noran would do what he wanted him to before he even realized what had happened. "No, you didn't do that. But if you had fulfilled your responsibilities as Sic's master and educated him according to his talents and status as your personal slave, he would have been wise enough to know that Damon was lying. But you only toyed with him. You gave him a collar but denied him the privileges that come with it. He was easy prey for the priest, and that's your fault alone."

Noran stared. As much as he resented it, the young man was partly right. If he had taken Sic's training more seriously, Sic probably wouldn't have been fooled by that bootlicker of the Good Mother. Also, Casto's expression made clear that he was determined to battle this one out to the bitter end. Noran's respect for him went up a few notches but was already shadowed by anger. Would this pretty boy really manage to outsmart a seasoned Emeris? Noran would be damned. With a sickly sweet smile, he agreed with Casto. "I acknowledge my fault. You're right, without my negligence, this would have never happened. So, you're asking for Sic's life as compensation?"

Casto nodded. Victory was at the tips of his fingers, and he had to remind himself to stay calm. "Yes. I do."

"Then let it be. I'll reclaim him as my slave. But since I can't stand working with a traitor, you'll have to take responsibility as well. I'll inform you about the details later."

Relieved, Casto exhaled. Noran was setting conditions mainly to save face, but Casto was willing to go along. The only thing that counted was that Sic got another chance. Casto had been thinking about it for a while and realized that his anger was simply too great. Because Sic had been Casto's only friend, his treason weighed heavier. But Casto had liked having Sic's friendship, and he felt nauseated.

He would have to face the fact that true friendship didn't exist. Having Renaldo as his lover and Lys as his brother would have to suffice. During his time in Ummana, that was more than he could have ever dreamed of.

Noran was looking at him expectantly. Hastily he bowed. "I thank you, Lord Noran. I deem your debt as paid in full."

The gigantic man smiled darkly. "I'm glad to hear it, Casto. I'll see you tomorrow."

"I'm looking forward to it."

The polite phrase left Casto's lips without him thinking consciously about it.

In the end, his political upbringing did have some merit. He left the smithy in the knowledge that he had just gained a victory he would have to pay a hefty price for in the future. Noran would surely not let it pass without comment or retribution.

ON HIS way to the stables, Casto banished his musings about possible consequences in favor of a more pressing problem. It had been almost two and a half weeks since he had been able to follow the training plans for the horses entrusted to him. Because the beasts had barely been worked during his absence, he would have to change, if not dismiss, his former plans.

He decided to start with the chestnut stallion Kalad had given to him. The steed was promising, teachable, and intelligent. Casto hoped to start the day with a positive experience that would help him deal with the drawbacks to come.

When he left the stables with the saddled stallion, he told one of the stable boys which horse he wanted to ride next. The boy nodded and promised to get the mare ready for him.

But upon his return, neither the horse nor the boy could be seen anywhere.

Instead, Sindal and Elwan, the demoted workers, were waiting for him with their arms folded. Casto steeled himself for a fight. The higher he had risen in the favor of his master, the more intense their hatred burned. They were his enemies for life. Acting as friendly as he could bear when faced with such open hostility, he asked after the horse.

It was no surprise when they ignored his question completely, but they shot him pejorative looks that began to get on his nerves.

Finally, Sindal said, "Look who's dodged his just punishment again, Elwan. It seems the arrogant tart has managed to soothe the Angel of Death once more. What a lucky guy."

Elwan chuckled maliciously. "I don't think that has much to do with luck. My guess is the pretty boy has just waved his ass and Renaldo, blinded by lust, spared him."

"When I think about all the things you've managed to pull with the lords, I'm asking myself whether the rumors are true and Renaldo only thinks with his dick where you're concerned."

Both men started to laugh and failed to notice the dangerous flame in Casto's eyes. He didn't care when the two idiots insulted him—he was used to far worse—but when they started involving the Barbarian, he lost his patience. Before he could show them their place, a cold voice resounded from the entrance, and it made Casto shudder.

"What's going on here? Who dares to speak in such a disgraceful manner about my brother?"

Canubis approached the three men, his amber eyes glinted as coldly as those of the two huge wolves accompanying him.

Sindal and Elwan kneeled immediately. Casto bowed low but refrained from getting down since the stallion he was leading wasn't too happy in the presence of the predators.

Canubis turned to Casto. "I ask again. What's going on here? And before you give me your answer, I want to stress that I'm no friend of lies, Castolus."

The prince stared at the master of the Valley in blind panic before he remembered that he'd told Renaldo his secret. Of course Renaldo had shared it with his brother. He straightened his back, unwilling to show weakness in the presence of the unrelenting warlord. "It's only a small incident, Lord Canubis. I ordered that a certain horse should be prepared for me, and those two thought I could do that on my own as well."

A dangerous glint entered Canubis's eyes His gaze almost stabbed Casto, forcing him to continue telling the truth. "For how long have there been—incidents between you?" Canubis's tone showed how aware he was of the understatement in Casto's words.

Casto felt crimson tinging his cheeks, but he had no intention of showing weakness. "Since I arrived here, Lord Canubis."

"Since you came back, or since my brother first brought you here?"

"Since your brother first made me his possession."

The lethal gaze now turned toward the kneeling men. "I understand." Then he addressed one of the wolves. "Get me two overseers. Tell them to bring whips."

The powerful predator dashed away with a threatening growl. Canubis looked around. "Hey, you!"

A stable boy who had tried to slip away unobtrusively froze in place.

"Take Casto's horse, and see to it that everybody in the stables gathers at the front."

The stable boy hurried off to do Canubis's bidding.

"And you, come with me." The cold, commanding voice was directed toward Casto.

Terrified, yet unwilling to admit it, Casto followed the demigod outside into the snow. He would never understand why most people in the Valley were more afraid of Renaldo than of Canubis. At that moment, the Wolf of War was so intimidating that Casto had to control himself not to fall down whimpering and begging for mercy. The warlord's sheer presence was like a hammer blow to the stomach.

Two overseers arrived at the stables and dragged Sindal and Elwan out of the building and into the semicircle where the other slaves had gathered. They all were on their knees, eyeing the Wolf of War with fear.

Canubis spoke in a voice devoid of emotion, a sure sign that he was seething with rage. "I had to observe a serious problem with discipline here in the stables. These two worthless creatures dared to badmouth my brother. Even worse, they've been denying his favorite due respect." His gaze lingered on the cowering slaves. "I'm not going to waste my precious time finding out who backed them in their obnoxious behavior, but rest assured, should I hear the slightest rumor of something like this again, you all will be put to death. I do not tolerate irreverence toward me or my brother. It's high time you all remembered who the masters are in this place."

With that, he nodded toward the overseers, who dragged Sindal and Elwan up. The two stable workers had been caught off guard by the sudden turn of events, but they finally realized that their lives were forfeit, and they started to beg.

At that moment, Casto couldn't say that their fate interested him in the least. The way they were trying to wiggle out of the situation was as dishonorable and pathetic as their previous actions.

Canubis seemed to think the same because he ignored their begging. Without mercy, he gave his verdict. "For your impudence, you both lose your tongue. After that, you'll be whipped and displayed for four days. Should you survive, you may stay in the Valley, but you will serve in the lowest positions possible."

He nodded to the two overseers, who pried open the mouths of the two men and adjusted pliers to their tongues. Then Canubis stepped forward, moving as fast as a striking snake, and with a sickening sound, two men's tongues hit the ground. Before the lumps of meat could color the snow crimson, the wolves were there.

Only with an effort was Casto able to suppress the urge to gag when confronted with the brutal punishment. He was used to Renaldo's quick dealings, but his elder brother was even more merciless.

When the overseers started the whipping, Sindal and Elwan screamed wordlessly through the cold air, like the voices of angry demons. Canubis grabbed Casto's wrist and dragged him back into the stables.

The coldness had gone from his voice, and now he let his anger show openly. "You little idiot! For five years those lowlifes have been acting like that and you never thought of telling my brother? How stupid are you? Do you think this is some kind of game? A pastime from the court of Ummana?"

The state of shock Casto had fallen into when Canubis had taken over so brazenly finally dissipated. Outraged by the accusation, he felt like a child who'd been scolded by an adult, and he didn't like it in the least. He met the demigod's gaze, and before he could think twice, he answered sarcastically. "Please forgive me, Lord Canubis, that I didn't talk to the man who had taken away my freedom more than absolutely necessary in the beginning. And yes, the behavior of those men did remind me of my life in court and warmed my heart. I enjoyed not being able to talk to anybody, knowing none of them would help me, that I was on my own in everything I did. Indeed just like at home. I'd have rather hacked off my right arm before admitting to the Barbarian that I was having problems with the other slaves. There are things that have nothing to do with you or your brother. That is my problem, and I'd have dealt with it in my way."

Canubis looked as if the earth had opened up and tried to swallow him. Never before had anybody dared to oppose him when he was angry. Not even Noemi would speak a word of defiance in such a loaded situation, and this young man had just told him very bluntly to mind his own business.

He was so thunderstruck his anger dissipated in an instant, a reaction his brother had already told him about where Casto was concerned. Suddenly Canubis understood in a completely different way why Renaldo loved the young man so much. Not only was Casto beautiful when angry, it was refreshing to be told an opinion so directly. Except for Renaldo, and occasionally one of the Emeris, nobody was bold enough to do something so outrageous.

Touched by Casto's bravery, Canubis explained the problem calmly instead of punishing him for his impudence. "As much as your stubbornness and independence suit you, this is definitely not your problem but that of my brother and, yes, mine as well. Here in the Valley we have a set of strict rules and laws that everybody who lives here has to obey. Those who break the laws lose the right to be protected by them. By not telling Renaldo about the actions of the men, you undermined his authority.

"You were his favorite, his lover. Now you're his heart. Whoever disregards you does so to my brother as well. That there weren't any consequences for the crime for so long has only increased the lack of respect. Creatures like those two wastes of space out there have risen above their rightful place. They're paying a hefty price for it, something that wouldn't have happened if you'd shown a little more regard to our customs."

Canubis expected the young man to give an angry answer, but Casto had turned pale.

"I've never seen it that way." Casto's voice trailed off as if he was talking to himself. "I always thought this was solely about me, and I'm used to solving my problems on my own. But you're right, I misjudged the whole situation."

Slightly lost, Casto stood amid the stalls. He eyed Canubis ruefully, his inner battle showing clearly on his features. Suddenly he knelt down. It was plain how much he resented being in the wrong, but it didn't keep him from doing what was right. "I beg your forgiveness for my willful behavior, Lord Canubis. I made a mistake and I'm truly sorry for it."

Casto lowered his gaze and waited humbly for the reaction.

Canubis felt a throbbing in his loins that he instantly suppressed. But the handsome young man who had no fear of opposing him and yet was willing to admit a mistake and submit to him was simply too alluring. Like a dream made flesh for which Canubis envied his brother. He cleared his throat. "I forgive you. But I expect you to tell Renaldo about what happened today. Unless you want me to do that."

With his gaze still cast down, Casto answered. "I thank you, Lord Canubis. I'll tell my master about this, even in your presence, should you so wish."

"I don't think that'll be necessary. You're a man of honor, Casto. Go back to work, we've already dallied enough as it is. I don't think you'll have reason to complain about lack of obedience in the near future."

Silently Casto got up, bowed once more to Canubis, and left the stables.

IN THE evening, Renaldo was already waiting for his lover when Casto entered the chambers, tense to the point of snapping. Renaldo knew immediately that something was off.

"Casto, what's happened? Has Noran refused you? I told you, the chances for that were great."

Casto shook his head as if he was trying to get rid of an annoying sound. "No, Barbarian. Everything went smoothly with Lord Noran. He's going to reclaim Sic as his slave."

Renaldo furrowed his brow. He had half expected Casto to be successful, but it was still a surprise. Changing Noran's mind was like talking to the weather—nothing would come out of it.

"That's good news. At least for Sic. Why aren't you happy?"

"Because I made a grave mistake today, one I know has to be punished, and I'm not looking forward to the discipline I'm going to receive from you. Plus I'm somewhat angry with myself for letting things get that far."

Slowly Renaldo was losing his patience. He hated riddles. "Casto, I don't intend to play 'guess and answer' the entire evening. You're telling me what happened right now or I promise I'll punish you without knowing your mistake."

Casto lowered his gaze. When he started talking, his voice was distant, as if he was retelling something that had happened to somebody else. It was obvious that he was trying to put some distance between himself and the situation at hand.

"Ever since I came to the Valley, I've been having problems with the other slaves, especially those working in the stables. They always viewed me as an upstart and meddler, and they only suffered me reluctantly. It went so far that they even sabotaged me openly. Today, the two who chained me in front of your tent started again. They first picked only on me, but then they started to slander you as well."

Casto rubbed his temples with the tips of his fingers as if he were an old man, tired of the ways people behaved. "And your brother heard. He was beyond furious. The men were punished brutally and everybody from the stables had to watch."

Remembering how ruthless Canubis had acted, Casto fell silent for a moment. Long enough to give Renaldo a chance to start yelling.

"Damn it, Casto! Why didn't you tell me? Are you aware of what you've done? How stupid you've been?"

Casto's chin went up and he glared at Renaldo.

"Your brother was kind enough to tell me about the consequences of my actions in detail. I'm afraid I told him quite bluntly that I don't share his opinion."

Renaldo stared at him in horror. What he had just heard made his anger dissipate like fog in the sun, and worry took its place. "You talked back to my brother?"

Casto concentrated on his hands, nervously playing with a tail of his shirt. Slowly but surely the severity of the situation was sinking in. "I told him to mind his own business. I was very impolite, but he refrained from sanctioning my irreverence. Instead he explained in detail the stupidity of my mistake. Then he left it to me whether I wanted to tell you myself or if he should do it."

"You told the Wolf of War to mind his own business?" Renaldo was aghast. "I can't remember when somebody dared that last."

"He was very sarcastic, which made me angry. I never planned on being so impudent, but he was very offensive."

Renaldo gently caressed Casto's cheek. "My brother's good at that, I know." He sighed.

Casto was still staring at the ground. He hated what he was going to say next, but there was no way around it. "What will be my punishment, Barbarian? I'm sure your brother expects something… lasting."

Renaldo lifted his lover's chin with his forefinger. He wasn't pleased about the way things had turned out. "I didn't envision the evening like this, my own."

The young man smiled weakly. "Me neither."

"For not telling me about the actions of the other slaves, I'll make you pay at a convenient moment. But I cannot ignore the impudence toward my brother. I'm afraid you won't be able to ride a horse for the next few days."

Casto nodded despondently. He'd anticipated as much. "The glass whip?" he asked, trying to sound casual about it.

Renaldo's face contorted in revulsion. "Surely not. You're my heart, and that protects you at least a little bit. No, I'm going to chain you and then you'll be beaten with the strap. That should satisfy my brother."

With a bland expression, Renaldo watched his beautiful lover undress. He'd definitely had plans for this night other than punishing his heart, but he couldn't just let slip what Casto had done. They'd been too lenient during the past years—how else could Damon have managed to gather so many traitors around him? It was high time the inhabitants of this world learned once again the meaning of respect.

But that also meant that nobody went unpunished when opposing the will of the demigods. Not even the heart of one of said demigods.

Naked, Casto stood in front of his master and awaited his punishment. As much as he resented allowing to be beaten, he also understood why it was necessary. The hatred of the other slaves partly stemmed from the impression that he never had to pay the price for his behavior, a dangerous message that was partly accountable for his journey to the mines.

It was a tricky situation, one that could be most easily solved by punishing him, although he didn't like the thought of losing control over his life so quickly. Everything inside Casto revolted against what was going to happen, and it took all his self-control not to fight back when Renaldo seized his wrists and guided him toward one of the walls in the main room where chains were fixed about two ells high.

HYPNOTIZED LIKE a rabbit in front of a snake, Casto stared at the dangling cuffs that would soon be embracing his wrists.

A scent assaulted his nostrils, one he had almost forgotten: a mixture of mold, decay, and very old wood rotting away quietly in the darkness and dampness.

And then he was back in Ummana, on his way to the cellar where the torturer would punish him. The man was holding his wrists in a merciless grip, shoving Casto toward the wall where Casto knew every stone, every bump by heart because he was chained there so often.

Suddenly defiance bubbled up inside. He was no longer a child but a man, a warrior. He would not allow the torturer to punish him for something he hadn't done, never again. With a guttural yell, the prince threw his head back. A *crunch* told him he had broken his captor's nose.

Surprised by the sudden pain, the torturer loosened his grip, a chance Casto didn't let go by. He wriggled out of the arms that held him and ran for the door that promised freedom. He only had to reach Lys, and then he was safe. Then they could escape, as swift as the wind. The door was drawing closer, but the torturer reached him just before he could touch the handle.

The monster of his childhood tackled him and held him with so much force that Casto was unable to move.

Terrified, he tried to escape, but the grip of those merciless hands only tightened, and finally he gave up, submitted to the fate he would never be able to escape. Tears streamed down his cheeks. A gentle touch on his head, which he tried to shake off, and then a deep, soothing voice that was a spark of light in the darkness consuming him.

"It's okay, my own. I'm here. Don't be afraid, nothing can happen to you. Shush. I'm here."

Slowly reality returned. Casto was cowering on the floor of Renaldo's chambers, not far from the exit. Renaldo had slung his arms around him and was rocking him like a child. Casto had just had a panic attack. Sobbing, he clung to his lover. "I'm sorry, I'm sorry. I—I…."

"Shh, my own. Be calm. Everything's fine. Everything's good."

When Casto had calmed down a little bit, Renaldo helped him up. Startled, Casto put his hand in front of his mouth when he saw that Renaldo was covered in blood. "My lord, I'm sorry. I didn't mean to do that, please, I—"

"Casto, first, it's not as bad as it looks." Again the demigod had interrupted him. His voice was dry, and he tried desperately to hide his worry. "You broke the nose cleanly and it's already almost healed. Second, if I thought you had done this on purpose, by now you'd be back at the wall.

"Can you tell me what just happened? One moment, I was contemplating how to get this over with quickly, the next you had smashed your head into my face."

Ashamed and agitated, Casto looked down. "I'm not entirely sure myself. I was suddenly back in Ummana, in the cellar where I used to be punished. It was so overwhelming I panicked and tried to escape."

"You called me Voltara. My Ummanian is not worth mentioning, but I remember that word. You used it toward the man from your dream, the one I decapitated."

"I thought you were him, the torturer. He is my father's right hand and the one who always beat me."

Renaldo sensed that Casto was hiding more from him than he was telling. Involuntarily, he tensed. "What else, Casto? How often did that despicable pig hurt you?"

"Since the day I was officially given to my father till the moment of my escape, at least once every day. Depending on his mood, he did it more often."

Casto shuddered in his arms, his voice was the lost whisper of a small child. Seeing him so helpless stoked to a blaze Renaldo's fury toward those who had done that to his precious lover. Renaldo felt the vein in his forehead thumping. Heat flared around him like a coat of pure wrath. "Ten years?" he screamed. "For *ten years* you were beaten up daily?"

"Yes, for ten years. Most of the time he used the strap, but sometimes it was a cane. He had to be careful, since he wasn't allowed to leave any visible or lasting traces."

"My own!" Renaldo hugged Casto closely. "What have they done to you?"

The pain in Renaldo's voice snapped Casto out of his shock. "It's fine. It's in the past. I guess I overreacted because of the combination of wall, chains, and strap. It made the memories vivid. I don't think I'm going to lose my composure like that again."

"After all this, I surely won't beat you, my heart. I'm going to explain the situation to my brother. He'll understand."

Casto shook his head. As much as he resented feeling the bite of the strap, as much did he know that this punishment was necessary to restore balance in the Valley. If he really wanted to build a future with the Barbarian, he had to learn how to bow to Pack rules. "I can't believe I'm saying this, but it really is all right, Barbarian. I made a grave mistake. I deserve punishment, and I don't want you to fight with your brother because of me."

Casto smiled darkly. "It's enough when I do it. I'm ready."

Renaldo regarded his heart for a long time, then kissed him on the forehead. Witnessing even this tiny glimpse of the hardships Casto had gone through had hardened his resolve. No matter how much he deserved to be punished, Renaldo simply couldn't do it. He couldn't hurt this proud, brave man anymore. He slung his arms around his lover and carried him to bed.

"You better lie down and rest. I'll go wash off that blood. Then I'll join you."

The azure eyes pinned him. "Are you sure about this? Defying your brother?"

"I know I'm going to regret it, but I'd regret it even more if I hurt you."

Casto sighed. "I can't say I'm not relieved. As of late, there have been too many beatings."

Renaldo smiled gently. He always enjoyed it when Casto allowed him to come close. "Don't worry. I can promise you, there won't be any more of those—unless you wish it."

"Get your mind out of the gutter, you fiend! It's still too early for that."

Renaldo gave him a sad smile. "And here I thought you liked me being suggestive. How disappointing."

Casto returned the grin. He may not be there yet, but he was on his way. "Go and wash yourself, Barbarian. I want to sleep."

With crackling laughter, Renaldo went into the bathroom. He was immensely relieved that Casto had regained his composure so quickly. After everything that had happened, Renaldo still worried about his heart's mental well-being.

CASTO WOKE because a stinging pain assaulted his nerves. In his sleep he had rolled onto the book he'd been reading the day before, and the sharp, hard corner had left a bruise on his back. With a whimper he turned onto his stomach and tried to ignore the painful throbbing. He had to be grateful that it was only the small spot where the book had pressed into his flesh that was hurting and not his entire body, as would have been the case after a thorough beating.

When the Barbarian had come back from the bath, he had hugged Casto tightly until he'd fallen asleep, still confused and agitated, but at least reassured about Renaldo's feelings.

Casto closed his eyes and tried to fall asleep but then gave up. Thinking about what had happened the other day had woken his whirling thoughts and he was unable to stop the torrent. A little awkwardly he climbed off the bed, searching for Renaldo, but he couldn't find him.

When Casto entered the main room, Renaldo was awaiting him. He looked pale, and his gray eyes were full of worry as Casto sauntered toward him.

"My own, how are you feeling? Did you get enough sleep?"

Casto smiled. Renaldo's concern touched him more than he wanted to admit. "Good morning, Barbarian. It's fine. I'm just feeling emotionally challenged at the moment. I'm still not sure whether it was a wise decision to let me go unpunished—not that I'm inviting you, but well…. Your brother can be scary sometimes."

Renaldo pulled his heart close. "I did it because I love you. And because I like your temperament—most of the time. After everything I've done to you, I just couldn't bring myself to hurt you yet again."

Casto's smile broadened. "I'm with you on that one. You do have a heavy hand, and I'm grateful that you've usually been lenient during the past five years. I mean, you could have punished me pretty badly for some of the things I did, but except for when I escaped from the Valley, you always held back. Even when you thought I had betrayed you, it was your chambers that bore the brunt of your wrath, not me."

A grim smile appeared on Renaldo's face when he thought about the damage he'd done to his own rooms. It had been so bad that the traces were still there, a reminder of the worst mistake in his life. Renaldo stroked Casto's cheek gently. "It was my pleasure. Fighting with you beats every other pastime I know. Speaking of which, how did you manage to convince Noran? I'd have bet a fortune that the sun would sooner rise in the west."

Casto's face hardened. "He said something similar. But luckily I was able to get my way."

"Are you going to tell me how you managed to do that?"

Casto shrugged. "Is that so important? He agreed to my wish. There's nothing more to it."

Tactfully, Renaldo refrained from prying further, but he did make a mental note to talk to Noran about it. Because of Casto's explosive temper, Renaldo sometimes forgot that Casto also had a sharp mind. A mind, as he knew now, that had been trained to think in the crooked strokes of high politics at a very young age. Renaldo would have to be very careful what his heart was up to in the future and which concessions he made to him.

Casto might be young, but he was dangerous in more ways than one.

To get rid of the unpleasant thoughts, Renaldo pulled him closer and kissed him fervently. Casto snuggled up, groaning and ready to get down to business. On this field, at least, they were in perfect harmony. But before Renaldo could repay himself for the past night, a knock interrupted their games.

With a sigh, Renaldo went to the door. "It seems as if we won't be granted any intimacy today either." He opened and stared into Canubis's smiling face. "Brother! What a nice surprise! Have you come to see how I punished Casto? If so, I'm afraid I have to disappoint you."

The smile vanished from Canubis's predatory features. "Why should you punish him?" He furrowed his brow. "Is this about the incident at the stables? That's already settled."

Both men looked at Casto, who was glaring at them. "If this is meant as a joke, I fail to see the punch line." Casto's voice was tense, a sure sign that he was about to explode. "I did what you wanted and told the Barbarian everything."

Canubis looked questioningly at his brother, slightly taken aback by the sudden change in temperature. "To be honest, I don't see the problem. You obviously haven't punished him, so why are you both so tense? I mean, it wasn't too bright what he did, but there's no need to grow gray hair about it either."

Canubis gestured at the prince's naked, unmarred body that was proof of Renaldo's lenience.

Renaldo didn't seem happy. "Casto told me everything. I thought you left his punishment to me."

Canubis turned toward Casto. He still had no clue what was going on, but now he was determined to shed some light on the situation. "What did you tell my brother?"

"Everything that happened. The punishment of Sindal and Elwan, my impudence, how you explained everything to me and left me the choice to tell the Barbarian myself." Casto was calmer, but a spark of suspicion remained in his eyes.

Canubis shook his head. "And you forgot to mention that I've forgiven you?"

Renaldo's eyes shot daggers between his brother and Casto. "You've what?"

"What do you think, brother? It's been a long time since a human dared to oppose me. To be frank, I found it a refreshing experience. Anyway, Casto apologized very nicely. For me, the matter was done."

Like an avalanche, Renaldo came down on his lover. "Why didn't you tell me? We could have avoided a lot of trouble if you'd been a little more aware!"

Casto's blue eyes were now almost black with anger. "I apologize for not seeing through your brother's intentions and thus preventing you from the inconvenience of making a decision on your own. I'm sure it was a traumatic event for you!"

"Shut your mouth, Casto. Between the two of us, I was the one who bled!"

"My heart's breaking," Casto sneered. "It must have been a couple of terrible minutes until everything was healed again."

"Hold it!" Canubis intervened in the fight that was gaining momentum by the minute. "Casto beat you up?"

Annoyed, Renaldo glared at his brother. "He had a panic attack. I realized too late, and by that time he'd already broken my nose with his unbelievably thick head."

Canubis started to cackle. "Let me get this straight. A human, your lover, broke your nose? How could such a thing happen? The mighty Angel of Death, the master fighter, knocked out by his own lover! That's too good. Noemi's going to split her sides when she hears this!"

Renaldo regarded his brother with a menacing look. It was obvious to everyone how pissed he was. "Let it go, brother. It was an accident, bad luck. You wouldn't have fared any better if you'd been in my place."

Canubis turned to Casto, who was still standing with his fists clenched. The mood in the room was so overheated he felt like doing some damage control. "I'm sorry, Casto, that I wasn't clear yesterday. I thought you knew that I hadn't asked for punishment."

Slowly the night-dark eyes returned to their usual color. The transformation was so extraordinary that Canubis couldn't help but stare.

Casto inhaled deeply before he bowed his head. "No, I didn't realize that. You were so angry, I thought you'd left the punishment to the Barbarian because you'd have killed me otherwise."

Canubis shook his head. "Casto, you're my brother's heart. Your life is as precious to me as his. You're a part of me, as much as Noemi is a part of Renaldo. We're a very close-knit family, the four of us. I could hurt you just as little as Renaldo can since the spell dropped. It's virtually impossible for us."

Renaldo stepped toward Casto and slung his arm around his neck. "I'm sorry. If I'd known that my brother had forgiven you...."

He didn't finish the sentence. Casto slumped his shoulders. "This is truly embarrassing. It seems I'm unable to understand the finer parts of your barbarian society."

Renaldo blew him a kiss. "It's not as complicated as you think. And wasn't it you who always looked down on me because of my primitive ways? Evolution is not necessarily desirable. Let's forget about the whole thing and consider it a cultural misunderstanding."

When Canubis saw Casto's disgustedly high brows, he couldn't suppress a grin. It was the first time he'd directly witnessed a fight between his brother and his wayward lover. The speed with which they returned from raging fury to casual banter took his breath away.

Absentmindedly Renaldo stroked his heart's cheek. "Why are you really here, brother? Surely not just to ruin my morning, am I right?"

Canubis shook himself for a moment to get his thoughts back on track. "We need to talk about the execution. I want it to be tomorrow, and there are some details we haven't discussed yet."

"Then we'd better get it over with. Casto, can you pour us some wine?"

Casto bowed his head slightly to show his consent.

The demigods relaxed on two opposite lounges while Casto offered them the wine cups with his usual grace.

When he was done, Renaldo thanked him with a nod and sent him on his way. "You can leave now, Casto. Take a bath. That should soothe your mind."

One of Casto's brows went up. "I thank you, Barbarian. Lord Canubis." His voice was full of sarcasm, but he bowed to the Wolf of War, who nodded at him kindly.

"I'll see you later, Casto."

When Casto had vanished into the adjacent room, Canubis chided his brother. "What exactly was that all about? Not that I didn't get some fun out of this, but you really had me worried for a moment."

Renaldo's gaze was dark. "It was merely another exciting day with Casto. You just had the bad luck to get in between. But now I'm really glad I didn't punish him as I'd planned. He would have never forgiven me. Damn, this is all so messed up. Treating you like he did should get him a serious spanking, especially when I think about how much we've been slacking off on discipline recently. But I couldn't do it. I was literally unable to harm him."

Canubis patted his little brother's hand. "I agree with you. And I understand better than you might think. I couldn't hurt Noemi either. I had to wait for her for too long."

Renaldo nodded. "Same for me, and I've literally just gotten my heart. But it's so difficult to find the right balance. There's no way in the world I would want Casto to become a frightened yes-man. But he has to learn to voice his will in a politer way."

"Surely not an easy task given his short temper. I'm still fascinated about how fast he can work himself into a frenzy."

Renaldo took a deep sip from his cup. "Not any faster than I do. The only problem is I often have no clue what he's getting angry about. He's unpredictable."

"I hate to tell you this, dear brother, but your heart isn't easy to read at all. I've always thought I was a good judge of character, but Casto shows me my limits. The only thing I'm definitely sure about is that he loves you. Everything else is guesswork. He's a very mysterious man."

"He is indeed hard to understand. Sometimes I don't know why he's doing things the way he does, and to be frank, I'm glad he's one of us. He's dangerous."

Amber eyes lit up menacingly for a moment. Canubis always knew when his brother was serious, and right at that moment, the Angel of Death was deeply worried. "What do you mean?"

Renaldo returned his brother's gaze with the masklike expression he always wore when he didn't want his feelings to show. "He's a prince who has grown up under horrible circumstances in a city synonymous with power and schemes. He survived because he was stronger than his opponents at a time when he was nothing more than a child. What will become of him when he reaches a position that grants him real power?"

"You mean a position like being the heart of a god?"

"Yes. He already managed to convince Noran to take in Sic again. What will he be capable of once he realizes how much power he commands as soon as he's validated?"

Canubis put down his wineglass with a click. That was indeed a problem. "Is this the reason why you wanted to punish him? Because you think he could develop in an unwanted manner? Except for his short temper, Casto has a good character. He's a man of honor. And don't forget, you're his master and god. In the end, it's your will alone that counts."

Tiredly, Renaldo buried his face in his hands. The past days had been exhausting and he was no longer able to suppress his fears. "I wouldn't be so sure about that, brother. During the past five years, I've broken so many of my own rules where Casto was concerned that I sometimes forget who the master in our relationship is. I'm afraid I'm no longer who I have to be to win this war."

Never before had Canubis seen his brother so vulnerable, so disheartened. Renaldo was voicing the exact same fears Canubis had harbored ever since he met Noemi. Were they about to lose the severity they needed to defeat the Good Mother? The events of the past days seemed to confirm that.

He placed a hand on his brother's shoulder. "I know exactly what you're talking about, Renaldo. I, too, am more lenient toward Noemi than I should be as a God of War. And I'm asking myself, just as you do, whether this is a good thing. But when you listen deep inside you, what does your heart tell you?"

His little brother looked at him with clouded eyes. "It's been some time since I last listened to myself."

"Then let's do it together and find out whether we've strayed from our path."

They joined hands, amber predator eyes lost themselves in the gray depths of Renaldo's gaze, and together they plunged into the stream of memories, so old and deep, its roots were already forgotten in the land of legends.

Their birth and youth in the Green Lands, their coming of age, the loss of their hearts when Ana-Isara had burned in anger about the inhabitants of Ana-Darasa, the feeling of emptiness that followed and overcoming the problems they had adjusting to it, their first tries as leaders of an army, their victories and defeats, their relocation to the Valley, and the long, lonely years as absolute rulers, feared gods.

Then, some eight hundred years ago: Kalad and Aegid, the first Emeris and brothers like they were; the first reluctant softening of the rules that had been set in stone; and the insight that loyalty could also mean resistance.

Some fifty years later came Hulda, Mother Superior of the Sisters of the Night, a powerful Emeris, a strong female who taught them the true meaning of family. Then over the course of the centuries, Bantu and Cornelia, who brought order and consistency; Wolfstan, who changed their attitude toward the mercenaries; and finally Noran, whose acute sense of aesthetics helped them to understand the beauty of the world.

About a hundred years ago, Noemi Amerasu, the snake witch, appeared. Canubis's heart and a personality as unrelenting as Hulda, she showed the brothers the value of life.

Every Emeris had taught the warlords something, made them a little more human, taken a small part of their divinity and replaced it with understanding. The demigods had gotten softer over the centuries, more lenient because they no longer viewed the creatures who were born to do their bidding as faceless slaves. But their fight against the Good Mother was a fight about dominance over Ana-Darasa, and everything the Emeris had given them could be swept away as soon as they regained their true powers.

Because that was what this world deserved, according to the will of the Mothers: two absolute rulers, unrelenting gods of war whose merest whim would change the fate of nations. They realized it was immaterial whether they showed mercy or not. In the end, all of them—hearts, Emeris, and humans too—would bow to the will of their gods.

Renaldo spoke first. "Do you think things would have been different if Mother hadn't taken our hearts?"

Canubis shrugged. He'd pondered that question many times before and come to the conclusion that it didn't make a difference. Losing their hearts hadn't changed their nature, only enhanced it. The lenience they showed toward Noemi and Casto was nothing but an expression of their soft side that was nevertheless still ruled by their true nature.

"I don't think so, brother. But to be honest, I'm glad she did, because otherwise I wouldn't have gotten to know love so intensely and deeply. The feeling of happiness when Noemi smiles at me compensates for every sacrifice we had to make during the centuries. Perhaps we would have never learned to love if Mother hadn't done it. Knowing her, it could have been part of her plan.

"You know as well as I do that we aren't like Ana-Isara and Ana-Aruna at all. Those two are creators, while we bring death and destruction."

Renaldo sighed. Of course he knew. The Holy Mothers had created themselves, while he and his brother carried the essence of Ana-Darasa inside them and were also defined by it. "You're right. We're different. And I love Casto so much, it's driving me crazy. Knowing he's mine alone is more than I can describe with mere words."

Smiling, Canubis placed a hand on Renaldo's shoulder. Seeing his brother so happy almost made him forget the gloomy reason for their discussion.

But only almost.

"So we're in agreement. We've become softer but haven't lost our bite. Tomorrow at the execution, everybody will see that."

So saying, Canubis, the Wolf of War, got up and turned to leave. "You'd better take care of your heart. Casto gave the impression he needs some love." Canubis's eyes lit up in plain hunger. "I'm going to get my wife."

Renaldo laughed and turned toward the bath. He, too, needed some loving attention from his mate.

Casto was in the water. He had made himself comfortable on one of the stone lounges. His eyes were closed, and his hair swam like a carpet of exotic seaweed around his head, moving slightly in the swell caused by his breathing.

"May I accompany you?"

The young man opened his eyes lazily, the blue so clear it almost hurt. A challenging smile darted over his lips. "But of course, Barbarian."

"For someone who so narrowly escaped serious punishment, you're remarkably saucy."

The smile deepened on the full, sensuous lips. Casto was definitely on his way back to his old self. "Your advice concerning the bath was very helpful. I'm already feeling a lot better."

"Obviously well enough to be sarcastic."

"I'm always like this. I thought you knew that by now." Casto's voice was dreamy. "It's like a reflex. I'm not really accountable for it."

"Then you should learn to control your reflexes. Among other things, my brother and I have discussed the fact that we're too lenient toward our underlings."

Casto got up abruptly. "I wouldn't care to label what happened yesterday as lenient."

Now it was Renaldo who flashed a challenging smile. "To tell you the truth, it was bordering on merciful. I can recall times when we left slaves to the wolves with their bellies slit open for far less."

"Are you threatening me, Barbarian?"

Now Casto stood. The water cascading down his naked body seemed to caress him, something Renaldo was planning to do himself. He smiled disarmingly. Casto's change of tone hadn't escaped him. "No, my fierce one, I don't threaten you, since I already know how futile that is. But in the not too distant future, we're going to have a discussion about appropriate behavior, you and me."

Suspicion filled the blue gaze. "Why not now?"

Renaldo darted his tongue hungrily across his lips. "Because right now I have different plans."

The impact of those words on Casto was overwhelming. A soft red tinged his cheeks, his breath sped up, and his eyes turned cloudy—something that told Renaldo better than words about the state his capricious heart was in, and his cock came alive under Casto's burning gaze.

Renaldo quickly got rid of his clothes, his own hunger on the verge of animalistic. He looked at Casto. He could count on one hand the few occasions in which they'd had gentle, loving sex. Being with Casto always woke the beast in him, something that didn't seem to faze the stubborn youth at all, but today Renaldo was feeling merciful and willing to give his lover a choice. "I'd love to take you hard and brutal. But considering all the things that have happened recently, I'm willing to spare you."

Casto laughed mockingly. "And why would you do that? It's not as if you're able to restrain yourself. But if you need a reason, I can give you one."

Renaldo's eyes narrowed. "What was that?"

"You understood me well, Barbarian. I was bold and irreverent."

With a growl, Renaldo seized his lover and pulled him close. "I thought as much. But I'll give you the chance to make up for it. Submit, and I'll show you mercy."

"I should submit to you? Why on Ana-Darasa would I do such a thing?"

Renaldo leaned forward and kissed Casto, invading the young man's mouth brutally, claiming him completely.

Groaning, Casto snuggled up to him and glided his hands up and down Renaldo's back, while his nails left burning traces on the skin. Renaldo shoved him against the edge of the pool, wove his right hand into Casto's wet hair and then bent his head backward to expose Casto's throat. With his other hand he stroked Casto's cock and then started to pump while his lips and teeth were busy at Casto's neck.

A whimper escaped from Casto's throat, and he bucked his hips into his lover's hand while Renaldo calmly led him to orgasm. Casto came with a shudder, but Renaldo did not stop stimulating him, knowing full well where Casto's weak points were. Renaldo grazed Casto's artery, and in response Casto started to shiver.

Soon, Casto started to plead. "Please, Master, I'm begging you. Take me. I can't endure this pain any longer."

Renaldo smiled contently at his lover's neck. As soon as Casto stooped to calling him master, he had won.

"Are you going to submit to me?"

"Yes. Everything, I'll do everything you ask. What do you want me to do?"

Renaldo let go of him. He suddenly felt the inclination to draw out the sweet agony. "Get out of the water." Shivering, Casto obeyed. Renaldo followed him. "Take the oil and apply it. Everywhere."

Trembling, Casto did as instructed. The oil glistened between his fingers, was warmed by his body heat, and left a silken layer on his skin that felt like a lover's caress. His master watched every move with the attention of a cat that had discovered a mouse. The hunger in Renaldo's gaze, the knowledge that he was stoking this hunger with his every movement, forced Casto to the edge of sanity. The familiar lust never grew boring; it inflamed them deeper the more they gave in to it. Now, too, Casto couldn't wait to submit to the urge. But before he could start begging once again, his master gave him new orders as if he knew exactly how Casto was feeling.

"Now kneel in front of me. Open your mouth."

When Casto's soft lips closed around his cock, Renaldo had to gather all his self-restraint not to release immediately. Groaning, he threw his head back. "That's a good boy. Serve me."

Those words, which only half a year ago would have caused Casto to use his teeth instead of his lips, now only heightened his lust. Casto glided his tongue hungrily over Renaldo's shaft; he sucked at the tip and tried to take in as much as possible. Briefly, he remembered the times when he had thought it beyond his dignity to service Renaldo in such a manner. That was a thousand years ago. Now he simply enjoyed the knowledge of how much power his lips and tongue wielded over the Angel of Death, how much lust he was able to give. Lust his lover paid back a hundredfold.

With a guttural sound that expressed regret, Renaldo withdrew from his mouth.

"Good. You can stop. Get up, we're going to the bedroom."

With his knees trembling in anticipation, Casto walked in front of his oh so skilled lover to their bed. He could feel Renaldo's presence and his muscles tensed in happy excitement.

"Kneel down again, with your upper body on the bed, facedown."

Purring contentedly, Renaldo watched Casto obey once again. Seeing him so obedient, so compliant, woke feelings inside him that were so animalistic they almost terrified him. Renaldo had never felt like this before, hadn't even believed an emotion could be so intense that he thought it would burst him from within. He stepped behind fate's perfect gift, caressed the exposed buttocks gently, and decided to take a risk. He slapped Casto. It was only a light touch, barely hard enough to bring some color to the skin. It was his way of asking for permission to go further. All Casto had to do was tell him to stop and he would revert to other means of bringing them both pleasure, but deep in his heart, this was what he really wanted. When Casto neither stiffened nor invited him to go on, he slapped him again, this time a bit harder. A choked whimper was his reward. Casto was obviously willing to give this aspect of their sex life a second try. Renaldo would do everything to make the experience perfect for his lover, because that was the best part, when they spiced up their lust with some pain and aroused each other even more. He was careful, though, not to be too brutal. He didn't want to scare Casto away. "What does it feel like, slave? Does it hurt?"

"Yes, Master."

"What, yes?"

"Yes, it hurts. You have a heavy hand."

"Do you deserve it?"

One more blow before Casto answered. "Yes, Master. I deserve it."

"Why would that be?"

"Because it's your will."

That surprisingly obsequious answer drove Renaldo past the limits of his patience. Three blows, quicker and harder than the ones before, one short break in which he playfully bit his prey's nape, and then four more blows.

Casto whimpered. "Please, Master, I'm begging you. Take me. Please!"

Abruptly, Renaldo entered Casto's ass with his fingers; Casto was still slick from the oil he had applied earlier. "Is it this you want?"

"Yes, oh, yes. Please, don't stop."

"Who do you belong to?"

Casto groaned in protest. His master's fingers moved relentlessly inside him and broke any resistance he might still have felt. Defeated by the skillful ministrations, he gave in. "I belong to you, Master. I'm yours alone."

Renaldo felt shivers of righteous ownership racing along his spine. That was how things were meant to be. "That's right. You're mine—mine and nobody else's. Never forget that, slave. Do you understand?"

A helpless sob was the answer. Casto was so caught up in their game, so consumed by passion, that he didn't register the severity of what Renaldo had just said. All he could do was gasp his consent. "Yes, Master. Never. Please, release me."

With a growl, Renaldo grabbed Casto's hips and entered him fast and deep. From Casto's lips flowed a stream of approval, his back muscles tensed. Renaldo lost himself completely in the rush of owning his lover. He took him hard and long until Casto collapsed from exhaustion beneath him.

Then he picked up the trembling, sweating human bundle who had shown him such ecstasy as he had never known before, and placed him on the furs. He slung his muscular arms around the young man and kissed his nape. "You see what happens when you're irreverent? I have to discipline you."

With a sigh, Casto leaned into his lover. "I'd love to be able to promise more obedience toward you in the future, but this was simply too good. I thank you, Barbarian."

Gently, Renaldo kissed his heart on the mouth. Now that his first, greatest desire was sated, he could take the time to fondle him. "It is me who has to thank you. I know how hard it must be for you to trust me again. What you just did—it humbles me." Happy about the way things had turned out, Renaldo pulled Casto closer. "Considering that you're normally so defiant, your obedience in bed is remarkable."

"That's only because of you, Barbarian. Even when I try to fight it, you always manage to get me to the point where all I can think of is belonging to you. In these moments, you could ask anything from me. My whole being is concentrated on feeling you, being yours."

Renaldo felt a strange discomfort. Now that he was thinking with a clear head again, Casto's statements were no longer blurred and he was able to see the deeper meaning behind them. He slung his arms tightly around Casto, unsure whether he should voice his fears.

But Casto wasn't stupid. It was better to have the matter out in the open. "I only hope you won't regret this one day."

Oblivious, Casto snuggled even closer. "Why should I? You make me feel good. Really, really good."

"I know, but that won't always be the case, my sweet one."

Casto tensed in his arms. Casto might not possess Renaldo's divine insight, but he was intuitive enough to realize when something was amiss. "What do you mean?"

"Casto, I was born a god. And my brother and I, we'll become gods again. Once you're confirmed as my heart, we only have to await the arrival of the last Emeris before we enslave this world. Our powers will grow. We'll lose the humanity we've gained during the time after Mother took our hearts. When that happens, we'll return to being what we were born as, and your will is going to be insignificant then. You'll be mine, doing my bidding in everything you say and do. Chances are that even your thoughts will be mine. That's what it means to be with a god."

"I know."

Casto had only whispered those two words, but they couldn't have shocked Renaldo more if he had screamed them into his face. "You know?"

Casto pried himself from Renaldo's grasp, straightened up, and looked calmly at him. "I've known ever since you ordered me in my dream to come back home. Why should I have done that, knowing what kind of punishment was waiting for me? But I acquiesced to your will because I had no other choice."

"Oh, Casto, my poor love! You endured the fear of punishment, the terror of losing me, and the knowledge that your freedom turns to dust in my hands? And still you came back to me?"

Casto smiled crookedly. "Of course. Even though I don't always like it, you're my life, my home. I can't resist you."

Renaldo pulled him close and kissed him hungrily. "But still you defy me."

"Whenever I get the chance. It gives me the feeling of having at least some control over my life."

Renaldo touched the prince's left ear with his lips. "I love it when you defy me. I like your strong character, your stubbornness. If you weren't as truculent and strong as you are, you'd never be able to bear me."

"You're not the first to tell me that. You're obviously not very successful when it comes to lasting relationships."

"My reputation is disastrous. Ask Hulda if you're interested."

Casto's smile vanished. "Did you ever love somebody? I know you had countless partners for sex, but in all that time, there must have been someone who meant more to you than just the satiation of your lust. I want to believe that you aren't such a beast."

Renaldo was too busy thinking to react to the challenge of the last words. "Once there was a young woman. It's been so long I've forgotten her name. She was intelligent and funny, and like you, she wasn't afraid of me. I liked her because she was able to pass the time for me not only in bed. But she left me after only two months. She knew she had to go, because otherwise I would have destroyed her with my hunger. That was the longest relationship I ever had that wasn't purely sexual." He traced Casto's face with his fingertips. "I don't like to admit it, but I really was a beast. I had a man or woman with me almost every night, sometimes more than one. It was an unsteady, poisonous time. Nobody managed to catch my interest for more than a few days. They were all vessels for my frustration and despair. I felt empty, shallow. The continuous sexual joinings led me to believe in a closeness I couldn't hope to know. My looks, the fire inside me—all that had isolated me. Although I was never literally alone, I tasted bitter loneliness.

"Then you came. You weren't afraid. You stood up to me openly, and my looks didn't interest you at all. That bothered me, but I also found it impressive. Our first kiss was almost more than I was able to bear. Never before had I felt so intensely, had I been so alive. And you weren't repulsed by me, neither by my anger, nor by my jealousy, nor my love."

Casto laughed drily. "That's not necessarily a compliment. Not knowing when to give up is one of my weak points."

"And I'm glad about it. I couldn't stand it if you left me. Or if you were afraid of me."

Mischief lit up Casto's features. "How could I ever leave you, Barbarian? Since you're giving me such nice orgasms on a regular basis."

Growling, Renaldo pressed his lover into the furs. His right hand traveled boldly over the outstretched body; his left hand prevented Casto from getting up. "It seems I haven't exercised you enough. If you can be cheeky again, you aren't really exhausted."

"Please, Barbarian, I was only joking. I'm really done."

"You should have thought about that before you challenged me. Now it's too late. I'll only stop when you've truly run out of steam and can't cheek me anymore."

Casto tried weakly to wriggle free of his master's grip, but when Renaldo held him all the harder, he gave up.

HEYDAY

1. MERCY

THE DAY of his execution sent some lost sunrays into his cell that danced across the stone floor as if they didn't know that today his life would come to an end. With a trace of sadness, Sic watched the light spinning, knowing it was the last time he would see true beauty. But he was also glad, because the day also meant the end of the nerve-racking wait.

Sic had no illusions that his execution would be anything but painful. He knew the Angel of Death had invested a great amount of time in the planning of the due punishment of those who had almost killed his heart.

He was just glad that he'd told the truth in the end. At least he could meet his death with his head held high. Although his master had a different opinion on the matter and had told him clearly what he thought of him, Sic had managed to preserve a last scrap of dignity for himself. In light of the misery of his entire existence, it was enough.

The heavy iron door to his cell opened, and a guard entered to unchain him. He wanted to drag Sic, but the young smith shook his head.

"Please, I won't try to run away. But I'd like to walk on my own."

For a moment Sic thought the guard hadn't heard him, but then the man gave an almost imperceptible nod and stepped back. Sic passed him unsteadily—he had been chained to the wall for almost a week and had problems making his feet obey him.

In the dimly lit passage, the other traitors were already waiting, including Damon and Assani, all bound with iron chains. Sic followed the gloomy procession as it slowly made its way out of the dungeons.

Outside, he blinked rapidly under the bright morning sun, whose rays were reflected by the snow and made the Valley look as if it was covered in diamonds. The stinging cold attacked him like a hungry animal, but Sic was glad about that, since it meant that he was… still… alive.

The path to the place of execution wasn't long. Everybody in the Valley had gathered around an oval with a canopy erected at the south side under which the divine brothers and their Emeris sat on throne-like chairs. Sic recognized Casto; the young man was standing behind the Angel of Death's chair. Noran was there as well, sitting between Hulda and Bantu. His gaze went through his former apprentice as if he didn't exist. Sic wasn't surprised that it hurt him more than any torture he'd endured so far.

Knowing he had disappointed his master, the most important person in his life, was like a knife constantly twisting inside him, a pain reaching deeper than anything that could be done to his body.

In the middle of the oval, eight crosses had been erected. Each of the convicts, with exception of Assani, was now bound with their arms stretched wide to one of the wooden poles. Nobody had thought it necessary to tell the convicts the details of their punishment, except that their end would be excruciating. Sic didn't know what was awaiting them.

Assani was led right in front of the brothers. Two overseers held the struggling female with unrelenting hands. When all the traitors were in position, Lord Renaldo raised his hand. Immediately everybody fell silent.

The Angel of Death's voice echoed coldly through the air, a sound that reminded Sic somehow of the darkness of the grave.

"The scum you see bound here have dared to raise their filthy hands against me and my brother. They've tried to harm my precious heart, and they've worshipped the false goddess here in the Valley. There is no punishment imaginable to compensate for this kind of crime, but be assured, the suffering of those who challenge us doesn't end with death. Ana-Isara, our beloved mother, will speak her verdict on the other side, once the traitors have left this world."

For a moment his gaze wandered aimlessly around the crowd. The inhumanly beautiful face had frozen to a mask that made it impossible to guess the emotions behind it. When Renaldo spoke on, his tone sent shivers down the spines of everybody present. He picked Assani first because she and Damon were the leaders.

"Assani, because you dared to lie to your god and wrongly accuse his heart, you don't deserve an easy death. The pain and suffering your actions have brought shall be reflected in the way you die."

The Angel of Death then nodded toward the two men who had been waiting at the edge of the oval. Shuddering, Sic watched as they threw Assani to the ground. One of them held her down while the other grabbed her left foot around the ankle and held it up. An overseer stepped forward. He had a whip in his hands. Almost gently, he touched the sole of Assani's foot with the leather before he swung his arm back and let the whip crack. Assani screamed like a demon from the other realm when blow after blow rained down on her exposed foot. After twenty strokes, the men changed to her right foot and repeated the action. Renaldo and Canubis observed with expressionless faces how the slave was tortured. Casto, who was still standing behind Renaldo's chair, was white as linen, but his face didn't betray any of the emotions raging inside him.

Noemi Amerasu, who was standing right behind her husband, stared intently at Lord Canubis's back, unable to bear the brutality unfolding in front of her eyes.

The other Emeris showed no sign of emotion. If anything, the faces of Kalad and Aegid displayed their boredom.

The sun had already risen quite a bit when Assani's screams grew hoarser and finally died down to a whimper. The men let her go but didn't allow her to get up. The woman was panting and her blood dripped in a steady stream into the snow. One of the overseers stepped behind her, yanked her upper torso back brutally, and slit open her abdomen in one swift movement.

The once proud, merciless woman roared in pain, the new source of agony successfully bringing back her voice. The man who had hurt her now stepped back and let her bleeding, twitching body fall into the snow, where she curled up into a tight ball. The diamond glittering was instantly covered by a thick stream of red.

A growl resounded behind Sic when the wolves entered the oval. The powerful predators sauntered toward Assani, who lay dying on the cold ground. The alpha wolf licked the bloody snow, and then the glowing, predatory eyes turned to the slave. With a forceful motion, the wolf turned its prey onto her back and with its paws prevented the hysterically screeching woman from getting free.

The female alpha approached. Her silky gray fur shone in the sun like polished silver. Her muzzle descended to the open wound, pushed inside the abdomen of her prey, and emerged bloody and with entrails dangling left and right from her jaw.

Assani's screams were no longer human: they sounded like the wailing of a vengeful spirit. The remaining pack members, which had waited respectfully at a distance, joined the alpha couple and the feast started. It didn't take the wolves long to strip Assani's corpse of all its flesh. After only a short time, all that was left of the slave were the bloody bones with which the pups began to play.

Again Lord Renaldo made a gesture, and Sic felt movement at his back. Out of the corner of his eye, he saw several overseers stepping forward with glass whips in their hands. Even before his ears registered the angry buzz of the especially brutal instrument of torture, the first wave of pain hit his body. The man who was whipping him knew what he was doing. He thrashed him with all his strength, methodically, from top to bottom to cause maximum damage. Sic had the feeling that his muscles had peeled from his bones, blood streamed down his legs into the snow, and he soon stood in a puddle of the warm fluid. He screamed, unable to cope with the pain in any other way, but he didn't beg, unlike the other convicts.

At first, because he knew how useless it was, and secondly, because he deserved it. He had not only betrayed his god and his god's heart, even worse, he had disappointed his master. He deserved whatever the Angel of Death had in store for him.

After an eternity imprisoned in worlds of agony, the beating stopped. The overseers stepped back from their victims and two of them approached Damon. The once charismatic and cruel man was reduced to a whimpering, bleeding bundle of pain who was unchained and led to a cross lying on the ground. With his arms and legs spread wide, the priest of the Good Mother was bound tightly. One overseer wielded a knife that glinted cruelly in the sunlight. A guttural scream full of unspeakable anguish echoed through the oval while between Damon's legs, his penis and testes slithered to the ground in a heap of gory tissue. A hissing sound, closely followed by another howl and the stench of burned flesh marked the cauterization of the wound.

Sic saw and heard several onlookers throw up violently, but the gods' expressions remained unreadable.

Now the overseers lifted the cross up and positioned it on four posts so that Damon's ravaged body was presented to the sun.

When the first ravens started to circle in the sky, Sic knew that the priest's suffering had only just begun.

The other overseers stepped toward their respective victims again, all wielding knives like the one that had just castrated Damon. Sic fought desperately against the panic rising inside him, determined to keep as much of his dignity as possible when faced with such a humiliating way to die. That, at least, he owed to himself.

But while the other convicts suffered the same fate as their leader, except that their bodies were left to the wolves, not the ravens, Sic felt his torturer slicing the trammels fastening him to the pole. Whimpering, he dropped into the gory mud with blood dripping from his wrists where he had been bound so tightly. Strong hands seized him and dragged him across the oval to the place where the Emeris sat.

The overseer tossed Sic into the snow in front of Renaldo, then left. With an effort, Sic managed to get to his knees, but he kept his gaze down. He was terribly afraid of what the Angel of Death had in store for him. Out of the corner of his eye he saw Casto observing him with his amazing blue eyes as if Sic were some rare species of insect.

An all-too-familiar hand fell heavily on his shoulder. His master's voice sounded as if he had just found something unpleasant under the soles of his feet. "I thank you, Lord Renaldo. It's very courteous of you to give this slave back to me."

Lord Renaldo's perfect features didn't show the slightest emotion. "It's my pleasure to do my brother-in-arms a favor." The Angel of Death cast a quick glance at Casto. "I only hope we won't regret this one day."

Noran, too, addressed the young man next to Renaldo when he answered. "I hope that, too, my lord. Very much so." He pulled his slave up roughly. "You, come with me."

Noran's voice was so ominous that Sic involuntarily cringed. He almost feared his master's unbridled fury more than the cold, controlled anger of the Angel of Death. With long strides that had no consideration for Sic's hurt state, Noran hurried toward the smithy.

He tossed Sic to the ground in front of one of the forges. His voice was ice-cold and so hollow as if it were coming from a grave.

"Don't you dare make the mistake of thinking for even one moment that I've forgiven you. Against my better judgment, I grace you with the possibility to earn yourself a second chance, although I doubt you're worth such an honor. For the time being, I don't want to see your face too often. That's why you're going to spend your mornings in the compost heaps, and in the afternoons you belong to Casto. You're going to obey him as if he were your master, and he can punish you whenever and however he sees fit. Every morning and every evening you're going to be beaten with the strap until further notice. Five blows, every time.

"You'll sleep here, chained to the anvil like the dog that you are. In my presence you only talk when I explicitly ask you to. Should you feel the inclination to address me, for whatever reason, you kneel down with your forehead on the ground. Only if I give my consent are you then allowed to speak.

"And Sic, if you so much as touch a smith's tool, you'll keep Damon and the ravens company. I've already sent for a healer who'll deal with your wounds. After that, you can rest for a while. Tomorrow your punishment will continue."

Noran left the smithy without sparing his miserable slave another glance.

Only when his master's footsteps had died away did Sic allow himself to cry with relief.

THE NEXT morning Sic was woken by a brutal kick in the ribs. Noran was looming over him with a cold expression and a strap in his hands.

Sic hurried to his knees, looking down demurely.

"Get up, you worthless piece of shit." His master accentuated his order with another kick.

Sic hurried to obey, well aware that the other smiths were watching him with malicious gratification and couldn't wait to witness his punishment. But he was too occupied with the pain exploding in his body with each movement to pay the additional humiliation too much attention. Lady Noemi had healed him just enough so he could work.

"Strip and lean across the anvil. Brace yourself."

Obediently, the young man did as he was told.

"You count, aloud. Five blows. If you lose count, I'll start anew."

There was a hint of cruelty in the master smith's voice, a cruelty that terrified Sic far more than Noran's usual grumpiness. He'd always known that Lord Noran wasn't a kind man, but despite his strictness and gruffness, he'd never been unjust. Now he seemed eager to punish

Sic as brutally as possible. When Sic thought about how much he had disappointed him, he could even understand him.

When the first blow came, Sic concentrated on counting the blows correctly—which he managed to do, very much to his own surprise and Noran's dismay. After his master discarded the strap, he allowed him to get up. A dark bundle fell to Sic's feet.

"Wear this when working in the pits. Normal clothing is too good for that. The overseers there will give you something to wear for the stables."

With trembling hands, Sic opened the bundle and put on the abrasive, dirty, brown linen trousers, a similar work coat, and rough, worn leather boots. The cloth rubbed his wounds uncomfortably; the shoes were too small and compressed his feet. After he was done dressing, Sic knelt down in front of Noran, his forehead on the ground.

His master watched him ungraciously. "What do you want, slave?"

Sic inhaled deeply. He knew how unreasonable and dangerous it was to talk to Noran when he was in such a dark, unforgiving mood, but he wanted to thank him, although he knew his gratitude wouldn't be welcome. "I want to thank you, Master, because you let me live. You're very generous."

A derisive snort was the answer. "Don't get any ideas. You're only here and not raven's fodder because Casto demanded repayment of a debt. If he hadn't asked for your life, you'd be dead by now."

Sic swallowed hard. So it wasn't his master who valued his life even a little bit, but the young man he'd almost killed. He seriously wondered how foolish he could be.

How could he have ever thought that he meant more to his master than the mostly worthless—as Noran never tired of emphasizing—work force he provided. His heart sank.

The man Sic had built his world on would rather see him dead for what he had done than grant him a second chance.

Defeated by that insight, he waited for further instructions and then went on his way to the pits.

THE PITS held the secret of the immense, never-ending fertility of the Valley that bestowed regular, rich harvests to its people. It wasn't a very pleasant secret, because there the waste of the inhabitants, the dung from the stables, and every other kind of organic muck was collected, mixed in an elaborate way, and turned, under constant care, into the precious black soil that made the Valley's crops grow like crazy. It was hard, stinking work to break up the rotting mixture, transport it from one pit to the next as it developed, and cart the mature soil to the fields. During summer the smell was almost intolerable, but it was easier to work the soil. In winter the smell wasn't so bad, but the frozen ground presented a different challenge.

Sic hacked at the stone-hard earth with a spade. With every movement, his pitiful coat chafed the wounds that had reopened at his jerky motions and were sending trickles of blood down his back. The cloth of his coat was so old and worn, it absorbed the fluid only slowly, which caused Sic additional pain when his sweat came in touch with his torn skin. But he didn't dare to stop for a moment; he knew all too well that the overseers had every right to punish him should they deem it necessary. They all knew he was a traitor: the iron collar Noran had put on his neck a couple of days ago screamed his disgrace to the world.

Grimly he worked to wrest obedience from the obstinate ground, strangely glad about the monotonous task that kept him from thinking too much about the encounter waiting for him that afternoon.

Sic was afraid to meet Casto, not because he feared the punishment he was sure to suffer at his hand, but because he didn't know how he could endure looking him in the eyes after his betrayal.

Sooner than he liked, the sun reached its zenith and an overseer led him to a trough of cold water. He was given a piece of hard soap and a bundle of fresh clothes. He washed in the freezing cold, grateful that it stopped the bleeding. After he finished, he went to the stables.

On his way Sic passed the place of execution, which he would have preferred to leave behind in a hurry, but a soft, pained whimper stopped him dead.

All that was left of the traitors who had been bound to the crosses were bones in the muddied, bloody snow. The wolves had obviously had a great feast. But Damon on his elevated poles was apparently still alive. The ravens had taken his eyes, and in some places his bones shone through, but the cold had slowed his bleeding. Against all odds, there was still a spark of life.

Shuddering, Sic wanted to go on his way, but a vitriolic voice stopped him in his tracks.

"Look closely, traitor, because this should have been your fate as well."

With his head bowed low, Sic knelt in front of the Angel of Death. The powerful warrior approached him. Without warning, he kicked him so hard that Sic fell backward into the snow. Then the Angel of Death placed his boot on Sic's throat.

"If it had been up to me, you'd be serving the ravens as a feast right now. I'm warning you, should you cause Casto the slightest trouble, you will answer to me. And believe me, when I'm done with you, you'll wish to change places with that damn priest. Did you hear me?"

Sic nodded in silent terror. He didn't want to imagine what would happen should he challenge the Angel of Death's wrath again.

The demigod released him, turned around, and left. Trembling, with agonizing pain in his back where he was kicked, Sic staggered toward the stables.

Casto seemed to have waited for him. He was just giving orders to a stable boy and motioned his former friend to come closer.

Sic obeyed with a downcast look. In front of Casto, he knelt. "Master."

Casto watched him coldly, but the expected outburst of anger didn't come. Instead, he talked to Sic as if he was nothing more than a worker who served in the stables.

"There's always a lot of work around here. Starting today, you'll clean the tack. That should keep you occupied for the next few days."

Casto turned to leave, but Sic stopped him. "Please, Master, am I allowed to talk?"

"If you insist."

Sic looked up, directly into those beautiful blue eyes that had laughed with him so often in the past but were now cold and distant. His stomach churned guiltily. "I wanted to thank you, Master, for speaking on my behalf. I know an apology from me is not worth much, but I still want to tell you how sorry I am."

Casto's expression was frozen—not his usual arrogance that kept others at bay, but a protective mask that barely hid the pain Sic had caused him. "You're right, your apology is worthless. I've spoken to Lord Noran on your behalf because I think you deserve a second chance, but it doesn't mean I care for you. Because of you, I almost died. You betrayed me, and I don't think I'll ever be able to forgive you for that. I want you to do your work diligently and to not give me a reason to beat you, but should your behavior call for it, I won't hesitate."

"Yes, Master."

"Then get to work."

Defeated, Sic got up to obey Casto's commands. The chill in his former friend's eyes reminded him that death was not necessarily the worst punishment.

2. PROPOSAL

Casto's gaze followed Sic when he went to do his bidding. The smith's apology had almost softened him, but just in time he remembered what the young man, who he had once thought his friend, had done. Still, he felt an overwhelming emptiness, as if he'd just rejected something unbelievably precious.

He didn't doubt Sic had been sincere about his apology, and he didn't deny the necessity of his actions. But Sic had betrayed and almost killed him. Casto couldn't, wouldn't, simply ignore the hideous deed, although it had been partly his own stupidity that had made the betrayal so unbearably painful. If Casto had trusted the lessons learned in the course of his life, he would never have let Sic get close enough to him to cause such pain.

But he had done it, and now he was paying the price for his naiveté.

Whenever Casto thought about his time at the mines, he felt cold fear claiming him. It wasn't death that terrified him, but the insight of how much he depended on Renaldo, how his entire being was tied to him. He had told Renaldo that he knew about his fate as a heart. What he had kept secret was the panic he'd felt when he imagined what it would be like to lose himself in Renaldo.

With his betrayal, Sic had forced Casto to face this fear straight on, and Casto didn't like what he saw.

Slightly irritated, he pried his thoughts from the gloomy topic to deal with more pressing matters in the stables.

When evening came, he bid Lysistratos good night, secured the doors of the stalls, and returned to Renaldo's chambers.

Renaldo was already waiting for him, his eyes glinting hungrily, something that immediately fired Casto up since he knew very well what that gaze meant. His breath started to accelerate, a soft crimson colored his features, his hips canted in silent invitation.

A lazy smile appeared on his lover's face. "Good evening, my own." Renaldo purred the words, a sound like velvet and silk that overwhelmed Casto's senses.

"A good evening to you as well, Barbarian." His voice was breathless, and he was glad to be able to say the words correctly.

The grin deepened. "We'll see how nice this evening is going to get."

At that innuendo, Casto's blood rushed to his loins. Renaldo got up from his lounge. With the confident grace of a cat that knew its prey couldn't escape, he sauntered toward his lover.

Renaldo took Casto's face in his hands and kissed him passionately. When he retreated a step, he watched with satisfaction as Casto stumbled and had problems regaining his balance. His voice got even gentler, more cajoling. "Undress, my own. Slowly."

Unable to withstand Renaldo's wheedling, Casto took off his clothes, turned whenever the Barbarian asked it of him, offering free sight of his body, of even the most intimate parts of his anatomy. Finally he stood naked, deeply aroused, willing to do anything Renaldo might ask of him. The fire between them had taken control, burned away every sensible thought, and choked off the last bit of resistance Casto might have harbored.

Renaldo held up a black silk cloth. "Do you trust me?"

It wasn't a question but a challenge. Casto gulped. If he was honest, the reply to that question was no, and if Renaldo had asked only a few moments earlier, the answer wouldn't have been sure, but now Casto had just one choice that his body demanded. "Yes, my lord. I trust you."

With a satisfied smile, Renaldo stepped behind him. The silken cloth descended coolly over Casto's eyes and excluded the world.

"Place your arms behind your back."

Unable to resist, Casto obeyed. Another soft cloth was wreathed around his wrists, binding him, making him helpless. Involuntarily, Casto tensed and took a step forward, a first attempt at escape from whatever the Barbarian had planned for him.

Renaldo held on to him, his lips grazing Casto's nape lovingly. "It's fine. That's just cotton. You can rip the cloth at any time. But I want you to submit to me, to trust me. I need to prove to you that I am worth this sacrifice. I promise you won't regret it."

Trembling, Casto forced his muscles to slacken, although every fiber in his body screamed defiance, then relaxed further. Instinctively he realized how important this was for Renaldo. They both were still struggling to find common ground, and Casto knew how much Renaldo beat himself up for the things he'd done. Renaldo's self-loathing helped Casto a lot. As twisted as it sounded, the emotional pain Renaldo inflicted on himself calmed Casto's anger more than any apology. With each passing day, he felt himself regaining his trust in the Barbarian. He would never forgive him, that was not in his nature, but they could return to their old ways. For that, Casto was willing to take another risk.

"Very good, my love. Now come, I wish to bathe you."

Casto let Renaldo lead him to the bath. The warm water caressed him like a soft coat, and his master's hands seemed to be everywhere at the same time, stroking, soothing, demanding. He felt shampoo massaged into his scalp, and the touch made him feel cherished. Renaldo's hands were beyond skilled and rubbed the last shred of resistance from Casto's body.

With a pitcher that he filled time and again with fresh water, Renaldo washed the foam from Casto's hair, then started soaping him all over.

Casto was already so excited by then that he reacted to the smallest touch. He submitted to his master's will with soft groans and gave in to the lust Renaldo so artfully stoked.

Renaldo guided Casto, quivering, to the bedroom. There he placed him on his belly and stuffed several pillows under his hips until Casto's backside was at a position agreeable to him. Casto's skin gleamed wetly in the candlelight, his flawless body an invitation Renaldo planned to use. He poured oil generously onto Casto's back and started massaging it into the skin. The muscles he touched gave in to the pressure with a shudder, relaxed obediently. Soon, Casto was begging to be taken. He arched his back so his cheeks opened alluringly; he whimpered and pleaded until it took all of Renaldo's self-control to hold back.

Renaldo bent forward and whispered into Casto's ear. "I don't want this to be about sex, Casto. I want this to be about us. About the things I can do for you. About how I should treat you. I want to show you how much you mean to me. Do I have your permission?"

Not knowing what Renaldo had in mind, all Casto could do was nod. Renaldo sighed with relief. Then he undid the cloth around Casto's wrists. "I want you to feel me, just like I feel you. I want to explore who we are without sex. I want you, Casto."

Shuddering, Casto reached for Renaldo, the man's body heat guiding the way. Casto was still blindfolded, but the lack of sight only enhanced his other senses. When his fingers touched Renaldo's hot skin, Casto was overwhelmed. He had to fight the passion that was threatening to erupt from his body. As Renaldo had said, this was different, and Casto didn't want to ruin it. Instead he concentrated on the feel of Renaldo's skin, on how smooth it felt, on the softness of the man's body hair. After a few minutes of exploring, Casto felt his lust turning into something else. He was still turned on, but now he also wanted to have more of Renaldo. The satisfaction of his baser needs was no longer at the forefront of his mind. That was now filled with the presence of his lover. As if to reassure him, Renaldo mimicked Casto's movements, touched the same places the prince did. It was like a sensual dance, and Casto was the one leading it.

They kept on exploring each other, growing more confident as they went along, reveling in the intimacy they shared. As hot as the sex was, Casto thought the touching-and-feeling game they were now playing was at least as good. He felt a closeness to the Barbarian he hadn't thought possible. Renaldo's touch had him melting, and before he knew it, Casto was lost in the sensations, unable to stop himself from running his hands over the Barbarian's body and drowning in the sensual onslaught. He lost all sense of time while Renaldo kept on pouring his love into him. Casto didn't even realize when he finally fell asleep and Renaldo removed the blindfold.

"WHY DID you do that?" Casto was still tired. He had napped for about an hour, and when he woke, Renaldo lay curled around him, his hands still moving lazily over his skin as he breathed into Casto's neck.

"Didn't you like it?"

Casto sighed. There was tension in the Barbarian's voice, and he didn't want to argue. "It was very nice. Different and—intense. I'm not sure what to think."

Renaldo propped himself up and stared directly into Casto's eyes. He was just contrite enough to put Casto on edge.

"Like I said, it was about us. I wanted to show you how much more we can be. How much more we already are."

"And?"

"And I may have tried to propitiate you."

"Why on Ana-Darasa do you feel the need to do that?"

His rather gruff tone made it obvious how quickly Casto's spirits were reviving. Obviously he had decided not to be too happy about his treatment.

"I thought you would have a harder time throwing a hissy fit when I relaxed you completely. And I want you to think calmly about the offer I'm going to make you."

Curiosity got the better of the rising anger. "Tell me."

Renaldo's face turned serious. "You're my heart, Casto. My life. I'm very glad that you're with me, but I'm also worried. The mere thought of losing you frightens me more than anything else in the world. That's why I want to make you irrevocably mine. I want you to belong to me and for everybody to see it. I want you to marry me."

Casto stared at him, his heart thumping so loud in his chest, he was sure Renaldo could hear it. That was indeed unexpected. "Why are you asking me, Barbarian? As far as I understood, the whole issue is already decided no matter what I want."

Renaldo started cursing in the language of the Ancients. His choice of words was most definitely not meant for Casto's ears.

Casto watched him with raised eyebrows, deciding for the sheer fun of it to reveal his knowledge of the tongue. "Those are some very nasty words you're using. I thought a god always knew how to keep his cool?"

Renaldo was rendered speechless. He had pondered for a long time how to address the difficult topic, since he knew very well how stubborn Casto could be when he felt left out, and now it turned out he'd already known? "Sometimes I'm not sure whether I think it's a good thing that you're so knowledgeable. How come you know about the wedding?"

Casto rolled his eyes. "I've read the prophecies, I have ears that function surprisingly well, and in case it has escaped you, Barbarian, I'm not stupid. Since it was announced that there is a high probability of me being your heart, the Valley knows only this topic—when you're going to marry me."

"You never mentioned it."

"Well, as I said, I didn't think I'd have a say in the matter." *And I'm in no hurry to swear my undying loyalty to you in front of witnesses*, he added in the privacy of his thoughts.

With his thumb, Renaldo caressed Casto's cheek. "So you are going to marry me?"

Casto returned his gaze with a hint of melancholy. He hated the predicament Renaldo's words were causing him. "Of course I'm going to do it. Just as little as I could escape you, can I evade your will now."

Renaldo didn't miss the petulance in those words and hurried to soothe him. "I'm sorry, my own. I didn't want you to feel overlooked. I wanted you to be able to make a decision. We don't have to do it this winter either. Next year is fine as well."

Casto snorted. "Don't make a fool of yourself. I can feel your tension, Barbarian. You're not entirely sure whether I'm your heart. Waiting one more year won't change this but will make you even more insufferable. And as much as I like fighting with you, I've no inclination of being accused of having said no to you for the entire year."

"But you aren't completely happy about the situation either."

Casto closed his eyes. Of course he wasn't. How could Renaldo think differently? "No, I'm not. But I love you, you know that. It's just— I'm realizing how I'm slowly losing all control. That frightens me. And what if the goddess doesn't recognize me? If I'm not your heart?"

"Stop it, Casto. You are my heart. I'm absolutely sure."

Casto cocked an eyebrow. "Absolutely?"

"Well, not absolutely. That's impossible so long as you're protected by the spell that hides the hearts' identities. Not even the Holy Mothers themselves can recognize you before I tell them my decision. After that, they're able to see through the veil, and once they recognize you, it becomes obvious to everybody else. But I'm as sure as I can be. And it would be nice if you trusted me a little more."

"I do trust you." Casto rolled his eyes ironically. "I've just proven it to you." Although he still sounded a little snippy, he got a wolfish grin as an answer.

"Yes, you did. Let's stop talking about this. Since you think that you don't have a say in this, it's probably futile to ask you when you want to hold the ceremony."

Despite his exhaustion, Casto sat up. "Do I really have a say, or are you only doing this to placate me?"

"A little bit of both. The proceedings during the ceremony are pretty much set in stone because you're marrying a god." He grinned saucily. "But there are some decisions that have yet to be made. I'm willing to give you a free hand in those."

"I'll only believe that when it's really happened," murmured Casto. "You think I can't do it?"

"Barbarian, we've known each other for almost five years now. I don't *think* you can't do it—I know. You're so dominant it borders on being ridiculous."

"So, I'm dominant and ridiculous?" A dangerous glint entered Renaldo's eyes.

Not in the mood to have a fight about his way of phrasing things now, Casto hurried to downplay his statement. "Not ridiculous in the sense you're thinking, surely not. I just wanted to say that I can hardly imagine you handing control over to somebody else. It's simply not in your nature."

Renaldo was neither happy nor content with that answer. "So you do think I'm ridiculous?"

"No, Barbarian, I don't. I'd never dare to suggest something so outrageous."

"And that, my cheeky prince, I don't believe. You always mean what you say and have no problem whatsoever to dare as much as you please. You just earned yourself some punishment."

Casto flinched. He wasn't in the mood for another round of sex. He reverted to pleading, which never came easy to him. "Please, Barbarian. I'm truly exhausted. I didn't mean to insult you."

Without listening, Renaldo grabbed his arm and drew him close. Despite their strenuous games, he wasn't sated yet. "You should've thought about that before you were so impudent. Even though you're so intelligent, you're a slow learner in this regard. I'm almost a little disappointed in you."

Casto's eyes betrayed his anger. He was only a breath away from snapping. "Then let me rephrase it, Barbarian," he hissed. "I don't want to do it with you today. You should be happy that you've outmaneuvered me regarding the wedding. Leave it be."

Before he could go on with his tirade, Renaldo kissed him long and deep until Casto's anger dissipated. When Casto was again soft and slinky in his arms, ready to be taken, Renaldo whispered hoarsely into his ear, "Who am I?"

The prince trembled in his arms, and overwhelmed by the superior personality of his future husband, he spoke the truth that had taken roots deep in his heart a long time ago. "You are my lover, my master, my lord, and my god."

"Good boy. Relax, I'm going to please you."

With a sigh, Casto submitted to his will.

DURING THE following weeks, Sic got used to the never-changing rhythm of pain his punishment was causing him. In the morning he was beaten by Noran; then he worked in the pits, where the continuous, debilitating movements with which he tried to conquer the frozen soil made his wounds reopen on a regular basis. Bleeding and in agony, he went to the stables at noon, where Casto usually assigned him simple tasks that allowed him to recover slightly for the evening, when his master beat him again and then chained him to the anvil.

That Casto still showed him so much consideration after everything he had done, hurt Sic almost more than the wounds all over his body, which healed only reluctantly and kept him imprisoned in a world of agony.

He received food in the mornings and evenings, right after his beating. It was simple, meager fare that gave him just enough energy to survive the coming day.

That evening, Noran had beaten him particularly viciously, the master smith's mood as black as a raven's wing. With a careless motion, Noran had thrown the plate of food down in front of him, tipping over the jug of water in the process. Sic watched desperately as the precious fluid vanished into the hard-packed earth of the smithy. He hadn't had anything to drink since morning and was so thirsty that he'd started feeling dizzy. Trembling, he pressed his forehead to the wet ground.

Noran watched him coldly. "What do you want, you piece of shit?"

For a moment, Sic contemplated keeping his mouth shut, but his parched throat forced the words out of him. "Please, Master. Could I have another jug of water?"

A long silence followed the simple request, a silence in which Sic cursed himself for his forwardness.

A silence in which Noran vividly remembered a scene from the past. A beautiful, raven-haired woman knelt in front of him, asking in a husky voice for a new dress. He saw himself giving in to that request, blinded by love as he fulfilled every wish pouring from those red, sensuous lips.

Noran remembered the humiliation when he finally realized what his brothers-in-arms had known all along: that the beautiful creature was only using him, taking advantage of his power and rank to enrich herself. Back then he had sworn that something like that would never happen again. No slave would ever rise high enough to get the better of him.

And the little traitor kneeling in front of him, the scum that by all rights should be dead by now, was making demands of him! As impertinent as if nothing had happened, asking for fresh water as if he, Noran, were the servant. He would show this insolent worm, as well as his brothers-in-arms, that he had learned his lesson, that nobody was able to get the better of him now. He would also show them how well he could play the game of manipulation for personal gain. After all, Arja had been the perfect teacher.

With a kick he shot the plate of food into a corner of the smithy, and then seized Sic mercilessly. He quickly loosened the chains that bound him to the anvil. "How dare you even think about addressing me with a request? Why should I do anything for you? You betrayed me, trampled the trust I put in you just when I had thought about allowing you closer to me. You could have become my right hand, even my lover, given time, but you threw that away. I can't even begin to tell you how disappointed I am."

Noran felt a dark satisfaction when he saw the pain his words caused Sic. They held more truth than he was willing to admit to himself.

Sic's betrayal had shocked him on a level the young man would never be able to understand.

Tears slid down Sic's face. "I'm so sorry, Master. All I ever wanted was to be close to you, to serve you well. I never meant to betray you. Please believe me. I know you can't forgive me, but please believe me."

The desperate pleading almost managed to move Noran's frozen heart. He'd known Sic long enough to know that he meant what he said. All of a sudden, Arja's face appeared in front of his eyes, and any mercy he felt evaporated. No matter how beautifully he begged, Sic would never change Noran's decision.

Determined to get his revenge on both Arja and Sic, he put on a cold smile. "As you can imagine, it's hard for me to believe anything you have to say. Trust is something one has to earn, and I can't see how you could accomplish that, not after everything you did."

That wasn't outright denial, and a desperate, impossible hope started to bloom in Sic's eyes, a hope Noran intended to use to his advantage.

"I'll do anything, Master. Anything you ask of me. Please."

Noran pretended to think about this request. The despair in Sic's face made the moment all the sweeter. "Well, I did intend to make you my lover one day. I can't say I have any feelings for you at the moment, but I don't need them for you to take care of my needs. Do I, Sic?"

Sic only stared at his master while the deeper meaning behind his words sunk in. He swallowed hard. Noran was playing with him, testing him, and to his own dismay, Sic was desperate enough to go along. Except for Casto's forgiveness, he craved nothing more than returning to Noran's good graces. For that to happen, he was willing to do whatever it took. "If that is your wish, Master, I will do as you please."

"Then strip and show me how you intend to please me."

With his head lowered, Sic started to undress. He was nervous and frightened and out of his mind because of the emotions warring inside him. He also didn't know what exactly Noran expected of him. Sic was still a virgin, although growing up in the Valley had been educational. He knew about all the things that would make Noran feel good—at least in theory.

When he was naked, he approached his master and sank to his knees in front of him. Trembling, Sic reached for Noran's belt and opened it.

The master smith didn't say anything, just watched him with a heated gaze.

Sic freed Noran's cock, which was already hardening in anticipation, something Sic counted as a win. He stroked the shaft with his right hand, momentarily distracted by how big it was. An impatient sound from Noran brought Sic back to his task. Hesitantly, he licked over the slit where precum was already leaking. Noran bucked against his lips, and his cock grew even harder. Emboldened, Sic took the tip into his mouth and inhaled the musky scent of his master. Even though he wasn't doing this entirely of his own free will, he still felt a sliver of arousal. Not enough to distract him from the emotional blackmailing Noran had used, but enough to help him with his task.

Sic worked his tongue up and down Noran's cock until the man pulled free of his mouth.

"That's enough. As wonderful as your mouth feels, I want to bury my cock someplace else." Noran nodded toward the worktable in one of the corners. "Get the oil from my workplace. You know where I keep the bottle. Then come back here, lean over the table, and prepare yourself for me."

Sic felt his cheeks redden in shame while he did as he was told. Once he was back at the table, he spread his legs far apart, poured a generous amount of oil on his fingers, and then bent forward and started to loosen himself. He could feel Noran watching him. The feeling of being violated grew stronger. This was not how he'd imagined his first time to be. Noran had always played the main role in his sexual fantasies, but Sic had never imagined him to be so detached and cruel. His dream Noran had always treated him with the utmost care and love; he had never just stood there and watched Sic do all the work.

When Sic thought he was ready to accept his master, he simply spread his asscheeks with both hands.

Noran approached slowly. If there hadn't been a slight hitch in the man's breathing, Sic would have doubted the whole situation affected Noran at all.

At least he's feeling something.

Sic couldn't help but feel despair. Noran entered him swiftly, taking just enough time to allow Sic to accommodate to his size.

Once he was completely inside, Noran whispered in Sic's ear, "This feels good. Maybe I should have done it sooner."

Sic shuddered in fear. He wasn't sure if the man talking to him was still the master he had come to adore when he was a child. Darkness had always surrounded Noran, but the cruelty showing in his words was something new, and Sic didn't like it. Noran started to move, and while he didn't hurt Sic, thanks to all the oil, he didn't give him any pleasure either. He just pounded into Sic until he found release.

Once Noran was done, he left Sic's body and the young man could hear the clinking when Noran closed his belt.

Sic turned slowly, his gaze cast down, unable to look Noran in the face.

The master smith made a shooing motion. "Get back to the anvil. Since you satisfied me quite well, I'm willing to give you some water."

Against his will, Sic felt a wave of gratitude wash over him. Noran was pleased enough to be lenient. What was happening between them was twisted, and Noran was using him, but Sic had no choice. Of course he could always deny Noran, and with luck the master smith would respect Sic's *no* even though he was a traitor and free game, but it would also mean that Noran would never forgive him. The mere thought made Sic shudder. After all he had done, he'd been given a second chance. Sic was determined not to waste it.

When Noran brought him a fresh tray with food and, more importantly, a jug full of water, Sic lowered his head demurely. "Thank you, Master. You're very generous."

Noran huffed but didn't say anything in return. He simply placed the food on the floor and left Sic alone.

THE NEXT morning, his master woke him as usual with a kick before he beat him. Sic lost count twice because he was so nervous about what would come after the punishment. So instead of the usual five blows, he received twelve. When Noran was done, he cast the strap aside.

Sic could hear him opening his belt.

"Last night was adequate. Let's find out if you have improved."

With tears stinging in his eyes, Sic knelt and started licking his master's cock. This time, Noran fucked Sic's mouth until he came. Hot seed poured down Sic's throat, and he tried desperately to swallow it all to satisfy Noran.

After Noran slipped his now-soft cock from Sic's mouth, the young man stayed on his knees. He didn't dare to look at his master or even move.

Noran looked down on him and couldn't help but feel glee. The slave would learn to submit completely to his will, and very soon, Sic would understand that the center of his world was Noran's pleasure. A tiny voice in the back of his head told him what he was doing was wrong, but Noran only had to think of Arja's cold smile and the voice died down.

He shoved another tray with bread and water toward Sic. "Eat, and then get going."

Sic's voice was nothing more than a whisper. "Yes, Master."

3. RECONCILIATION

HOW HE managed to get through the morning, Sic couldn't tell. He felt like he was caught in a nightmare. The ever-present pain in his back was accompanied by an almost unbearable agony inside his heart. He dreaded the afternoon in the stables and the evening when he would surely have to indulge his master again. His emotions were in such turmoil he no longer knew what he was thinking or feeling. Only the pain in his soul and body seemed real. Like a marionette, he moved through the day, grateful for the hard work that at least allowed his mind to get some rest.

CASTO HEARD shoes shuffling quickly over the icy ground and looked up in surprise. Sic was hurrying past him, looking as pale as the snow, which was still several ells high. With furrowed brows, Casto followed him into the stables. It wasn't like Sic to simply ignore him. If anything, he was hell-bent on not giving Casto the slightest reason to beat him.

From one of the tack rooms, the monotonous rushing of running water was interwoven with hoarse, desperate sobbing. Casto entered the room, unsure whether he should feel anger or pity. Sic was standing with his back turned toward Casto, in front of the small basin at the wall. Sic had taken off his clothes and was washing his body with rigid motions.

When Casto saw the trickles of fresh blood from Sic's beating that morning, the raw, badly healed wounds, and the uncontrollable shivers running down Sic's back, he felt his stomach turn. He suddenly realized that he wasn't angry at Sic but at himself, and that he had already forgiven Sic from the bottom of his heart.

He locked the tack room door so nobody could disturb them. "Sic!" Casto's voice was soft. "What happened?"

Sic spun around, his eyes wide with fear. "Please, Master, it's nothing. Please don't hit me. I promise I'll go back to work immediately. I promise!"

"Shh. It's okay. Don't be afraid." As if he was calming a frightened horse, Casto approached slowly, with extended arms. "I only want to help you."

Sic retreated until the basin pressed into his back. "It's nothing, Master, really," he affirmed with a shaking voice.

Casto lifted an eyebrow. "In my opinion, 'nothing' doesn't look like this. You look terrible, and I'm not only talking about your physical wounds. What happened?"

Sic stared intently at his wet, bloodstained hands. "Nothing I don't deserve. Nothing I didn't choose for myself. You said it yourself, you don't care about me, so don't let it bother you."

Casto's heart constricted with guilt. Without thinking any further, he pulled Sic close and hugged him, trying not to hurt him again. "I was an idiot. Can we leave it at that? I wasn't angry at you, Sic, but at myself, about the whole situation. Being sent to the mines forced me to face a truth I didn't like much. Still don't, to be honest. But that isn't your fault. Even though it's late, Sic, I accept your apology. I forgive you. It would be nice if we could become friends again."

This unexpected kindness was too much for Sic. He collapsed.

Casto comforted him until he calmed down a bit.

Still sobbing, Sic looked up at him. "You're very generous, Master. I thank you."

Casto's eyes were tearing up as well. Sic's chaste gratitude touched him more than he wanted to admit. For the first time in his life, Casto got an impression of what it really meant to call somebody a friend. To his surprise, the feeling was as intense and overwhelming as the love he felt for Renaldo. "As far as I know, my name is Casto. Friends do call each other by their names, don't they? And now, tell me what has happened."

Sic's gaze darkened. The memory of how he had been manipulated assaulted him like a predator. "My master found a very effective way of making me pay for my sins."

Casto's eyes drilled into the bent nape, disfigured by iron, within his arms. It took him some moments until he realized what Sic was trying to tell him. Once he did, he screamed in rage. "He *raped* you?"

Sic stayed silent for a moment. "No, he didn't. He just made it clear that his forgiveness, should he ever grant it to me, is bound to the way I serve his needs. I hate to admit it, but I'm desperate enough to do anything he asks."

Dark, all-consuming fury bubbled up in Casto's chest. "Don't worry, Sic. I'm going to talk to Noran. This has gone too far. There are rules here in the Valley, and he, too, has to follow them."

Sic shook his head in panic. "Please, don't do that, Casto. It'll only make him angrier. Besides, it's not like he's actually breaking any rules. He hasn't forced me."

"Nobody deserves something like that. Nobody."

"You may be right, but I'm a traitor." Sic's fingertips brushed over the iron around his neck. "The laws of the Valley no longer protect me. If my master wishes, he can even leave me to entertain everybody in the Pack. I have to be grateful when it's only him using me and that he's not actually hurting me."

Casto stroked Sic's shoulders. His anger had slightly dissipated at Sic's words and he was able to assess the situation with a clear head. "I'm afraid you're right. There isn't too much I can do for you."

Casto closed his eyes for a moment. When he opened them again, they shone so brightly, Sic had to avert his gaze. "First, we're going to clean you up properly. I'll just leave for a bit to get you some fresh clothes, okay? You stay here and wait for me."

Without waiting for an answer, Casto got up and hurried away.

Only a short time later, he was back with a bundle of clothes, a jug of tea, and a bag full of bread, bacon, and cheese. He carefully closed the door of the tack room again, took the sponge from where it had fallen to the ground, and started to wash him carefully. At first, Sic wanted to struggle, but then he gave in to Casto's will. It had been too long since anybody had treated him kindly, not to mention touched him without beating him. He enjoyed being pampered by somebody who saw more in him than just his ability to work.

After Casto had cleaned all Sic's wounds, he wanted to use a healing salve on him, but Sic shook his head. "It's better if you don't do that. I don't think my master would appreciate it."

Casto's eyes darkened in anger. "Leave that to me. I'm going to inform Noran that your wounds have to be treated because otherwise you're useless as a worker."

With determined movements Casto took care of him. When he was finally done, he tossed Sic the bag with the food and a jug of water.

"Enjoy your meal." Then Casto's expression darkened. "I'm going to talk to your master now."

Sic eyed the delicious meal warily. He should refuse it because it was Noran's will that he should go hungry. But he was so starved and the food looked so delicious, he couldn't resist. Hungrily he started to eat while Casto got ready to battle it out with Noran.

THE MASTER smith was in his private rooms. He looked relaxed, sitting in a comfortable chair, his feet resting on a bench and a glass of wine in his hand.

But his looks were deceiving. Noran was nervous. What he had done to Sic violated all the rules in the Valley, not to mention his own set of morals, and even though it was his right, a last streak of common sense was protesting loudly against the perversion of the Holy Mothers' gift. That was why he was almost relieved when Casto approached him and interrupted his inner dispute. "Casto, what a pleasant surprise!" Noran made his tone cheerful, almost shrill. Casto wasn't paying him a courtesy call. "How can I help you?"

Casto appraised him coldly. "I've come to tell you that today I was busy treating Sic for almost two hours. He was bleeding from fresh wounds and some of the old ones had opened up, as you surely know. I took the freedom to treat him with salve, and I'd be very obliged if, from now on, you'd send him over to me in a better condition. It takes time to pamper him, and he's not really useful as a worker when he's bleeding all over the place."

Noran's eyes lit up. He wasn't sure what Casto was up to and cursed the fact that his god's lover was so hard to read. "Don't tell me the little rat voiced a complaint?"

Casto shook his head. "On the contrary. You might be pleased to hear that he even asked me to not look after him because you don't want it. I had to explain to him how in the afternoons he's officially, and according to your will, my possession, and I take care of the things I own. That way they are of use for a long time."

Casto had spoken very calmly. An uninvolved bystander could have mistaken it for a polite conversation between two men who didn't know each other well. But Noran had known Casto long enough to interpret the steely undertone in his voice and the ominous darkening of his bright eyes as a clear warning that he had to slow his pace down if he didn't want things to escalate. Casto went on almost absentmindedly.

"Of course I respect your right to punish your possession as you deem fit, but I want you to keep in mind that I cannot make any use of him when he's too badly hurt—nor can you."

"So, what do you suggest?" Noran's voice was sly, asking himself whether Casto knew about the emotional blackmailing and what he was thinking about it.

With narrowed eyes that betrayed no emotions, Casto gazed at him. "I'd say it would be good to stop the beating until the wounds have healed. If you feel like it, you can beat him thrice a day or give him more blows afterward, but at the moment it's unproductive when you break open the wounds time and again."

"And who's going to look after him? I don't feel the slightest inclination to play healer to a filthy traitor."

"And I would never ask it of you. I'm going to do it myself, since I'm the one who'll profit most once he's better. Perhaps I can use him for more than just cleaning the leather, then."

Noran tried to read Casto's words and expression, but his face was an impenetrable, beautiful mask that reminded Noran in an unsettling way of Renaldo. Those two were alike.

He dipped his head slightly. There was no use probing further today. It was better to wait and see what would happen. He would react then. "I agree with you, Casto. It's unwise to wantonly damage the slave's ability. It was my mistake not to think about it. I'll stop the beatings until the skin has healed enough not to be torn by the strap anymore."

Graciously, Casto bowed to him. "I thank you, Lord Noran. Your comprehension is only outdone by your talent. I do wish you a nice day."

Casto left the smithy, followed by the musing gaze of the master smith.

Of course Casto's request had been prudent. Noran had been thinking about the matter as well, if only briefly, since the traitor didn't deserve such consideration. But he still couldn't shake the feeling that Casto had managed once again to outmaneuver him. Unfortunately he didn't have proof, just an evanescent suspicion, which probably wasn't worth investigating.

Sic had escaped his punishment for the next few weeks, but that didn't mean Noran couldn't hurt him then, even more cruelly. When he thought about the things he still had planned for his slave, he felt a shiver of anticipation running down his back that drowned the nagging voice of his conscience.

WHEN CASTO returned to his master's chambers that evening, he was still angry and in turmoil.

Confronting Noran had helped him to let off some steam, but whenever he thought of Sic, he saw the barbaric wounds the young man had had to endure. It simply wasn't right how the master smith punished his slave so mercilessly, but Casto's hands were almost completely tied. He had barely enough scope to get his friend some slightly more bearable conditions, and he wasn't clinging to any illusions about what Noran was probably making Sic do right then.

Exasperated, Casto entered the chambers. He was as jumpy as a young horse during its first ride.

Renaldo didn't seem to notice. With an alluring smile he got up from the lounge he had been resting in and extended his hand to Casto.

"My own! I've missed you today. Come and let me show you how much."

Casto sidestepped him, his face forbidding, his tone grumpy. "I don't want to today. I'm too tired."

He moved to pass Renaldo and head for the bath, but Renaldo retained him. The pressure of his fingers on Casto's arm had only slightly more emphasis than necessary.

"What's the matter? Since you returned to the Valley, you haven't told me no so blatantly even once."

"Then it's a first today," Casto spat, angry that Renaldo was holding him so tightly. He wasn't furious enough to try wrenching himself free in earnest yet, but it wouldn't take a lot more until he raised his hand against his god.

Said god was now inhaling deeply and had closed his eyes for a moment. When he talked again, his voice was a lot gentler than before, but the steely undertone was a clear warning. "I'm asking you again, Casto, what has happened? It's been some time since I last saw you so irritated."

Renaldo's attempts at soothing him only served to make Casto angrier. "It's nothing that concerns you. And I doubt you'd understand. Just leave me alone."

Renaldo's eyes lit up in fury. Not the most patient person to begin with, his temper was easily stoked by Casto's dismissive tone. "Watch your mouth, human. You may not be a slave anymore, but I'm still your lord and master. Even though you share my bed and will be my husband soon, I still expect you to show me respect. Apologize this minute. Then we may be able to turn this situation around."

While talking, he tightened his grip on Casto's arms and pressed him against the wall, trying to subjugate him with his physical presence as well as with words.

Casto's gaze was so dark, his eyes seemed almost black. He knew exactly what Renaldo was trying to do, and he hated it from the bottom of his heart. "All of you be damned!" he hissed and kicked Renaldo's left knee with all his might. An ugly sound was heard; Casto had aimed very well.

The sudden impact of pain loosened Renaldo's grip enough to give Casto a chance to escape. In two quick strides Casto was at the door; he pried it open and was gone.

Renaldo got up, cursing vividly. A pop sounded again when his dislocated kneecap returned to its original position. For a moment, Renaldo seriously contemplated following his wayward lover and bringing him to justice, but he dropped the plan because chances were he would kill the young idiot.

Instead he hit the wall of his chambers with all his might and listened to the furious crackling of the logs in the fire, which flared like some monster from the realms of stories when he fed it with his fury.

At the same time, Casto ran to Lys with tears of anger in his eyes.

The stallion greeted him with an expectant snort, and the dark, intelligent eyes regarded him intensely.

Casto buried his face in his brother's soft hair and told him what had happened this time. "We had a fight, Lys, a bad one. It's not my fault that I wasn't in the mood for sex today. But after I'd seen what Noran has done to Sic, I couldn't imagine doing it. And if I'd told him why I wasn't in the mood, he'd have gotten angry as well, and we'd have fought about that. What should I do? Will this relationship ever be normal?"

Lys snorted imperatively.

"I know. But I never thought it could be so difficult to be obedient all the time."

Another snort, accompanied by a stamping of hooves.

"You're right. But angry as he is right now, he's probably going to beat me black-and-blue. Can't I stay the night with you?"

Soft nostrils nudged Casto out of the stall. One last time Casto started to say something, but Lys pointedly showed him his back.

Casto's shoulders slumped in defeat. "I thought you hated Renaldo? Very well, I'll go and apologize. But I don't want to hear any complaints when I'm not able to ride you for the next week."

Apparently bored, the stallion started chewing his hay. Lys had known Casto for so long and so intimately that he knew how his recalcitrant brother could stand in his own way. Sometimes Casto had to have happiness forced on him.

Casto returned to his master.

When he opened the door, Renaldo was pouring himself some wine. He didn't face Casto but contemplated the red liquid swishing in the glass. "Have you come to raise your hand against me one more time, slave?" His voice was cold. He'd used *slave* on purpose to show Casto how enraged he was.

Casto inhaled deeply. He was still too agitated to feel truly sorry but didn't want a full-scale fight either. So he swallowed his resentment and forced his voice to sound even. "No, my lord. I came to apologize. My behavior was stupid and irreverent. I'm sorry."

The glass was put down with a click, and then Casto heard steps approaching. Strong hands seized him, and gray eyes bored into his own. For some time, neither of them spoke, each lost in the gaze of the other and their own thoughts. Both were pondering the same question: whether their love was strong enough to endure their difficult characters.

Abruptly, Renaldo let go of his lover. "I'm sorry too, Casto. You set me a clear boundary and I ignored it because I wanted to have things my way. That was wrong of me."

Casto shook his head. Now that Renaldo was giving in, he could feel his anger dissipating. "You had every right to ask me. You're my lover and master. I've promised to be open with you."

Renaldo smiled weakly, glad that the mood was swinging toward reconciliation. "Let's agree we both had our part in this, okay?"

Casto's forehead wrinkled in thought before a smile appeared on the full lips. "I agree, Barbarian."

Gently, Renaldo pressed a kiss on his mouth. "Then you should lie down. It was a long day. We can talk tomorrow."

Blue eyes sparked in mischief. "You're sending me to bed?"

"What else should I do? It's late."

Casto's tongue darted nervously across his lips, something Renaldo couldn't help but notice.

"We had a fight, Barbarian," Casto murmured. "Don't you think we should… make up?"

"You were very gruff before. I assumed you did not wish to be touched by me."

Instead of an answer, Casto started to undress, caressing Renaldo randomly time and again. When Casto was naked, he fondled his pierced nipples, a challenging gaze trained on Renaldo. "I haven't bathed yet. Do you want to watch?"

With a growl, his lord pulled him close. "I've got a better idea. I'm going to wash you, my own."

Like a storm, Renaldo's lust swept him away, burying everything else—the anger, the guilt, the fury—beneath it.

Panting, Casto allowed him to regain control and take him to the bath, where Renaldo washed and caressed him until Casto thought he would burn to cinders. Renaldo took him twice in the bathroom, once on their way to the bedroom, and then, when Casto was already close to exhaustion, one more time on the bed. Afterward the young man fell asleep in his god's arms, too tired to ponder the day's events further.

RENALDO WATCHED his lover's relaxed face while he was sleeping.

It never ceased to amaze him how Casto could be so arrogant, stubborn, and belligerent sometimes and then so willing and obedient where the bed was concerned. It was as if there were two souls living in the prince's chest, one sent to annoy Renaldo, the other to please him. He wondered whether it would ever change—and how he would like it if his proud lover submitted to him completely.

Sighing, he pulled the sleeping Casto closer. He would find out one day. In the end, the only thing that mattered was that the young man was his.

CASTO WOKE during an intensive, overwhelming orgasm. Dazedly he opened his eyes to realize that his master had rolled him sideways and entered him deeply. Renaldo was holding him tightly in strong arms from which there was, as Casto knew very well, no escape unless Renaldo wished it so.

"Barbarian."

"Good morning, Casto. Did you sleep well?"

"Until just now, yes." A hard thrust, which made him whimper, was the punishment for his small unruliness. Then Renaldo turned him on his belly without losing contact and started taking him earnestly. Groaning, Casto came twice before Renaldo let him go.

They went to the bathroom together, silently enjoying the feeling of intimacy, which was even more precious because it was still rare and fragile. During breakfast, Renaldo interrupted the peaceful silence.

"Why did we fight yesterday, Casto?"

Casto blushed, staring at his cup of tea as if he hoped to be aided by it. When he spoke, his voice was nonchalant and dismissive. "Because I acted like an idiot. I thought it would be easier to be obedient to you, but it's really hard for me."

Renaldo caressed his cheek fondly before tilting his head to meet his gaze.

"You didn't act like an idiot. You were just agitated, and I didn't realize it. So, what happened yesterday?"

"If I tell you, you're going to be angry, and I don't want to fight again."

Renaldo furrowed his brow. "I promise I'll restrain myself. Besides"—an ironic smile appeared when he continued—"if you don't tell me, we'll fight anyway."

Casto lifted his chin. It was plain how much he resented Renaldo's insistence. "It's because of Sic."

As he had expected, the smith's name sent Renaldo's temper flaring. He might have shown mercy toward Sic, but he would never forgive him. "What has that despicable little traitor done? Was he disobedient? I knew I should have killed him!"

Casto hurried to soothe the ranting warlord. "No, Barbarian, you're doing him an injustice. He hasn't done anything wrong. When he came to the stables yesterday, he was confused and out of his mind. It took me almost two hours to take care of him."

When he remembered the wounds, all the blood, and his friend's despair, Casto fell silent.

For once, Renaldo realized immediately that the topic was worrying Casto so he kept his mouth shut, although he would have preferred to give him an angry shake. After some time, Casto started talking again, his voice troubled.

"Noran blackmailed Sic into sleeping with him. Sic knows what Noran is doing to him, but he doesn't see another way. All he wants is for Noran to forgive him. He was so desperate, so ashamed. And I'm sitting here, warm and safe, and enjoying being touched by you. It doesn't seem fair."

Renaldo inhaled deeply. To his surprise, what Casto was telling him had affected him as well, and not just because Casto was clearly upset about it. Manipulating somebody into a sexual relationship was rape. Even though it was Noran's right following Sic's sentencing—a bad aftertaste lingered.

"Casto, I did warn you. Sic has been declared a traitor, and he has no right to be protected by the laws he has broken. Noran can do with him whatever he pleases. As I see it, Sic should be grateful that Noran isn't forcing him."

Imploringly, Casto looked up at him. "Isn't there anything I can do? I feel so sorry for him."

Renaldo shook his head. "No, you can't do anything for him. He pays for his sins."

"You don't seem to care a lot."

"No, why should I? I'd lie if I said that I'm even interested. Because of him, I almost lost my heart. So whatever is done to Sic has my approval."

Renaldo anticipated another fit from Casto, but the prince remained calm. His eyes were clouded by sadness. Renaldo had never seen such an expression on Casto's face before, and it took him some time before he knew what it was. When he realized Casto truly felt pity for the traitor, he felt a wave of black jealousy crushing him. It took all his willpower to fight against it.

Casto's next words didn't help in the least.

"I understand, my god."

They resumed their breakfast in silence. Casto dressed himself with erratic movements that mirrored his inner turmoil, told his master to have a nice day, and then vanished to the stables.

Renaldo was left alone in his chambers, his head filled with a whirlwind of contradictory emotions and thoughts. When he had felt Casto's sorrow, his first impulse had been to go to Noran, buy Sic from him, and give the smith to Casto. That would have been an elegant, acceptable solution to the problem. More importantly, it would have made Casto happy. But he remembered that the traitor had almost cost him his heart and his life. Sic deserved whatever Noran was doing to him, no matter how deeply it went against Renaldo's own sense of justice.

But Casto didn't deserve to feel bad because of it. Renaldo thought harder. He assessed the problem from various angles and finally reached a conclusion.

4. TRAPPED

WHEN SIC was called away from work by an overseer, he feared the worst. Although his master had already used him twice that morning, it didn't seem to have been enough. Why else should he have been called to one of the toolsheds, which were the only buildings around the pits? That's why he was almost relieved when he saw the Angel of Death awaiting him instead of his master.

The feeling didn't last long. Before the overseer had shut the door behind him completely, the powerful master of the Valley had seized Sic by the scruff of his neck and pressed him hard against the wall.

"I warned you, you piece of shit. If you cause Casto trouble, your ass is mine. How dare you burden him with your petty problems? In case you haven't noticed, you're nothing, a nobody in the Valley. Be grateful for still being alive and learn to live with the punishment your master has given you, but stop pestering my heart.

"When Casto asks you the next time how you're doing, you give him your sincerest smile and tell him everything's fine even if Noran has shoved a hammer crosswise into your ass five minutes before. Do you understand?"

Hypnotized, Sic stared into the god's perfect face, which didn't fit the brutish threats flowing from his lips. The pressure of Lord Renaldo's hands on his shoulders worsened as the expressive gray eyes sparked in anger.

"Did you hear me, slave?"

Sic forced himself to concentrate. "Yes, Master, I understand."

Without another word, Renaldo pulled him forward, rammed his knee into his stomach, and then dropped him carelessly. While Sic fought desperately for breath, the demigod who was the personification of physical perfection left the shed.

It still came as a shock when Lord Renaldo used violence, as if the crust on a stream of lava cracked to reveal the lethal, burning stone beneath. Everybody expected violence from Canubis—he emitted cold, unwavering determination—but his younger brother was like a book written in a foreign language. You only saw the precious binding, and it was impossible to comprehend the words of destruction written inside. Once you understood, it was already too late because Lord Renaldo was as unforgiving and lethal as he was beautiful.

Arduously, Sic got up. The pain from the merciless kick distracted him somewhat from the other agonies assaulting his body. It was almost noon, so the overseer allowed him to wash up and go to Casto.

Casto greeted him with apprehension. "You're early today, Sic. Is everything all right?"

Sic forced a smile. "I'm fine, Casto, thanks to you. My master didn't beat me yesterday. I'm really grateful."

Suspiciously, Casto's clear blue gaze bored into him, but Sic straightened his back and kept his cool.

"Then I'm at ease. Until your wounds have healed, you'll be having fun with cleaning the leather. After that, I'll make sure to find more interesting work for you."

Sic touched his friend's hand. "Thank you, Casto. I'm so glad that you've forgiven me."

Casto smiled. "It's my pleasure. I'll see you later." He made a face. "I still have to ride about a thousand horses before evening."

"Then I won't detain you any longer. I already have my own work cut out for me."

Casto reached for the reins of the light chestnut mare a stable boy had brought him, mounted her, and started to mechanically go through his program.

His thoughts were racing. He knew Sic wasn't well. That he was trying to convince him otherwise could only mean somebody had threatened him. Nobody besides Renaldo and Noran could have done that, and Casto was sure the Barbarian was responsible for Sic's behavior. But it would only cause his friend more pain should he pursue the matter further, although he didn't want the Barbarian to think a Prince of Ummana was so easily led by the nose.

It was more than enough that he had lost all means of control regarding the wedding. He didn't want to show weakness with this as well.

When talking to Renaldo, Casto had pretended he didn't mind his freedom being gradually lost, and in a sense, it was the truth since he loved Renaldo to distraction. But it didn't keep him from panicking outright when thinking about the wedding. At that moment, he could still lie to himself; he could convince himself that he was staying with his master of his own free will, that he could leave him anytime. It was still his decision whether he chose to stay or leave.

As soon as he swore loyalty to Renaldo in front of witnesses, that fragile web of lies would rip once and for all. Then he would belong to Renaldo, the Angel of Death, in every way.

Casto felt his chest tightening when he thought about it. There was no escaping for him now, but he was still afraid to admit that publicly. He also didn't know a lot about the ceremony, something that only heightened his fears.

If he wanted to make an educated decision, he had to know all the facts.

"CASTO, I'VE been wondering when you would grace me with your presence." Bantu smiled kindly.

"Am I that easy to read, Lord Bantu?"

The older man's smile deepened. "No. Believe me when I tell you that you're a mystery to all of us, including the Angel of Death. But your mind is a precise and logically working machine that I can comprehend. You're here to learn more about the wedding ceremony, isn't that so?" Casto nodded. "You're lucky, I've already prepared everything in advance. Here are the details about the ceremony, and this"—Bantu placed a small leather-bound book on the table—"is a summary of the future. Or to be precise, your future, should you really be Lord Renaldo's heart."

"I thank you, Lord Bantu."

"I'm always willing to serve those who seek wisdom." The Emeris patted Casto's head in a friendly way, placed a cup of tea next to the safety lamp, and left him alone.

Casto started to read with a sigh. The wedding ceremony itself was a ritual that followed strict rules that didn't allow any variance. The only thing that was flexible was the exchange of gifts after the vows. Usually both partners gave presents of a certain value to show their mutual respect. If one party was much richer than the other, it was also acceptable if only the wealthy partner gave away gifts while the poorer could take them without losing face.

All Casto owned was the clothes he had worn when Renaldo had captured him. And since his escape, they were more rags than clothes. He only kept them out of a sense of sentimentality, not because they were still usable or worth anything. In a small, worn leather bag, he kept some gold coins he'd received as payment while he rode with the caravan. Compared to the riches Renaldo owned, it was a drop of water in an ocean.

If they were in Ummana, Casto could use his private fortune—treasures that outdid even the possessions of the Angel of Death. But this was the Valley, and his title, and everything attached to it, had no worth there.

It went against everything inside Casto to enter a relationship as the obviously weaker person. So he decided to give the Barbarian a present that would outshine everything he could bestow on him.

After having read the prophecy and about the formalities regarding the ceremony, Casto was starting to get an idea of what his gift would be like, but he still had to think it through properly. Already tired of reading the heavy text, he went for the smaller book Bantu had given him. That had been written by a seer of the Ancients, a female who hadn't recorded a vision on the pages, but a dream that had haunted her every night.

The dream told her the role of the hearts in the lives of the divine brothers.

And once the Masters of the World acknowledge their Hearts, they will return to their former glory. Their splendor will blind this world and all those living in it, and the nations will kneel in front of their Masters. The Hearts will be the first to bend their knees before the glory of the Gods, and they will set the example the world will follow. The humility of the Hearts will be the humility of the world, their obedience absolute.

And the Masters will know the thoughts of their Hearts, just as they will know the thoughts of all people. The will of the Masters will be the will of the Hearts, their bodies the temples in which the Masters enjoy the ultimate worship. And thus the fate of the Hearts is an example for the fate of the world.

All will bow to the will of the Masters.

Suddenly drained of all emotion, Casto stared at the lines that had voiced his innermost fears. It was as if the seer had talked with him before writing those lines. Getting his fears validated by somebody who'd been dust for several centuries was like a slap in the face. All his life Casto had focused on being free, but in the end, he'd only traded a ridiculous human tyrant for a terrifying divine one.

He looked around the small room. The candle threw flickering shadows against walls that suddenly appeared to draw closer. The air around him was getting thicker; the whole Valley seemed to suffocate him with its narrowness.

Casto got up hastily and, without speaking to Bantu, hurried out into the cold air of the afternoon. The sun was already about to sink behind the mountaintops, the last rays a mocking reminder of how far off summer still was. Casto abhorred the cold, the snow, the fact that for even short trips he had to wear several layers of clothing.

It was too much.

The betrayal, their fights, the reconciliation with Renaldo, Sic's suffering, the wedding, the still-lingering doubt about whether he was truly his master's heart, the maneuvering with Noran, his own aspirations…. Casto felt the pressure weighing him down, forcing the air from his lungs and rendering him helpless.

There was only one thing that could help him now.

He ran to Lys, who was contentedly standing in his stall munching oats. But when he saw Casto approaching him, looking so confused and helpless, he immediately stopped eating. Casto buried his face in the black stallion's neck, his tears staining the silken hair. "Please, Lys. I want to be free."

The Emperor of the Storms gave his consent with a snort, and at that same moment, Casto was on Lys's back. With a shrill whinny like a challenge to the whole world, Lysistratos charged out of the stables, galloping in long, measured strides toward the exit of the Valley.

When they reached the plains, Lys's ears perked up. A storm was brewing, darkening the evening sky with ominous shades of gray. It was probably the last one that winter, the time for them being already over.

But at that moment, Casto was very happy to see it. He placed his hand on his brother's muscular neck. "Let's defeat the storm."

Huffing, Lys accepted the challenge. He threw his head back and then stretched his neck before he started racing. When the first gusts yanked the hood of his coat off his head and the cold air engulfed him like a living creature, Casto closed his eyes. Now, at this very moment, he was alive and free. He braved the elements; he was his own master.

To that place, at the eye of the storm, nobody could follow Casto, nobody could order him, and no responsibilities could bind him. For a terribly beautiful moment, he wished for that state to never end.

But Lys wasn't called the Emperor of the Storms for nothing. He overtook the storm that was gaining more and more momentum, changed direction, rode through it again, and finally returned to the Valley with his flushed, exhilarated rider.

When the steep cliffs of their home embraced them protectively once again, Casto had tears streaming down his face. All that was left of his dream of freedom—a storm on the plains that couldn't disturb the unshakeable walls of his home.

He took Lys back to his stall and got him new hay and more oats. "Thank you, my brother. As always, it's been a pleasure to run with you."

Soft nostrils blew warm air onto Casto's cheeks. Lysistratos was content: he had beaten the wind again.

He knew how deeply his brother was suffering, but he also knew he couldn't help Casto. Just as little as Lys was able to escape his own destiny could the prince deny what was determined for him. Lys would always be there for him, but Casto had to learn to accept the inevitable.

STILL AGITATED by his ride and the feelings he couldn't understand, all Casto wanted was to have a bath and find oblivion in sleep. But Renaldo had different plans. With folded arms, Renaldo waited for his lover, his eyes cold and clouded, his expression frozen. He imperiously extended a hand, and faced with his lover's unforgiving mask, Casto realized that this time it was better to be obedient.

Demurely he stepped into the warrior's arms. Renaldo grabbed him violently and kissed him hard. There was no gentleness in the kiss, and no passion. It was an assault Casto accepted nonetheless. What other choice did he have?

Renaldo kissed him for a long, long time before finally dealing with Casto's clothes. He opened Casto's trousers and ripped his shirt.

Judging from the violence Renaldo used, he had to be beyond furious. It reminded Casto of the time when the Barbarian thought Casto had betrayed him. The mere memory sent shivers down Casto's spine. There was no way he would subject himself to the wrath of his lover again.

Without warning, he kicked Renaldo in the place where it would hurt most. When Renaldo toppled over, Casto grabbed his hair and rammed his knee into Renaldo's face. The ugly, crunching sound when Renaldo's nose broke was like a balm to Casto's confused mind.

And that could have been that, had Renaldo not been a god. He recovered a lot faster than Casto had anticipated, and his retribution was swift. The Angel of Death closed his fists around Casto's upper arms, forced him against the wall, and lifted him. "How dare you raise your hand against me, slave! How dare you!"

"And what was it you were doing, Barbarian? It sure as hell was no loving welcome!"

"How I welcome you is entirely up to me, you insolent little worm! You really need to be taught some manners!"

"Ha! A barbarian teaching manners? Don't make me laugh!"

Renaldo was about to do something he would surely regret later, when a crackling sound made him spin around. Both lounges, the thick carpet, and one of his tapestries were on fire. Renaldo let go of Casto so quickly that Casto lost his balance, but the warrior didn't care. He had his hands full with reining in the inferno that was threatening his home. Once the flames were doused, he turned back to his unpredictable, infuriating lover.

Casto's piercing gaze made clear he wouldn't bend, wouldn't give in. It drove the demigod crazy. The young man was oblivious to how much he was trying Renaldo's patience; he didn't understand how hard Renaldo had to hold back not to subjugate him. Knowing it wouldn't be of any help no matter how much violence he used didn't improve his mood.

"What's gotten into you, Barbarian? I thought we had left this kind of behavior behind?"

As rational as the words sounded, the tone was vitriolic. Renaldo saw no reason to budge either. "I could ask you the same thing, Prince Castolus. You promised not to run from me anymore!"

"What are you talking about?"

"As if you didn't know! Where have you been this afternoon?"

Casto's eyes widened. "Don't tell me this is about my ride with Lys?"

"Is there anything else?"

"So it is about the ride." Casto sighed. His anger had cooled considerably. "I didn't try to run from you—you should know that. I just needed to calm down, nothing more."

"You left the Valley. Without telling me. After we had a fight. What was I supposed to think?"

"We have fights all the time! Regarding that, I should already be gone for good, but I'm still here."

Renaldo closed his eyes. He knew Casto was right, but the beast inside him was still not placated. "This may be the case, but you still have no right to leave the Valley without my permission. I won't allow you to go where I can't protect you. You're mine, I can't lose you!"

"I'm not your possession! I never was and never will be! If you want me to stay, you better not try to punish me with your body again. You know damn well how hard it is for me to yield to you. Forcing me doesn't make it easier."

The last sentence had been said with a little less venom, and Renaldo finally realized how close he'd been to losing his heart for the second time. Determinedly he reined in the beast and took the peace offering. "I'm sorry, Casto. You're right, it wasn't fair of me to try and discipline you like that. But I didn't know what you were about to do. I was blinded by rage and fear. The mere thought of having to be without you...."

Casto smiled crookedly. Renaldo's admission made him feel generous. "In this regard, you're one lucky barbarian, because being without you is the one thing I'd never be able to stand."

"That's a relief." Renaldo sighed. "You know, I'd very much prefer it if we spent more time in harmony." Gently he caressed Casto's face with his thumb, anxious to keep the fragile peace. "I want to lie naked on the furs in front of the chimney with you, drinking wine, perhaps reading a good book. Bedding you whenever I feel the urge, loving you as you deserve."

Casto leaned into the touch like a content cat. He was far too exhausted to keep up the fight. "That sounds fantastic. But I don't mind when you take me roughly either, when you let me feel that I'm a god's lover. I just don't want to be a toy or a lapdog. I couldn't bear that."

Renaldo's expression turned serious. "I swear to you, my own, you're neither. Even though I don't always act like it, I do respect you and mind your will."

Casto allowed his lover to embrace him. He returned Renaldo's kiss with passion, willing to reconcile with his difficult mate despite his exhaustion, but wistful because the bed seemed to be the only place where they really got along.

When Renaldo laid him down on the furs, his affection showing openly in his angelic features, Casto touched his cheek. "Who am I, Barbarian?"

Renaldo smiled, full of love; his voice was firm, with only a hint of regret. "You are my life, my love, my heart." He hesitated for a moment. "And my possession. Nothing will ever change that."

"Are you going to take good care of me?"

"How can you even ask that? Of course I'll always be there for you. Now shut up and kiss me. I've got to make up for a mistake."

WHEN CASTO finally fell asleep, Renaldo returned to the main room to assess the damage the fire had caused.

Despite the losses, he was thrilled, for it hadn't been his doing. In his anger, his heart had drawn the power from him without even noticing it. Under normal circumstances, Casto shouldn't have been able to do that before being confirmed by Ana-Isara, but since everything about his lover was unusual, he wasn't really surprised. They both had been highly agitated, and it was entirely plausible that Casto had managed to tap into Renaldo's powers and unleash them—the last proof Renaldo needed, and he was more than relieved about the assurance.

Casto *was* his heart, his destined mate.

All that was left to do was marry him, and thus bind them for the rest of eternity.

5. PRESENTS

"Sic, do you have a moment? I need your help."

Sic put aside the leather strap he was repairing. He smiled happily. "Of course, Casto. It's an honor to be of help to you."

"Good, then come. This is private business."

Casto led Sic along into one of the tack rooms and closed the door. Then he unfurled the two sheets of paper on which he'd sketched his present for Renaldo. "Please tell me honestly what you think about this."

Sic leaned curiously over the sketches. His eyes went wide when he realized what he was staring at. Drawn on the paper, with black coal, was a curved *R* flanked on both sides by a half-spread wing. There was only one explanation for the sketch, and Sic didn't like it. He frowned. "What exactly is this, Casto? These are sketches for a branding iron. Why on earth would you need something so horrible?"

"That's going to be my present for the Barbarian. At the wedding. You know?"

Sic looked confused. "What would the Angel of Death want with a branding iron?"

Casto hesitated. When he started explaining, he sounded defiant. "At the wedding I don't want to be a supplicant to the Barbarian. That's completely out of the question. But in order to achieve that, I have to give him something valuable, and the only thing I own is myself."

It took a moment, but when Sic understood what Casto was implying, he staggered back. "That's madness, Casto! Do you have the slightest idea what kind of pain you're asking for? A burning iron on your skin, that's… that's… completely and utterly crazy! And as big as this one!"

"The size is perfect. And I really don't mind the pain. Don't you understand, Sic? I have to do this. I've lost control. I'm like a ball some kids randomly toss at each other. This is for me, for my confidence. I'm not going to be a supplicant to my groom-to-be. I simply can't do that."

Sic looked aghast. "You don't want to appear weak, and that's why you're letting yourself be branded like an ox at the market?"

"Believe me, I've really thought this through. It's the only possibility. Here in the Valley, I have neither power nor money. I may have been freed, but for all intents and purposes, I'm still at the Barbarian's mercy. All that's been left to me is myself. That's why I'm giving away the only thing I have—myself. Luckily, I'm also my most precious possession. I simply have to do this."

Sic listened in surprise to the desperate undertone in his friend's voice. He suddenly realized how little he knew about him.

Sic had been a slave all his life. For him, it was only natural that everybody in the Pack was richer and more influential than him. Therefore, he was having problems understanding Casto's dilemma. "But he's your master. Even more, he's your god. Of course you're a supplicant to him. He's Lord Renaldo, the Angel of Death, master of this world. It's your destiny to be his possession."

Casto's eyes flashed dangerously. "God or not, I'm not a mere slave, I'm a prince. There's no way I'm going to be humiliated like that."

"You're *what*?"

"Don't tell me you didn't know? I thought that news had already gotten around in the Valley."

"No, it hasn't. Like everybody else, I assumed you're a rich merchant's son."

Casto shook his head. "No. I'm Prince Castolus of Ummana, the rightful heir to the Twin Cities." He smiled gently to calm Sic. "And future husband to a conceited, arrogant barbarian god who is suffocating me with his dominance."

"I'll never understand how you can talk so irreverently about your lord. Don't you fear his wrath?"

Casto thought about that for a moment. "No, not really. I've never been truly afraid of Renaldo. Not even when he thought I was cheating on him. I was surprised because the beating was so savage, but I was never afraid."

Sic sighed. "I don't know whether I admire your guts or mourn your stupidity. After all, we're talking about a god here. Still you act as stubbornly as if he were no more than a nuisance you can brush off with a wave of your hand."

Casto ignored that. "No matter what he is to me, the question remains whether these sketches are any good?"

"So, you're determined to see this foolishness through?" Casto nodded. Sic rolled his eyes. "Well…." He examined the sketches. "The basic idea is not too bad, but if you want to use it as a reference, you have to change some details. Do you happen to have some coal?"

"I had hoped you'd say something like that, my friend." With a relieved grin, Casto handed him a piece of coal. "I have to get back to work, but I'll see to it that you're not disturbed. And Sic? Not a word to anybody."

Musingly, Sic stared after his friend when he left the tack room. It had barely surprised him to find out that Casto was a prince; somehow he had always suspected that behind the perfect façade was more than a mere merchant's son. He could even understand why his friend was so eager to give Renaldo such a precious, though unbelievably stupid, present.

He hoped Prince Castolus's stubbornness wouldn't get him into serious trouble one day.

IN THE late afternoon, Casto escorted his friend back to the smithy, the improved sketches under his arm.

Noran raised his brows in question but left it to Casto to address him first. He couldn't deny himself that small triumph, not after everything that had happened.

Casto didn't waste time mincing words but cut right to the core, knowing full well that the master smith didn't view him favorably and would surely try to refuse his request. "I have here sketches for a branding iron, Lord Noran. I want it to be a gift when the Barbarian takes me as his mate. Sic has already explained to me that this work is not very complicated but will be time-consuming. I want to ask you to take a look at the sketches and tell me if eight pieces of gold are enough to pay for it."

Noran stared at Casto with deep suspicion. He had expected something, but not this request for help—if it was one. Casto's tone was as polite as always, but Noran had learned to listen to the undertones, and those were in an entirely different melody. Casto's choice of words made clear that he wasn't expecting to be refused.

Casto wasn't asking him as a member of the Pack, not even as a customer, but as the future mate of his god, and to top it off, it was also something that would please said god. Technically there was no way for Noran to refuse the request.

He extended a hand. "Show me the sketches."

Wordlessly, Casto handed him two rolls of paper, and Noran opened them on one of his worktables. He took a quick glance and saw immediately that Sic had been right: it wasn't complicated work, just time-consuming. Eight pieces of gold was a suitable price, but because Casto had outmaneuvered him before, Noran decided to make him wait. "The sketches are good, I can work with them, but I want to look at them closely before I make a decision. Is it okay if I give you my answer tomorrow?"

Gracefully, Casto bowed to him. "Of course, Lord Noran. I can wait. I wish you a pleasant evening."

Noran nodded benignly. "I wish you the same, Casto."

Casto said a friendly good-bye to Sic, who'd been demurely kneeling next to an anvil during the entire conversation.

When Casto was gone, Noran turned to his slave. "Did you know about this nonsense?"

"Yes, Master."

"And it didn't occur to you to talk him out of it?"

"He showed me the sketches only today and asked me to correct them. I had to obey him."

Noran watched the traitor angrily. "But it didn't really faze you, did it? Although you had to know what I'd think about it. But that's immaterial, because I won't do it. Eight pieces of gold aren't enough to pay a master's work."

Sic looked up in alarm. "But he wants it to be a wedding gift."

Noran smiled cruelly now that he'd managed to trap his slave. The evening would be more entertaining than he'd anticipated. Since he couldn't attack Casto directly, he would use this worthless worm to get back at him.

"You seem to be very eager to get Casto that iron. Of course, there's always the possibility to delegate the task. Unfortunately all my apprentices are booked solid. The only one remaining is you." Satisfied, Noran watched as hope and suspicion fought for dominance in Sic's features. "For that, I'd have to reverse your punishment of not touching any smith tools for the time being. I'm asking myself whether that's a good idea or not."

The hope vanished from Sic's face, eliminated by despair. "What's the price I have to pay, Master?"

The complete hopelessness in his slave's voice made Noran complacent. Deep inside, he knew that he'd lost his footing and was sliding endlessly downward. But another, grimmer part of him accepted the darkness, even welcomed it because it offered oblivion. His sins, no matter how obnoxious, couldn't reach him there. He was free to do whatever he pleased.

"Well, you're going to make a branding iron. Back in the old days, I was a great friend of this noble tradition. It's somewhat poetic to burn a slave's degraded standing into his flesh, don't you think?"

Sic only stared at him silently, full of despair. Noran sighed theatrically, then went to one of the cabinets at the wall and selected the two irons he had used to mark his slaves when it had still been practiced in the Valley. He shoved them in Sic's face.

"I'm feeling merciful today. You can choose which one you want." When Sic reached for the smaller one, Noran shook his head. "But you should keep in mind that this isn't only about being allowed to do Casto a favor. You surely want to get a chance to take part in the ceremony. Or am I wrong?"

Sic's hand froze, and his shoulders slumped in defeat. Trembling he chose the bigger iron, which showed an *N* inside a circle.

Noran grinned triumphantly. "You're obviously not as dumb as I always thought. Undress and lie down on the table, on your back. Bend your legs and spread them."

Noran shoved the iron into the glowing embers of the forge. He watched as Sic obeyed. Finally he pulled the red-hot iron out of the embers and approached Sic.

"If I were you, I'd concentrate on not moving. I'm going to brand you on the inside of your right upper thigh, and we don't want you to get hurt in other places, do we?"

Sic nodded, his gaze glued to the gleaming steel. Noran stepped forward and brought the iron perilously close to Sic's inner thigh, and Sic screwed his eyes shut. When the stench of singed body hair assaulted his nose, Noran yanked the iron back and tossed it to the ground. He watched as Sic slowly opened his eyes again, utter disbelief written across his features. "Master?"

The smile Noran flashed Sic was devoid of feeling. "I may be a cruel and strict bastard, but I'm not that much of a sadist."

When he saw the guilt shining in Sic's eyes, Noran knew he had not only assessed Sic's feelings right but had also managed to twist the young man even more. Now Sic thought Noran still had some last shreds of humanity inside his soul when nothing could be further from the truth. Noran's deception was perfect. And if he kept on telling himself so, he might even believe it.

Sic got up from the table and reached for Noran's belt. There was still a look of despair in his face, but also a glimpse of hope. Maybe his master would forgive him one day.

After his first climax, Noran musingly traced his victim's back. "Your wounds are almost healed," he murmured happily. "You're surely delighted to hear that I can start beating you with the strap in a day or two. I guess you can't wait to accept your just punishment."

The words reminded Sic that even though Noran had just shown him mercy, he was still far from forgiving him. He swallowed hard. "Yes, Master."

Noran grunted. He gripped Sic's hips harder as he started thrusting again.

THE NEXT morning, Noran visited Casto at the stables to tell him personally that he would allow Sic to make the iron.

Casto looked at him with open disgust. "This is very *generous* of you, Lord Noran. I do thank you."

The smith smiled cruelly. "You should do that. For eight pieces of gold, I don't even start working. Neither do my apprentices. You're lucky that Sic is such an untalented loser. His work is free."

He gave Casto back the pouch with the gold and enjoyed the anger sparking in his eyes. That would teach the arrogant idiot to go against an Emeris. And because he was in such a good mood, Noran decided to top it off.

"Please take a look at the traitor's back today. I'm planning to resume his beating starting tomorrow, and I'd love to have your opinion. We don't want that piece of trash thinking we're not in agreement."

"Of course, Lord Noran. How thoughtful of you."

Noran had to give it to Casto, his face was completely devoid of expression. If he hadn't seen the angry sparks in his eyes just a moment ago, he would have doubted if Casto wasn't still angry with Sic. But now he was sure the arrogant little twerp was interested in the well-being of the traitor.

He was going to show the two presumptuous young men that nobody went against Lord Noran, master smith and an Emeris in the Pack for almost two hundred years, without paying the due price.

In silent fury, Casto watched the bulky figure of the smith retreat from the stables. And all the while he cursed under his breath in Ummanian. "That damn bastard. I'm starting to lose my patience with him. Beware, Lord Noran. I am Prince Castolus. I do not forget nor will I forgive."

WHEN SIC arrived at the stables sometime later, Casto took him into one of the tack rooms, closed the door, and regarded him critically.

"I want you to tell me the truth, Sic. What price did you have to pay to be allowed to make the iron for me?"

Sic lowered his gaze. "It's all right, Casto. I wanted it."

"Sic, please. It's enough that Renaldo and Noran think they can take me for a fool. You're my only friend, so please, don't do that to me. I already know that Renaldo threatened you and that is the reason why you're no longer telling me about the things Noran does to you. But I'm not blind. I can see how much you're suffering, and I know Noran has used my request to play one of his games. So, what did he ask of you?"

Sic looked wide-eyed at his friend, unsure what to do. Obviously, they'd all underestimated Casto once again. Hesitantly, he started to speak. "My master hinted at the fine old tradition of branding slaves, and I assumed he wanted me to wear his. I really thought he would brand me when he held the iron in his hands, but he didn't do it. I think he enjoyed my fear. He certainly was pleased with the way I showed my gratitude."

"Holy Mothers! Sic, I'm so sorry! That's entirely my fault. Me and my damn pride. Believe me, I never wanted, never thought it possible, that Noran would do something like this to you. I anticipated he would try to stall me to show me his power, but I never thought he'd use you like this."

Sic managed a weak smile. "It's fine, Casto. It gave me the chance to pay off some of my debt toward you. He said he wouldn't make your brand because this kind of work was unworthy of a master. And he refused to let somebody else do it. He knew it was important to you, and I was foolish enough to show him that I cared about you. If I manage not to annoy him too badly during the next two weeks, then I might even be allowed to witness when you swear loyalty to Lord Renaldo. That's definitely worth it."

Without saying a word, Casto hugged his friend. His voice was a raw, emotional whisper at Sic's ear. "There's no debt to pay to me, not any longer, my friend. Please, never think something like this is necessary. I'm glad to know you, happy and grateful to have you in my life again, and I swear to you, Noran's going to pay for what he's done. It may take some time, but if I've learned anything in my life, it's that it always pays off to wait for the perfect opportunity. Your suffering won't go unpunished."

Sic sobbed. "Please, Casto, our god is going to kill me if he hears you talking like that."

"Don't worry, Sic. I know very well. I'm not going to give Renaldo reason to hurt you, but I'm going to seize my chance should it present itself. And now let me pamper you for a bit. You look terrible."

Hiccupping, Sic leaned against the wall, glad that he had a single friend in the Valley. "It does hurt a lot. Here." He indicated his heart. "I'm not sure how much more I'm able to take."

"You won't be alone. I swear."

AFTER HE had tended to Sic and ordered him to take some rest, Casto went to see Aegid and Kalad. In the late afternoon, the warriors could be found at their chambers since they hated the cold as much as Casto did. Now that he knew his gift for Renaldo would be finished in time, Casto had to take care of the presentation, and for that he needed the help of the brothers.

After knocking at the impressive oak door, he heard Kalad's voice, careless as ever. "Daran, cutie pie, go and look who it is!"

Only a short time later, the door opened to reveal the young man who was Casto's best—albeit only—pupil at the stables.

Daran's black hair was hanging in a braid down his back as usual. His dark brown eyes brimmed with intelligence. "Hello, Daran. Nice to see you."

The young man, who had come to the Valley one year after Casto, but who had assimilated a lot faster and more smoothly than his capricious teacher, bowed elegantly. "Casto, welcome."

Casto entered and flashed the slave a friendly smile. Daran was a very easygoing young man, who he barely saw beyond lessons because Aegid and Kalad kept him in their chambers most of the time. They watched jealously over their thief's acquaintances and preferred to keep him hidden.

Casto could understand them up to a point since Daran was a very agreeable and charming person who wasn't aware of his own charisma. He was simply friendly by nature, although fate hadn't been too favorable with him until he came to the Valley.

Once every day he went to the warriors' training hall to work out, but during that time he was unapproachable because the program the desert brothers had given him to form his body to their liking left no time for breaks.

Casto wasn't sure what the warriors were planning for the young man and hadn't dared to ask either. Although Kalad in particular had been very open toward him since the battle of Ki't, there were still things Casto deemed too private to discuss with the brothers. At any rate, Daran didn't seem to be unhappy.

Kalad smiled, genuinely pleased to see Casto. "What a nice surprise. What brings you here?"

Casto grinned. "The warmth."

Kalad laughed heartily. It was an old joke between them, but one with a sad background. "Renaldo still doesn't understand how to use a coal pan or the chimney, does he?"

Casto shuddered. Not that it wasn't warm in the Barbarian's rooms—Renaldo was anxious to create an atmosphere that agreed with his lover—but his interpretation of *warm* was that of a man who'd grown up in the North. Like Aegid and Kalad, Casto was a child of the south and of the sun. Before Renaldo had brought him to the Valley, Casto hadn't understood that for many people the word *winter* meant they had to wrap themselves in the furs of dead animals. His first snow had come as a shock. It never snowed in Ummana.

As children of the desert, Kalad and Aegid had the same problem, which meant they were holed up in their chambers most of the winter, heating the rooms so much they could've easily gone naked.

Casto sighed in bliss. "He'll never understand. He thinks I'm effeminate."

"Don't fret it. If you're effeminate, we are as well. We've been living here for so long, but we haven't gotten used to the cold yet. So, why are you giving us the honor of your visit?"

"I'm here to ask a favor of you two."

Kalad's eyes sparked with interest. Casto as a supplicant was unusual and aroused his interest. "Then my brother should hear it as well. Daran! Get Aegid. Tell him we have a guest. Then you can pour us some wine, do you get me?"

The young man bowed low. "Yes, my lord."

Proudly, Kalad watched his slave retreat. "Isn't he wonderful?"

Casto coughed slightly. From his time in Ummana, he was used to people talking about others as if they were things. Not for nothing were the Twin Cities the center of business on the continent. While he was still very young, Casto himself had made some nice profits in the trade of high-class slaves for the amusement of the wealthy. Before he'd become property himself, he had never given much thought to how it felt to be a possession—it was just something that happened everywhere. Now that he had experienced what it was like firsthand, he couldn't return to the same loftiness Kalad showed. Especially since Daran, because of the horse training, was closer to Casto than the rest of the faceless slaves in the Valley.

"He's easy on the eyes, if you mean that. And he's making remarkable progress in the saddle."

Kalad laughed. "I was talking about his tight ass. Every time I look at him, I get the urge to bed him, which is rare, even for me."

Casto concentrated on his nails; the topic was awkward for him. He knew Daran served both warriors between the sheets, but whenever he tried to imagine it, his fantasy abandoned him. He could only guess how much stamina was required to satisfy two masters instead of one. Seen like that, it was a small wonder that Daran was able to stand on his own two feet during the day. Before his thoughts could run further in this disturbing direction, Aegid entered the room, followed by Daran, who filled three cups of wine.

After Daran handed them to Kalad, Aegid, and Casto, he waited with his head bowed, ready to obey further instructions.

Kalad patted his backside. "You can leave now, Daran. Strip and go to the bedroom. We'll join you as soon as we're done here."

The young man bowed again and vanished soundlessly through one of the doors that branched off from the main room.

"So, Casto, what can we do for you?" Aegid looked happily at Casto. He was still fascinated that Renaldo had managed to bind this stunning, arrogant young man.

He had been sure those two would be at each other's throats within weeks and that their relationship would go the same way as all the others Renaldo ever had. But Casto had stayed.

Casto defied a man Aegid wouldn't provoke if his life depended on it; he fought with a warrior who was infamous for cruelly punishing his enemies and those who dared to oppose him, and he bore the love of a god who, before Casto, had burned so many to ash. And he did it all without seeming conscious of it.

"I want to give the Barbarian a wedding gift, and for that I need your help. As you know, the exchange takes place right after the vows, and then everything has to be ready. I need to rely on you. I need two men who are stronger than me to hold me down."

"What in the name of the Holy Mothers are you planning?" Kalad's voice was lively with interest.

Casto couldn't suppress a smile. "I'm planning to give the Barbarian the most precious thing I own—myself."

Aegid whistled lowly. "How are you going to do that?"

"I've designed a branding iron, which I'll give to him so that he can brand me."

Silence.

Kalad was the first to regain his speech. "Casto, this is madness. Romantic madness, but madness. Do you have the slightest idea what kind of pain you'll be facing—and on your wedding day, to boot?"

"Yes." Casto's voice didn't waver.

Aegid's eyes narrowed. "I don't think this has anything to do with romantic feelings, am I right, Casto? You want to show the world you're Renaldo's equal, isn't that so?"

Casto's face turned into an expressionless mask that scarily resembled his master's. "And if it is?"

"Then I understand you very well. What do you want us to do?" Aegid's voice was soft. He did understand only too well, and his respect for Casto had just gone up a few more notches. It took guts to allow yourself to be mutilated like that, and in front of an audience as well. And it was pretty shrewd to turn an obvious gesture of subjugation into the exact opposite.

Casto definitely wasn't an idiot, and it paid to never forget that.

"I need a coal pan that deserves the name to heat up the steel quickly. You should own something suitable, am I right? And then I need your strength to keep me down. I won't use ropes—that would be inappropriate at such a moment. Do you think you can restrain me?"

The two warriors shared a long look. Then Aegid said, "Yes. You can count on us. We won't let go of you, no matter what happens."

A beaming smile brightened Casto's features. He suddenly seemed a lot younger and more relaxed than only a few minutes ago. "I thank you from the bottom of my heart. You're taking a load off my shoulders. Oh, and I probably don't have to tell you that this is a surprise, so not a word to anybody."

Aegid grinned. "Just leave it to us."

Casto got up from his seat, thanked the brothers once again, and left their chambers to return to the cold of the stables.

Kalad watched him go, lost in thought. "He's going to be a good, strong leader. And dangerous."

Aegid nodded. "I find it harder and harder to believe he's a mere merchant's son. He's way too cunning for that. Do you think Renaldo knows?"

"If not, then he at least has a suspicion. He's no idiot either."

"No, but he is madly in love."

Kalad glanced at his brother. "He's found his heart, of course he's in love. Do you remember what it was like when Canubis finally found Noemi? He grinned like a fool for ten years straight."

"Oh yes, sweet love. It turns all of us into idiots."

"Speaking of which, I think there's a pretty, very willing slave waiting in our bedroom. I'm sure he's already feeling bored."

Aegid's eyes betrayed his hunger. "Then we should keep him occupied. We don't want him to get ideas, do we?"

Laughing, Kalad followed him into their shared bedroom.

Daran was waiting for them, naked and indeed eager, his brown eyes full of devotion for his masters while they got ready for a night of passion.

THE CLOSER the day of the wedding approached, the more insufferable Renaldo became.

It all started when he got it into his head to ask Casto at every given opportunity for the phrases he had to recite during the ceremony. Then he gave the order that nobody was allowed to train with the prince anymore so that he wouldn't be injured or overworked. The last strain was when Renaldo commanded Casto to stop riding.

Until then, Casto had shown remarkable patience with his future husband's whims, but now he let his anger get the better of him. "Forget it! I surely won't sit around doing nothing for the next five days while everybody around me starts going crazy."

"Casto, that was no request. It was an order."

"To be frank, Barbarian, I don't care. I have a tough training schedule, and I'm going through with it."

Renaldo was getting angry as well. "Watch your mouth, slave. In case you have forgotten, you're mine and you do as I say."

"No, I won't! I'm done with your irrational fears. In case *you* have forgotten, I'm a prince. Knowing complicated phrases by heart comes as natural to me as breathing. I'm absolutely fluent in your language and can probably speak it even better than some of your mercenaries. There's absolutely no reason to distrust me! Stop finding problems where there are none."

Growling, Renaldo grabbed his future mate by the shoulders, pressed him against the wall, and held him in an iron grip. "I'd love to beat you for your irreverence, slave. Thinking about it, I'd say you deserve to taste the whip."

"Go on, don't hold back! Whip me, but stop pestering me with ridiculous orders."

Rendered speechless by such cheekiness, Renaldo stared at his unruly lover, then suddenly bent forward and kissed him.

As if he had been waiting for it, Casto snuggled against him, his tongue fighting Renaldo's intent, his hands stroking Renaldo's back hungrily. It was like the beginning of their relationship, when intercourse had always been a fight for dominance, bearable only because of the all-consuming passion they felt for each other.

But Casto was no longer an inexperienced youth. Almost five years of sharing the Barbarian's bed had turned him into a skilled lover who was able to stand his ground against Renaldo. And thus the fight was more fierce, more brutal, and more merciless than anything they had done before. In the end, Casto only submitted to his god because of Renaldo's untiring stamina. When it became obvious that Casto would bow down, Renaldo used his advantage to drive the young man to the brink of exhaustion. He made love to him until Casto was totally submissive to his master's wishes.

Only when he was sure his lover wouldn't challenge him any more did Renaldo allow himself to find relief. Then he carried the now-obedient Casto into the bathroom, slipped into the water with him, pulled him close, and kissed him gently. "I'm sorry, my own. I'm aware that I'm telling you that way too often at the moment, but that doesn't make it less true. I hope I haven't hurt you?"

Casto leaned his head against Renaldo's shoulder. "No, the orgasms were great as always."

His tone was crisp. It was obvious that he wasn't pleased with the way things had gone.

Renaldo caressed his arm. "I know I'm making a fool of myself, but I'm terribly nervous."

Casto turned to him in surprise. "Why? You're a god. This whole ceremony is basically held to celebrate your glory. There's no way you can do anything wrong."

"Casto, I've lived for so long, I lost count a few hundred years ago. This is my first and only wedding, a feast I will hopefully remember fondly in the years to come. I know you aren't entirely happy with the circumstances, and that's why I want it to be perfect for you as well. It disturbs me, knowing that I'm asking something of you that makes you unhappy."

"You're aware that this is even more ridiculous than forbidding me to ride? I admit I'm not overjoyed about the way my consent was presupposed by everybody, but that doesn't change the fact that I love you. In four days, when I stand next to you to say my vows, you can be sure that I'll do it of my own free will, because I truly love you and can't imagine a life without you. If I didn't want this, I'd be sitting on Lys's back by now, escaping in the heart of a storm. I surely wouldn't be here with you, fighting about every trifle we can think about."

Renaldo hugged his heart close, his voice raw. "Holy Mothers, I love you so much, my own. I'll never be able to tell you in words."

Casto bit his tongue keep the sarcastic comment he had in his mind from giving him the slip. He preferred enjoying the peace between them, which was still new and rare. To be fair, he had to admit that his lord tried really hard to treat him the way he deserved, but the dominant god took the reins at regular intervals, and it always provoked Casto's opposition, leading to a heated fight that ended in passionate, brutal sex. Casto was glad that there were only four days left until the ceremony because he wouldn't be able to bear the emotional strain much longer.

EXCLUSIVE EXCERPT

Ummana

Gods of War: Book III

By Xenia Melzer

In war, loss is the price of victory, and the cost of love is sometimes pain.

After Renaldo and Casto finally celebrate their marriage, the time has come for revenge against the followers of the Good Mother who tried to kill Casto—though this time, the Gods of War won't use bloodshed to take Medelina.

As a member of the Confederation of the Plains, Medelina answers to Ummana, the head of the alliance… and Casto is heir to the throne of Ummana. Accompanied by their most capable mercenaries, Canubis and Renaldo travel to Ummana to make Casto king.

They'll face the Council of Elders, Lord Aran, Casto's father, and Princess Anesha, Casto's sister—none of whom are happy about the king's return. For Casto, the city is a reminder of a terrible childhood, and Renaldo can only helplessly watch his beloved fight a seemingly hopeless battle.

Through trickery and political scheming, vengeance against the Good Mother is finally within their grasp—but their success might be bittersweet. Not everyone will return to the Valley with Casto and Renaldo.

Coming Soon to
www.dsppublications.com

1. WEDDING DAY

THE DAY the Pack celebrated the wedding of Lord Renaldo, the Angel of Death, with his heart, Prince Castolus of Ummana, dawned in splendid glory. The sun's rays cut through the chilly air like swords ripping an enemy's body apart, and they transformed the snow into a sparkling carpet of diamonds.

Excited anticipation that nobody could evade ruled over the huts, the stables, and the main building. Even the slaves were affected by the nervous energy permeating the morning.

In Frankus's chambers, Casto stood in front of a huge, almost man-sized mirror and studied his body that, in only a few hours, would be scarred in the most barbaric way imaginable. Behind him, Frankus was busy arranging all kinds of oils and ointments on a table. While doing this, he kept rambling on in hushed tones.

"I explicitly told you to drink some wine so you could have a good night's rest. But why listen to somebody who's had as much experience with weddings as me? You had to brood the entire evening as if today wasn't the happiest in your life. You probably wanted to put my skills to the test, didn't you?"

Completely unfazed by the scolding, Casto kept staring at himself in the mirror. Since he had fled from Ummana, his body had changed dramatically. During his year on the run, he still resembled a child, with the long, slender limbs of a newborn foal, but already showing signs of his later build. After the Barbarian had taken him prisoner, the awkward body of an adolescent had transformed into a muscular, elegant weapon already steeled in battle.

His skin was still as flawless and soft as back then, and the only difference was the studs in his flesh. Of course Frankus was right: he had seen better days, ones without those dark circles that told of a night spent in useless musings, deprived of sleep. Then again, how often did one marry a god? If anything, those circles were well earned.

Frankus pushed him away from the mirror, prying him away from his useless pondering. "To the bath! You've got half an hour to clean yourself. Then we'll see what I can make of this disaster."

Without a word of protest, Casto obeyed Frankus, knowing that the man was probably even more nervous than Casto himself. The wedding was important in more than one respect, and Frankus was aware of all the implications that came with it.

The warm water managed to soothe Casto a little, and his thoughts went back to the day when he fled from Ummana.

Most of his memories about that night were blurred because he had been so emotionally high-strung, not knowing what would become of him when he left the only home he'd ever known. The one thing he could remember clearly was the agitating mixture of wild triumph and utter fear swamping his senses as Lys galloped through the storm he had summoned.

At that time, Casto had been used to the feeling of being powerless. His father and Voltara had seen to that. While the gusts had tugged at his cloak as if they wanted to tear him apart, Casto had experienced what it was like to control such powers through his connection with Lys. The ambiguity of those emotions had left a deep impression on him, one that had influenced his actions more than he wanted to admit.

Now, too, he felt as if he were riding a storm, but this time he was alone, without Lysistratos to calm and protect him. And it wasn't an escape either, or at least, not a proverbial one. It was a step—no, a leap—into a whole new life that would permanently sever him from his past. Perhaps it would even banish the demons still haunting him, or so Casto hoped.

At the end of that day, he would be the mate of a barbarian god from the North. This fact would from then on shape and change everything Casto had ever been, his entire personality. His whole identity was going to be created anew, not by himself, but by the people around him. By the way they looked at him. It hadn't been easy becoming who he was, and Casto wondered whether he could make that change a second time. He was deeply afraid of losing himself to the Barbarian, of drowning in a different kind of helplessness.

Renaldo was just too much of everything, too intense, which was also the reason Casto loved him.

When he was honest with himself, all these thoughts were idle, an endless repetition of his fears that he hoped to escape today. Becoming the mate of a man as overbearing and dominant as Renaldo would help him slay those demons from his past. Determined, Casto left the bath to let Frankus take care of him.

An hour later, Kalad and Aegid arrived to escort Casto to the main hall. The desert warriors were wearing identical clothes dyed in a vibrant, dark green, their personal color. The seams of their shirts, as well as the jerkins, were embroidered with golden threads, the heavy coats and the black boots were lined with otter fur. Both men had superb ceremonial swords tied to their hips and golden vambraces, which were decorated with emeralds, strapped to their arms. They bowed to Casto, and he was almost sure they meant it. With those two, one could never tell.

"You're stunning, Casto." Kalad's voice was full of unrestrained admiration.

Casto wore dark blue silk trousers that caressed his body like a lover's touch. His black boots, dyed blue at the seams, were made from mountain deer leather lined with rabbit fur. The cream-colored shirt and dark blue jerkin with golden embroidery told Renaldo's story in the runes of the Ancients, and were also made of silk. Casto's eyes, highlighted by kohl, looked almost innocent in this get-up. His wheat-blond hair was tamed by a broad leather strap, and the ends dipped in gold dust made the light explode every time he moved.

The contrast between Casto's stunning appearance and his contradictory character posed a deception Aegid deemed fitting on this important day. It emphasized how perfectly suited the young man was to become Renaldo's mate.

"Just now I'm regretting we weren't able to defeat Renaldo five years ago." There was a hint of longing in Aegid's voice.

"My words, brother." Kalad grinned.

"Perhaps you want to rethink your decision, Casto? We would take good care of you."

Only a few weeks ago, that saucy comment would have made Casto furious for two reasons. One was that he was regarded as a trophy; the other was the implication that back then he had chosen slavery freely. Luckily for Kalad, Casto had learned to see the words for what they were, a compliment wrapped in good-humored banter.

He bowed to them in mockery. "It would be my pleasure. But it would be your task to explain to a notoriously short-tempered and jealous god why the object of his desire has chosen to elope with two male hookers."

The desert brothers made indignant faces.

"Uh, that hurt. Hookers? I'd call us sexually open-minded." Kalad grinned when he said this, fully aware of his and Aegid's reputation.

Casto snorted. Kalad's and Aegid's promiscuity was legendary within the Pack. "Please, when we first met, you were changing your bed partners so fast, you didn't even bother learning their names. You were worse than the Barbarian!"

"That's not true—not entirely." Kalad managed to let his voice sound hurt, although the twinkling in his eyes betrayed his amusement. "And since we've met Daran, we're fidelity incarnated."

"It's the truth!" Aegid came to his brother's aid. "The little thief is special in many ways. Ever since we got him, I haven't longed for diversion."

Casto rolled his eyes. He would never admit how much he enjoyed their relaxed bickering. Among all the warriors of the Pack, Kalad and Aegid came closest to what Casto would have wished for as brothers. "All right, I understand. You're the embodiment of sexual fidelity and devotion. Nevertheless, I have to decline your generous offer. I'm fully occupied with one self-righteous Barbarian and have no intention of trading myself double trouble. It's my pleasure to leave that honor to Daran."

Kalad and Aegid started laughing out loud. Their amusement was like a breath of fresh air in Casto's tense mood.

"Then we better get you to your barbarian while you're still determined. I've no intention to chase you through the snow should you get cold feet." Aegid sounded a little too serious for comfort.

"Those, I already have. Why does it have to be so cold today?"

Casto hadn't planned to start lamenting, but he still resented the cruel irony that made the days with the most radiant sunshine those where the cold was especially biting. It almost seemed as if nature itself was having a good laugh at his expense.

Aegid and Kalad nodded in silent agreement. Aegid grabbed Casto's wrist. "Let's go. The sooner we start moving, the sooner you're in the main hall, and if nothing else, it's warm there."

Beaten by this truly valid argument, Casto followed them out into the cold.

THE MAIN hall was almost bursting at its seams. Every warrior in the Valley, as well as many of the slaves, were present to witness their god taking his mate.

When Aegid opened the gigantic doors, the excited murmuring from hundreds of voices was like a wall forcing Casto back a few steps. Then all noise died. The silence was so heavy, it made him wonder whether his heartbeat could be heard.

Aegid and Kalad left his side to take their seats next to the other Emeris at the far end of the hall.

Casto stood alone in the aisle. The stares from all the people almost hurt his body. All the expectations tied to his person threatened to weigh him down. He felt as trapped and chained as he had been in Ummana, confronted with a burden he was not ready to take on. If he started to run now, he could probably make it to the stables and Lys before anybody realized what he was doing. He could leave it all behind—

No, he had already tried that. There was no turning away from Renaldo, not anymore. Casto straightened up. He had come this far; backing out now would be even worse than staying. After all, this was no different from the official appearances he'd made in Ummana. He would neither shame himself nor the Barbarian.

At the end of the aisle, Renaldo and Canubis were waiting. They had gotten up from their wooden seats as a gesture of respect and were watching him expectantly.

Casto glimpsed the hunger in the features of his future husband and everything besides Renaldo vanished from his sight. The Barbarian was breathtaking. His eerie perfection was enhanced by his dark blue ceremonial clothes.

Renaldo's shirt was made of the finest silk, highlighting the outline of his muscular arms, broad shoulders, and chiseled abdominal muscles without being vulgar. The leather trousers hugged his slim hips, and the black boots enhanced his long legs. Renaldo's only jewelry was a headband made from pure gold, formed like two wings holding a blue diamond between them. His eyes were smoldering, a mirror of the lethal fire blazing inside the demigod.

Casto was the only one who did not fear that fire. On the contrary, he loved it since it was so incredibly similar to his own.

Gravely he proceeded along the lines of the warriors toward the two demigods, every inch a royal prince. When he reached them, he bowed. Only when Canubis and Renaldo had returned the formal gesture did Casto bend his knee to swear his fealty as a free warrior of the Pack.

"I plead my loyalty to you, Lord Canubis, and to you, Lord Renaldo, as my leaders and commanders. I swear to follow your orders and fight by your side until Ana-Isara claims me for the Green Lands."

In return, Canubis and Renaldo promised to protect and help him whenever he needed their aid.

"We accept your pledge, Casto. We offer you the protection of the Pack and swear to look after you until your time has come to return to the Mothers."

Once the words were spoken, the other warriors in the hall celebrated the pact they all had made with the Wolf of War and the Angel of Death with deafening applause. It was the pledge that bound them all as brothers and sisters under the sword.

After the cheering died away, Canubis approached Casto with a blade in his hands, the symbol for the alliance they had just made. The forbidding Wolf of War girded the sword around Casto's hips. His voice was loud and clear. "Welcome to the Pack, Prince Castolus of Ummana. You are most welcome."

The agitated hush following these words was proof that the brothers had kept Casto's identity a secret until today. It was one of the oldest, most effective, tricks in politics. Always stay one step ahead of friend and foe alike, and surprise them when they are least expecting it to demonstrate your superiority. Casto nodded at Canubis in silent recognition that was met by a conspiratorial wink. Then Canubis stepped aside to make room for his brother, who took his place next to Casto.

As a greeting, Renaldo pressed a kiss on Casto's temple. "You're doing really well, my own."

"I've told you so. I'm used to presenting myself."

Smiling, Renaldo rolled his eyes before he turned his attention to his brother. Canubis regarded the two men standing in front of him with affection. It was an emotion that seemed alien to the usually unrelenting man and showed how much he loved his younger brother.

When the Wolf of War started to speak, the people in the hall fell silent again. "Some hundred years ago, it was me standing in front of Renaldo, harboring the same love and probably the same fears in my heart. Yet it was the happiest day in my life, and I can still recall it as if it happened yesterday."

He made a short pause to give everybody the chance to realize how important the moment was.

"I wish you, my brother, and you, Castolus, the same. That in a hundred, or two hundred years' time, even for the rest of your life, you will think of this day and it will be as crystal clear in front of your inner eye as if it had happened only yesterday. You are about to take your vows of fidelity and love, with phrases given to us by the Mothers themselves. May these vows see the end of time, unsullied by treason or hatred."

Canubis took a silken cloth, dark blue and embroidered with golden runes, and wove it around Renaldo's and Casto's intertwined hands. Casto looked at Renaldo with a mixture of love and defiance when he started to recite the ancient vow.

"Ne, ana blod brester stratatos, renosor an treano net aremao te memoso net elendio, ana Renaldo muaro. Ne rono unemaso la na re anoso tare. No risuo, ne ledeto. Ne ratodio an no."

I, the kindred of the wind, swear my undying love and fealty to my mate and god, Lord Renaldo, the Angel of Death. I will be your heart from now on until time itself will end. Your will shall be my command. I belong to you.

Casto was not too happy about the wording of the vows, but seeing the love igniting in Renaldo's eyes made him bear them a little more easily.

"Ne, ana elendio muoro no Ana-Isara te Ana-Aruna, elendio da nort, paretao no adeso. Ne torinos memoso te aremao net uromeo da adoso an anas net permaso da unemaso. An anoso tere, no heloso da ne."

I, Angel of Death to the Mothers, God of the North, accept your vow. I welcome you as my mate, and I swear to love and protect you as asked by the Mothers and as is befitting for my heart. Till the end of all time, you are mine to cherish.

Renaldo's voice was clear and steady. He had waited all his life for this moment.

Canubis placed his hands on the ribbon between his brother and Casto.

"Ne, ana elendio remaro no Ana-Isara te Ana-Aruna, elendio da nort, tureano elene te irao asuendo. Ne torinos brester unemaso da riano."

I, Wolf of War to the Mothers, God of the North, bless this union and recognize it as eternal. I welcome my brother's heart to the family.

Heralded by the thunderous applause from their fellow warriors, Canubis took the ribbon away and hugged first Renaldo and then Casto before he turned back to the audience.

Renaldo raised a hand to get everybody's attention, ready to start with the next part of the ceremony, the presenting of the gifts.

Casto took a deep breath and touched his mate's arm. "May I have a word, my lord?"

Renaldo furrowed his brow in surprise, then nodded almost imperceptibly and retreated a few steps. The interruption wasn't planned, but he doubted that even his capricious prince would ruin a moment like that.

For a few heartbeats, Casto contemplated the sea of faces in front of him before he turned to Renaldo, because what he had to say was mainly for him to hear. "As you all know, we didn't have an easy start."

Laughter erupted in the hall, accompanied by whistles and howling. Renaldo smiled lovingly at Casto, who went on.

"Neither of us is what you might call easygoing—" More comments from the crowd interrupted Casto, only this time he ignored them and kept on talking. "Which is why I'm still surprised that I'm standing here today. Truth be told, I've gotten used to our arguments, and no price in the world can tempt me into living even one day without your love. You gave me a home when I was without an anchor, you showed me consistency when all I knew was insecurity and doubt, and you loved me before I even knew I was able to feel so strongly myself. My life truly began when I met you, and I will always be grateful for that. To show my appreciation, I have prepared a gift for you."

That was Kalad's cue to hand Casto the box. Casto gave it to Renaldo, who regarded him with love and a hint of suspicion in his gray eyes. Even though the occasion did call for some pathos and a certain amount of subservience, Casto's unusually tame statement had alerted Renaldo. Casto's following words did nothing to ease his doubts.

"I do hope you are pleased with my gift, my lord."

"I'm sure your gift will please me plenty." Renaldo's voice was soft, with a barely audible strain in it. He opened the lid.

His eyes widened. Silently he stared at the content of the box, his jaw muscles clenched visibly. When he looked up, the perfect, impenetrable mask he normally wore was gone. "You shame me, my mate."

Casto smiled, satisfied. He enjoyed making the Barbarian uncomfortable in front of all his followers. It was a small revenge for all the things he'd made Casto endure since they met. "It is my gift for you, my lord."

Behind Casto, Aegid and Daran brought the brazier. Kalad approached Casto to help him get out of his jerkin and shirt. Renaldo took the iron from the box and buried it under the glowing coals with a rushed gesture. His face betrayed nothing of his feelings.

When the assembled warriors realized what kind of gift Casto had chosen, they started applauding again. After what seemed like a small eternity to Casto, Canubis made a gesture and absolute silence ensued. Only the sizzling of the iron and the soft crackling of the coals were still audible.

With his chest naked, Casto knelt in front of his mate with his back to him and swiped his hair over one shoulder. Aegid and Kalad grabbed his upper arms. Renaldo took the iron out, exchanged a glance with the desert warriors who tightened their grip around Casto's arms so brutally he thought his bones would break any moment. In the audience, the mercenaries started hammering a dark, steadily increasing rhythm on their shields with the hilts of their swords.

Renaldo hesitated for one more moment, then pressed the glowing red iron between Casto's shoulder blades. Casto tensed in agony. His body jerked forward and a muffled whimper escaped his lips but was swallowed completely by the noise in the hall. Casto had known he was facing serious pain when he decided to make this move, but he hadn't anticipated how bad it would be—worse than being whipped in public, *a lot worse*. Even the broken arm he'd had to endure at his father's court could not come close to the white-hot agony flashing through his body, assaulting his nerve endings and swamping all his senses with the burning desire to scream and somehow escape the pain. If it hadn't been for the audience and his own unbreakable pride, Casto would have given in. But he would not scream, not in front of so many witnesses, not after he had forced Renaldo's hand to get his way. And so he gritted his teeth until he thought they would crack and imagined how good his triumph would feel once the pain subsided.

Mere agonizing moments that felt like a lifetime later, Renaldo tossed the iron aside and helped Casto to his feet, surreptitiously wiping away the involuntary tears. The warriors started cheering again as Renaldo kissed him.

His voice was raw, only audible to the young man who was still shivering from the pain he had just endured. "We're going to talk this out later, O husband mine."

Casto's answer was equally challenging. "I'm counting on it, my lord."

Renaldo turned to the mercenaries. "Since my precious mate has gifted me so generously, I can only hope my presents for him are equally suitable."

He waved his hand imperiously, at which the great doors swung open and row after row of slaves started carrying heavy wooden trunks into the hall, the lids open so everybody could see the contents. First came twenty chests with clothes: silk and linen, velvet and exquisite leather, everything of the finest quality, all dyed in the dark blue color that was Renaldo's own. After the clothes had been carried outside again, twenty more chests were brought in, filled with gold and gems; expensive, intricately crafted wine cups; cloak pins, rings, sumptuous necklaces, and other jewelry. Another twenty trunks followed, and those were filled with books, each bound in leather with golden lettering on the cover. Then the slaves brought a complete set of war equipment: several swords, daggers in various lengths, bows and arbalests, an array of spears, chain mail, leather jerkins, and solid leather boots.

These unbelievable riches were followed by forty slaves, bringing twenty of the best horses Renaldo owned, each with its own saddle, bridle, and several blankets.

Lysistratos was the last to enter the hall. His majestic appearance was highlighted by the gifts Renaldo had bestowed on him. The stallion wore a saddle made of dark blue chamois leather, one of the rarest and finest in the world. His bridle was of the same material; the headband was pure gold studded with three blue diamonds. The saddle fittings were gold too, and the stirrups were ornamented with lapis lazuli.

Speechless, Casto took in all the riches spread in front of him. The Barbarian had just made him one of the wealthiest men in the Pack, announcing his status with the highest impact possible. The assembled warriors felt it as well, for the looks they were giving Casto were no longer just admiring. Now they carried a kind of awe that would soon turn into the respect Casto deserved as the mate of their god.

For once truly overwhelmed by Renaldo's generosity, Casto knelt in front of him, the gesture less graceful than usual due to the pain in his back. "You're the one shaming me, my lord. You're spoiling me."

Renaldo helped him up, genuinely pleased with this honest reaction. "I'm only giving you what is rightfully yours, my own." He smiled radiantly.

"I think it's time to declare the feast officially opened."

With his arms stretched wide, he turned to his brothers-in-arms. "Let's celebrate!"

The invitation was met with frenetic joy. The doors opened once more and this time slaves brought food and wine. Renaldo led his mate to the waiting Emeris, and Noemi was the first to hug Casto. He could feel a soft prickling from her, and the pain in his back subsided into a tolerable throbbing. Noemi couldn't heal him completely, because then the branding would be gone, but with her power she sped the process along so that it felt as if the wound had already healed for days. He flashed her a grateful smile.

"I'm so happy for you two, Casto. My best wishes to both of you!"

"I thank you, my lady. As always, you're as kind as you're beautiful."

Pleased with the answer, Noemi kissed him on the cheek. "You're so cute! What have we done all these years without you?"

Hulda pulled Casto into her arms. "We were appalled by our men's lack of manners. But truth be told, before we met you, we didn't even know what we were missing."

Casto took her hand in his own and kissed the back. He enjoyed this little game immensely. "How can anybody be unruly when confronted with so much grace?"

Wolfstan stepped up to his wife, smiling broadly. "Casto, stop it already! You make us look bad!"

"Don't fret it, darling." Hulda caressed her husband's arm lovingly. "You do realize this is all a game, don't you?"

"Of course, my precious, but it's fun to catch you off-balance now and then."

On and on it went. Casto drowned in congratulations and good-humored banter. Even Noran added his good wishes, though still rather grumpy, as always. Sic had been allowed to follow the ceremony from the farthest corner of the hall, and he expressed his joy with a nod and a broad smile before he left. Casto was sure the young smith had paid a high price for his participation, but that was a topic he would address once the time was ripe. Until then, Casto maintained a mental list of everything Noran made his slave suffer, so that he would not forget even one insult when he took his revenge.

The feast quickly turned into an orgy, which was the hallmark of any group activity in the Valley, as Casto had come to accept by now. It was not as bad as during the Spring Ceremony. Most of the warriors stuck to one partner and nobody was completely naked yet, a fact that would change as soon as the alcohol consumption reached a certain level.

Renaldo, like Casto, let his gaze wander through the hall, touched his hand lightly, and nodded at him reassuringly. There had been a major fight between them about the question of whether they should share intimacies during the feast, something that was considered mandatory for a wedding by many members of the Pack. Casto had finally won the argument by phrasing an ultimatum: should the Barbarian insist on that part of the ceremony, he could go and find himself another fiancé. Knowing there were some lines Casto would not cross, Renaldo had wisely acquiesced to his demand and promised not to lay a finger on him in public.

Around midnight, Renaldo took his husband's hand, wished the other warriors a pleasant night, and then retreated to his chambers, where they would be undisturbed for the next three days. The time span was considered sufficiently long for the newlyweds to test their compatibility. Once it was over, the pair was expected to either confirm their union or annul it straightaway.

That was not an option for Casto, but he and Renaldo would still have their time of retreat.

The door hadn't completely closed when Renaldo slung his arms around Casto. His lips closed over Casto's, and Casto had some trouble evading the sudden assault.

"What do you think you're doing, Casto? I want you right now. Ever since you entered the hall this morning, I've been craving your body. Waiting this long was torture."

Casto couldn't suppress a smile. Renaldo's eagerness was a promising start to their wedding night. "I want you too, Barbarian. But before we get down and dirty, I want to give you something."

Renaldo glared at him. "I'd say you've given me plenty already. And don't you dare think I don't know what you've done."

Casto looked down, slightly flustered. He knew that forcing Renaldo's hand as he had done was in stark contrast to the vows he'd made. "I had to do it, Barbarian. For myself, for my self-esteem."

"Believe it or not, I do understand you. But I warn you, don't ever push me like that again. Do you have any idea how hard it was for me to hurt you in such a brutal way on our wedding day?"

Casto raised his hands in a conciliatory gesture. "I'm sorry, really. I'll make it up to you, I promise. Here, this is for you."

"Another present?"

Renaldo glared at the package in Casto's hands with open distrust. Finally he took it and opened it. He wasn't able to hide his surprise. "Are you serious?" Renaldo held up the leather cuffs Casto had sewn for him.

Casto held his gaze steadily. "I'm deadly serious. We both know why I allowed you to brand me today, and love or subservience has nothing to do with it. But as I said, I do love you, and I want this day to be as perfect for you as it is for me—well, most of it, anyway. We always have fun between the sheets, and I'm aware of how much you have to hold back. Tonight you don't have to do that. I'm going to do anything you ask of me. I'll be whoever you want. Tonight, you can let go."

Renaldo shook his head as if somebody had hit him. Deep in his eyes, a hunger awoke, so irresistible, so terrible, it aroused Casto immediately and dragged him into depths he'd avoided till now.

"You're going to do everything I ask?"

"*Yes*. Everything you want. You can do with me as you please. I've sworn fealty to you today, and I don't want anything to stand between us, not even unexplored sexual fantasies."

"What about tomorrow night?"

Renaldo had put his finger on the crucial point. Casto treated him to a lazy, seductive smile. "We'll see, Barbarian. If I were you, I'd concentrate on the here and now."

Snarling, Renaldo pulled his mate closer. There was no doubt about Casto's sincerity. "I will, my gorgeous victim, you can bet on it."

His hands trembling with excitement, Casto helped Renaldo out of his ceremonial clothes and then undressed when Renaldo ordered him to.

As soon as he was naked, Renaldo fastened the cuffs around Casto's wrists, put his arms at his back, and locked the iron rings sewn to the leather. "You're completely helpless now, my own. How does that feel?"

Casto whimpered. He felt strange and a lot more vulnerable than he'd anticipated. His own strength was no match to Renaldo's, a fact Casto was always aware of, but it was a huge difference between just knowing and actually *experiencing* it. The lust Renaldo was practically oozing seemed more intimidating to Casto, more threatening—and also more arousing. Before he knew it, Casto was caught up in the insatiable passion that made his relationship with Renaldo so fulfilling.

"Please, my lord, don't torture me."

"Oh, but we're just getting started—slave."

Renaldo's lips caressed Casto's right cheek, then started wandering down, grazing his neck, pausing for a moment at his throat before Renaldo playfully bit the tight muscles at the junction between neck and shoulder. Casto squirmed in his embrace, trying to rub himself on Renaldo's thigh.

Renaldo kept him at a distance. "Don't rush it, my own. We have all the time in the world. Literally."

He started to push Casto toward the bedroom, never stopping with the kisses. Although Renaldo felt as if he were about to explode, he placed his mate gently on the bed and took his time to explore every inch of Casto's skin until he begged to be taken. With the aid of some cushions, Renaldo lifted Casto's rear to a height he found appealing. Then he entered him with first one, then two oiled fingers, massaging and teasing Casto until his hips started to buck in helpless pleasure. It was a heady feeling, seeing how the proud young man succumbed to the pleasure only Renaldo could give him— as only Renaldo was *allowed* to give to him. Moaning, Casto lifted his lower body, presenting it to Renaldo like a gift.

"Please, my lord, I'm begging you! Stop with the torture. Please!"

Satisfied, Renaldo withdrew his fingers, knowing from experience that his difficult lover would not refuse him anymore. He nudged Casto's entrance with his hard cock; his muscles bulged with the strain of holding back, of drawing out the teasing. "Is this what you want?"

"Yes, please!"

"What do you want me to do?"

"Take me. I'm begging you."

Renaldo shook his head. He enjoyed this game immensely. "If you want me, you have to go into more detail. *What* do you want me to do?"

Casto groaned in frustration. He already doubted the wisdom of his actions, but it was too late to back out now. He was too aroused, too eager. With only a hint of resentment in his gaze, he indulged the Barbarian. "I want you to enter me deeply. Take me hard and brutal. I want to feel that I belong to a god. I want to beg for mercy, knowing I won't get it. Hurt me, be cruel."

"As you wish, my delectable property."

Renaldo had been determined not to lose control completely, to keep that last strand of restraint, but when he heard Casto begging so deliciously, when his lover welcomed him so willingly, all reason evaporated in a red haze. This was not the ecstasy he'd felt the first time they had sex, and it wasn't the feeling of happiness, bordering on insanity, that swamped him every time he took Casto. This was a torrent that buried everything underneath, that only knew his hunger, his wish to own Casto, to mark him as his property for all time. Renaldo wasn't capable of clear thought. All he knew was that Casto was his, and his alone. Laying Casto facedown, with brutal thrusts he took what nobody else was allowed to have. When Casto came for the first time, the fever running through Renaldo's body increased.

Renaldo dragged him up, glided his teeth over Casto's throat, then bit down hard enough to draw blood. Casto yelled and reared up, forcing Renaldo's cock even deeper into his body as he was overcome by his next orgasm and shook like a tree in a storm.

When Casto's muscles tensed again, Renaldo pushed harder, forcing his own rhythm onto the young man as his lips bathed in the delight of Casto's blood running hotly down his throat. It was the most feral part of him, the beast slumbering deep inside that reveled in this brutal consummation of their marriage.

It was what they had been made for: Renaldo to possess Casto entirely, Casto to absolutely belong to the demigod.

Renaldo continued to take Casto with regular movements, subduing him like a young horse that had to learn how to yield to its rider's will. It was no gentle teaching; for that, their need was too urgent. Renaldo reached his own climax and made Casto drown with him in the void of unrestrained, all-consuming lust.

Exhausted, they lay between the cushions, still connected, panting and sated.

When his breathing finally slowed, Casto gave a soft groan. As Renaldo came back to himself, he retreated from Casto's body, and his heart constricted with guilt when he assessed the damage he'd caused. Casto was covered in sweat. Even though Noemi had sped the healing along, the wound from the branding had turned a deep, angry red in reaction to their salty fluids and the chafing of the sheets. The bite wound was swollen and a thin trickle of blood ran down Casto's shoulders; the skin on the inside of his thighs was covered with Renaldo's semen. Renaldo hastened to open the cuffs and turn Casto around.

Tears stained Casto's eyelashes, and Renaldo was close to beating himself up for what he'd done.

"Casto, my own, my precious, I'm so sorry! I lost control. Is everything all right?"

Casto cocked an eyebrow. He was always hard to read, and right then he didn't seem to know what he should think himself. "I feel a little sore. I have to admit, I'm overwhelmed. You've never taken me like that before."

"And for good reason. I'm sorry for pushing you so far."

A puckish smile was the answer to that. "It's fine. I hardly felt any pain since I was busy having the greatest orgasms of my life."

Renaldo didn't seem to hear him. "That's the first time I ever subjected somebody to my full power. I simply don't know what to say. I've never lost control like that before."

Much to Renaldo's surprise, Casto seemed satisfied with that answer. "Good. I wouldn't like it if you had any means of comparison for what we just did."

"You're not angry? I thought you'd lose it completely."

"Why should I? It was my idea. I explicitly asked for it. Besides, I was curious what it would be like when you could do whatever you want. I'm surprised how much I liked it."

Overwhelmed, Renaldo pressed a gentle kiss on his lover's temple. "When will you stop surprising me?"

"Never, I hope. I don't want you to get too comfortable."

Renaldo furrowed his brows. There it was again, the slight discomfort he felt whenever Casto challenged him, even when it was hidden in a joke. Since Renaldo had no intention of ruining his wedding night by provoking a fight, he made his own words sound lighthearted.

"You've just been subjected to your god's full power and yet you dare be cheeky again? I can't fight the impression that you *want* to be punished."

Casto undulated alluringly, but his tone was dismissive. "I've been wondering when you'd realize it. Even though you're supposedly a god, you're not the sharpest dagger in the rack."

A growl escaped Renaldo's throat. Then he bent over his daring husband and kissed him.

Until the first rays of the sun tinted the sky a glorious shade of red, Casto got no more chance to defy his husband.

THE NEXT night, Casto woke because the bedroom was lit by a flickering light as if a candle were burning in the wind. Next to him, the Barbarian slept soundly, sated by their lover's games.

Just when Casto had decided to wake Renaldo, he glimpsed movement in the corner of his eye. A tall, beautiful woman emerged from the dancing shadows. Her white hair moved softly, like cobwebs caught in a breeze. Her equally white dress hugged her body like a living thing, and it was impossible to tell where the cloth ended and the hair began. Black eyes dominated her pale face, and her bloodred lips parted in a friendly smile. Her voice, when she spoke, was a melodic whisper, like the autumn wind when it caressed the trees.

"It is not necessary to wake my son, Casto." She eyed the sleeping Renaldo, her gaze full of love. "He is very tired."

Casto got up from the bed. "You're Ana-Isara, the Empress of the Dead." He bowed respectfully.

The goddess smiled again. "I am, Prince Castolus of Ummana, and I'm glad we can finally meet. It has taken us some time."

Involuntarily, Casto lowered his gaze. He had never met a goddess before, but he learned quickly that her presence did not allow any pretense. "I know. I was quite stubborn."

An amused laugh was the answer to that. "You were as stubborn as a mule and as defiant as a three-year-old child. In other words, you are my son's heart."

"Is that really true?" All of Casto's fear and all the hope he had nurtured were bared in that one crucial question.

Ana-Isara looked at him, rather surprised. "Don't you feel it, Casto?"

"I'm wishing for it so desperately I can't tell whether it's true."

"What would you do if I told you your doubts were justified, that you are not my son's heart?"

The pain reflecting in Casto's eyes moved the goddess, but it was the graceful dignity of his answer that made her bow to him.

"I would die."

Ana-Isara caressed his cheeks with her cold fingers. "You *are* my son's heart, there can be no doubt about that. And you are a worthy member of the Pack. I did not want to hurt you, Casto, but you had to find out certain things on your own. You know now that you can trust Renaldo, that you love him, and that you are able to obey him. Of course, first and foremost he is your lover, but he is also your god, and you owe him obedience."

Casto nodded. As much as he resented it, he could not deny the truth in Ana-Isara's words. "I know."

"This does not mean you cannot criticize him. On the contrary, it is your duty, or he would become too conceited. But once he has made a decision, you have to bow to his will."

Again, Casto nodded, slightly hesitantly. About that matter, the last word had not been spoken yet. "Yes."

The goddess flashed a radiant smile. "Come to me. I want to welcome you into my family."

She opened her white arms.

Casto approached her slowly. Cool like the grave was the embrace of the Empress of the Dead, but not uncomfortable. Casto felt safe and pampered, as if the world's challenges lay far behind him. Ana-Isara mumbled close to his ear, "Death is nothing to fear. It is the door to another truth. Those walking in my footsteps do not have to fear getting lost. In the end, every pain we endure is only an illusion on our way to ourselves."

After having spoken that riddle, the goddess pressed a kiss on Casto's forehead. It was unexpectedly warm, almost searing.

"Don't worry, my son. My sister and I are with you. From today, you will never be alone again."

The light flickered and winked out. The goddess's hair flew up like a flock of birds in a storm and then settled like a coat around her.

When she stepped away, the pain set in.

RENALDO WOKE when he heard Casto scream as he had never screamed before. His gaze darted wildly through the room and stopped at the sight of his mother, who was just about to leave.

"Why are you doing this to him? Hasn't he endured enough yet?"

Ana-Isara's features hardened. "Indeed he has, and it has made him strong. Strong enough for you. This will make him even harder, more unbending. He is what you need, what your brother needs."

"But it's not fair."

"It's never fair, my son. You should know that better than anybody else. Take care of him. He needs you now."

Renaldo turned away from his mother and slung his arms around his screaming lover.

Long after the sun had risen, Casto's wails finally subsided. Panting, he lay in Renaldo's arms. Shudders ran through his body in a desperate reaction to a pain he'd never even imagined before.

Renaldo stroked his sweat-soaked back soothingly. "Shh, shh, my own. Everything's fine again. It's over."

Casto snuggled closer, still overwhelmed by what he had just gone through. "I'm sorry, Barbarian. I thought I was stronger."

"You stubborn idiot. You've been touched by a goddess. That's no triviality. You've done well."

"If you think so."

"I do. And now get up. I wish to see how you were branded."

Groaning in protest, Casto got up. He just wanted to sleep, but he could sense how important it was to Renaldo to find out what Ana-Isara had done to him.

With his fingertips, Renaldo traced the two black runes carved into Casto's flesh, right above his heart. "The sign of the Mothers and the rune for a rider. How fitting."

Gently he turned Casto around so that he could see himself in the mirror. Gingerly, Casto touched the two dark symbols. Pride and resentment fought for dominance while he studied the signs that were proof of another person's will, not his own. "It doesn't hurt anymore."

"No. Being branded is brutal, but once it's done, the pain quickly becomes a fading memory. Look at your back."

Casto turned and stared at his back reflected in the mirror. The branding from the wedding was healed, the skin smooth and flawless again. Now the design glowed from within in the same color as the runes above his heart. Starting at the end of the *R*, a rune was engraved over every vertebra of his spine, telling the world that he was Renaldo's possession, his beloved heart.

Casto shuddered. This was too much to be pondered in his current state of mind.

Renaldo embraced and kissed him lovingly. "My precious heart. I am truly happy."

Sighing, Casto snuggled up to his mate and god. If, half a year ago, somebody would have told him that one day he would be branded like an ox, visible for all the world to see that he was the Barbarian's property, he would have thought the person insane. Yet here he was, bearing the marks of a barbarian god from the North, and he was not unhappy about it.

Casto fought this disturbing, atypical thought and tried to concentrate on the lust Renaldo was stoking in him anew. Strictly speaking, he was too tired to be in the mood, but all he wanted was to be with Renaldo again without wasting time on things too complex to consider after a night like that.

Xenia Melzer was born and raised in a small village in the South of Bavaria. As one of nature's true chocoholics, she's always in search of the perfect chocolate experience. So far, she's had about a dozen truly remarkable ones. Despite having been in close proximity to the mountains all her life, she has never understood why so many people think snow sports are fun. There are neither chocolate nor horses involved and it's cold by definition, so where's the sense? She does not like beer cither and has never been to the Oktoberfest—no quality chocolate there.

Even though her mind is preoccupied with various stories most of the time, Xenia has managed to get through school and university with surprisingly good grades. Right after school she met her one true love who showed her that reality is capable of producing some truly amazing love stories itself.

While she was having her two children, she started writing down the most persistent stories in her head as a way of relieving mommy-related stress symptoms. As it turned out, the stress relief has now become a source of the same, albeit a positive one.

When she's not writing, she teaches English at school, enjoys riding and running, spending time with her kids, and dancing with her husband.

Website: www.xeniamelzer.com
E-mail: info@xeniamelzer.com

CASTO
GODS OF WAR
XENIA MELZER

Gods of War: Book I

All is fair in love and war. Renaldo has lived happily by that proverb his entire life. But he has finally met his match, and he's about to discover how unfair love and war can be.

When demigod and warlord Lord Renaldo takes a beautiful stranger captive during an ambush, he is delighted to have found a distraction that will keep him entertained during the upcoming siege. Little does he know, Casto is keeping more than just one secret from him. Slowly, Renaldo gets sucked into a turbulent roller-coaster relationship with his mysterious prisoner, one that begins with hatred and soon spirals into a whirlwind of conflicting emotions. And when it seems that things can get no worse, an old enemy stirs right in the heart of his home.

Determined to keep Casto by his side, Renaldo has to find a balance between the capricious young man and his own destiny as a ruler and god to his people.

www.dsppublications.com